Praise for *Running the Rift*

"This is truly fearless writing: ambitious, beautiful, unapologetically passionate. Culturally rich and completely engrossing."   —Barbara Kingsolver

"[An] audacious and compelling first novel . . . It's a brave writer who takes a subject as historically complex and gravid with emotion as this one as the background to her first novel, and Benaron has to be loudly applauded for her bravura . . . It is an authentic and richly textured portrait of African life."
                                                            —*The Washington Post*

"A powerful coming-of-age story that highlights the best and the worst of human nature."   —*The Christian Science Monitor*

"[An] unflinching and beautifully crafted account of a people and their survival. In addition, she compellingly details the growth and rigorous training of a young athlete . . . Highly recommended; readers who loved Khaled Hosseini's *The Kite Runner* will appreciate."   —*Library Journal*, starred review

"Rich characterization and insights about Rwandan culture make this book a pleasure to read, and Jean Patrick impossible not to root for . . . *Running the Rift* is a profound display of imagination and empathy. Benaron writes like Jean Patrick runs, with the heart of a lion."   —*The Dallas Morning News*

"Benaron's compelling storytelling and extensive research creates an undeniably breathtaking work of historical fiction . . . No reader will finish this book unchanged."   —*Deseret News*

"Benaron depicts the rugged beauty of Rwanda, and the horror of genocide, vividly in these pages. She writes with an earnest clarity, bringing the boy to manhood and imparting to readers a culturally rich and unflinching story of resilience and resistance."   —*Chicago Tribune*, Editor's Choice

"Encourages us to see the world as a whole, despite the simmering divisions that threaten to erupt . . . [An] accomplished, comprehending and generous first novel."   —*The Kansas City Star*

"In a finely crafted story of dreams, illusions, hard reality, and reaching the other side of fear, Benaron has bestowed upon the world a story that illuminates events on a national scale by showing their effects at the personal level."
                                                              —*ForeWord Reviews*

"It is exceptionally difficult to fictionalize a relatively recent mass murder without either cheapening the tragedy or becoming bogged down in grim reportage—but Ms. Benaron does a smart, sober job of it . . . *Running the Rift* is well-paced but always makes time to demonstrate the apparatus of genocide."

—*The Wall Street Journal*

"This well-written and well-researched novel is an impressive debut."

—*The Seattle Times*

"Benaron accomplishes the improbable feat of wringing genuine loveliness from unspeakable horror . . . It is a testament to Benaron's skill that a novel about genocide . . . conveys so profoundly the joys of family, friendship, and community."

—*Publishers Weekly*, starred review

"Where Benaron shines is in her tender descriptions of Rwandan's natural beauty and in her creation of Jean Patrick, a hero whose noble innocence and genuine human warmth are impossible not to love."   —*Kirkus Reviews*, starred review

"Benaron sheds a crystalline beacon on an alarming episode in global history, and her charismatic protagonist leaves an indelible impression."   —*Booklist*

"Benaron successfully mitigates what could have been an unrelentingly grim narrative with a sympathetic main character, the love of family and country, the loyalty of friendship, the excitement of athletic competition, and the depth and purity of Jean Patrick's love for Bea."   —*School Library Journal*, starred review

"In *Running the Rift*, a novel full of unspeakable strife but also joy, humor, and love, 'hope always [chases] close on the heels of despair,' thanks to a writer who knows when to keep a steady pace and when to explode into an all-out sprint."

—*O: The Oprah Magazine*

"Novelist Benaron, with her fusion of research and firsthand observation of Rwandan society, knows how to tie the reader in knots as she develops Patrick's life-affirming story while the reader waits for the inevitable genocide."

—NPR's *All Things Considered*

Running the Rift

Also by Naomi Benaron
Love Letters from a Fat Man

Running the Rift

A NOVEL

NAOMI BENARON

ALGONQUIN BOOKS OF CHAPEL HILL 2012

Published by
ALGONQUIN BOOKS OF CHAPEL HILL
Post Office Box 2225
Chapel Hill, North Carolina 27515-2225

a division of
WORKMAN PUBLISHING
225 Varick Street
New York, New York 10014

"The Geology of Ghosts," a short story based on a chapter of this book,
first appeared in *Munyori Literary Journal*.

This is a work of fiction. While, as in all fiction, the literary perceptions
and insights are based on experience, all names, characters, places, and incidents
either are products of the author's imagination or are used fictitiously.

LIBRARY OF CONGRESS CATALOGING-IN-PUBLICATION DATA
Benaron, Naomi, [date]
    Running the rift : a novel / by Naomi Benaron.
        p. cm.
    ISBN 978-1-61620-042-8 (HC)
    1. Rwanda—Fiction. I. Title.
    PS3602.E6565R86 2011
    813'.6—dc23   2011026349

    ISBN 978-1-61620-194-4 (PB)

10 9 8 7 6 5 4 3 2 1
First Paperback Edition

FOR

MATHILDE MUKANTABANA AND ALEXANDRE KIMENYI,

WHOSE SPARK LIGHTS THESE PAGES. AND FOR ALL THE SURVIVORS

OF THE RWANDAN GENOCIDE WHO LENT ME THEIR VOICES;

AND FOR THOSE WHO DID NOT SURVIVE,

BUT WHOSE VOICES WHISPER TO ME STILL.

*A genocide is a poisonous bush that grows not from
two or three roots, but from a whole tangle that has
moldered underground without anyone noticing.*

—Claudine, genocide survivor,
from *Life Laid Bare,* by Jean Hatzfeld

Running the Rift

BOOK ONE

EJO HASHIZE (YESTERDAY)

Izina ni ryo muntu.

The name is the very man named.

1984

ONE

JEAN PATRICK WAS ALREADY AWAKE, listening to the storm, when Papa opened the door and stood by the side of the bed. Rain hissed at the windows and roared against the corrugated roof, and Jean Patrick huddled closer to his brother Roger for warmth. He remembered then that Papa was going to a conference in Kigali. He said it was a very important meeting; educators from all across Rwanda would be there.

"I'm leaving now," Papa whispered, his voice barely louder than the rain. "Uwimana will be here soon to pick me up." If even Headmaster was going, Jean Patrick thought, the conference must be top level.

The lantern flame glinted on Papa's glasses and on a triangle of white shirt; the storm must have knocked the power out, as usual. "You boys will have to check the pen carefully after you bring the cattle in. Make sure no earth has washed away in the rain." He tucked the blanket around their shoulders. "And Roger—you'll have to check Jean Patrick's lessons. I don't want any mistakes from either of you."

Turning his head from the light, Jean Patrick puckered his face. He didn't need Roger to check his homework; even Papa had to look hard to find an error.

"I'll be back tomorrow night," Papa said.

Jean Patrick leaned on his elbows and watched his father walk into the hallway on a beam of yellow light. His footsteps echoed on the concrete. "Be safe, Dadi," he said. "May Imana bless your journey." Gashogoro, the rainy season of November and December, often turned the roads leading from Cyangugu into muddy swamps. On the path, Jean Patrick sometimes sank in mud to his ankles.

All day the rain continued. Streams swelled and tumbled toward Lake Kivu. Rivers of red clay washed down from the hills, and by the time Jean

Patrick came home from school, mud had stained his pant legs the color of rust. After he finished his homework, Jean Patrick brought out his toy truck and steered it back and forth in the front room. His father had made the imodoka from coat hangers, scraps of wood and metal, and brightly colored bits of plastic.

Roger had a new watch, a gift from a muzungu missionary. He kept setting and resetting the alarm, beeping it in Jean Patrick's ear. The bell for the end of classes rang at Gihundwe, their father's school, and the students' voices bounced between the buildings, a river of sound muffled by the rain. Jean Patrick imagined the day he would leave primary school behind and be one of them, adding his uproar to the rest. Sometimes the anticipation bordered on fever, a feeling that slowed the passage of time down to the very tick of the clock.

"We better get the cattle," Roger said. "If we wait for the storm to end, we will be here, waiting, when Dadi comes home."

They put on their raincoats and rubber boots and took their switches from the side of the house. "Let's race," Jean Patrick said, taking off before Roger had a chance to respond.

The competition between Jean Patrick and Roger began this year, when Roger started playing football on the weekends with a small club called Inzuki—the Bees. He ran whenever he could to keep in top shape, and often he took Jean Patrick with him. He had taught Jean Patrick how to run backward, how to pump his arms and have a good strong kick behind him.

Since they lived at the school, Papa kept the cattle with a cousin of Mama's who lived near. Jean Patrick ran, keeping to the side of the road where the mud was not so churned. Each day, he'd tried to make it a little farther before Roger caught him, but today was impossible. No matter what line he chose, the road swallowed his boots. Roger passed him before the red bricks of Gihundwe's walls were lost to the mist.

From a distance, Jean Patrick spotted the wide arc of horns on the inyambo steer, their father's favorite. In the blur of rain, the horns dipped and turned above the small herd like the arms of an Intore dancer. The steer looked up, blinking his liquid black eyes, as they approached. Jean Patrick placed a hand on the steer's back and felt the wet quiver of his hide.

Led by the inyambo steer, the herd shuffled into motion toward the rickety collection of poles that marked the pen.

ROGER MADE IT to the gate at Gihundwe a good ten steps in front of Jean Patrick. He stopped and took off his watch. "Look—it took us twenty-seven minutes and thirty-five seconds there and back. I timed it."

Jean Patrick gasped for air. Mud clung to his clothes, his boots, his hands. "You lie. No watch can time us. Let me have it." He took the watch, and there was the time in bold numbers, just as Roger had claimed.

The smells of stewing meat, peppery and rich, came from the charcoal stove in the cookhouse. Jean Patrick and Roger stripped off their boots and raincoats and went inside. In the kitchen, a snappy soukous tune by Pepe Kalle played on the radio. Jean Patrick's little sister did some kwassa kwassa steps with Zachary in her arms. His legs dangled to her knees.

"Eh-eh, Jacqueline. You dance sweet," Jean Patrick teased.

Jacqueline spun around. "Aye! What happened to you? Did you drown?" She pointed to the dirty water that pooled by Jean Patrick and Roger's feet.

Roger took Zachary from Jacqueline, and the three of them danced. Jean Patrick swung his hips the way he had seen on the videos. He was still swinging them when he heard the knock at the door, quiet at first and then louder, and still when he opened the door to two policemen. Mama ran into the room, Baby Clemence bundled at her back.

"We're so sorry to bring you this news," they said.

MAMA BROUGHT THEM TEA, her back straight and tall. Clemence began to whimper, and Mama picked her up to comfort her. Zachary played with the truck on the floor as if the only difference between this afternoon and any other was that men had come to visit.

There were six of them traveling together, the policemen said, all headmasters and préfets. The urubaho was out of control—they always were—going too fast down the mountain with a load far too heavy for such a flimsy truck. It swerved around the corner on the wrong side and crashed head-on into the car. Two people dead from Gihundwe—Jean Patrick's father and the préfet de discipline. Two others dead and two badly injured. It was a miracle anyone survived, and the urubaho driver with barely a scratch, obviously drunk. He hit a boy on a bicycle, too; the sack of potatoes he carried on the handlebars scattered across the road. The bicycle was found, but not the boy, the cliffs too steep and dangerous to search in the rain.

The policemen clucked their tongues. It was always the best of the country—Rwanda's future—that died like this. The body was in the hospital at Gitarama. With their permission, the headmaster from Gihundwe would bring him home.

Mama stopped her gentle rocking. "Uwimana wasn't in the car?"

It was one of those strange occurrences, the policemen said, that revealed Ikiganza cy'Imana, the Hand of God. At the last possible minute, there had been an emergency at school, and Headmaster had stayed behind. "Uwimana asked us to fetch his wife from the Centre de Santé as soon as she finishes with her patients."

"Angelique," Mama said. The name came out as a long, trembled sigh. "Yes—I will be glad to see her."

The policemen rose. "We knew your husband—a good, good man. Thank you for the tea."

After they left, Mama stared so hard out the window that Jean Patrick looked to see if someone stood there in the storm. He half believed that if he closed his eyes hard enough, he could blink the afternoon away, look up, and find Dadi there, returned from his trip, pockets full of cookies as they always were.

Mama knelt by him. "Don't worry. Uncle Emmanuel will be a father to you now."

"I hate Uncle Emmanuel," Jean Patrick said. "He's stupid, and he always stinks of fish."

The sting of Mama's slap made his eyes water. "Be respectful of my brother. He's your elder."

Jean Patrick couldn't hold it back any longer. He wailed.

Mama drew him close. "We have to be strong," she said. "Think of your namesake, Nkuba. You must be as brave as the God of Thunder."

The door opened, and Angelique came in, still in her white doctor's coat. Mama collapsed into her arms.

BY MIDNIGHT, THE RAIN had stopped, the moon a blurred eye behind the clouds. Neighbors and family had been arriving since early evening with food and drink. Students and teachers from Gihundwe crowded into the tiny house. The night watchman drank tea inside the door.

The table was set up in the front room, covered with the tablecloth reserved for holidays. There were plates of ugali and stews with bits of meat and fish to dip it in, bowls of isombe, green bananas and red beans, fried plantains, boiled sweet potatoes and cassava. There were peas and haricots verts sautéed with tomatoes, bottles of Primus beer and Uncle Emmanuel's home-brewed urwagwa. Angelique had not stopped cooking, bringing Mama tea, wiping everyone's eyes. The power was off. Candles flickered; lanterns tossed shadows at the walls. Jean Patrick and Roger sat on the floor with Jacqueline, feeding Clemence bits of stew wrapped in sticky balls of ugali.

A wedge of light beckoned Jean Patrick from Papa's study, and he went inside. The lantern on the desk turned the oiled wood into a pliable skin. Papa's books surrounded him and comforted him. Books on physics, mathematics, the philosophies of teaching. Papa must have been writing in his journal; his pen lay across the leather-bound book. The cap rested beside a half-full cup of tea as if at any moment he would enter the room, pull out his chair, and pick up the pen once more. Jean Patrick put the cup to his lips and drank. The sudden sweetness made him shiver. Flecks of tea leaf remained on his lip, and he licked them, tasting the last thing his father had tasted. The house groaned and settled in the night.

Mama joined him. She held a tray of urwagwa, and the banana beer's sweet, yeasty tang tickled his nostrils. "Are you tired? You can go to bed if you want."

He shook his head. He thought of his father sitting in his chair on Friday evenings, drinking urwagwa and eating peanuts. He could almost reach out and touch the glitter of salt on Papa's lips.

"He must have been writing his talk for the meeting," Mama said, stroking the journal's skin.

Jean Patrick read. *Everything in the universe has a mathematical expression: the balance of a chemical reaction, the Fibonacci sequence of a leaf, an encounter between two human beings. It is important*—the sentence ended there. Jean Patrick envisioned a noise in the bush, his father putting down the pen and peering through the window. It seemed at that moment as if not only his father's words but the whole world had stopped just like that: midsentence.

THE MEN WERE still drinking, some sharing bottles of urwagwa through a common straw, the women still replenishing empty bowls, when Uwimana came with the coffin. A procession of Papa's family from Ruhengeri followed. Dawn, ash colored, came through the door behind them.

"Chère Jurida," Uwimana said. He held Mama's hand. "Whatever you need, you can ask me. You know François was my closest friend."

A line of people formed to say good-bye. Mama sat by the coffin, her family and Papa's family beside her. The women keened.

"Are you going up?" Roger pressed close to Jean Patrick.

"Are you?" Neither of them moved. "We can go together," Jean Patrick said.

Papa was dressed in an unfamiliar suit. Dark bruises discolored his face, and the angles his body made seemed wrong. Jean Patrick could not reach out to touch him.

"That's not your dadi anymore. Your dadi's in heaven," a small voice said. Jean Patrick looked down to see Mathilde, Uncle's daughter, beside him. She wedged her hand in his. "When my sister died, Mama told me that. I was scared before she said it. I came for Christmas—do you remember? You read me a book."

Of course Jean Patrick remembered. Since she was small, Mathilde had had a hunger for books and loved to listen to stories. When Uncle's family came to visit, she would rush to Papa's study, dragging Jean Patrick by the hand. She would point to a tall book of folk stories on the bookshelf. "Nkuba, read me the one about your son, Mirabyo, when he finds Miseke, the Dawn Girl." It was always this same one.

Even before Jean Patrick could read the complicated text, he knew the story well enough to recite it. "Some day, like Miseke," he would say, "you will laugh, and pearls will spill from your mouth. Then your umukunzi, your sweetheart, will know he has found his one love." Each time he said this, Mathilde released a peal of laughter. "You see?" Jean Patrick would say, pointing to her lips. "Pearls! Just like your Rwandan name, Kamabera." And Mathilde would laugh again.

"You have to tell your papa you love him," she whispered now, "so he'll be happy in heaven." She stood on tiptoes and peered inside the coffin.

Jean Patrick looked at Roger, and together they approached the coffin. They knelt down to recite Papa's favorite words from Ecclesiastes.

"Whatever your hand finds to do, do it with your might; for there is no work or device or knowledge or wisdom—"

Jean Patrick stopped. If he spoke the word *grave,* tears would stain his Sunday shirt.

UWIMANA CANCELED CLASSES on the day of the funeral, and all the teachers and students from Gihundwe escorted the coffin to the church. Cars packed with people wound through the streets, followed by crowds on foot. Children ran on the paths in a cold, drizzling rain. Mud splattered their legs and shorts.

A brown kite swooped from a branch; its sharp cry hung in the mist. Jean Patrick wondered if Papa's soul had wings, too, like the paintings of angels in church. Mist rose from Lake Kivu. Fishermen emerged and disappeared in a gray space that belonged to neither water nor sky. Long-horned cattle grazed in the green hills. As the procession passed, farmers watched from their fields. Some signed the cross; others stretched out a hand in farewell.

Instead of the chapel at Gihundwe, where Jean Patrick's family worshipped every Sunday, they went to Nkaka Church. The harmonies of the choir and the steady beat of drums poured through the open doors. All the pews and chairs were filled. Behind them, people stood shoulder to shoulder. Above the coffin, the Virgin Mary wept tears of blood onto her open robe. The whiteness of the Virgin's skin, her wounded heart, the reverberating drums and clapping, combined to fill Jean Patrick with terror. He shut his eyes and tumbled back in time until he arrived at the moment when he had lain warm inside his bed and wished his father a safe journey. He undid the wish and told his father instead not to go.

1985

Two

UWIMANA HAD PROMISED that Jean Patrick's family could stay on at the boarding school until a new préfet was found, but every day Jean Patrick waited for a man in a pressed suit to walk up the path and claim the house from them. In his dreams he heard the new préfet say, I am taking your father's job. Get out of my house.

It was the first clear afternoon since Itumba, the long rainy season, had begun, and sunlight pooled on the floor where Jean Patrick gathered with his brothers and sisters to enjoy the warmth. Zachary pushed the wire truck across the floor. Jacqueline sat in a swath of sun, spooning sorghum porridge into Clemence's mouth. Clemence tried to catch a wavering tail of light on the floor. She giggled, and porridge ran down her chin.

Jean Patrick hid behind a chair. As Zachary went past, he roared like a lion and pounced, waving his hands like paws. At that moment, the window exploded in a spray of glass. Jean Patrick thought it was something he had done until he saw the rock by Zachary's feet. Clemence screamed, and Jacqueline hugged her close. Jean Patrick grabbed Zachary and pushed him away from the window. A second window splintered; the rock would have caught Jean Patrick's head if he hadn't ducked.

"Tutsi snakes!" The shouts were as close as the door. Laughter followed. A rock thudded against the house. Mama burst in, running barefoot across the broken glass, and scooped Clemence into her arms.

"Next time we'll kill you!" The laughter trailed off.

A wild noise filled Jean Patrick's head, and at first he didn't realize it came from his own throat. He burst through the door as the boys disappeared into the bush. He heaved a rock at their backs, grabbed a walking stick that leaned against the wall, and ran after them. Sprinting furiously, the stick clutched in his hand, he followed the fading sounds of their movement. Stones stabbed his bare feet. At the top of a rise, he shaded his eyes to scan the vegetation below. Nothing stirred. If he saw the boys, he knew he could catch them. If he caught them, he swore he would kill them.

The land poured in rolling folds of terraced plots toward Lake Kivu. Banana groves dotted the bush, leaves shining with moisture. Sweet potato vines, lush and green from the rains, claimed every spare scrap of earth. Jean Patrick picked up stones and threw them, one after another. The women in the fields looked up from weeding and hilling to rest on their hoes.

"Eh-eh," they teased. "Who are you fighting? Ghosts?"

He pretended not to hear. His legs burned from his effort, and he pressed his hands to his thighs to keep them from shaking. When he caught his breath, he picked up his stick and tore down the path toward home in case the boys had doubled back to attack again. Several times he lost his way on goat trails that petered out in a web of new, thick growth.

A red sunset smoldered in the clouds over the lake, and the day's warmth fled. He hadn't realized how far he'd run; he'd have to hurry to beat the fast-approaching dark. The brush stretched before him, the silence broken only by the calls of tinkerbirds in the trees. *Who-who?* Jean Patrick couldn't tell them. Taking off at a dead run, he crashed headlong into Roger.

"Hey, big man! What do you think you're doing?" Roger held him firmly by the shoulders.

"These guys—they threw rocks—"

"Mama told me. She said you chased after them like a crazy man. Reason why I came to find you."

"I didn't see their faces, but they weren't from Gihundwe. They had dirty rags for clothes." Jean Patrick spat. "Abaturage—country bumpkins."

Roger blew out his breath. "You ran fast. I saw you from a long way off, but I couldn't catch you. What did you think one skinny boy could do against a gang of thugs, eh?"

Jean Patrick shrugged. "I didn't think. I just ran."

"Superhero, eh?" Roger tapped Jean Patrick's shins. They were scratched and bleeding, his bare feet spotted with blood. "You should take better care of your special gift. You won't get another one," Roger said.

In the waning light, Jean Patrick couldn't see his face to tell if he was joking.

THE SUN HAD disappeared by the time Jean Patrick and Roger returned. Jacqueline was sweeping glass from the rugs. Papa's office door was open, and Mama stood by the desk, packing papers and books. Jacqueline held out a hand to warn him, but Jean Patrick hurried across the room. A shard of glass burrowed into his foot.

"We'll have to leave now," Mama said. She had a look of fear on her face that Jean Patrick could not recall ever having seen.

"Why? This is our home." He sat on a chair to dig at the glass in his foot. Events were happening too fast. Jean Patrick could not keep up in his mind.

Mama knelt beside him. "Let me." She cradled his foot in her hands. "We live here by Uwimana's grace. What if someone comes to burn down the house?"

"But Mama, it's only kids. We can't fear them."

Mama shook her head. "There are things you don't understand. Each time I believe this country has changed, I find out nothing changes. I'm glad your dadi didn't live to see this."

Jean Patrick didn't know what she meant. "If Papa was alive," he said, "this would never have happened."

"There." A sliver of glass glistened on Mama's finger. "I'm saving Papa's books for you. When you're a teacher, you will have them."

"I can't be a teacher now."

"Who told you that? Your father was."

"Dadi can't help me anymore."

Mama picked up Papa's journal and held it out to Jean Patrick. Since Papa's death, it had remained open, as he had left it. "Take it." She removed the pen and closed the book.

Jean Patrick took the journal and pen and went outside. Opening to a random page, he tried to read what was written, but it was too dark. What he needed from his father was a clue, something to help him fit the fractured pieces of the afternoon together.

Before his first day in primary school, Jean Patrick had not known what

Tutsi meant. When the teacher said, "All Tutsi stand," Jean Patrick did not know that he was to rise from his seat and be counted and say his name. Roger had to pull him up and explain. That night, Jean Patrick said to his father, "Dadi, I am Tutsi." His father regarded him strangely and then laughed. From that day forward, Jean Patrick carried the word inside him, but it was only now, after the windows and rocks, after the insults, that this memory rose to the surface.

The first stars blinked sleepily from the sky's dark face. The generator at Gihundwe intoned its malarial lament. If Jean Patrick had powers like his namesake, Nkuba, he could have breathed life into the inert pages, sensed the leather skin stretch and grow into a man's shape, felt once more his father's strong, beating heart. Instead he dug the pen into his flesh until blood marked his palm. *François,* he wrote, his father's Christian name.

THREE

"We'll be like beggars," Roger had said, and even though Mama pinched him for it, Jean Patrick thought he might be right. Now the final week of school had come, and he wished he could drag his feet in the dirt, slow time down to a crawl so that they wouldn't have to move to Uncle Emmanuel's when classes ended. Some days he had to force himself to care that he was at the top of his class, bringing home papers to show Mama with hardly any red marks at all.

Roger was waiting for him beneath the broad brim of an acacia tree behind the house. They bent to take off their shoes. A drift of yellow pollen swirled to the ground.

Jean Patrick rubbed at a yellow spot on his school shorts. "Mama would kill us if she saw us going barefoot to school."

"She would talk so that cows leave their calves," Roger said. "But she should get used to it when we move to Uncle's."

"Don't talk like that," Jean Patrick said, and he pushed his brother. "You don't know."

He started out toward school at a steady jog, a shoe in each hand. There were five more days of school, six more until he found out whether Roger's complaints came true. That was the day they would pack up their belongings and close the door of the house for the last time. Come September, who would sleep in his and Roger's room? Who would write at Papa's desk?

"We have to hurry," Roger said, patting Jean Patrick's bottom with his shoe. "Sister said she had a surprise for us today, remember?"

Jean Patrick looked over his shoulder. Since the boys had broken the windows, he watched out for them. Sometimes he thought he caught sight of them disappearing into the brush, vanishing in a curl of cook smoke. It was silly, of course; unless they wore the same rags, he probably wouldn't know them if they walked up and shook his hand.

THE SURPRISE WAS that a famous runner was coming to speak to the class. Not just any runner—an Olympian. After Sister made the announcement, Jean Patrick could not keep his mind on the path of his studies. For the past few weeks, he hadn't thought anything could lift up his spirits. Not Papa's books, not the igisafuria and fried potatoes with milk that Mama cooked for him, not the songs Jacqueline played full force on the radio. But Sister had managed to succeed where all else had failed. All morning long, his mind traveled back to the runner. His eyes wore out a spot on the window where he searched for the speck that would turn into the runner's fancy auto. Finally, just as he finished his sums, he saw a shape materialize from a swirl of dust. The car was not fancy; it was a Toyota no different from a hundred other Toyotas on the roads. A man thin as papyrus unfolded his legs into the yard, stood up, and stretched.

Jean Patrick had expected a big man, but the runner stood not much taller than Roger. Jean Patrick wondered if he was umutwa, one of the pygmy people who sold milk and butter in clay pots to families that didn't keep cows. The momentary disappointment vanished as he watched the runner move, flowing rather than walking from one place to the next, as if his muscles were made of water. He wore sunglasses. His shirt snapped in the breeze, zebras and lions racing across the shiny fabric.

"Muraho neza!" the man said to the class. "I'm Telesphore Dusabe, a marathon runner representing Rwanda in the Olympics. I am blessed to be here in Cyangugu to talk to you today." Jean Patrick asked him to write his name on the board, and he copied it into his notebook, framed by two stars on either side.

Telesphore spoke about running barefoot up and down Rwanda's hills. "We call our country the land of a thousand hills," he said, his face lit from the inside as if by a flame, "and I believe I have conquered every one." He talked about the lure of the Olympics and a feeling like flying that sometimes filled his body when he ran.

Jean Patrick raised his hand. "Did you say *sometimes?*" he wanted to know. "What about the rest of the time?"

"Smart boy," Telesphore said, and he chuckled. "I will tell you a secret. Sometimes it is all I can do to go from one footstep to the next, but for each such moment, I make myself remember how it feels to win."

Jean Patrick felt the man's eyes on his face alone, and his body tingled. *How it feels to win,* he repeated in his head. He wrote the words in his book of sums.

"We're going to have a race," Sister said, taking two thick pieces of cardboard bound with tape from behind her desk. She slit the tape and held up a poster of Telesphore breaking the finish-line ribbon at some official meet. "And the winner will have our runner to watch over him." She smiled. "Or her."

Telesphore lined up the students in the dusty schoolyard behind a starting line he drew with a stick. "According to age, youngest first," he said. That put Jean Patrick two rows from the back and Roger in the back. Telesphore brought two wooden blocks from his bag. "This is how we start a race," he said. "Now take your marks."

Jean Patrick wanted the poster. He wanted it more than he had wanted anything in a while. He heard the sound of the blocks clacking together, and for the second time that day, some small balance tipped inside him. When he stretched out his legs and sprinted toward the far end of the fence, passing one student and then another, the earth his bare feet touched was not the same red clay as before Telesphore began his talk. When he reached the far end of the fence three steps in front of Roger to claim first place, he understood that the earth would never feel the same again.

"Look at that lean! A natural!" Telesphore shouted. He pushed his sunglasses onto his forehead and pulled Jean Patrick closer. "What is your name?"

"Jean Patrick Nkuba."

The runner squinted into the sun, and a field of wrinkles mapped his eyes. "No wonder, then. Do you know who you are named for?"

"The god who brings the thunder," Jean Patrick said.

"Yes—Nkuba, Lord of Heaven, the Swift One." Telesphore touched Jean Patrick below the left eye. "I see it there: the hunger. Someday you will need to run as much as you need to breathe."

Sister brought the poster and gave it to Telesphore. Balancing poster and cardboard on his knee, he wrote with a flourish, *To our next Olympic hero, Jean Patrick Nkuba*. He signed his name, Telesphore Dusabe, in a large, scrolling hand.

Jean Patrick took the poster and looked out toward the hills. The storms of Itumba were behind them now, the days sparkling and polished by the rains into a brilliant blue. In the steeply terraced fields, women harvested beans and sorghum. The berries bowed the stalks, decorating the lush landscape with necklaces of red beads. Soon the rains would dry up completely, and Iki, the long dry season, would warm the young plants cultivated during the rains, coax them to grow tall and strong. Now it was four more days until Jean Patrick's time in the house at Gihundwe would come to an end, but he would not think about that. Instead he looked at the runner's face and felt his words as truth—a prophesy.

Four

THE LAST THING JEAN PATRICK did was to roll up his poster of Telesphore Dusabe, wrap it in two layers of paper, and tie it with string. He looked around the bare room. All traces of his family's life had been swept away like the dirt Mama cleared with her broom.

Outside, bees hummed in the acacia. Mama had picked the last ripe tomatoes and beans, a few chili peppers, from her garden, and it was the time to sow a new crop of beans and squash. It had always been Jean Patrick's job to help his mother, but for the first time he could remember, they had not knelt in the earth to plant. Like the house, the garden looked bare—already forgotten. Jean Patrick hefted his knapsack and tucked the family's radio under his arm. He followed Mama through the door and closed it behind him.

Jacqueline, Zachary, and a few students from Gihundwe were helping Uwimana and Angelique pack the family belongings into his truck.

Uwimana took Mama's hands in his. "I wish I could change your mind, Jurida," he said. "The house will be empty until the start of school." Clemence, bound in a cloth at Mama's back, made kissing sounds in her sleep.

Mama shook her head. "I can't look at those windows without hearing glass break. My brother's home is our home now."

"François believed Hutu or Tutsi made no difference anymore. His students loved him, and his dreams gave us hope. We must hold on to that hope in spite of what happened," Uwimana said.

"For my husband's sake and yours, I will try to keep it alive."

Angelique took Mama in her arms and then hugged Jean Patrick, Jacqueline, and Zachary. "Gihundwe will seem so empty without your voices to fill the days," she said.

"We'll come visit," Jacqueline said. Jean Patrick saw her bite her lip and knew she was not far from tears.

Angelique knelt beside Jean Patrick and lifted his chin with her finger. "You will come back for secondary school," she said. "This will be your home again; you must believe in that."

"Come, Jean Patrick." Uwimana opened the truck door. "Sit next to me."

"I need to help Roger with the cattle," Jean Patrick said. He took the radio's plug and held it to his ear. "Jacqueline—they're playing your favorite song." He made clowning faces and mimicked Pepe Kalle until they both laughed.

"How will you make the radio play at Uncle's? By Imana's electric power?" Jacqueline said.

Jean Patrick wiggled the dials and sang a few words at top volume. "Maybe Uncle will get electricity soon." He wedged radio and knapsack between two mattresses in the bed of the truck. Then he gave his poster of Telesphore to his mother and said good-bye before he, too, found himself close to tears.

He stood until the truck became a speck in the red swirl of dust. When even the speck had disappeared, he broke into a run down the road, where life paraded on as if nothing had changed. Men strained up the hill, sacks of sorghum and potatoes draped over bicycle handlebars or stacked in rickety wooden carts. Children herded goats fastened with bits of string, lugged jerricans filled with water, trotted with rafts of freshly gathered firewood on their heads. Women chatted on the way to and from the market, basins filled with fruits and vegetables balanced like fancy hats.

Jean Patrick had not gone far when a student from Gihundwe hailed him. "We heard you were leaving," he said. "So sorry."

"I'll be back once I pass my exams. I'll be a student here," Jean Patrick said, echoing Angelique's words. He shook the boy's outstretched hand and sprinted away, charging the hill until his chest was on fire and spots danced in front of his eyes.

He found Roger in the shade of a banana grove. The cattle lolled beside the trees, tearing off mouthfuls of young urubingo. The inyambo steer stood apart from the rest as if he knew he was descended from the cattle of kings. His arc of horns supported a corner of sky, and his oxblood hide glowed in the sun. On his head were two white patches like countries on a map. He sported a beaded necklace—blue and white like an Intore dancer's—and bells tinkled when he shook his head. When Jean Patrick was small, Papa used to hold his tiny hand steady while the steer licked sugar off it with his hot, rough tongue.

Roger looked behind him, toward Gihundwe, his face lost in shadow beneath the brim of Papa's felt hat. How many Sundays Jean Patrick and Roger had watched as their father put on his hat, took his traditional carved staff from its place by the door, and said, "Tugende, my sons. Let's go for a walk."

As if reading Jean Patrick's thoughts, Roger touched the hat's brim. "Everything is finished now. We'll be nothing but poor fishermen, running around dirty and eating with our fingers like the rest of Uncle's children."

Jean Patrick patted the steer's dusty rump. "We'll still go to school. Papa always said that, and Mama promised. Anyway, Uncle Emmanuel isn't poor. Look at all his boats."

"Eh—stupid! Who'll pay for our school? Uncle has his own children to worry about."

"I'm not stupid," Jean Patrick said. "You already have your scholarship for Kigali, and I'll go to Gihundwe. After, I'll go to college in America. I'll get a scholarship to run. Everyone does it there."

Telling the boy on the path he would be back at Gihundwe, Jean Patrick had doubted himself, but when he heard Roger challenge him, Angelique's words lodged in his heart as a prize he was determined to claim, whatever the price. He crouched on the grass the way Telesphore had shown the class. "Come on. I think today I will beat you," he said.

"You think so?" Roger said. "See that tree at the top of this hill? I'll give you a head start."

"I don't need a head start," Jean Patrick said, springing up the trail. He kept his tempo fast, his kick high, the way Roger had told him. The familiar burn settled into his lungs, and he pushed harder toward the ridgetop. He felt Roger at his back. Just to the tree, he told himself. I need to beat him to the tree. He gritted his teeth and dug in deep, but Roger drew even before the last rise and kept pace easily beside him.

At the tree, Roger tackled him. "You can't beat me yet. You're close — I had to work hard — but it will be a while before you take the wreath from me."

"You're talking foolishness. I already beat you once — the day Telesphore had us race."

Roger sucked his teeth. "Number one, you started two rows in front of me. Number two, that was too short to count."

"Let's keep running. Maybe I will do it now."

"Aye-yay! I don't want you to collapse." Roger cuffed Jean Patrick's head and then helped him to his feet.

Jean Patrick heard the tinkle of the inyambo steer's bells behind them. He turned to see the steer trotting in front of the small herd, regal as a king.

"Go easy," Roger said. "We don't want to lose our herd."

Jean Patrick and Roger let gravity take them down the backside of the trail. In the distance, the dark eye of Lake Kivu winked.

By the time they reached Gashirabwoba, where Uncle lived, Jean Patrick's legs felt like stones. They stopped on a ridge above Uncle's urugo. Below the compound, two eucalyptus trees marked the path, towering above the rest of the forest. It was afternoon already, the heat lazy around them. Bees hummed in the hives that perched in the high branches.

"We're here. Let's go down and greet them," Roger said.

Two cypress trees formed a gateway in a fence of dried sorghum and maize stalks. A cassava patch spilled down the slope. Beneath a lean-to, a pirogue rested on two halves of a fifty-gallon drum. Fishnets hung between branches like strange, mossy growths. Sheets of corrugated metal, propped against a shed, threw back the sunlight. The main house, shaded by a large jacaranda, was a sprawling collection of mud and brick, as if the rooms had sprouted like extra arms and legs from a central body. Since the last time Jean Patrick had visited, the front door and the window frames had been painted a bright blue.

A procession of children ran from the house, led by Uncle's little twins, Clémentine and Clarisse, in matching dresses. Mathilde burst through the door and charged after them, cradling Jean Patrick's radio in the crook of her arm. "I've been waiting for you!" she said, and she held the radio aloft. "How can we play some tunes, eh? I want to hear that morning music, Indirimbo za buracyeye, they play." She shook Roger's hand formally but threw her free arm around Jean Patrick.

A girl in a ragged skirt approached, and Mathilde yanked her forward. "This is my friend Olivette. She lives just there." She pointed to a ridge where a woman and boy descended. The woman balanced a large basket on her head. "That's Olivette's mama and her brother Simon coming just now. Mama says put the cattle in the pen until they get used to it here."

The children surrounded Jean Patrick and Roger as they herded the cattle through the gate. They chattered and wiped at runny noses with their sleeves.

Aunt Esther came from the garden. "Welcome," she said. "You're home now." She wore a new-looking pagne decorated with colorful fish. Around her close-cropped hair she had tied a scarf with glittery threads that caught the light. Jean Patrick wondered if she had put on her good clothes for the occasion of their arrival. Between her feet, a red puppy, more bones than flesh, chased invisible prey. Jean Patrick tried to pet it, but it scurried away.

"Don't worry," Auntie said. "She'll be following you around soon enough."

Olivette's mother came into the yard. "Ego ko Mana!" she said. "Look at these skinny boys!" She set her basket on the ground. Inside, Jean Patrick saw brilliant blue eggs, a small pale pumpkin, and a giant papaya. She embraced Roger and Jean Patrick. "I've brought some food to fatten you up." Cupping her hands to her mouth, she called after her son. "Simon! Come and meet these boys properly, eh? Don't act like the muturage you are."

Simon scowled and pushed himself up from the tree where he had been leaning. His hand in Jean Patrick's felt cold and limp, like one of Uncle's fish.

"Mukabera," Aunt Esther said, "these are smart schoolboys — no husband for your daughter here." She kissed Mukabera's cheeks — right side, left side, right again.

Mukabera laughed, showing a mouth full of large teeth stained brown from chewing sugarcane. She bent down to Jean Patrick. "Have you ever seen a blue duck egg before?"

Jean Patrick shook his head and took it from her extended hand.

"When you need to be strong, come see Mukabera, and I'll cook one for you," she said, and she pinched his shoulder. "Now you need to rest, and I need to get back to my fields." She placed the basket in Jean Patrick's arms and strode up the hill. Simon set off after her. He said something under his breath that Jean Patrick didn't catch.

STANDING OUTSIDE THE DOORWAY of Uncle's house, Jean Patrick felt woozy from the odor of the kerosene lanterns. Dusk painted the lake aubergine; mist blurred the horizon. Enormous bats glided between the trees. The air held an unfamiliar, wild smell, and he missed his home, bright and cheerful with electric light.

Uncle Emmanuel sat in the yard in a plastic chair. He was mending a net, a bottle of urwagwa by his side. The needle wove in and out like a darting insect. He sang a song, and when he forgot the words, he looked toward the lake, hummed and smiled. His rubber-booted foot kept time. He took a sip of his banana beer. "I made a new pirogue," he said. "Now that I have you and Roger to help me, we can catch more fish."

Roger gave Jean Patrick a look. Jean Patrick stared at the ground.

"We'll lash two pirogues together and drag the nets between them," Uncle said. "And I'm fixing up a house for you. See that corrugated metal? That's the roof."

"Aye, Emmanuel, so much money—you didn't have to," Mama said. Tears turned her eyes bright. Jean Patrick couldn't understand why such a dusty shack made her proud.

Mathilde called to Jean Patrick from the house. In her hands was Papa's folktale book. "Will you read me the one about Rutegaminsi and the mole?"

He settled beside her on the couch. "Ko Mana! You always want to know about love. But you're a big girl now. Can't you read it for yourself?"

Her mouth tried out the letters. "It's hard. "I'm only first year."

Roger looked up again from his homework. "Do you like school?"

"A lot. But when I get older I might not be able to go."

"Why?" With a snap that made Jean Patrick blink, Roger closed his book.

"Papa said Tutsi have to be first in the class and maybe even then they won't get in."

Roger frowned. "That's not true. Anyone can—Hutu or Tutsi. You just have to pay, that's all. *Our* papa said that."

Uncle Emmanuel set down his net and stepped inside. "Is that what he taught you? You think Hutu and Tutsi are the same in Rwanda?"

"Papa was the préfet in charge of teachers at Gihundwe," Roger said. "He told us President Habyarimana wants equality."

"How old are you, Jean Patrick?" Uncle Emmanuel asked.

"Almost ten."

"And you, Roger?"

"Twelve. Thirteen next month. And *I* got into secondary school even though I'm Tutsi."

Jean Patrick winced as their mother crossed the room. "Be respectful in your uncle's home." She slapped Roger hard above his ear.

Uncle Emmanuel held up a hand as if silencing an audience before a speech. "So. Do you boys know about the last massacre?" He glared at Mama.

"What massacre?"

"Nineteen seventy-three, the year Habyarimana overthrew Kayibanda. All over the country, Hutu rose up to murder Tutsi. They burned down our house, killed your grandparents and your uncle, our youngest brother." He turned to Jean Patrick. "You were named for him. No one told you?"

Jean Patrick knew the shocked expression on Roger's face mirrored his own. Whenever they had asked about their grandparents, Mama had said, "When you're older, you'll know." Suddenly the month's events fell into place: her terror when the boys smashed the window, the hastily packed boxes, the puzzling comments about changing and staying the same.

Mama stepped in front of Emmanuel. "Why are you frightening them? The past is the past; leave it be."

"It's dangerous to sleepwalk, Jurida. You've come back to Gashirabwoba now. Here, we live up to our village name: *Fear Nothing*. You don't need to keep secrets anymore." He swept his arm across the hillside. "Do you think it won't happen again?"

"It can't," Mama said. "Habyarimana won't allow it."

"Look what happened to you—on school grounds."

Zachary careened across the room with his wire imodoka, Clémentine and Clarisse close at his heels. Uncle watched him and shook his head. "The hate runs too deep. Sooner or later the government will find it convenient to let it boil to the surface again." He held out a closed fist to Jean Patrick and Roger. "Here is our president's hand. Do you know where the Tutsi are?" Uncurling his fingers, he jabbed at his upturned palm. "Right here where Habyarimana wants us. To him, we're nothing but inyenzi."

Roger tapped the invisible bug. "But Uncle, a cockroach can't be crushed."

The light disappeared, taking the lake with it. Uncle left to fish with his neighbor, Fulgence. Jean Patrick walked out into the grass to look for the dog. The forest came alive with the animals' night songs, their musky scents. Emmanuel's words crashed through his head. He wondered how old his unknown uncle had been when he died. As old as he was now? As old as Roger? How strange that Mama had named him for his uncle yet never mentioned him. Jean Patrick envisioned boys sneaking through the bush, hurling torches instead of rocks. He had to blink his eyes to clear the image.

Whistling after dark was bad luck—country people said it called evil spirits—so he made hissing sounds and called out, "Puppy!"

The red puppy barked at him from a scooped-out patch of earth. Jean Patrick pulled the fried sardine he had saved from his pocket and held it out. The puppy sniffed the air and crawled forward. Before the fish hit the ground, it was firmly in her jaws. He moved to stroke her head, but once more she skittered away.

AT FIRST LIGHT, Jean Patrick creaked open the door of the shack that was to be his and Roger's home. Mouse droppings and insect shells speckled the floor. He picked up an old broom from the corner and swatted at spiderwebs. Twigs from the broom rained down on him.

"That's for girls to do. Let me help you." Mathilde stood behind him, the red dog by her feet. The puppy slunk closer, but when Jean Patrick crouched to pet her, she jumped back.

"What's her name?"

Mathilde giggled. "Dogs don't have names." She took a bite from the piece of boiled cassava she held in her hand.

"This one will. I'm going to call her Pili, like pilipili."

Mathilde burst into a fit of laughter. "She's not a hot pepper; she's a dog."

"But I gave her fish with pilipili, and she loved it."

Mathilde broke off a piece of cassava. "Here. Some for you and some for Pili. If you feed her this, she'll like you."

He reached too quickly, and the dog scooted away across the yard.

"Don't worry. She'll come back." Mathilde ducked through the low doorway. "When Dadi fixes this up, it will be fancy. Luxury hotel." She wiped her hands on her skirt. Her skin had a golden color, and her hair crowned her high forehead with a feathery, red-dusted cap. "I'm going to study here, too," she said. "Dadi can build you and Roger desks."

"I don't think he wants us here. He got so mad at us last night."

"Eh! Do you have eyes in your head? It's all he's talked about since we knew you were coming." She leaned closer. "Every night when he goes fishing, he says it's to pay for your roof. He says corrugated metal costs like gold."

"He did that just for us?" Jean Patrick suddenly felt mean for all his negative thoughts.

"Dadi says we are finally going to have brothers. He calls you his sons." She touched his finger. "So now you have to call me Sister—promise?"

"I promise." Jean Patrick passed his hand across her hair. It was as soft as feathers.

1987

FIVE

WHEN JEAN PATRICK'S FATHER WAS ALIVE, the path to secondary school had seemed easy. If you did well, you succeeded. After all, Roger had done well, and now he was in school in Kigali. Mama and Auntie had made a big celebration for him the day he left, everyone from the hillside coming to talk and eat. Jean Patrick could have burst from pride for his brother, but watching Roger's face in the bus window, his waving hand getting smaller and smaller, he had wanted only to run after him, to catch hold of his arm and beg him not to go.

Jean Patrick remembered that first night in Gashirabwoba, when Roger had boldly contradicted Uncle's views. He hated to admit it, but Uncle had been right. With the quotas for Tutsi, he would have to come in first in his class to get a financial award. If he didn't, there would be no secondary school for him. Now that he had taken both the national exam and the exam at Gihundwe, staying up nights, studying until his chin dropped to his chest, his future was in Imana's hands. All he could do was wait. And wait some more.

It was always on his mind, the first of August, the date they would start announcing exam results. That morning, he awoke early, moving carefully to keep from waking Zachary, who slept beside him now that Roger was gone. He felt in the darkness for the lantern. His hand brushed Pili's fur, and he cupped her warm, wet muzzle. Lantern in hand, he walked out into a stillness as dark as the bottom of Lake Kivu. Now that it was school vacation, Jean Patrick spent his days fishing with Uncle. Fulgence and a few cousins were working for him, so Uncle could stay home nights while his crew fished.

Just before daybreak, Uncle and Jean Patrick paddled their pirogues out to help with the last loads of sardines and take them to market. Then the two of them checked their lines and trolled for tilapia. Jean Patrick was strong enough now to keep the canoe steady in the fast-moving current that flowed from Lake Kivu into the Rusizi River and on to Burundi.

There were three large capitaine fish waiting for them when Jean Patrick and Uncle reached the green plastic bottles that marked their lines. They lashed their pirogues together, and Jean Patrick held them steady in the swiftly flowing water.

"God is good," Uncle Emmanuel said. He slid the hook from the first fish's mouth and wound the line on its spindle. A kingfisher, harassed by pied crows, darted across the water and disappeared into the trees. Uncle hauled in the other two fish and dropped them into the bilge. "If the fishing stays like this, we can buy a motorboat by Christmas."

"I should hear about school soon," Jean Patrick said. "Maybe even today."

He thought of the shops and cabarets where radios blasted from sunrise to sundown. Exam results were announced on Radio Rwanda, but his radio, with its useless plug, remained silent on his shelf, and Uncle's transistor had broken last month and had not been replaced. Unless he was lucky, hearing his name by chance on the street, Jean Patrick would have to wait to see the results posted in town.

Uncle stripped to his shorts, dove into the current, and came up grinning. "Did you say something about school?" He disappeared, resurfacing with a rusted axle. Dropping the prize into the bilge, he said, "That's worth a few hundred francs." He went under again and brought up a bent rim. "Sorry. You were speaking to me. What was it?"

"It's not important, Uncle," Jean Patrick said.

IN THE AFTERNOON, when Jean Patrick came home, there was a large box on the table. "Open it," Mama said. She slid her iron over a pair of trousers, and the scent of Omo soap rose from the fabric. She added charcoal to the iron with a tong. The inside glowed, a field of tiny suns. With so little money for all of them, Mama spent mornings cleaning houses, washing and ironing for the rich people by the lake. Afternoons, she pressed the families' clothes with an old-fashioned iron, no magic switch to keep the bottom hot.

Inside the box was a transistor radio the color of a lemon. Carefully,

Jean Patrick lifted it out and set it on the table. "I want to hear your name announced when you win a scholarship," Mama said, as if success were already written in the sky.

Jean Patrick turned on the radio and twisted the dial until Radio Rwanda crackled through the speakers. He felt his father's presence close beside him. *Ntawiha icyo Imana itamuhaye,* Papa whispered. Nobody can give himself what Imana has not given him.

"There's something else," Mama said. "Didn't you see?"

Behind the box was a package tied with string. Unwrapping it, Jean Patrick found a pair of new shoes and a note in Uncle's careful hand. *Me, I am certain your news will be good. You have made me very proud.* He held them to the light and saw his face reflected back at him.

ON THE SECOND Wednesday of August, Jean Patrick opened his eyes with the thought firmly in his head: Today the results will be announced. He threw on his clothes and went straight to the house. Only spits and crackles came from the radio when he turned it on.

"What did you expect?" Mama looked up from stirring hot milk and sugar into a thermos of tea. "Not even Imana can give Radio Rwanda life before the appointed hour," she said.

ALL DAY FISHING, Jean Patrick could not keep still. He dropped hooks into the bilge and spilled his tea. Paddling home, he sprang into the water too early and sank to his neck.

"Eh! What's the hurry?" Uncle dismissed him with a wave of his hand. "Go, then. I'll take care of the boats."

No announcements floated from the town radios into Jean Patrick's ear, but when he saw Uwimana's truck parked at the bottom of the path, his heart jumped. He knew it wasn't right to ask Imana for help, but he couldn't stop himself, over and over, until he came through the door.

Inside, Aunt Esther, Mama, and Uwimana were dancing, the radio so loud the speakers buzzed. Clemence twirled Baby Pauline, Auntie's new daughter. There was a plate piled with cookies on the table, the same kind that filled Papa's pockets on special occasions. Zachary and the twins stuffed them into their mouths.

"Congratulations," Uwimana shouted. He danced over to Jean Patrick and grasped his hands. "First place! Your science score was in the top three percent in the country. Math: fifth percentile. Welcome to Gihundwe."

Jean Patrick was afraid if he moved the wrong way or blinked too many times, the news would hop back into Uwimana's mouth. "First place," he repeated. "Are you sure?"

Mama and Uwimana laughed. "I heard it with my own ears," Mama said. She had to shout to be heard above Papa Wemba's raucous tune. Jean Patrick fell into a chair and let out his breath as if he had been holding it for weeks.

"What's this?" Uncle Emmanuel stood by the door, pulling off his rubber boots.

"First place!" Aunt Esther sang, pulling Jean Patrick up for a dance.

Emmanuel leapt like an Intore dancer. "What did I tell you, eh? I knew you earned those shoes. You make every Tutsi proud."

"Papa is smiling today," Mama said.

"And there's more good news." Powdered sugar drifted onto Uwimana's suit jacket. "The new préfet de discipline is starting a track team. I told him about you, and it turns out he's a big fan of your brother's. He used to watch him play football on weekends with the Inzuki."

"Did you know Roger's the best player in his school? He's in Kigali, playing for a club."

"Of course I know. Your family is like our own."

It was true. Uwimana and Angelique had been a constant presence, bringing books and clothing, coming for tea. How often had Uwimana stooped in his baggy suit to play with Zachary and Clemence? How often had Angelique come to the house after her work, still dressed in her doctor's white coat, to bring medicine and take care of them?

Jacqueline and Mathilde danced through the door, hips swaying. Mathilde threw up her hands, first fingers pointing at the ceiling. "Wabaye uwa mbere! You're number one!"

Jacqueline kissed Jean Patrick's cheeks. "A neighbor boy came running out to the fields to tell us."

"Me, I never doubted it," Mathilde said. She took Jean Patrick by the wrists and spun him around. "My brother is the smartest boy in all Rwanda," she sang. Then suddenly she stopped, and tears tumbled down her cheeks.

"Why are you crying?" Jean Patrick wiped her tears with his palm.

"I don't want you to go away."

"Little Sister, I never will. I'll be just there, down the hill."

Uwimana clasped Jean Patrick in his strong embrace. "Welcome back," he said.

JEAN PATRICK TOOK Papa's journal from his shelf and sat on his bed. He let the book fall open where it would, as if Papa himself had chosen the entry. Although he could pick out themes, this particular page, like many, was filled with scientific terms and formulas Jean Patrick couldn't comprehend. Soon he would begin to decipher them. The thought filled his heart with pride.

He turned to the final entry. Once again, he imagined the scrape of Papa's chair, saw him search the darkness outside the window for the source of the noise that had interrupted his thoughts. He saw him rest the pen on the page, the pen he would never pick up again.

"I did it, Papa," he said. He listened for a whisper, a rustle of leaves. Only silence responded. He closed his eyes and inhaled the journal's smell of musty paper, the same scent he remembered from when his father held him.

Beside the journal was a powdered-milk tin where Jean Patrick kept Roger's old watch. The day Jean Patrick had finally beaten him running, the watch had been his prize. Jean Patrick thought Roger would be mad, but instead he clapped him on the back. "Here," Roger had said, fastening the watch on Jean Patrick's wrist. "You've earned it."

The strap was frayed, the face scratched, but it still kept track of his progress. Thirty seconds to the cypress trees, three minutes to the rock shaped like a bird, eighteen minutes to school—all his times recorded on the back pages of his notebook. Tonight, he thought, I'll write Roger and tell him the news. He zeroed the timer and put on a warmer shirt. Right now, he was going out to break his own record.

JEAN PATRICK SPRINTED as hard as he could up the ridge. Halfway, he had to stop, hands on his knees, lungs emptied. A reddish haze hung in the air and coated the brush. A blue turaco exploded into flight, its beak a flare of red and yellow. A bell tinkled in the clearing. It was Papa's inyambo steer, watching him with sleepy eyes, a clump of grass between his teeth. The beast dipped his head, horns radiant in the sun. Jean Patrick jogged to him and stroked the quivering skin. With a flash of understanding that took his breath, he saw that his father lived in all that surrounded him, and that every breath of wind contained his father's blessing.

Six

ON THE DAY JEAN PATRICK was to leave for Gihundwe, he opened his eyes to bright daylight, a mountain oriole's whistle in the distance. He must have slept, although he was not aware of having closed his eyes. All night he kept popping up, checking his folded uniform by feel in the dark, listening to Zachary's quiet breathing beside him. It would be the last night for a while that he would hear it. Lightly he touched the small knobs of Zachary's curled spine. Careful not to wake him, he took his clothes, walked out into the cool air, and climbed the path to the house, Pili following close behind as if she understood he would soon be departing.

In the courtyard, fresh laundry hung on the line. Aunt Esther sat on a mat beside the cookhouse grinding sorghum, a pile of red berries spread before her. Mathilde and Jacqueline swept, the *scritch-scritch* of twig brooms accompanying the bend and sway of their movements. In the small, rickety stall at the back of the courtyard, Jean Patrick stripped, held his breath, and poured a basin of icy water over his body. Instantly he awoke.

When he came out, Mama held out a steaming cup. Drops of milk fat glistened on the tea's surface. "Drink," she said. The tea was sweet and tasted of flowers.

Jean Patrick sat in a chair and watched the morning unfurl from the darkness. The mountains glowed red, and the forest canopy turned slowly to green and silver blue. He remembered a page in his father's journal about the dance of life. Here it was, all around him. He drew it deep into his memory so he could call it back at will.

Tonight he would sleep in a strange bed. Tomorrow he would wake without Zachary pressed against him or Pili curled by his feet. Mathilde set down her broom and disappeared into the house. He would miss her studying beside him, her feet tracing circles in the lantern's orb. Who would she ask now to explain a problem of geometry or the meaning of a French phrase? She reappeared at the door with a bundle of cloth.

"Here—I made this for you," she said. She thrust the bundle into his lap.

The cloth held a little red dog, the scent of grass still strong in the fibers. He recognized the fishhook curl of the tail, the attentive half-up, half-down set of the ears. "It's Pili!"

"So you won't be without her." She grabbed the cloth from Jean Patrick's fingers and unrolled it with a snap. It became a pair of running shorts.

"You made these, too?" He held them to his hips. "Eh—so pro!"

"I saw a pair in the market and copied them. Look inside."

Sewn into the waist was a pocket. "What's this?"

"So you can hide your money or keep your identity card when you run," she said.

Jean Patrick kissed her cheek. "All my big-big money."

"When you go to America to run, you will pick it from trees. I heard this."

"Then it must be true." Jean Patrick sipped his tea, curling his tongue around the taste. It was strong, at once bitter and sweet.

In an hour's time, Uwimana and Angelique would arrive. They would sit down to the traditional feast to mark a journey and then pile into the truck. They would walk with him through the pine archway, festively decorated for the arrival of new students as custom dictated. The statue of Saint Kizito would greet them as it had greeted Jean Patrick when he was small and went to visit his father at school. Exhilaration and fear balanced inside him like the two baskets of a scale.

ONLY THREE OTHER Tutsi stood at the beginning of class: Noel, a light-skinned boy from Gisenyi; Jean Marie from Gitarama, who stammered as he said his name; and a boy called Isaka, who shouted out, "I come from Bisesero, in the Prefecture of Kibuye." He was thin as a wire, quick and nervous in his movement. Jean Patrick wondered if Papa had made the Tutsi students stand when he was a teacher.

The classrooms seemed smaller and shabbier than Jean Patrick remembered. Boys crowded onto the rows of benches, and ink stained the long, scarred wooden desks that they shared. Sounds echoed in the room, every whisper magnified by the cement walls and floor.

The priest's scalp shone beneath thinning red hair. A mass of tiny freckles dotted his face. Cloaked in his white robes, he looked like a stork, and when he spoke, a lump moved in his throat as if he had just swallowed a fish. He picked up a stack of books. Before passing them to the boy on the end of the front row, he stroked a cover lightly with his fingertips, a gesture of tenderness Jean Patrick remembered suddenly from his father.

The priest began his lecture, and his complexion turned fiery. Jean Patrick thought of his father's journal, the pages he would now learn to decipher. Light streamed into the room. Beyond the window, Saint Kizito overlooked Gihundwe from his brick perch, arms open in blessing, the black wood of his skin gleaming.

THE TRACK AT Kamarampaka Stadium was a dirt path circling the football field. The runners stood barefoot, waiting for the coach to dismiss the football players. A boy kicked a wild shot at the goal, and the ball spun out of play. Jean Patrick watched the coach's fluid movement as he sprinted to retrieve it. I can learn a lot from him, he thought. He studied each of the runners in turn. Only Isaka, the skinny boy from Kibuye, worried him. That one, he thought, has a lot of energy that could turn to speed on the track.

A squat, chubby boy came up to Jean Patrick and shook his hand. In the sun, his skin gleamed like blue-black ink. Beneath his nose was a perfectly circular mole, as if God had taken a brush and applied a dot of paint. Jean Patrick inspected his legs; despite the boy's chubbiness, his calves looked muscular and strong.

"I'm Daniel," the boy said. "From Kigali." When he smiled, a dot of tongue poked out between his two front teeth like a piece of eraser. "Have you run track before?"

Jean Patrick shook out his legs. The football players had quit, and they lazed at the edge of the grass. "Not track, but I've run some. Me and my brother, before he left for secondary school." He did not want to give too much away in case this boy with the strong legs surprised him. The coach looked up and caught Jean Patrick's eye. A tingle traveled from his toes up his spine.

"I don't like to run. I like football," Daniel said. He jutted his chin toward the coach, who was now making his way toward them. "After tryouts, he said I was fat and lazy. He said I needed to suffer before he let me on the team. What is that crazy talk, eh?"

Isaka had joined them. "Me, I don't want to suffer. I ran a long way every day to get to school. I don't go fast, just far." He flicked a clump of earth from his toe. "I ran halfway to Cyangugu from Kibuye to take the test for the government scholarship."

Jean Patrick laughed. "Why didn't you take the Onatracom bus?"

Isaka shrugged. "It broke down. I started running, and it was a very long time before the next bus came." A grin spread on his face. "But as you see, I won the scholarship." A whistle shrilled, and they all jumped. "Hey-yey-yey!" Isaka said. "Here comes Tough Guy."

The coach wore white shorts and a blue and green football jersey that still looked crisp and freshly starched after a hard practice. His close-cropped hair accentuated the angular shape of his face, the hard line of his jaw. Jean Patrick recognized the Nike swoosh on his running shoes.

"Welcome." The coach motioned them onto the track. "My name is Rutembeza, Gihundwe's coach and préfet in charge of discipline, so you'll see a lot of me—especially if you behave badly." A toothpick wiggled between his teeth, and Jean Patrick couldn't tell if he was smiling or squinting. "How many Tutsi?" Jean Patrick and Isaka raised their hands. "Good. You'll be strong for distance."

Isaka looked at Jean Patrick and grinned. The coach took a stopwatch from his pocket. "Line up behind here. Let's go. Then once around to warm up."

Jean Patrick took off, quickly passing everyone. Each time he checked, the coach was watching him with that same odd expression. After warm-up, they ran short sprints. Excitement kept him at the front. He kept glancing at Coach, but the tight curl of his lips never changed.

"Now, four hundred meters: once around the track." Coach pointed at Jean Patrick. "You."

"Me?" Jean Patrick waited for praise.

"Yes—you. Do you know what *pace* means?" Jean Patrick opened his mouth to respond, but no answer came to him. The squint or smile passed from Coach's face. "I didn't think so."

Halfway around the track, Jean Patrick's chest tightened and strength left his legs. The feeling came out of nowhere, and it took all his will to keep him moving forward. Isaka passed him. Then another boy and then another, then Daniel, the chubby one, went by him with his lazy trot. Jean Patrick tried to respond, but a cramp brought him to his knees.

Daniel stopped and held out a hand to help him up.

The coach blew his whistle. "Leave him. Never stop in the middle of an interval. And you—I don't care if you have to crawl, but get back on that track and finish."

Jean Patrick struggled to his feet. Driven half by pride and half by a desire to punch both Coach and Daniel, he limped across the line.

SQUEEZED AGAINST THE tailgate in the back of the school truck, Jean Patrick stared out at the traffic and wished he could disappear. The boys' chatter burned his ears. Daniel squatted beside him on the wheel well. "Hey. I'm sorry if I got you in trouble."

Jean Patrick shrugged. A packed green bus honked and passed them. Painted in blue on the rear was the saying IMANA IKINGA UKUBOKO. God shields us from danger. A chicken scurried out of the way, squawking a saying of its own.

The truck pulled into Gihundwe. "I'm next to you in the dorm," Daniel said, his tongue peeking from between his teeth. "I saw you put your things away—so neat. My papa's in the army, so you'd think I'd be orderly, but sorry—I am not. I have three sisters, and my sloppiness drives them crazy. Maybe we'll have to draw a line between your bed and mine to keep my sloppiness away from your good order."

In spite of himself, Jean Patrick laughed. "Maybe we'll put up a fence," he said, jumping down from the truck. Still rattled by his failure, he did not pay attention and landed with one foot in a rut. His ankle gave, and he stumbled.

A firm hand held him up. "Are you all right?" Coach's grip tightened on Jean Patrick's arm.

"I'm OK, Coach. I'm sorry about what happened on the track."

"I've made that mistake myself. It humbles you." From Coach's look, Jean Patrick saw there was nothing accidental about the choice of words. "What did you say your name was?"

"Jean Patrick Nkuba."

The coach took the toothpick from his mouth and grinned. "Of course! Roger's brother. He's a good footballer. Why don't you play football? Running has no future in Rwanda. You have to go to Kenya or Tanzania for that."

"I want to run in the Olympics." The words slipped out. After his performance, they seemed silly, but Coach didn't laugh. The sun slid below a ridge of clouds. In his wet clothes, Jean Patrick felt the evening breeze go right through him.

"You're shaking. You should towel off and put on dry clothes."

Jean Patrick started back toward the dorm, but Coach stopped him. "You're good," he said. "I can see that. You have a lot of heart. But you also have a lot to learn. *Pace:* I want you to say that word in your sleep."

The muscles in Coach's jaw tensed and relaxed rhythmically. That's a smile that could cut you in two, Jean Patrick thought, as easily as wish you good morning or good afternoon.

SEVEN

JEAN PATRICK TUCKED HIS IDENTITY CARD into the pocket of his running shorts and zipped his thin jacket. When Mathilde began the tradition four years ago of sewing these pocketed shorts, she could not have foreseen how handy the design would become. She could not have predicted the checkpoints, the soldiers and policemen with their hands out demanding indangamuntu—identity papers—and harassing anyone with a high forehead and narrow features, anyone tall and skinny, what people thought of as Tutsi.

"Are you ready?" Jean Patrick whispered.

"Two seconds, eh?" Daniel said. "Let me sleep two seconds more."

Jean Patrick poked at the lump of blanket and sheet. "Two seconds more and we won't get back before someone is up and catches us."

Behind the chapel, they squeezed through the gap in the wall and started off down the path. It was just over a kilometer to the start of the hilly forest trail; by now, they knew the pace they kept, and they knew the ground well enough to run in darkness. Only the occasional crack of a branch, the rustle of a small animal through the undergrowth, broke the silence. They kept an easy tempo, Jean Patrick shaking out his fingers, tapping into the signals from legs and lungs. He felt good. At the trailhead, they stopped to recuperate before the start of their intervals.

"Are you going to take it easy, my friend?" Daniel put a hand on Jean Patrick's shoulder. "You'll need to save some energy for later."

"I'll be all right. I'll catch you on the way back. Don't forget to run."

"Be mindful," Daniel called after him. "My papa says soldiers everywhere have orders to arrest anyone they consider suspicious."

Jean Patrick did not need to be reminded. He zeroed his watch and took off. There was no moon, but he knew every rut and root by heart. Letting the sound and rhythm of his footfalls fill his head, he tried to push out all thoughts of his current troubles. Today the burgomaster was coming to Kamarampaka Stadium to watch him race. If he won, he hoped such an important person could help him with his Olympic dream. Perhaps keep open one of the doors that were closing for all Tutsi.

It seemed impossible that life could change so quickly. Since that day the previous year when the priest had come running into the classroom to announce that rebel soldiers had attacked Rwanda, his papa's dreams of unity had vanished as rapidly as mist in morning sun. The rebels, mostly Tutsi refugees who had fled to Uganda, called themselves the RPF, Rwandan Patriotic Front. Uncle said this was just the excuse the government had been looking for to stir up anti-Tutsi venom, and despite what his father had taught him, Jean Patrick had to agree.

Overnight, all Tutsi became ibyitso — accomplices. President Habyarimana declared war and announced reprisals. Accusations on Radio Rwanda blared from every shop and cabaret. Two of Auntie's cousins were arrested, and one day, policemen came to Uncle's house and accused him of helping the RPF. They searched in every corner, left clothes and cooking utensils and torn-open sacks from the larder strewn about the floor.

At Gihundwe, students who yesterday had been their friends looked at Jean Patrick and the other Tutsi as if they had suddenly transformed into devils. Word of Tutsi massacres filtered down through radio trottoir, sidewalk radio, the news that traveled on the streets.

"What did I tell you?" Daniel had said. "My papa knows what he's talking about." With every letter, Daniel had some dire warning to pass along to Jean Patrick.

Jean Patrick sucked his teeth in disgust. "Sidewalk gossip can't be trusted." But since that time, he had kept his eyes on the gangs of ragged boys who roamed the marketplace in town.

Jean Patrick picked up his pace. Dead sprint to the banana grove, slow to the cassava field. After the third interval, he unzipped his jacket. After the fourth, he turned back to run the course in reverse, his jacket fastened about his waist. First light turned the sky lavender. The exhilaration of speed, of plucking the taut string of his capability, coursed through his body. He caught Daniel on the last hard effort. "You are supposed to be running, not walking so," he said.

"I am running. It just seems like walking to you."

They would have to push to make it back in time. It was a little game they played, courting the risk of discovery. Jean Patrick gave Daniel a playful spank. "Put in some effort, OK?"

The gate was in sight. Jean Patrick's pulse drummed in his ears. He stretched out his legs as they slowed to an easy jog. The campus remained quiet, nestled in the wing of sleep.

IF IT WEREN'T for the cold, Jean Patrick would have been dozing by second period. By third period, the chill was no longer enough. The motion of his chin hitting his chest startled him awake. He shook his head and took off the outer of his two sweaters. If he wanted to keep his scholarship, he needed to pay attention. In two hours' time, he needed to win a race.

The last thing he remembered was answering Father Paul's question about the classification system for tilapia. He had mixed up the genus and the species. Every day, Jean Patrick recited his lessons while he ran around the track. At night, he studied until he couldn't focus, and then he fell into a sleep that felt like drowning. Coach had been right; it would be better to play football like Roger. A football player had a chance to succeed in Rwanda.

With Roger, Uncle's political seeds had taken root. He was at university now, in Ruhengeri, and he hoped to be a journalist. In his spare time, he wrote for a student opposition newspaper. When he came home to visit, he always brought a copy of *Kanguka* for Uncle to read. Emmanuel read the newspaper cover to cover. "I like the name of this paper—Wake Up," he said. "That's what you need to do, Jean Patrick. Open your eyes. See what's going on." But when Emmanuel mentioned politics, all Jean Patrick wanted to do was close his eyes and sleep.

His father had always said that Hutu and Tutsi were one people living together in one country. After Jean Patrick first uttered the words *I am Tutsi*, Papa had asked, "What does that mean? Can you tell me how we are different?"

Jean Patrick could not. Some Hutu had coffee-and-cream complexions, long, delicate fingers, and sculpted features, and some Tutsi were short and round-faced, with black-coffee skin. If he just saw Roger on the street, with his broad, muscular body and shorter stature, could he say? They had been mixed up together for so many years; two of Papa's sisters had married Hutu men. Did their husbands love them less because of the ethnie written on their indangamuntu?

It was not until rocks shattered his windows, the word *Tutsi* crashing through the glass, that the two were torn apart in Jean Patrick's mind. Since the start of the war, ethnicity grew around him like an extra layer of skin. No matter how he tried, he could not shed it.

"Be proud," Uncle said. "Your heritage is the heritage of the mwamis, the Tutsi kings. If it weren't for the Belgians and their meddling, we might still be ruled by the mwami today." But pride didn't protect Jean Patrick from glares in the dining hall, on the paths, in class. When he had been home the month before for Christmas, he had overheard Zachary asking Imana why he hadn't been born Hutu.

Jean Patrick shifted his weight on the hard bench and tried to focus on the diagram Father Paul had drawn on the board. Somehow the class had left the animal kingdom behind and entered the world of plant taxonomy. Glancing at his watch, Jean Patrick traveled forward in his mind to his race. He felt the fire in his lungs, saw the finish line approaching, the burgomaster standing to cheer him. A chill that came partly from fear, partly from excitement, made the hairs on his arms stand on end. He was still caught in the moment when a barrage of fists pounding on the classroom door jerked his attention back to the present. The door flew open, and a group of boys swarmed in.

"Mana yanjye!" Daniel whispered, pulling on Jean Patrick's sleeve. "It's starting."

"What craziness are you talking now?"

"Are you blind? They're coming to kill Tutsi." Daniel squeezed Jean Patrick's arm so tightly he nearly cried out.

There were five of them. They walked down the rows shouting and kicking the benches. Fumes of banana beer rippled in their wake.

"Sit down, Father," one of them said. "We're taking over the lesson."

Father Paul sat and opened his book.

Three of the boys wore the red, yellow, and green pajamas of a new group called Hutu Power. Jean Patrick had seen them hanging around the cabarets, walking through town with machetes and clubs. The one who spoke wore a boubou of the same colors over his pants. The shirt, flowing almost to his knees, looked sewn from a Rwandan flag and fitted him so loosely he swam inside it. A hat with a button bearing Habyarimana's picture sat crookedly on his head. When the light caught his face, Jean Patrick saw the zigzag scar that slashed his cheek, and he remembered his name: Albert. Mama once bought a charcoal iron from him at the market where he sold used appliances with his father. Uncle almost made her take it back because he didn't trust him.

Albert sat on the edge of the priest's desk and clapped his hands above his head. "Inyenzi, stand up!" No one moved. "What? No Tutsi cockroaches in this class?"

The air sagged with the weight of the question. *Be proud,* Uncle Emmanuel whispered in Jean Patrick's ear. Roger's fingers pressed at his back. He stood.

"Are you stupid?" Daniel hissed. "Sit down."

Jean Patrick stepped clear of the bench in case he had to run or fight. "Yego. I'm Tutsi."

"We're Tutsi, too," Noel and Isaka said. They stood and held their joined hands high.

Jean Marie hunched in his seat. He leaned over his notebook and pretended to write until the pencil fell from his fingers. The thugs circled the rows of desks, two of them stopping in front of Noel and Isaka. A third yanked a tall, skinny boy from his chair. "Hey, Inyenzi—stand up! What are you afraid of?"

"Leave that guy alone—he's Hutu," a classmate said.

"Sorry, man." The Hutu Power boy laughed wildly, showing rotten gray nubs for teeth. He let his captive go and walked drunkenly over to Noel and Isaka. "So you're proud cockroaches?" He twisted Noel's arm behind his back and shoved him facedown onto the desk. Jean Patrick heard a crack. Noel struggled to raise his head. Blood dripped from his nose.

"He's Tutsi, too," a student in the front row said, pointing at Jean Marie.

Rotten Tooth pulled Jean Marie to his feet. "Did you eat your tongue?" He shook Jean Marie until he cried.

Father Paul turned the page of his book and adjusted his glasses on his nose.

Albert jumped from his perch and confronted Jean Patrick. The reek of his breath made Jean Patrick recoil. "You're that runner guy." He jabbed his thumb into Jean Patrick's chest.

Jean Patrick smiled. "That's me."

His heart thudded against his ribs, and blood surged into his legs as if he were at the start line, waiting for the bang of the blocks. Albert slapped him and then brought a boot down on his foot. The pain, immediate and sharp, brought flashes of light to Jean Patrick's eyes. His knee buckled, and he collapsed against the bench.

Daniel put his arm around Jean Patrick. "He's crazy from lack of sleep, this one. Everyone knows he's Hutu. His father was préfet des maîtres here, and he helps the whole class with homework. Eh? Am I right?" No one contradicted his word.

Albert seized Daniel by the shoulders. "Are you icyitso?" He sucked his teeth. "Stupid boy, don't you know the Ten Commandments?"

Jean Patrick held his breath. Since December, when the Hutu Ten Commandments were first published in *Kangura,* the new Hutu newspaper, they had been broadcast on the radio, quoted in the streets, tacked up on walls. *Any Hutu man who acquires a Tutsi wife, a Tutsi secretary, a Tutsi business partner, is icyitso — a traitor. All Tutsi are inferior and must be kept out of schools and important positions. The Hutu male should be united in solidarity against his common enemy, the Tutsi. All Hutu must spread this doctrine wherever they go. Any Hutu who persecutes his brother for spreading and teaching this ideology shall be deemed icyitso.*

"You should know your enemies," Albert said. He pushed Daniel hard against Jean Patrick, jumped onto the desk, and walked from one end to the other, listing precariously. In front of each of the five students sharing the desk, he stopped and stared. Jean Patrick gave him a mental push so he would lose his balance and fall, crack his head on the floor.

"Let me tell you the news from Radio Rwanda," Albert shouted. "The

RPF have attacked Ruhengeri and slaughtered hundreds of innocent Hutu. Now Hutu Power wants vengeance."

He jumped down and waved his arms toward his friends, who then dragged the Tutsi and Daniel into the aisle. Some Hutu students sprang up, ready for action, railing against all Tutsi. Frantically, Jean Patrick looked around for someone to come to their side, but no one did. Father Paul remained seated at his desk, calmly reading.

Bodies pressed in. A book thumped against Jean Patrick's back, hard enough to knock the wind from him. Fists hit his head, but his attention was on protecting his legs and feet. The pain in his foot made even standing difficult, and shifting his weight brought a rush of dizziness. Albert grabbed him by the sweater and twisted until the collar squeezed his throat and he struggled to breathe. From the corner of his eye, he saw Daniel lifted like a sack of sorghum.

At that moment, Uwimana burst into the room, two policemen behind him. Suddenly, Jean Patrick was back at his old house on a December afternoon, hearing these same two policemen tell him that his papa had died.

"Let those boys go!" Uwimana shouted.

The stranglehold eased, but Albert still held on. His lips brushed Jean Patrick's ear, and Jean Patrick smelled the rank, hot breath, sharp with urwagwa. "Don't forget me, because I'm going to kill you," Albert whispered. "That's a promise."

"This is still my school," Uwimana said. "Your justice isn't welcome while I'm in charge. All of you, get out."

The boys circled Uwimana. The policemen moved toward them, hands on their sticks.

"Beware, icyitso," Albert said, pointing at Uwimana. "Hutu Power memories are long." They backed out the door, and the policemen followed. On the way out, one of the policemen nodded to Jean Patrick and gave him a hidden thumbs-up.

Father Paul cleared his throat and peered out from behind his book as Uwimana approached his desk. Uwimana removed his glasses, cleaned them, and put them back on, speaking to Father Paul in a voice too low for Jean Patrick to hear.

"What could I do?" Father Paul said loudly. "They were so many. And drunk. I could smell urwagwa from here."

"Class is canceled," Uwimana said. "All Tutsi and anyone else who is hurt, stay behind."

Jean Patrick pressed against Daniel. "Help me walk. I have to fix my foot so I can run." While Uwimana tended to Noel's bloody nose, Jean Patrick leaned on Daniel and limped out.

"They could have really hurt you for defending me," Jean Patrick said. He pulled off his shoe, and the wave of pain made him sweat. "Daniel, check my foot, eh? I'm afraid to look."

"Aye! So swollen!" Daniel said.

"Let's get some tape. I have to race."

Daniel clucked his tongue. "Hutu Power tries to kill you, and all you think about is running."

"Hutu Power." Jean Patrick spit into the grass. "They're just trouble-makers. I don't want to think about them anymore."

"If you want to survive, you better think about them. Let's find Coach." Daniel stood and offered Jean Patrick a hand.

Thick gray-black clouds descended over the forest, blocking the sun. Jean Patrick inhaled an oily smell. He sniffed again, and the stench hit him: not clouds but smoke darkened the sky. Houses were burning in the hills. Columns of smoke rose in all directions. Students and staff came running from the buildings.

"What's happening?" someone asked.

"They're smoking out Inyenzi one by one," another student replied, laughing.

Jean Patrick lunged at the student and swung wildly. A blast from a horn froze him.

"Get in," Uwimana shouted. The truck's smashed headlight glared like a punched eye. Noel sat beside him, head tilted back, a bloody cloth held to his nose. Somber-faced Tutsi students squeezed together in the bed of the truck. "Isaka says you're hurt."

Jean Patrick shook his head, but Daniel spoke up. "Yes, Headmaster, he is."

"Sit inside, then. Angelique will see to you. All Tutsi are coming to my house for the night. I'm not taking any chances."

"Headmaster, I need to get home right away." Jean Patrick gestured toward the hills. Panic gripped his chest. "Can you ask the burgomaster to come another day?"

"Ah, Jean Patrick. Don't worry about the burgomaster now. Track is canceled. Everything's canceled. Cyangugu has gone mad."

IN THE MORNING, Uwimana drove Jean Patrick to Gashirabwoba. With his long legs, it was impossible to get comfortable on the seat. "No need for X-ray; they're both broken," Angelique had said when she splinted his toes. "Probably a bone or two in the foot as well, but I'm afraid there's nothing we can do but bandage it and give you crutches."

The smoke of burning houses was gone, replaced by the haze of cook fires. Roads and hillsides bustled with morning traffic. At a small spring in the rocks, children filled jerricans with water. A young boy walked down the road balancing two filled cans nearly as big as he was. Jean Patrick almost wondered if yesterday had been a bad dream.

The truck backfired and strained on the hill. Jean Patrick searched the landscape. Beyond the welcome sign for Gashirabwoba, he saw the first charred ruin. In the valley below, in the eucalyptus grove where meetings were held, he counted a second, a third. His heart contracted. As the truck lumbered forward, his eyes did not leave the spot where Uncle's compound should soon have come into view.

His attention was so singularly focused that he didn't see Uncle and Mathilde until Uwimana slowed and called out. Although he was relieved to see them, he knew something was not right. Uncle was dressed for town, with his jacket and wide-brimmed hat, when he should long since have left to tend his fishing lines. Mathilde should have been in school.

Mathilde was already talking loudly as she hopped into the truck. "Jean Patrick! You're safe! Ko Mana—we were so worried." She flung her arms around his neck.

"Me, too. I hardly slept all night, worrying. Is everyone OK at home?"

"Thanks to God," Uncle said.

"And the house?"

"Untouched. But what about you? We heard there was trouble at Gihundwe. We were on our way to check."

Mathilde squealed and touched Jean Patrick's bandaged foot.

"Tsst! What happened? They beat you?"

"It's not bad," Jean Patrick said, shifting his weight. The movement made him wince.

Uncle whistled. "Who did this?"

"Just some boys from town. I'm all right."

Mathilde pointed to a dark purple bruise on her arm. "Me, too. Some girls in my class said it was my fault the rebels attacked. They called me Inyenzi. I don't care; it didn't hurt too much." She touched her lips to Jean Patrick's ear. "I pushed them down when Madame wasn't watching."

"Good girl," Jean Patrick whispered back. He plucked a piece of grass from her hair. "What's this?"

"We're all dirty from sleeping in the forest," Mathilde said. She rubbed her scalp, and flecks of leaves and grass fell onto her blouse.

"We saw the smoke," Emmanuel said, "and I sent everyone into the bush. Then I sat all night in the chair with my machete. I wasn't going to leave our safety up to chance."

At the bottom of the trail, Uwimana got the crutches from the bed of the truck. They were heavy wooden things with thickly padded armrests and handles, a few sizes too small. Jean Patrick limped stubbornly up the slope before Uncle had a chance to help him. Aunt Esther, Clemence, and Jacqueline ran to embrace him. Zachary and the twins came out behind them. Clémentine still had dirt on her face; Clarisse had one flip-flop on and one in her hand. The familiar chatter of family hummed around Jean Patrick. He couldn't remember another time when he had been so glad to hear it. He kept expecting his mother to come and greet him, but when he reached the house and looked inside, he still had not seen her.

"Where's Mama?" he asked, apprehension returning.

"She went to work. None of us wanted her to go, but what could we do?" Auntie said. "Uwimana, come eat with us. So late, and we are just now sitting down."

"I would love nothing more, but I have a school full of hotheads to attend to. I told Jean Patrick to stay home and rest."

With a sick feeling in the pit of his stomach, Jean Patrick recalled his missed race. "The burgomaster! What will happen now?"

"He won't run away. Not when he can hear the jingle of gold coins in his pocket," Uwimana said.

"Now you see I'm right," Uncle told Jean Patrick after breakfast. "Habyarimana is no change. Buhoro, buhoro, little by little, the Hutu will pick us off until we have all disappeared."

"Papa taught me to believe in Habyarimana," Jean Patrick said without conviction. "Those RPF shouldn't stir up trouble."

"Listen to you! Like Radio Rwanda. Habyarimana is no different than Kayibanda, the first murderer to lead this country. If you ask me, nothing has changed since the Hutu rose up against the mwami and drove him out. That's when they started killing us, and they haven't stopped. The RPF are *our* people. Their families did not leave by choice; they fled for their lives. They're not *stirring up trouble,* Jean Patrick. They just want to come home."

The familiar discomfort stirred in Jean Patrick's chest. Who was right, Uncle or Papa? The question tired him more every day. He struggled to his feet and put on Papa's felt hat. It was only now, after the start of the war, after the insults and name-calling had started, that he began to understand that a felt hat and a herder's staff branded a man as Tutsi, a keeper of cattle, despised by the Hutu tenders of the fields.

"I'm going to look for Mama." Jean Patrick took his crutches and closed the door on Uncle's protests.

Jean Patrick found her on the road above the lake, a basin of fruit on her head. He waved, and she hurried toward him.

"Mana yanjye—what happened to you?"

"Hutu Power broke my foot. I'll be OK."

"I can see it hurts—let's rest a minute." They sat together on a log and shared a mango.

Jean Patrick looked out at the lake, its rippled surface. "Why did you never tell us about your parents?"

Mama's eyes shone with the same coppery flecks as Mathilde's. "Your father thought the troubles were over for the Tutsi when Habyarimana seized power. Habyarimana promised the Tutsi equality. He said there would be no more killing, and we believed him. The past was the past, Papa said—why frighten the children?"

"And what do you think?"

"Papa loved you so much. He just wanted to protect you."

They sat and watched the fishermen, tiny flakes of pepper floating in the soup of the lake. A peaceful silence took over Jean Patrick's mind. He was worn out from thinking, tipping the balance back and forth, one side winning and then the other. The tumult was too much.

Mama refastened her scarf and placed the ingata on her head. Even this small thing made of twigs to cushion a load was a crown when she wore it. "Are you ready to go, my son?"

"Yes. I think I can walk now."

She balanced the basin on top of the ingata, and they started up the slope. A breeze chased purple clouds across the sky, a hint of rain swelling their bellies.

"What about Papa's parents? Did the Hutu kill them, too?"

"*The Hutu.* You sound like your uncle now. Not every muhutu is a killer. Your grandmother died of cancer. Grief killed your grandfather two months after."

"Do you agree with Papa? Is the killing in the past?"

Mama let out a long sigh. "I don't know. When talk heats up Hutu heads and they start burning our houses, I have to question." She faced Jean Patrick, her gaze even with his. "You are old enough to understand now. A shadow of fear follows me wherever I go. I can't remember a time since I was a young child when both my eyes slept at the same time." She stepped across the rutted earth, the basin steady atop the ingata. "We can never forget we're Tutsi, eh? It's a curse but also a blessing." She leaned her weight into the hill as if pushing against an opponent.

Jean Patrick found a rhythm of movement, swinging crutches and then body to keep up with her. The padding on the handles had started to unravel. In the distant fields, women bent and swayed with the rhythm of their hoes, their pagnes splashes of bright color in the gray air. The countryside quivered, everyone waiting for rain.

IT DIDN'T TAKE long for government forces to beat back the RPF or for Jean Patrick's bruises to fade and then disappear. But the incidents of January 23 had changed Gihundwe for good. The peace at school, like peace in the country, remained an uneasy one. Jean Patrick's bones were healing. After four weeks of rest, two weeks of slow running, and three weeks of hard training, Coach finally said, "I think you're ready for the burgomaster now." Practice had ended, and he was rubbing a minty-smelling oil into Jean Patrick's legs. "Your rebel friends are making everyone's life hard." As if it had been the RPF that had burst into class, turned the afternoon upside down, and stamped on his foot.

A fierce breeze drove trash across the track. Itumba, the long rainy season that spanned Easter, knocked at the door, and rain weighed heavily in the air. Jean Patrick looked over at the scratched-out oval of dirt where he felt most at home in his life. "Me, I don't care about the RPF," he said. "I care about racing. About winning." He waited for Coach to dismiss him, hoping the subject of politics was finished.

A thin smile cracked Coach's face. "I like you, Jean Patrick. You're a true warrior. I believe you will show the burgomaster what you're made of."

"Eh? You think I'll win?"

"I would guess that you have only just begun to win." Coach helped Jean Patrick to his feet. "OK. For now, we're done."

Released, Jean Patrick jogged toward the truck. Daniel was there, waiting for him. His baby fat had disappeared; he was trim and solid now, a real footballer. At least their friendship had endured. Jean Patrick knew he could always count on that.

ON THE WAY to the dorm, Daniel grabbed his arm. "Walk a minute, eh?"

"What's up?" Jean Patrick fell into step beside him.

Daniel walked toward the chapel. "It's probably nothing," he said, "but I wanted to tell you what I heard. There's been talk of expelling all Tutsi from school."

Jean Patrick swallowed. "Who told you?"

"No one. I overheard the priests talking."

The path seemed suddenly close and dark. "Headmaster won't allow it. Neither will Coach. He knows it's me the burgomaster's coming to see."

"I heard Coach's voice," Daniel said. "He was there with them."

"You heard wrong." Rage bubbled in Jean Patrick. Mama had been right when she said being Tutsi was a curse. About the blessing, he was not sure. But he knew one thing: in Rwanda, it was the Hutu who drank the cream from the igicuba — the milk jug. If Imana were to come down this minute and ask him to choose his ethnicity, he couldn't say for sure how he would answer.

"You didn't let me finish," Daniel said. "Coach also said it was because of you — only you — that he couldn't agree."

EIGHT

JEAN PATRICK CLOSED HIS NOTEBOOK and packed up his books. Father
had kept the class late, so he needed to hurry or Coach would be mad.
Charging toward the door, he nearly collided with Coach.

"I thought I'd find you here," Coach said. PLAY TO WIN, his football
jersey proclaimed. He handed Jean Patrick a pair of green Nikes.

"What are these for?" They felt as light as air in Jean Patrick's hands.

"Try them."

Jean Patrick slid a foot into the sneaker. His body tingled. When his
toes hit something hard, he tried to force them in. Coach laughed. "I forgot. There are socks inside."

The socks were thin and soft, and with them on, Jean Patrick's feet
slipped into the shoes as if gliding through butter. He took a few prancing
steps. The soles were springy; he almost lifted from the ground with his
toe-off. The sides held his heels like a firm hand.

"Ko Mana. Like this I could run forever." He fingered the strange fabric, waiting for Coach to explain.

Coach explored a space between two teeth with his toothpick. "They're
yours, so get used to them. I'm taking the team to a meet in Butare next
month—a real track. I want you to qualify for Nationals next June in
Kigali. This year you'll have some true competition. It's going to be staged
as a two-country meet: Rwanda and Burundi."

Nationals—the first solid step on Jean Patrick's Olympic journey! He
tasted the word like the first bite of a pastry, savoring the anticipation of
the sweet in the center, made all the more tempting by the thought of
extra competition.

Coach squeezed Jean Patrick's toes. "A little big, but at the rate you
grow, they'll be fine by next week." He relaced the shoes. "If your Inyenzi

friends would stop making trouble, it wouldn't be such a struggle to get you recognized."

"The RPF are not my friends. I don't want to make trouble. I just want to run."

"Let's go," Coach said. "You ride with me. We have a few things to discuss."

ON THE WAY to practice, Jean Patrick flexed and pointed his foot inside the Nikes—*his* Nikes. First the shoes and now this place of privilege in the cab. Each time Jean Patrick stole a glance, Coach's eyes were on him, Coach's mouth frozen in his familiar, inscrutable grin. He knew Coach was toying with him, knotting the silence into a noose of anticipation. Coach sped up and passed a slow-moving car, barely avoiding a head-on collision with a bus. Jean Patrick's stomach rose to his throat, and instinctively he gripped the door handle. The bus horn's wail followed them.

Coach laughed. "I want you to concentrate on middle distance—specifically the eight hundred. Those stocky Hutu guys have more muscle in one calf than you have in your body, and they'll pound you into the ground for shorter sprints. You won't slow down no matter what I tell you, so you'll fade for anything longer, but with your determination, twice around the track you can hang on and win."

A cloud of dust swirled toward them, and Jean Patrick rolled up the window. It was Umuhindo, the small rainy season, and in the hills, women planted beans, peas, and maize. Through the haze he picked out the treetops along the far wall of the stadium, then the rusty galvanized panels over the seats, the walls, and finally the white line of a goalpost. The afternoon sun stained the brick walls pink. Even after four years, this first glance caused an extra little skip of his heart.

"I like the eight hundred, but I can win any distance," Jean Patrick said, touching a fingertip to his Nike swoosh for luck.

Coach parked the truck in a scrap of grass. "Let me do the thinking, eh? You just run." He took his stopwatch and whistle from the glove box, committed to forward motion before his foot hit the ground. The rest of the runners headed toward the track, feet swishing through the dirt. "I'll make a star out of you yet, but you have to listen to me," Coach said. "Have patience." He aimed a finger at Jean Patrick's chest. "*Buhoro buhoro ni rwo urugendo.*" Little by little a bird builds its nest. Jean Patrick recognized the proverb with a chill. It was the same one Uncle had quoted to describe how the Hutu would wipe the Tutsi off the face of the earth.

☙

THE TRACK AT National University in Butare was an oval of swept red dirt encircling the football field. Unlike the track at Kamarampaka Stadium, the ground was leveled, wide enough for eight runners. Spectators filled the seats and sprawled across the grass. When Jean Patrick saw the crowd, adrenaline rushed through him. Runners jogged around the track, practiced drills and sprints down the straights. Jean Patrick watched a group of girls doing lunges and high-step drills in the grass.

"You look like you're trying to figure out their genus and species," Daniel said.

"Eh! I think some of them could beat you."

"Watch it! Come on—let's warm up together." A dot of pink tongue showed between Daniel's front teeth.

Isaka caught them. "Hey-yey-yey! Can you believe this? I wonder how many runners in the fifteen hundred."

They took an easy jog around the track. In the final turn, a group of runners closed in behind them. Two came up on either side, and two stayed back, on their heels. Jean Patrick nodded a greeting, but in response they only tightened the space between them. The hairs on the back of Jean Patrick's neck stood up.

"Something smells," one of them said. He made a show of sniffing the air, and they all laughed. "You're Nkuba Jean Patrick, right? That Inyenzi from Cyangugu who thinks he's a star?"

Jean Patrick quickened his pace. "Maybe I am a star."

"You tea pickers think you're good, but you haven't been to Kigali."

"Don't talk stupid," Daniel said. "I come from Kigali."

The boy sprinted in front and spun around. "Take a good look, Inyenzi," he said. His nose veered crookedly to one side, giving his face an off-balance look. "It's all you'll see of our faces. After this, it will be our backsides you look at." The four hooted and peeled off down the straight.

Isaka chased them down and ran on their heels. Jean Patrick started after him.

"Stay focused," Daniel said. He pulled Jean Patrick back. "They want to wear you out. They're scared."

"They should be. If I am Inyenzi — cockroach — I have six legs to run on." Jean Patrick turned his attention to the girls on the track. "Who goes first, them or us?"

Six runners remained for the eight-hundred-meter final, including three of the four Kigali boys. Crooked Nose mouthed something to Jean Patrick that he didn't catch. Jean Patrick looked him in the eye and laughed. Coach had instructed him to let Crooked Nose win the semifinal. It took every ounce of willpower, but he did it. Now came revenge.

The starter banged the blocks. Jean Patrick drove off the line, rising quickly from his crouch. He expected to leave the boys behind, but after breaking for the inside, the four of them ran together. Crooked Nose crowded him toward the pole. Jean Patrick stepped it up. Two boys faded from the pack. Jean Patrick surged again, but Crooked Nose hung on.

By the second turn, Crooked Nose had fallen back, and Jean Patrick ran alone. His chest compressed; his lungs burned. When he passed the start for his second lap, Coach was on the sidelines, stopwatch strangled in his hand, signaling, Slow down! Dig, Jean Patrick told himself, but his legs would not respond. His new Nikes felt more like lead than air, and his rhythm began to desert him.

By the time he reached the back turn, all three Kigali boys had caught him. They hemmed him in, sprinting when he sprinted, blocking him when he tried a move. They approached the final turn. Jean Patrick looked for an opening and prayed he had the strength to take it. Shoulders jostled. Elbows bumped.

A hundred meters to go. Let's go, Jean Patrick chanted in his head, as if there were two of him, the runner of his spirit, who could fly, and the runner of his body, who teetered on the edge of surrender. Crooked Nose forced him to the edge of the track. Shouts and cheers came from the crowd in waves, like echoes down a long hallway. Beads of sweat from the boy's face splashed Jean Patrick's arm.

With the finish line in sight, Crooked Nose drifted to the outside. It was little more than a suggestion, but Jean Patrick saw it as a ray of sun piercing the forest canopy. He pounced and started his kick. A second wind filled his lungs. He leaned across the line a half step in front and then collapsed to heave in the dirt. Coach ran toward him.

"Nkuba Jean Patrick. One forty-eight eleven," the announcer bellowed. "A new school record by almost two seconds. All top three runners break the old record." The stadium erupted.

"Victory lap!" Coach shouted. "You're going to Championships in June!"

Jean Patrick wobbled to his feet and jogged around the track. He was giddy and trembly, utterly spent. Half of him basked in the wild cheers, everyone standing and clapping—this was the unity Papa believed in—but the other half could not shake the heat of the Kigali boys' breath, still stinging his neck.

JEAN PATRICK TOOK the steps two at a time. The electricity of his win, his record-breaking time, still buzzed in his head. Daniel and Isaka stood on the top stair. They were shouting something, but it was lost in the ruckus. "I'm just coming," Jean Patrick shouted back. He heard footsteps close behind, and he moved aside to let the person pass. The Kigali boys surrounded him.

"You think you can just win like that?" Crooked Nose said.

"I think I did," Jean Patrick said. He searched for an opening. Momentum carried the crowd upward. He shifted his gym bag on his shoulder to use as a weapon if he had to. Daniel and Isaka struggled to reach him, fighting the opposing tide. Jean Patrick knew it would be better to keep quiet. A Tutsi boy could not stand and fight in a crowd. He had learned that lesson well at Gihundwe, but he could not let it go.

"Hey—we don't want trouble," Daniel said from the step above.

Crooked Nose grabbed him by the jersey. "You look Hutu to me. Are you Hutu?"

"I'm Rwandan," Daniel said.

"You're icyitso—a traitor." Crooked Nose shoved Daniel full force into Jean Patrick.

The force sent Jean Patrick spinning. Daniel grabbed his wrist but could not hold on. The concrete step rose to meet Jean Patrick's face. The last sensations he had before darkness engulfed him were of warm blood and gritty bits of tooth against his tongue, the dizzy relief as Coach lifted him like a baby into his arms. Coach was saying something about Championships, but the words drifted by without sticking. Jean Patrick let himself sink into the waters of Lake Kivu, Uncle's face like a drowned, dark moon above him.

1992

NINE

ALTHOUGH IT WAS THE MIDDLE of Itumba, the rainy season, clouds failed to gather, and the earth remained dry and wrinkled as a grandfather's skin. Lake Kivu had withdrawn, leaving a ring of black sand where waves had tickled Jean Patrick's feet the year before. The fish had disappeared, taking Uncle Emmanuel's motorboat dream with them.

Some days, before dawn or late in the evening, storms erupted across the peaks, and people began to hope. But when the sun climbed high and no rain materialized, the women clucked their tongues and went back to hacking the thirsty ground with their hoes. Red dust stained their pagnes and settled like a blanket over the entire countryside.

Jean Patrick, home for Easter vacation, stood with Mathilde among the hilled rows of beans. Skinny pods drooped between the leaves. Pili lay in their scant shadows and chased lizards in her dreams. "What do you call inyanya in French?" he asked.

"Ça s'appelle tomate."

"Fruit or vegetable?"

Mathilde wrinkled her nose. "Tomato is a vegetable. No, wait. It's so sweet. Maybe a fruit." She groaned. "I don't think I have to know this to pass secondary school exams."

"You're Tutsi. You have to know everything. You have to get first place." Two pied crows clucked from a branch in the jacaranda. Jean Patrick heaved a rock, and they flew away, complaining loudly.

"Ko Mana! I forget. It has something to do with seeds." Mathilde sighed. She took a mango from the basket of harvested fruit and vegetables, peeled back the skin with her teeth, and took a bite. "This one is so sour." She made a face and threw it back.

"You have to finish it now. No one wants a mango with your teeth in it." Jean Patrick tossed it back to her.

Laughing, Mathilde inspected the bitten place. "I don't see any teeth."

Jean Patrick picked the last of the beans and moved to the rows of peas. He shook a dried pod in Mathilde's direction. "What is the taxonomic system of classification?"

"*Kingdom, phylum, class, order, genus, family, species.*" Mathilde accompanied each word with the strike of her hoe.

"Which comes first—*genus* or *family*? You're mixed up."

A lizard scurried into the vines, and Mathilde chased after it. "I'm too tired. I still have three weeks before exams. You can help me tonight."

"Lazy! One more. What's the genus of our tilapia?"

Mathilde didn't answer. Jean Patrick followed her gaze. She was watching someone on the path climb briskly toward them. It was Roger.

Jean Patrick whooped and bolted toward him. "So many days no word of you, and now you just come dancing home?" In his embrace, Roger's body felt hard and spare. He wore blue jeans, and beneath a beret, his hair stuck out in an Afro.

"Look at you!" Roger wiped his brow and made a show of looking up into Jean Patrick's face. "You are *Little* Brother in name alone."

With a shock, Jean Patrick realized his eyes were even with the top of Roger's forehead. Only six months before, they had stood eye to eye.

Mathilde sprinted toward them. "You're back from Ruhengeri! And only last night I dreamed you'd return."

Jean Patrick smiled at her fluid quickness, her muscular kick. "Here she comes, Mathilde Kamabera, our new Olympic hero!"

Roger spun her around. "Are you studying hard, little bird?"

"Of course." Mathilde danced. "Jean Patrick beats me if I don't. I take placement exams after vacation."

Roger cupped his hand to his ear. "What's this? The wind tells me you'll get first place." He patted Jean Patrick's back. "And you—ready for the Olympics? I've told everyone you're Rwanda's best runner."

The first suggestion of a beard graced Roger's chin, and Jean Patrick ran the tip of his finger across it. "Not Olympics, but Nationals in Kigali in June. Come and watch. You'll see how fast I've gotten, even without you to chase me."

Roger frowned. "I'll do my best." Then the frown was gone and he flung one arm around Jean Patrick, the other around Mathilde. "Let's go to the house. It's hot, and I have walked a long way. I'm thirsty."

LATE IN THE afternoon, rain clouds rolled down the hills. Across the lake, thunder rumbled. Jean Patrick and Roger leaned against the eucalyptus, waiting for Mama.

"I don't like her doing other people's housework," Roger said.

Jean Patrick shrugged. "Fishing is bad. Jacqueline is already in secondary school, and Mathilde is going next year. What can we do?"

"Why should we suffer more because we're Tutsi? Jacqueline came in near the top of her class, and still she didn't get a financial award. Why should Hutu get all the scholarships, all the best places for jobs?"

"Everyone is suffering. Neither Tutsi nor Hutu can make rain."

"Our government is not suffering. Have you seen how Habyarimana grows fat?" Roger slapped his forehead. "Tsst! I forgot your present." He jogged to the house and came back with his knapsack. "Look—it almost fits in your hand." He pulled out a box with a transistor radio inside.

Jean Patrick extended the antenna to its full length. "So fancy! But we have a radio."

"This is for you alone, to keep with you wherever you are. I think at night you could catch Radio Muhabura, the RPF station. I tuned to it in Ruhengeri, but you may have to adjust a little."

Funnels of dust chased across the ground. Thunder resonated across the lake from Zaire. "Why would I want to listen to them? Radio Rwanda's bad enough."

Roger leaned in close. "If I tell you something, will you promise to keep it to yourself?"

"I swear."

"I'm joining the RPF."

Jean Patrick sank back against the tree. He touched Roger's wrist, seeking the familiar feel of his skin. "The rebels? Why?"

Roger took a rolled-up newspaper from his pack and tapped it against his palm. "After all that's happened, you still think the RPF are troublemakers?"

"It's because of them the country is suffering, and I'm tired of being blamed for it. All day long I hear *icyitso, Inyenzi.* Traitor, cockroach. Twice, some guys beat me." He showed Roger his chipped tooth.

"What guys? Boys I know?" Roger slapped the newspaper hard.

"It doesn't matter. I could take care of it, just me and them, but because I'm Tutsi I can't fight back. I could lose my scholarship or get hurt so I can't run. Me, I can't take a chance. I wish the RPF would go back to Uganda and leave us alone."

"This country is theirs as much as it's yours or mine," Roger said. "Exile was not something any of them chose, and all they — *we* — are asking for is an end to government corruption and the right of return, to participate in the political process here in our motherland."

Jean Patrick felt the first bubbles rise to the surface in the pot that boiled over whenever talk turned to politics. "I'm not getting you. Uncle told me the same thing, but I don't understand. Those RPF — they were born in Uganda, right? Rwanda is not their home, so why, all of a sudden, do they come down here and invade?"

"Some were born here, some are the children of refugees, born in Uganda or Tanzania. Every time Hutu massacre Tutsi, more Tutsi flee the country. It wasn't just in 'seventy-three, when our grandparents were killed. It started in 'fifty-nine with the first Hutu uprising when the mwami, King Kigeli the Fifth, fled. Then again in 'sixty-three and 'sixty-seven. No one wants to live in exile forever. And if you opened your eyes, you'd see it could happen again, *is* happening again." He slapped the newspaper open and gave it to Jean Patrick.

It looked like *Kanguka,* the name just one letter different: *Kangura,* Wake *Them* Up, instead of *Kanguka,* Wake Up. Next to a drawing of a machete and a photo of Kayibanda, Rwanda's first president, was the headline, SPECIAL. WHAT WEAPONS SHALL WE USE TO CONQUER THE INYENZI ONCE AND FOR ALL??

"So this is what the paper looks like," Jean Patrick said.

Roger watched him closely. "Tricky, eh? At first people bought it thinking it was *Kanguka.*"

Jean Patrick nodded slowly. "I knew about it from the Ten Commandments, but before now, I never held it in my hands. If I saw someone had it, I turned away." He sucked his teeth. "I got my foot broken because of those stupid commandments."

Lightning arced across the ridges. Current thrummed between the high branches. The pages of *Kangura* rippled as if the wind wanted to tear them from Jean Patrick's grasp.

Roger snorted. "It's time to stop looking the other way, Little Brother. I've done a lot of studying, and I've discovered most of the history we learned in school is a lie. It's by listening in the street that you learn the truth." He pulled a book in English from his pack: *Decolonising the Mind.*

"You can read that?"

"It's hard, but I manage." Roger took a photograph of a woman from between the pages. "Her name was Anastase. We were planning to marry."

"My brother getting married! You never said a word." Jean Patrick studied the shine of her skin, a polished ocher brick. He liked her makeup and stylish Western clothes. "When?"

Roger caught the first drops of rain in his cupped hand. "I think finally we'll have a storm." He looked up toward the thickening clouds. "Have you heard about Bugesera?" Jean Patrick hadn't. "After Kayibanda gained power, many Tutsi were put in trucks and dumped in the swamps there, to live however they could, because the new government wanted to give their good land to the Hutu.

"Anastase's family was among them. They settled in Nyamata. Last month, the government claimed some RPF were planning to murder Hutu leaders there. They broadcast the story on Radio Rwanda, screaming and shouting that it was time to kill or be killed, getting Hutu heads so heated up they took up clubs and machetes. By the next day, there were Tutsi bodies lying in the streets." He pointed to *Kangura.* "A few days before the massacres, free copies of this issue were distributed in Bugesera. It was not by chance." His eyes flashed. "Anastase had gone to visit her family. I went to join her, not knowing what had happened. I planned to ask her father for permission to marry her. Instead, I found their house burned to the ground. No one survived. Right there, in front of those blackened bits of timber, I made my decision to fight with the RPF."

A white heron wheeled across the sky, pushed by the storm. Jean Patrick imagined soaring to freedom, shedding the gravitational force of his country and lifting into the air. "What are you saying? The government planned it?"

"This wasn't the first time. Anastase told me it has been going on in Bugesera since she was small. One year, two or three killings; another, forty or fifty. Maybe some talker on Radio Rwanda lit the fuse, or maybe some Tutsi cattle trampled a Hutu field. Peace between Hutu and Tutsi was uneasy from the beginning, and in this swamp, there was always conflict over land. The government knew how to exploit it. What I am saying is, think about the situation. Be prepared."

Jean Patrick looked again at the photograph. Anastase's hair was pulled back from her face to show off her thin, arched eyebrows. Her lips were parted in a shy half smile as if she were about to speak. "She's so beautiful. I'm sorry."

Hard drops of rain spattered the earth, breaking the air's eerie stillness. Mama appeared on the path below, walking toward them.

"We better hurry to meet her," Roger said.

They had walked a short distance when the sky ruptured, thunder and lightning simultaneous. The bark on the eucalyptus exploded, shreds flying into the air. The force knocked them to the ground. Smoke rose from the tree, and Jean Patrick's skull rang like a struck bell. Roger lay on his back, knapsack twisted to the side.

"Are you all right?" Jean Patrick's tongue was thick in his mouth. He touched Roger's shoulder, and current sizzled in his fingers. Rain came down in a sheet.

"Such stupid little calves," Roger said. "Lying in the dirt with our mouths open." He helped Jean Patrick up, and they abandoned themselves to laughter. Mama called to them, her voice frantic. "How much will you bet me," Roger said, "that if we looked hard enough, we could find our souls seared into the tree?"

Jean Patrick glanced back in awe at the scarred trunk. At Christmas, Roger had still moved in the circle of family, his identity merged with theirs. Today, he had stepped from the circle. He had taken Jean Patrick by the hand and walked with him to the edge of his new life. But when Roger left, he would jump alone into its dizzying possibility. Soon enough, Jean Patrick would follow his own path, an oval tarmac four hundred meters around, to wherever it took him. Until then, Jean Patrick would have this tree as proof that this day had really happened. He could put his hand against the bark and feel Roger's soul, his heart with its steady beat of love.

JACQUELINE CAME HOME from school in Gitarama in the morning, the family complete for Easter once more. Jean Patrick marveled at her long, straight hair, its iridescent sheen. As she walked up the path, the breeze lifted it from her ears and blew spidery strands across her face. Like Anastase, she wore Western slacks and a smart Western blouse.

On Easter Sunday, they joked and ate the afternoon away, sharing news in a constant onslaught of noise. A stream of neighbors and cousins filled the house. Jean Patrick traveled back through the years, carried on the steam from pungent dishes, all his favorites. For that moment, his worries seemed small and far off. He remembered the morning he first arrived, how he and Roger had stood on the hillside above the compound and quipped about Uncle's family. How much this book of life changes, he thought. And we are not the ones to write the pages.

WHEN DAWN BROKE on Wednesday, Roger was packed and ready to leave. "Stay one more day," Jean Patrick pleaded. "Mama is so happy with you here."

Roger hoisted his pack. "That will only make it harder when I leave."

Jean Patrick had noticed the way Roger lingered at the table and held Mama's arm as if afraid he would never touch her again. In the mornings, he stood at the door and inhaled deeply, looking out toward the lake. Jean Patrick imagined the land absorbed into the tissue of Roger's lungs so that when he marched through the mountains, cold and hungry, it would warm him at will.

"Did you tell her your news about becoming RPF?"

"That is for your ears, and your ears alone."

"Then what will you tell them when you disappear into thin air?"

"That I am going to Kenya with a friend to work. Make some good money."

"I'll walk you to the road and wait with you for the bus," Jean Patrick said. "Uncle won't mind; there's nothing to fill our nets."

Mukabera met them on the path, a machete balanced on her headscarf. "I am going to harvest my three beans." She laughed, hoarse and hearty, showing her large brown-stained teeth. "I wish you the peace of God." She waved and walked on. Dust swirled at her feet.

AT THE BUS stop, Roger bought two ears of corn from a vendor stooped over a charcoal grill. They moved into a private corner of shade to eat. "Are you going to the Virungas?" Jean Patrick asked. "Everyone knows RPF is hiding there."

"You'd be surprised. We're everywhere."

"Will you finish the school year first? You will never be forgiven if you don't."

"Don't worry," Roger said. "I'll finish."

"What about National Championships? Will you come to Kigali to watch me win?"

Roger picked a kernel of corn from his teeth. "So many questions." He smiled in his familiar way, wrinkling his nose. "I'll try."

A pang that felt like hunger twisted Jean Patrick's insides. He embraced Roger a final time. "I better get back, in case Uncle needs me," he said.

A civet hurried out from the bush, a mosaic of shadow and light falling across its body in the same crazy patchwork as its fur. It froze, stolid and doglike, a bristled ridge of hair on its back. Its sweet, dungy scent hung thick in the air. Roger motioned as if to strike it, and it bared its teeth. "That's the spirit: brave and stubborn," he said. He stomped, and the creature retreated toward the undergrowth. "Don't worry about me. I'm like him. Listen for Radio Muhabura and think of your brother." He pulled his beret out of his pack. "We're getting stronger every day." He saluted and jogged off toward the approaching bus. The civet surveyed the scene warily from its haven, as if it, too, found this small occasion worthy of committing to memory.

TEN

ON THE DAY OF National Championships, Jean Patrick felt strong and confident but, he had to admit, a little nervous. He put down his running magazine and flipped onto his back, head dangled over one side of the bed and feet over the other. He poked Daniel's shin with a toe.

"How long to Kigali?"

"The same as when you asked me yesterday and last week and ten minutes ago—maybe six hours. I don't think it will change."

"Aren't you going to class?"

"There's nothing to do but review for exams," Daniel said. "I'd rather wait with you."

Jean Patrick peered out the window. "Do you think Coach has a wife?"

"Coach? A wife? Mama weh!" Daniel roared. "He's too mean."

"Maybe he had one and killed her."

Daniel grabbed Jean Patrick's jiggling thigh. "Be still, eh? If this is what Championships does to you, maybe you shouldn't go."

Laughing, Jean Patrick pushed his hand away. "Why don't you come with me?"

"If it was three weeks later, I would. Then you could come to my home and meet my mama and my sisters." Daniel aimed his finger at a noisy bird beyond the window. "Papa could teach you to shoot."

"Aye-yay. What do I need a gun for? Me, I fight with my legs."

"When Hutu Power gets guns, you better have one, too—and know how to use it."

"Always your serious talk." Jean Patrick covered his ears. "Let me rest now, eh?" He threw his magazine at Daniel's head, flipped back over, and closed his eyes.

JEAN PATRICK WAS still asleep when Coach burst in, jingling his keys.

"Ready?" A camera hung from his neck. "We have a long drive."

Jean Patrick pointed to his gym bag. His Nikes, now more rust than green, peeked from a side pocket.

Daniel grabbed him in a headlock. "Pretend I'm chasing you, and you'll run fast."

"What? If you chase me, I can walk." Jean Patrick followed Coach out the door.

On the walkway, Coach stopped suddenly and pulled Jean Patrick into an empty classroom. "Stand beside the board," he said. Jean Patrick had a fleeting vision of an execution. Coach aimed the camera at him. Light flashed in his eyes as the shutter clicked.

"Is that for the newspaper?"

Ignoring the question, Coach half jogged to the car. He pointed to something shiny on the seat. "For you."

It was a tracksuit with GIHUNDWE in large letters on the jacket. Jean Patrick passed his hand over the slithery cloth. He slipped on the jacket, pleased with the crackly sound it made when he moved. He ran the zipper up and down, up and down. "Now I am ready for the Olympics, eh?"

Coach squinted through the windshield. The engine sputtered and then whined into life. "Not yet."

EVERY POTHOLE SENT shock waves through Jean Patrick's skull. Without room to stretch his legs, he fidgeted to find a comfortable position. Coach honked at farmers, cars that drove too slowly, trucks he roared past while navigating blind curves. In the valley below, a woman paused to wave. The laundry she spread over the shrubs formed a tapestry like bright flowers. The green dazzle of tea plantations disappeared from the rearview mirror, and the blue haze of Nyungwe Forest rose before them. Out of the forest's shimmer, the first checkpoint appeared.

A bored-looking officer sauntered to the car. "Indangamuntu," he said. A crumpled five-hundred-franc note from Mama fluttered to the floor when Jean Patrick took his identity card from his pocket. The officer peered at the picture and then at Jean Patrick. "Step out." A second soldier opened Jean Patrick's door and motioned to him. "Open the trunk," the officer said. While the soldier poked at bags and blankets, the officer studied their papers. "What is your business, Mr. Rutembeza?"

"We're going to National Track Championships in Kigali," Coach said. "I'm this boy's coach. Remember his name, Sergeant. He's Rwanda's finest. Our Olympic hopeful." His smile could have cut through stone.

The officer hooted, showing off several gold-capped teeth. Out of the corner of his eye, Jean Patrick saw the second soldier pocket Mama's five-hundred-franc note.

"You can go now," the sergeant said. "Make sure that Inyenzi wins. I'm going to place a bet on him."

Coach started the car and accelerated slowly. The soldiers' trailing laughter left a sour taste in Jean Patrick's mouth.

"Soon Rwanda will win the war," Coach said, rolling up his window with swift, certain strokes. "And then this nonsense will be over." He looked intently at Jean Patrick. "Don't you ever wish for a Hutu card?"

Jean Patrick was sweating in his jacket, but he didn't want to take it off. He closed his window, then opened it again. What was the proper answer to such a question?

"You'll get malaria," Coach said, aiming a toothpick at Jean Patrick.

"How can I?"

"From the wind." Coach popped the toothpick between his teeth. "Isn't that what villagers believe?"

"I don't know." Jean Patrick left the window down. "That soldier took my money," he said, focused on the blue-green river of scenery that rushed by. "It was all I had to buy food in Kigali."

"This would never happen in Butare or Kigali. I'm known there. And never mind about the money; I can feed you." Coach attacked the horn and sped past an old farmer pushing a cart loaded with sorghum. "Nothing but bumpkins around this place." He rolled down his window and flung the toothpick in the farmer's direction. In an instant of revelation, Jean Patrick saw that Coach, too, had been humiliated, and it was because of his shame that he turned on Jean Patrick, the old man, the countryside.

"THERE ARE TWO runners—and only two—I want you to pay attention to tomorrow," Coach said as they crested the hill. He smiled easily again, as if he had left all his anger on the farmer's cart. "They're on the Burundi national team. Stick to them like a tick—if you can."

Jean Patrick ran his tongue over his chipped tooth. "What about those Kigali boys?"

"They have a new coach to keep them in line." Coach smirked. "He's Tutsi."

Jean Patrick laughed, imagining Crooked Nose and his friends taking orders from a Tutsi. "What about the running part? I haven't raced against them in a while."

"You've already shattered their times." Coach grinned. "Tomorrow you'll be the best eight-hundred-meter runner in Rwanda. Ever." He was looking at Jean Patrick, taking a corner too fast. Until Jean Patrick shouted, he paid no attention to the branches set across the road to warn of an accident. Bark and leaves flew into the air, scraped against the skidding tires. They barely missed the truck sprawled on its side across the road, wheels still spinning, the wooden sides of the truck bed shattered.

Jean Patrick tried to look away, but he couldn't. A dark stain spread on the asphalt. Already a crowd had gathered, some gesturing wildly, others collecting pieces of wood and spilled cargo. With a sigh of relief, he saw the barefoot truck driver stagger by the side of the road, arm held close to his body, hand dangling at an odd angle. A stream of curses poured from his mouth.

This is how it must have been with Papa, Jean Patrick thought. Trying to slow his runaway heart, he thought how life was decided by the most inconsequential decisions: a second here to get a drink, a minute there to stop and stretch your legs, and either you arrived at the turn at the same out-of-control moment as the truck, or you saw the branches and came to a stop, the catastrophe already in the past.

THE SUN HAD started its quick descent toward the horizon when they entered the sugarcane fields and marshes along the Nyabarongo River. Jean Patrick closed his window against the fetid, sulfurous air. Birds flitted in the papyrus and umunyeganyege. In the dusky light, the hills ringing Kigali were like flared pleats of a dancer's skirt.

At the edge of town, Coach stopped at one of the many small kiosks by the roadside and bought two Fantas. The cold and the sweet went straight through Jean Patrick's chipped tooth and into his eye. Coach chuckled, the tension gone from his face. "You look like you've never left your rugo before, staring like that."

They were in the thick of Kigali traffic. A jumble of sound filled Jean Patrick's ears: car horns, radios, shouts, and whistles. His nostrils burned with the odors of exhaust, charcoal, the stench of rotting garbage. But beyond the noise and the reek, there was also a sense of excitement that quickened his heart, and he marveled that Daniel had grown up with the pulse of such a place in his veins.

"WE HAVE ARRIVED. École Technique Officielle. Do you want to see the track?" Coach honked, and a rheumy-eyed man opened the gates. He was thin and bent, like an ancient tree whose trunk no longer supported the weight of its branches.

Coach hooked Jean Patrick's arm and guided him down the walkway. A group of girls coming from a classroom split and walked on either side of them. Jean Patrick called out a greeting, and they turned around and giggled.

The Burundi runners were the only ones on the track. They wore red, green, and white jerseys, Burundi's colors, and on the back was the Burundi flag. They moved together with long, stretched-out strides, as if they had been fashioned from a single piece of clay and split into two. One was at least as tall as Jean Patrick; the other, shorter, a wiry bundle of muscles and bone. They talked as they ran, gesturing and laughing. Jean Patrick visualized running beside them. Comparing his pace to theirs, he didn't think they would be that hard to beat. The first tease of victory tingled his lips, and he quickened his pace.

"Where are you going?" Coach tightened his grip on Jean Patrick's arm.

"To greet them."

"Stay here and watch instead. Keep them guessing."

"What do you mean?"

"Psychology. To you, they have become human, but to them you are still a mystery. Stay here and watch; learn their pace, their stride. Let them worry about you."

"But I've never raced against them. How do they know about me?"

In the waning light, Coach followed their movements. "News of someone like you travels quickly. Trust me—they know."

THE FIRST RUNNERS Jean Patrick saw in the morning were the Kigali boys. He sat on the bench to watch them warm up while he put on his shoes. His toes pressed against the tops, and he loosened the laces to make a little more room. Crooked Nose tapped his friend's shoulder and pointed in Jean Patrick's direction. Jean Patrick waved, and the boys laughed and turned away.

"Jean Patrick?" The voice behind him made him jump. "It's nice to finally meet you. We've heard a lot of talk." The Burundi runners held out their hands in greeting. It was the taller boy who spoke. "I'm Gilbert." Sweat glistened on his nearly bald head.

"And I'm Ndizeye. Come warm up with us."

Jean Patrick settled into a comfortable jog between them, resisting the urge to test the boys by pushing the pace. They chatted about this and that, and Jean Patrick was surprised to learn how running was encouraged in Burundi—unlike in Rwanda, where you had to fight for every little scrap of recognition. For a moment he imagined leaving his life behind to start fresh in that country. He knew many Tutsi did.

When Jean Patrick returned to the bench, Coach was pacing. "Did you forget what I told you? You just gave away your advantage." Jean Patrick retied his shoes with singular concentration. "I want you this far from them in the prelims and semis—no more, no less." Coach held his hands shoulder wide in front of Jean Patrick's face. "Do you hear?"

"What about the Kigali boys?"

"Can you listen for once? The Kigali boys are not worth worrying about."

Jean Patrick followed Gilbert and Ndizeye with his eyes. Caught in the sun's dazzle, they looked like two swimmers gliding in the lake. "What if they're not near me?"

"Don't vex. They'll be there."

NONE OF THE Kigali boys were in Jean Patrick's heat for the semi. As the Burundi runners rounded the first turn and came out of their lanes, they closed at his heels; Coach had been right about that. By the back straight, only the three of them remained in the lead pack.

Jean Patrick had been too wound up to eat, and the trip had left his muscles stiff and cramped. In the prelims, he felt unbalanced — feet slapping, timing slightly off — but now that he ran with Gilbert and Ndizeye, his legs cranked like a perfectly turning gear. They passed the start line together and headed for the final lap, Jean Patrick slowly increasing his lead. The Burundi runners melted into a single shadow behind him. His last acceleration went unanswered.

"I can beat those guys," Jean Patrick said, sitting down on the bench. "Did you see my last kick? I felt great, like I wasn't even working." His foot drummed a war beat. "And I ran a personal best by — how much?"

"Half a second." Coach handed him a bottle of water, his face set in his usual mask. "In the final, I want *you* behind *them*. Breathe down their necks. Make them lose stride. Don't pass before the last two meters. Then turn it loose." He flashed his smirk-smile. "If you are able."

"Eh? Coach, I can break them. Let me run free."

"You're not understanding me. This time, do as I say." He rubbed out Jean Patrick's calf. "There is more at stake here than you can know." From Coach's expression, Jean Patrick understood he was not to ask any further questions.

JEAN PATRICK HAD lane five for the final, the Burundi runners on either side. Crooked Nose and one other Kigali boy remained, staggered to the outside. Jean Patrick's nervous energy boiled over, and he falsestarted, committing to motion before the sound of the blocks. Crooked Nose jeered. Taking a deep breath, Jean Patrick walked in a circle, shook out his legs, resumed the set position: body cocked, weight balanced. The starter banged the blocks, and he drove off the line. By the time he rose to his full, upright stride, Gilbert and Ndizeye were halfway through the turn. He sprinted furiously to catch them, but his step was too short or too long or too choppy — he couldn't tell which. He was used to people at his back, not the other way around. His Nikes squeezed his feet until all he felt was the pulse inside his toes.

The pack too far behind to help, Jean Patrick ran alone. He watched for a labored breath, a missed step. The two Burundi flags floated calm and steady, farther away with every footfall. He dug as deep as he could and then deeper. Four hundred meters to go. From somewhere, he found the strength to keep them in sight. Black dots danced in front of his eyes. The ground lurched beneath him. For an instant he thought he would pass out, but hope kept him surging forward. Never before had he experienced so much suffering. But by infinitesimal gains, he began to reel the Burundians back in.

Coming out of the final turn, he could almost touch the flags. Once more, the thought of victory floated into view. Then the Burundi boys kicked, and he had nothing left to answer. Utterly spent, he leaned across the finish line. He barely had the strength to shake Gilbert and Ndizeye's hands. The crowd roared, but he didn't pay attention. He only wanted to sit down and take off his Nikes, now soaked with blood, and release his toes from prison.

"So Gilbert and Ndizeye are on Burundi's Olympic team, and until now you don't tell me?" Jean Patrick stood with Coach at the Karibu Café in front of a buffet of endless choices. For the first time since leaving Cyangugu, Jean Patrick felt hungry. He scooped peas and rice, fried plantains, chicken and goat brochettes, onto his plate.

"Some things are better left to surprise."

"Those guys were a surprise all right."

"They've been at this game a little longer than you have." Coach maneuvered to a table by the window and signaled a waiter for drinks. "How is your brother Roger doing? Long time, no news. Does he still play football?"

The unexpected question sent a flutter through Jean Patrick's heart. He tried to center himself, calm the chatter in his mind, so he wouldn't give anything away. "He's in Kenya, working hard. He plays for a club there, but I don't think he has much free time."

Coach tore the last piece of goat from his brochette and pointed the skewer at Jean Patrick. Jean Patrick started. "You didn't hear your time, did you? You ran off to sulk before I could catch you."

"I don't need numbers to know how badly I did." The waiter glided to the table, opened their drinks, and poured. Jean Patrick watched the foam rise to the top of his Coke. His Olympic dream had burst as easily as these bubbles. That much he realized.

Coach took the watch from his pocket and placed it on the table. Jean Patrick peered at it. He picked it up, shook it, put it down again. "It's broken."

"What's wrong? Don't like what you see?"

"Something happened. It says one forty-five ninety-seven." Jean Patrick shook the watch again. "I guess my time's gone. Lucky for me."

"Luck has nothing to do with it. That's your time—I promise."

Jean Patrick dropped the watch as if it had shocked him. "Mana yanjye! That's under the A-standard time, isn't it? Does that mean what I think it means?" He barely took in breath, the commotion of the restaurant a blur. Slowly the implication sank in.

"Congratulations. Yes—you ran a qualifying time for the Olympics."

Jean Patrick touched the watch's face as if it were a talisman. "Still, I let two guys beat me. I came in third." He sipped his Coke, savoring the cool, bubbly slide down his throat. He felt a buzz, as if he were drinking beer. Next time, he promised himself, he would do whatever it took to come in first.

THE HIGH LASTED all the way out of Kigali. Now past its zenith, the sun turned the Nyabarongo River to slate. Coach braked for a checkpoint and held out his hand for Jean Patrick's papers. His eyes slid over Jean Patrick's body. "Relax." The line of cars slowed to a crawl. Coach drummed his fingers against the steering wheel. A thick and airless heat descended, fueled by the sun's glare through the windshield. Jean Patrick fanned himself.

At the checkpoint, a family stood nervously beside a cart of produce. The man carried a herder's staff and wore the traditional felt hat of the Tutsi cowherd. The woman carried a baby at her back, only its small, wooly head visible above the brightly patterned cloth. The smaller children scurried after a bleating kid, and a soldier shouted at them. The children cried.

"Why do they have to treat them like that?"

Coach snapped his head around. Jean Patrick wished he could grab the question back and swallow it. "They could have weapons under their vegetables. They could be Inkotanyi."

Jean Patrick was surprised to hear Coach use this term of respect. Inkotanyi was how the RPF referred to themselves, Roger had explained, the name given to the mwami's warriors.

There was an explosion in the distance—truck tire, mortar round, who knew?—and the man started, overturning his wobbly cart. Tomatoes, cabbages, and onions scattered. Jean Patrick felt the cowherd's shame on his own head. He could have grabbed the soldiers and shaken them. "Coach, I don't think they can be RPF. The mama has a baby on her back."

"You don't understand these things. These Inkotanyi—they'll strap grenades to a baby."

Jean Patrick thought of Roger picking up Zachary, holding Baby Pauline to his face and kissing her. Hand grenades on a baby! He didn't know if he would laugh or cry. The soldiers returned the family's papers and whisked them through. The farmer bent forward as if to kiss the soldier's hand.

Coach turned the blade of his smile on Jean Patrick. "It's like football. The game goes much easier when you play for the right team." The car crept forward. The family scrambled to collect the last of their vegetables. The baby wailed, and a little girl reached inside the bundle to comfort it. Coach flicked his hand as if swatting at a fly. "What can you accomplish when your life is reduced to that?"

Slowly, methodically, Jean Patrick smoothed the fabric of his track pants. *That,* he thought, is who *I* am. The soldier inspected their documents and waved them through, tipping his cap to Coach. As he forced air into his lungs, Jean Patrick wondered if this sharp edge of fear could ever be blunted. He wondered what it would feel like to play for the right team.

"You have a strong spirit," Coach said when the soldiers had vanished into the haze behind them. "How are your feet?"

"I'll have to pop the blisters again."

"Do you need new shoes? You've earned them. Why didn't you say something?"

Jean Patrick shrugged. It had never occurred to him that new Nikes could be his just for the asking.

"I've talked to the burgomaster. An Olympic runner would be quite a feather in his cap. Tell me—how would you like to be one of the chosen?"

It was as if a book written in strange symbols had become suddenly clear—the photo before they left Gihundwe, the pointed questions and comments: Coach was offering him a Hutu card. He could barely take it in. "But everyone knows I'm Tutsi."

Coach waved the words away. "It's not so difficult to invent a male Hutu relative somewhere in the past. Do you think it hasn't been done before?" Jean Patrick had heard the stories. "I've accepted a position at National University. No one else in Rwanda can train you to reach your potential, so I want you to follow me there after you graduate. You'll come to train with me on weekends next year, too. A Hutu card would grease all the wheels."

"I'm going to the Olympics; isn't that enough?"

"Not so fast," Coach said. "You have to run an A-standard time on a sanctioned track with an approved timing system between January 'ninety-five and the games. And you have to make it past the National Olympic Committee, the sanctioning body of Rwanda. If they choose, they can bypass a Tutsi with an A time to pick one Hutu runner with a B time."

Jean Patrick sank back against the seat. He had assumed all he had to do was run fast, and he would get to the Olympics. *We can never forget we're Tutsi,* his mother had said. They were climbing again, papyrus and umunyeganyege giving way to pine and eucalyptus. Coach honked at a group of children pulling a calf up the road, and they scurried out of the way. Clouds sailed across Bugesera, the hills stained with shadow. Whirlwinds of dust swirled in the valley. A truckload of boisterous soldiers passed them. Crowded together in the bed, they shouted and sang, rifles raised high.

Coach smiled. "Their team must have won." For a moment his eyes followed the men. Then he turned to Jean Patrick. "Someday a Hutu card could be even more important than the Olympics." His smile had disappeared.

Jean Patrick watched an ocher funnel swallow the children and their

calf. The dust had an almost human smell, like sweat and earth ferment-
ing in folds of skin. There was something else, too—a suggestion of iron
and rust, like the scent of dried blood that remained as a war wound on
Jean Patrick's Nikes.

THE DORMITORY WAS still dark, heavy with the sounds of sleep,
when Jean Patrick awoke. He rose quietly and slipped on his new shorts.
Mathilde had made them for National Championships, and he hadn't
had the heart to tell her he couldn't wear them at an official meet. His
muscles felt weak and wobbly, but he had too much shouting in his head.
He needed motion to sort things out.

Daniel stirred. "Where are you going, superstar? I heard Coach say to
take the day off."

"My legs hurt if I don't run." The sky grew light beyond the window.
Birds filled the dawn with shrieks and whistles.

"I'll come with you, then, make sure you don't go at some crazy pace."

At the door, Daniel held him back. "Do you have your card?"

"We won't be long. For once, I don't want to have to think, Am I Hutu
or Tutsi?"

They set off at an easy pace. Jean Patrick thought of Gilbert and Ndizeye
skimming around the track. Joyful songs of Sunday worship came from
the churches.

"Coach offered me a Hutu card."

"Let's walk a minute. I can't keep your *slow* pace and speak," Daniel
said, walking. He grabbed Jean Patrick's hand. "Of course, if you have a
chance, you must take it."

"But what about my family? How can only I be Hutu?"

"If you have a card that says you are Hutu, what can anyone do?"

"That's what Coach said. Still, I would feel like a traitor."

"I got a letter from Papa yesterday." Daniel slowed. He picked at the
mole above his lip. "The commander instructed them to start making
lists."

"What do you mean? What kind of lists?"

"Tutsi. They were ordered to drive through neighborhoods and identify
every Tutsi hut, every Tutsi house, every Tutsi business."

"And your papa did it?"

"What choice does he have? He's a soldier."

Jean Patrick shook off Daniel's hand and broke into a run, dodging between a group of chittering girls and a man on a rickety bicycle. From the steep, runneled cliffs that framed the road, skinny trees rose as if only hope held them in place. Sun shimmered on the hills, a blue haze rising from the eucalyptus. A stork, startled, rose from a field below. Daniel tried to keep pace beside him. Jean Patrick increased his speed until Daniel dropped back. If he didn't keep going, he would grab Daniel by the shirt as if everything was his fault: checkpoints and soldiers, Coach's needling insults, yesterday's lost race, the making of lists. He would shake his friend until he confessed what his papa would do if they told him to aim his gun at the Tutsi and shoot.

BY THE TIME Jean Patrick reached the edge of town, churchgoers filled the road. A little girl in a Sunday dress, a child on her back nearly as big as she, stopped to point and giggle. Suddenly he remembered his shorts and sweaty jersey. He found a goat trail and pushed as hard and fast as he could go. The knot of anger in his throat did not release until the dusty ribbon of earth leading to his compound rose before him. There, a man in a suit stepped jauntily down the path. A brown briefcase swung from his hand, and his glasses gleamed like twin stars.

"Mwaramutseho," Jean Patrick called.

The man waved and passed his hand over a cottony cap of hair. The gesture immediately carried Papa to Jean Patrick's mind. His hair would be turning white, too. When he died, Jean Patrick had reached barely to his waist. Now, he imagined, they would be amaso ku maso, eye to eye. He tried to journey through the years and pull back the details of Papa's face, but he realized he could not.

What would Papa say about his beloved president now? Would he tell Jean Patrick to take a Hutu card? What would he think of the names of his family inscribed on a government list? Jean Patrick stopped by a tree to stretch. No, he thought. That can't happen in Cyangugu.

Lake Kivu stretched, steel black and dazzling, below. A group of sisters came out from Ntura Church. "Eh-eh, Jean Patrick," they teased. "Running

on the Lord's day? And in such tiny shorts?" Peals of laughter followed, and
their chatter buoyed Jean Patrick's mood. There must be some explanation,
he reasoned, some necessity for having these lists in Kigali.

JEAN PATRICK FOUND Mukabera on the way to her fields.
"Amakuru, Jean Patrick?" Olivette smiled shyly behind her.

"My news is good." He was bursting to tell them about the Olympics,
but he held back.

"Where are your mother and your aunt?"

"I don't know. I'm just coming now from school. Didn't you see them
in church?"

"They weren't there. Please greet them for me." Mukabera shaded her
eyes and pointed. "Ah. Zachary is coming." Her broad smile disappeared,
and alarmed, Jean Patrick followed her gaze. He saw the reason and broke
into a run.

Zachary raced wildly up the path, shirttails flapping. He stumbled,
caught himself, stumbled again. "Fetch Angelique and Uwimana." His
chest heaved. "We have to bring them."

"What is it? What's happened?" Jean Patrick pulled him close.

"Mathilde's so sick. We went to collect firewood and she fell down and
started flopping around like a fish. Now she won't wake up. Auntie says
it's malaria."

Jean Patrick tasted metal on his tongue. "Don't worry. You just take the
pills and get well." He rested his hands on Zachary's shoulders. "I'll run
back to school. You go home. Tell Mama and Auntie you found me, and
I've gone to fetch Uwimana. Can you do that?" He ran his fingers across
Zachary's scalp. Zachary nodded. Once he disappeared into the eucalyptus, Jean Patrick ran as if his own life depended on it.

In the few minutes he had stopped, his legs had stiffened up. He pleaded
for one last burst of speed and careened down the hill. He had arrived at
the gate when his foot caught on a rock, and he fell.

"Are you OK?" A man offered his hand.

When Jean Patrick stood, he saw the hand belonged to a young soldier.
He reached for his card and with a rush of panic remembered he had not
taken it. "Thank you. I'm fine. I'm sorry, but I —"

"I don't care about that." The soldier pointed at Jean Patrick's bleeding knee. "You've cut yourself." He had a broad, friendly face, cheeks like a baby's, and sleepy eyes. He offered Jean Patrick his handkerchief. "That looks nasty, huh?"

The gesture nearly broke the dam that held back Jean Patrick's tears. He thanked the soldier and wiped his knee. Gingerly he took a step. Nothing hurt. He gave back the handkerchief. "Sorry," he said. "I've soiled it."

"No worries." The soldier hiked his pants over his round belly and resumed his stroll down the road. His arm remained in the air, locked in a farewell wave. Jean Patrick passed through Gihundwe's gates, and his welled-up tears broke through.

MATHILDE SHIVERED INSIDE a shell of blankets in Auntie's bed, Mama and Auntie beside her. They wiped her face and neck with a cloth that smelled of herbs. Uncle Emmanuel paced. They were all dressed for church.

Jean Patrick knelt beside Mathilde. "It's your brother, Jean Patrick. Can you hear me?" He put a finger to her brow. It burned like fire. Her eyes flickered open, then closed again. He offered a silent barter—he would never get a Hutu card if Mathilde got well. He heard Uncle's voice in his head. *Imana iraguha, ntimugura, iyo muguze iraguhenda.* God gives you, you don't buy. If you buy, he overcharges. But no price was too high for his sister's life.

"We can use the blankets to carry her to the truck," Uwimana said. "Angelique has gone to the Centre de Santé. They are expecting you."

Aunt Esther wrung out the cloth into the bowl. "Uwimana, we can't pay much."

"Don't worry about that. Jean Patrick, come help. The three of us can manage, I think." Uwimana wrapped the blankets tightly around Mathilde in a makeshift stretcher. She had no weight to her body when Jean Patrick and Emmanuel lifted her, only fire and air. Even so, the journey to the road took forever as they picked their way down the trail. Their feet stirred clouds of dust, and Jean Patrick covered her face to protect her.

At the truck, Emmanuel turned back. Jean Patrick watched his slow, uncertain steps. He stooped forward as if the weight of the years had suddenly landed between his shoulder blades.

THEY CRAWLED THROUGH traffic. Jean Patrick wanted to lean his head out the window and shout at the milling crowds to get out of the way. If only they had an ambulance with a loud, wailing siren. The four of them were squeezed into the front seat, Mathilde across their laps, the windows closed against the dust and wind. Mathilde's fever burned through the blankets. Every now and then, a quiver arched her spine.

None of them saw the checkpoint until a line of brake lights appeared around a curve. The soldiers seemed to be scrutinizing every car, every cart, every boy on a bicycle. Jean Patrick touched his hand to his shorts pocket and went suddenly cold. This time, the sin of his forgotten card would not go so well. They arrived at the barrier, and an officer demanded their cards. Uwimana, Auntie, and Mama already had them in hand, and they offered them up for inspection. Jean Patrick went through the motion of searching, afraid the officer would hear the blood that roared in his temples. The officer waved his hand in front of Jean Patrick's face. "Indangamuntu," he repeated.

His power of speech gone, Jean Patrick shook his head. He sensed the excitement of a lion circling its prey. "You don't have your card?" the officer asked, opening the door and beckoning Jean Patrick to get out.

"I was in a hurry," Jean Patrick said, unfolding his body to stand beside the truck. Although he knew it was pointless, he made himself smaller so the man would not know him for a Tutsi. "My sister has malaria, and I ran to get home. Until now, I didn't realize I had forgotten it."

Soldiers swarmed the truck. Mathilde whimpered. Behind them, drivers leaned from their windows to gawk. "Everyone out," the officer said. He gestured toward Mathilde. "That cockroach, too. Out." Already the soldiers were patting down the seat, going through the glove box. Mama and Auntie huddled together, motionless, their eyes on the road.

"Officer, the girl is burning with fever. We're taking her to the Centre de Santé. My wife is a doctor there," Uwimana said.

With Uwimana's card clutched in his hand, the officer swiveled around to face him. "What are you doing with a car full of cockroaches? Are you an RPF supporter?"

A soldier yanked Mathilde by her ankles, and she cried out.

"She's too sick," Auntie said, and she took a step toward the truck.

Another soldier pushed her back with his rifle, and she fell against Mama. A cry escaped Jean Patrick's lips. He did not know if it was from the wind on his wet clothes or the rage that swelled inside him, but he began to shake and could not stop.

The soldier pointed his weapon at Jean Patrick's heart. "I should arrest you, Inyenzi," he said.

"Officer, I believe I have a solution to this problem," Uwimana said, gesturing toward his inside jacket pocket.

For a moment, no one moved. Exhaust curled up, blue and noxious, from the line of cars. Jean Patrick held his breath, the soldier's finger still on the rifle's trigger. He understood that right now, only Uwimana had the power to help them. Then the officer gave a faint nod. "Put up your hands," he said. When Uwimana's hands were raised, he patted him down and reached inside his jacket. Jean Patrick saw the quick palming of bills.

"You may pass," the officer said.

Quickly they got back in the truck. Jean Patrick could touch the fear in the air, each of them praying that the soldiers would not suddenly change their minds. Uwimana put the car in gear, and in another moment, the checkpoint was behind them.

As if sensing the release of tension, Mathilde sat up. Her eyes wandered dully from face to face. The blankets had slipped to her waist. One sleeve of her shift fell across her arm, exposing the delicate hollow between neck and shoulder. Jean Patrick covered her, and her eyes focused. "Here you are." She smiled and leaned her head against him. "Don't leave me again."

With trembling fingers, Jean Patrick swept a stray curl from her forehead. Sweat had frizzed her hair, destroying the neat bob she had worked so hard to create in imitation of Jacqueline. He kissed her brow, tasted her salt. "Don't be afraid." He tried to calm the hammer of his heart against his ribs. "You're going to be well soon." But it was more a plea than anything he believed.

A SHARP MEDICINAL scent, the sour odors of disease and unwashed bodies, hit Jean Patrick as soon as Uwimana opened the door at the Centre de Santé. All the seats in the small front lobby were taken. Children played on the floor or wailed loudly in their mamas' laps. A grandmother rose from her chair and beckoned. "Bring that poor girl here. Let her sit."

Mathilde was awake. She smiled and thanked the woman, and Jean Patrick allowed himself a shred of hope. Uwimana pushed to the front of the line at the desk and spoke to a nurse. Soon Angelique appeared. "Come back," she sang. Hearing her cheer, so much fatigue flooded Jean Patrick's body that he thought he might sink to the floor.

They put Mathilde on a cot, and she drifted back to sleep. When Angelique touched her forehead, her brow pinched. "Let me get the stick." She pricked Mathilde's finger. Mathilde wailed, and Angelique smiled. "Good," she said, smearing the blood onto a glass slide. "That's a very good sign." She took Mathilde's temperature, shone a light in her eyes, hit her knees and elbows with a rubber triangle. She held the stethoscope to Mathilde's chest, her back, her stomach. She took more blood and gave her a shot. "Chloroquine," she said.

Mathilde opened her eyes, her brow wrinkled as a new puppy. "Good morning. Can you tell me your name?" Angelique asked.

"Mathilde."

Jean Patrick let out a sigh of relief.

"Let her rest while I look at the slides." Angelique embraced Aunt Esther. Jean Patrick caught the deep lines of worry in Angelique's reflection in the glass.

When Angelique returned, she carried a hospital gown and a gray blanket with a white stripe. "We need to keep her," she said. "She has a very high fever, and her malaria count is high. With the shot, she should be much better in a matter of hours. Esther, we'll find you a cot so you can stay with her. I am hopeful that in the morning you can bring her home." Esther clasped Angelique's hands and held them to her forehead.

Jean Patrick pressed his cheek to Mathilde's. "See you tomorrow," he said. "Ndagukunda cyane." I love you very much. The flicker in Mathilde's eyes told him she had understood.

MARKET GOERS CREATED a congestion through which the truck barely moved. In the dying afternoon, hawkers called out bargains, packed up unsold tools and clothing, used appliances held together with hope and string. Flies swarmed around carcasses of meat. The aromas of over-ripe fruit and gamy animal flesh made Jean Patrick queasy. A bicycle taxi swerved into their path, and Uwimana braked to avoid it. The woman on the back loosed a stream of insults in their direction.

The radio droned; the truck engine whined and coughed. Their bodies jostled together from the potholed road. Every now and then, Mama made a comment meant to cheer them up, pointing out a man who stumbled drunkenly, a woman scolding her husband on the street, but the day's events had left Jean Patrick numb. He could not shake the fear that the checkpoint's delay had tipped the balance against Mathilde's survival.

"I MUST REPAY you," Jean Patrick said. "I was so stupid to forget my card." They sat in the truck at the trailhead. The sun had plunged into the lake, drawing with it the last of the day's heat.

Mama reached into her purse. "I have some money here. Maybe enough."

"It was a small sum. You had more important things to think about."

"How much did it cost to make me Hutu for one minute?" Jean Patrick rubbed his arms against the chill; his legs prickled with cold. What would it cost to make him Hutu forever?

"I didn't count." Uwimana sighed. "Before the Belgians measured our noses and sealed our ethnicity forever, we didn't need our indangamuntu to tell us who we were." He pronounced the word as if he could barely stand it on his tongue.

Mama shook her head. "We can't go on blaming the Belgians forever," she said. "Now it is the Hutu themselves who brand us. You saw the disgust on those soldiers' faces."

Uwimana's gaze followed a bug on the windshield. "Can they prove we are two different tribes as they say, as we are taught in school? Isn't it possible that differences of feature came about as a function of livelihood and geography? After all, we have a common language and share the same original myths." He took out his card. Turning to his photo, he tapped the place where it said UBWOKO/ETHNIE. "This word here, the Kinyarwanda one, what does it mean?"

Jean Patrick puzzled over the question. "*Ubwoko*? It means ethnicity."

"Ah, Jean Patrick, you are mistaken. It was the Belgians who gave it this meaning. Before colonial days, the Kinyarwanda word *ubwoko* meant only clan. We had no word in our language for ethnicity." Turning the key in the ignition, he shook his head. "Enough lecturing. Stay with your family. School can wait until Mathilde comes home."

Reaching over Jean Patrick, Mama clasped Uwimana's hands. "Nothing we can say will be enough to thank you," she said.

Jean Patrick gathered the blankets and stepped into the evening. "You saved us this afternoon," he said. He helped his mother from the truck, and together they climbed the path.

No matter what Jean Patrick decided about the Hutu card — if it was even his decision to make — he wanted his family to be safe. Could Coach promise him that? He took his mother's arm and felt the strong, steady rhythm of her body.

Above them, a noisy troop of colobus monkeys leapt one after another through the high umuyove branches as if following a well-marked road, each flared mane a white flash against the purple dusk. Jean Patrick wondered if he could read the future from their path as the umupfumu divined events from animal grease. The meaning of the monkeys' flight eluded him, as did his future. As did the words that would come from his mouth when Coach asked him to choose between Hutu and Tutsi.

JEAN PATRICK TOOK his radio from the shelf and began his nightly search, moving the antenna, wiggling the dial, pressing his ear to the speaker. Zachary sat cross-legged beside him. The lantern swooped their shadows onto the wall.

"I miss Mathilde," Zachary said.

"I miss her, too. So much."

"Will she really come home tomorrow?"

"Of course." Jean Patrick moved the antenna left, right. He was ready to give up when he heard a faint signal through the static.

"Eh! I think I found it!" He tapped the dial, and the static became a song. Although the station was not clear enough to catch all the words, Jean Patrick recognized the old praise song for the ancient Inkotanyi, the soldiers who had defended the first Tutsi kings.

That was . . . , a voice said, fading out again. Then Jean Patrick heard, *Muhabura, station of RPF-Inkotanyi, broadcasting from free Rwanda.*

"It's them!" Jean Patrick felt Roger's breath in his ear, his fingertips on his shoulder.

The broadcaster launched into a story about the meaning of the RPF struggle. His voice was calm and steady, not like Radio Rwanda, always shouting, shouting. His Kinyarwanda sounded softer, his accents in slightly different places, and Jean Patrick realized he must have grown up in Uganda.

Hutu and Tutsi, hear us: we are all Rwandans. Inkotanyi are fighting to bring peace for everyone. Jean Patrick wondered how fighting a war could bring peace.

"This is what you're always looking for? RPF?" Zachary put his fingers in his ears. "Turn it off. I don't want to die."

"What nonsense is this? How can a radio station kill you?"

"Our teacher told us RPF will all be pushed into the Nyabarongo River, and so will anyone who loves them."

"She said that? Did you tell Uncle?"

"I didn't want him to know I was afraid."

"Don't worry. No one's going to push us into the river."

Zachary pulled his sweater close. Radio Muhabura faded into static.

"There. It's gone. Now go to sleep," Jean Patrick picked a stalk of grass from Zachary's sweater and tucked the blanket around him. "Don't ever forget—I'm here to protect you. I promise."

Zachary curled up again inside the blanket. Soon his breathing slowed and deepened. Jean Patrick remained awake. How could he keep such an oath? He was afraid if he let his watchfulness fade, the Hand of God would steal Mathilde and his brothers, too.

FULGENCE AND THE rest of Uncle's night crew had already come ashore when Jean Patrick and Uncle reached the lake. "Any news of Mathilde?" Fulgence asked.

Uncle shook his head, worry lined deep in his face. "How was the night?"

Fulgence sucked his teeth. The Saint Christopher medal he wore around his neck twirled as he moved, casting off tiny spears of light. "We could have stayed home."

Jean Patrick and Uncle went to check their lines. "Hardly worth a morning's work," Uncle said when the last one came up empty. "But yesterday, diving, I found an old propeller. Maybe it's enough to pay for the hospital." A brown kite sliced the lake surface and emerged with a small tilapia in its claws. Uncle laughed. "He's doing better than we are. Let's troll where it's deep and see if our luck improves."

While Jean Patrick paddled, Uncle beat the water with a long pole to bring the fish to the surface. Jean Patrick waited for the right moment to speak about the Olympics, the Hutu card.

"I've been thinking," Uncle said, speaking in sync to the pole's *slap-slap*. "Maybe it's time to cross to Burundi. My sister Spéciose would help us." Diamonds of water sparkled on his back. "Your mama told me about the checkpoint. Things can only get worse."

Jean Patrick baited a hook and cast his line. Just to their south, Lake Kivu funneled into a narrow channel to feed the Rusizi River. If it weren't for the rapids, they could have simply paddled until the current caught them. Uncle's muscles flexed with each strike of the pole. There would be no right time to speak.

"With everything that happened, I never got to tell you," Jean Patrick began. "On Saturday I ran fast enough to be in the Olympics."

Uncle Emmanuel dropped the pole into the boat. "The Olympics?"

"Yego." It sounded like a story in a book, not something that had happened to him.

Uncle whooped. "You're going to the Olympics, and until now you say nothing?"

"It's not quite certain. What if I told you I needed a Hutu card to make the team, and the burgomaster could get me one? That would make it easier for me to get into university and to travel as well. What would you tell me to do?"

"Look. You've caught a fish, and you don't even see." Emmanuel jerked Jean Patrick's line. "You must take the card, of course."

These were not the words Jean Patrick had expected. Hearing them, he understood that he had wanted Uncle to forbid him, to take the burden of decision from his shoulders. "How can I? I'd be betraying my ethnie. Turning my back on you."

"We all know who you are; a piece of paper changes nothing. If a Hutu card means you can compete in the Olympics, then seize the chance with our blessings. You are taking all Tutsi with you, not leaving your family behind." He picked up his paddle. "Let's go back, eh? We can't sell these tiny fish at the market, and I want to be there when Mathilde comes home."

Jean Patrick threw himself into each stroke. He felt the resistance of the paddle, watched the rainbow arc flung from its surface. The forward motion calmed his mind. It was only when he looked up, sensing the change as the bottom shoaled, that he noticed the truck parked beside the dock. Uwimana stood by the shore in his rumpled suit, eyes shaded against the sun. Jean Patrick knew instantly what he had come to say. Sometimes all the prayers, all the bargains offered up to Imana, escaped His outstretched arms. Sometimes love was not enough to cradle a sister safely inside the sphere of life. Uwimana had come to tell them Mathilde was dead.

THEY BURIED MATHILDE beside her grandparents in the family cemetery at the border of the compound, her grandparents on one side, her baby sister and her uncle—Jean Patrick's namesake—on the other. Mama and Esther surrounded her grave with flowers. Jean Patrick tossed purple blossoms of jacaranda onto the coffin. Emmanuel fell to his knees and wept. It was the first time Jean Patrick had seen him cry, and it unsettled him, as if human weakness had only now turned his uncle into flesh and blood. He remembered then how his father's body had terrified him, and he remembered who had given him the strength to say good-bye. He touched Uncle gently on the shoulder.

"When Papa died, Mathilde made me tell him I loved him, so he could find peace." He blinked to stop the tears. "I'm glad now, because those were the last words I said to Mathilde."

Uncle Emmanuel gave a little laugh. "Mathilde was always clever. I can't remember the last time I told her I loved her, but I know she understood." He rose and bent over the grave, and Jean Patrick saw the same delicate arch of spine he had watched so often in Mathilde, like a crane bending to water. "She made me so proud," Emmanuel said. "I always knew she would go to university—just as I know it for you."

A shiver of wind passed through the trees, and suddenly, Jean Patrick felt Mathilde's fingers on his shoulders. He knew she was whispering to him that she was all right. She was pushing him forward, telling him to go on with the business of living.

THE FOLLOWING WEEK, for no reason any of them could explain, Zachary found Papa's inyambo steer dead among the grasses on the edge of the cemetery. They buried him close by, his beads around his neck. Jean Patrick did not say aloud what he believed, that there was more grief in the world than the tired old steer could withstand. In his thinking mind, he understood this carried no substance, but in his heart, his soul, he knew it to be so. A stream of sunlight fell across Mathilde's grave, and he thought of Ukubo kw'Imana, the Arm of God, coming to lift her to paradise. Watching the dance of light, his skin prickled. He fell to his knees and begged Imana's forgiveness for the thought that came into his head. Since his bargain had not been accepted, he was free to take the Hutu card.

THE DAY BEFORE the term ended, Uwimana called Jean Patrick into his office. There on the desk was an identity card, open to the photo Coach had taken the day before Nationals. It was stamped over with the official seal. He recognized his mother's high forehead, his father's narrow nose, his own upthrust, confident chin. In the space marked UBWOKO/ ETHNIE, all groups but Hutu were crossed out.

Jean Patrick picked up the card. The lie burned his fingers. "How can I take this?" He waited for Uwimana to respond, but he seemed distracted by something outside, so Jean Patrick continued. "How can I be suddenly Hutu when every part of my face says Tutsi?"

Uwimana turned his gaze from the window. "If the burgomaster says it, then it is so."

"What about my registration with the commune?"

Uwimana pantomimed crumpling a piece of paper and throwing it away. "Disappeared. You've been reborn." Hands pressed together, he leaned forward. "One more thing. Tell no one but your mother and your uncle about the card. Present it at checkpoints as if you've had it all your life, even if it's a soldier or policeman who has known you since you were small, but no one else must know. And keep your old card. We plan, but only Imana decides."

"Umuhutu cyangwa umutusi?" Jean Patrick said. "Hutu or Tutsi— which am I now?"

"Think of it this way. Your identity is the key that opens a lock. At this moment in Rwanda, all locks open with a Hutu key."

A raucous highlife tune came from the yard, and Jean Patrick saw what had stolen Uwimana's attention. It was a group of students sporting Hutu Power caps. A radio perched on a student's shoulder.

"Today you are Tutsi. When you go to Butare to train with your coach this weekend, you will be Hutu. What a marvelous power you have now," Uwimana said, his focus on the boys. "One day Hutu, the next Tutsi. All according to your needs." Uwimana took off his glasses and rubbed them vigorously with his handkerchief as if they were impossibly stained.

Eleven

Jean Patrick looked up from his book and peered out the bus window at the thirsty fields of young maize. Although this short season of rain was known for its fickle nature, so far it had shown only its cruel teeth of drought. Soon it would be dusk, and they were only now climbing out of Nyungwe Forest, rocking over the bumpy road. Coach must be waiting for him already, pacing and annoyed. And it didn't make it any easier that Jean Patrick was suffering his first slump. Since Nationals, he had not repeated his qualifying time, and this cast a gloomy shadow over his usual anticipation.

There had been three checkpoints, and the soldiers made everyone step out. Each time, as Jean Patrick handed over his Hutu card, he swallowed fear. Each time, the soldier merely glanced at his picture and handed back his papers.

The man in the next seat peered over Jean Patrick's shoulder through crooked spectacles. "What are those crazy symbols? Is that the Muslim language?" He wore tattered brown trousers and a stained shirt that must once have been yellow, and he gave off a scent of must and urwagwa.

"Physics, muzehe. It's my schoolbook." A sudden bump threw Jean Patrick against the man's shoulder. *A body in motion tends to remain in motion. A body at rest tends to remain at rest.* In the packed, airless bus, Jean Patrick's knees pressed into the seat in front of him, and he had no room to move without hitting some part of the man's body.

The bus stopped, and two young women in makeup and high heels stepped aboard. They squeezed together into the single remaining seat. "Tutsi," the man spat in Jean Patrick's ear. "See how tall and slender? And look at those expensive clothes—like ParisFrance," he said, running the two words together as if he believed they were one. He tapped the cover of Jean Patrick's book. "Did you know the RPF run naked through the forests and have sex with monkeys?"

Jean Patrick coughed into his hand to hide his laughter. "I had not heard that."

"It's true," the man said, belching. "I read it in *Kangura*."

A grandmother in the seat in front turned her head. "And if you read in *Kangura* that gold could be found at the bottom of a lake, would you jump in after it?" She kissed her teeth.

"If I read a prediction there, I know within a week it will come to pass," a mama with a broad face and farmer's sturdy shoulders said. She poked her friend, a lady in a complicated head covering, for emphasis. The two women in the shared seat moved closer together. The already heated air heated up further.

The man leaned into Jean Patrick. "I also heard RPF have sprouted horns because of their evil deeds."

Jean Patrick pointed to his head. "No horns here."

"Ha-ha!" the man bellowed. "That's because you're not Tutsi," he said, as if he had just penned the last stroke of some grand mathematical theorem.

Jean Patrick angled closer to the window to escape his neighbor and catch the last light to read by. On the page was a graph of time versus distance with tiny red arrows along a curved line. *Instantaneous velocity is the limit as the elapsed time approaches zero.* He imagined red arrows shooting from his back to measure his speed. He peered out at the sullen sky, the swollen, skittish clouds that so far had delivered little rain. By next week, he believed, they would open with a vengeance. *Everything in this world,* his father had written in his journal, *has a mathematical expression.* Jean Patrick closed the book and watched the passengers sway with the movement of the vehicle.

"Good evening. Almost good night," Coach said. He stood by the open bus door, impatience written in his posture.

Jean Patrick pushed his way through the mass of descending passengers and jumped to the ground. "Sorry. Checkpoints, as usual."

Coach frowned. "Problems?"

"No, just slow. This war is making the soldiers nervous, and they take it out on us."

"Well, let's go and eat. We could both use it." Jean Patrick threw his bag into the backseat. He no longer had to ask to know that they were headed to La Chouette.

The radio played full force behind the bar. Coach guided Jean Patrick to his usual spot and ordered Primus and food for both of them. The latest Simon Bikindi tune, "Nanga Abahutu," "I Hate the Hutu," came on. *I hate them and I don't apologize for that.* Coach chuckled. He's talking about the Hutu of Butare. Have you heard it?"

"How could I not? Radio Rwanda likes that song too much."

The food came, and the waiter poured their beers. "So you see, as a Hutu from Butare, even a loyalist like me stands accused. I have made it onto Bikindi's hate list." He cut into a chicken leg.

"Even me, I have to laugh when I hear his songs. They're so exaggerated."

Coach shook a sauce-stained finger at him. "Don't forget—you're a member of Rubanda Nyamwinshi now. The great majority. Officially, you're playing on Bikindi's team."

Jean Patrick felt the hot flash of anger in his face. Could he calculate the *instantaneous velocity* of rage? In his mind, red arrows exploded from Simon Bikindi's music, sprang from the students talking in animated voices at the next table. They sprouted from a stalk of bananas on an old woman's head as she passed by the window. Arrows blazed from the cue sticks of the soldiers playing pool, calling out "Shot!," slapping hands.

JEAN PATRICK STRUGGLED through another eight hundred, wishing it would end. His times were not improving.

"Run from your belly," Coach shouted. Jean Patrick didn't get what he meant. "Your belly!" Coach repeated. He made Jean Patrick lie down on the grass and place a hand on his abdomen. He made him bicycle in the air on his back.

This is stupid, Jean Patrick thought. Frustration fueled his stroke. He forced his cadence higher until his stomach cramped. Then, out of nowhere, a jolt of energy went straight through his belly and into his hand as his legs connected to his core. "Coach, I got it!"

"OK! Now get up and run. Quickly, before it goes away."

The feeling was no more than a shift in his center of gravity, a subtle flow of force inside him. But it was enough. He knew that this time, when he crossed the line, Coach would hold up his stopwatch and smile.

AFTER THE WORKOUT, Jean Patrick sat on Coach's couch and watched him pace. His thighs still throbbed with a pleasant, tingly heat. President Habyarimana glared down from his portrait on the wall. Giddy from his effort and emboldened by the Primus beer he had half finished, Jean Patrick tipped his glass toward the president in a mock toast.

"What is that boy's name, the Tutsi in your class who runs distance?" Coach asked.

Jean Patrick's heart quickened. "Isaka."

"Do you still run with him? He pushes you—you push each other."

Jean Patrick averted his eyes from Habyarimana's gaze. "He left." Isaka had not returned to school in September. There were rumors that his family had been killed in an August massacre in Kibuye, rumors that they had fled to Burundi. Jean Patrick didn't take them seriously. He knew his friend's spirit. Whatever had happened in Kibuye, Isaka had somehow survived.

"No matter. You'll be here permanently soon enough." Coach jiggled a handful of peanuts. "There are two parts to the eight hundred: heart and head. You've got the heart, no question, but the head is where I come in. If you don't have the tactics, you'll never get out of the pack when you run with the Ndizeyes and Gilberts, the Sebastian Coes and Paul Erengs of this world. And starting next year, you'll be doing that." He listed off the dates of important meets, the times Jean Patrick should be running by then. "Strategy, Jean Patrick. More than any other race, the eight hundred is about strategy. Watch any national or international race and see how often the original leader actually wins," he said.

Listening to Coach's plans, Jean Patrick realized that, like Roger at Easter, he now stood at the vertiginous edge of his future. The Olympics became something he could touch and taste and smell. He took another sip of beer and enjoyed the rush, the sensation of falling and flying at the same time.

"Are you listening?" Coach poked Jean Patrick's toe.

Jean Patrick's head snapped up, his eyes immediately pinned by Coach's intense stare. He turned his attention to a copy of *Kangura* on the table beside him.

A COCKROACH CANNOT GIVE BIRTH TO A BUTTERFLY, he read from the open page, a cartoon with a Tutsi woman beckoning to a Hutu man. A machete dripped blood behind her back. What would the world see when he ran for Rwanda? Cockroach or butterfly? When his picture appeared on the front page of the paper, how would anyone know who — or what — he was?

ↄↄ

Father Julius wrote the equation for the behavior of springs on the board. It was the last few minutes of the last class of the day, and Jean Patrick couldn't concentrate. Looking out the window at the gray, rippled sky, he rubbed his legs, still sore from the weekend's workout. Rain weighted the air. Quietly he touched a hand to his belly, lifted his leg beneath the desk, and tried to feel the instant when muscle converted to action.

"Here is the work done by the spring when force is applied." Father Julius drew a diagram with a spring and a thick arrow to represent the force. He wrote the calculus beside it.

Jean Patrick copied the equation in his notebook. Then he added, *Like a spring, if someone pushes me, I push back. An equal and opposite force.*

A tentative *ping* sounded on the metal roof. Jean Patrick looked at Daniel. *Rain??* he scribbled on the corner of his page. Daniel grinned and shrugged his shoulders.

The raindrops came closer together. Father drew two blocks connected by a spring, arrows of force between them. Before he finished, a riotous downpour ripped the sky. *Yes!!! Rain!!!* Daniel scrawled below Jean Patrick's question.

A rivulet of rain dripped between ceiling and wall. It ran down the board through the middle of Father's artwork. The drumbeat of rain rode over his words. Finally the bell rang. "Class is finished," Father shouted, chalk-whitened fingers held high.

Everyone bolted from the classrooms, taking off their shoes to dance in the season's first storm. "Imvura!" they shouted, faces turned toward the sky, arms held wide. Rain! It was an occasion worthy of tradition, the best Intore dancers going to the center to leap and spin, mimicking the steps of the early heroes, the graceful women of the mwami's court. "Finally it's come!" they sang. Even the priests joined in, showing off their best steps, white frocks raised to their calves. The courtyard erupted in swampy celebration.

Jean Patrick could almost believe there was no war, no drought, no indangamuntu weighing down his pocket. Bean plants would sprout. Fish would fly onto hooks. Roger would come home from the mountains unharmed. From nowhere, a memory of Mathilde came to him, a day when her face gleamed like polished copper, her smile transformed by the simple miracle of rain. After her death, they found out she had come in first in exams. She would have started secondary school this year, but no miracle could make her rise from the dead.

A FEW DROPS still fell when Jean Patrick and Daniel walked back to the dorm and pushed through the ruckus of naked boys. Instantly, Jean Patrick knew his bed had been disturbed. He could smell it, sense it on his skin, taste it on his tongue. He felt between the sheets, looked under the bed. When he ran his hand beneath the pillow, he found what had been placed there.

It was a copy of *Kangura,* folded open to an excerpt from a speech by Mugesera. Two sentences were underlined in red. *If you are struck once on one cheek, you should strike back twice.* And *Your home is in Ethiopia, and we are going to send you back there, quickly, by the Nyabarongo River.* The word *quickly* had been crossed out and *dead* written in its place.

Jean Patrick put the paper back beneath the pillow and sat heavily on the bed. The euphoria of the rain had evaporated; in its place was a sense of shock and the eerie feeling of eyes at his back. He looked around the room but saw only the chaos of bodies and slapping towels.

"What happened, eh?" Daniel sat beside him, dressed only in a towel. Beads of water blinked from his skin.

"Leave it," Jean Patrick said, instantly regretting his harsh tone. "I'll be back soon."

"Wait! Where are you going?"

Jean Patrick ran outside without answering. It was forbidden to leave school grounds, but he slipped out the gates, still barefoot and in his soaked school uniform. Again he felt the prickle of eyes at his back. At the edge of town, he stopped at his father's favorite bakery. The yeasty warmth of baking bread enveloped him. Instantly he was a small boy again, holding his father's hand and pointing at the chocolate-covered biscuits.

"Ah, Jean Patrick, still enjoying your favorites?" The old baker opened the case with fingers like gnarled mahogany root. White flour coated his face, his arms and hands.

"And you still remember." Jean Patrick placed his coins on the glass counter. "The chocolate ones."

"How many do you need?"

"Five is what I can pay for, I think."

The baker put seven biscuits in a paper sack. He was still waving when Jean Patrick shut the door and set the little bell tinkling. He leapt down the stairs. Two boys from Gihundwe stepped out from a pathway at the back of the shop, and he hailed them before passing between them into the narrow lane. "I guess I'm not the only disobedient student," he called over his shoulder. He sensed them close at his back.

Too late, he realized the connection to his unease, and he quickened his pace. A guy emerged from the gate at the far end of the alley, blocking his only exit. His red and yellow boubou was familiar. When he approached, Jean Patrick saw the zigzag scar across his face.

"Do you remember our last meeting at Gihundwe?" Albert grabbed his foot and hopped. The Gihundwe boys snickered. "I told you I'd be back."

"We hear you've switched sides. Got tired of being Inyenzi?" one asked. Jean Patrick recognized him from the sixth form. The other one, he thought, was a year or two younger.

The older boy pushed him against Albert. A stale, penetrating odor invaded Jean Patrick's nostrils. Quietly he collected his energy into a coiled spring. "What are you talking about?" He stepped sideways so he could watch both Albert and the students.

"Uri umuhutu cyangwa umututsi?" The three formed a tightening circle around him.

"I'm Nkuba Jean Patrick. I haven't changed."

"Mbwira! Answer the question. Are you Hutu or Tutsi?" Albert slapped Jean Patrick's cheek. "These guys heard you have a Hutu card. Maybe if you're Hutu we'll let you pass."

"Or maybe we won't, since your family is on the list in *Kangura*." The older student drew his finger across his throat.

"I don't know that list. I don't read *Kangura*." He shifted his balance. Like breaking out of a pack, he told himself. Find the clearing. He coiled the spring as tight as it would go.

"It says your brother Roger's RPF. It says your family's ibyitso." Albert reached into his pocket. "Everyone but you is mentioned by name."

"How would you know?" Jean Patrick asked. "I bet you can't even read." He was bargaining for time, praying an opening would reveal itself.

"We can read," the younger student said. "Here's what else was in *Kangura: Know that anyone whose neck you do not cut is the one that will cut your neck.*"

Jean Patrick heard the click before he saw the blade. Albert had dropped into a crouch, the knife loosely balanced in his hand. He lunged, and the coiled spring at Jean Patrick's center unleashed. He sliced the space between them as a diver slices the water. The blade grazed his arm, and the sack of biscuits tumbled to the ground. He burst through the rotten gate, splitting the wood from its hinges.

As he surged up the hill, blood trickling down his arm, he knew he must apologize to Uncle because his own name was not on the list. He would also have to apologize to the children because he had no sweets to give.

Twelve

THE MUZUNGU WAS SITTING at one of the tables set up for guests outside l'Hôtel du Lac Kivu. He had placed rocks all along the edge. Jean Patrick and Uncle Emmanuel watched him as they checked their tilapia lines beneath the sluice gate. The muzungu inspected the rocks with a small eyeglass he held in his hand, then wrote in a notebook. In the center of the table, an omelet and a basket of bread remained ignored, and the sight of the food made Jean Patrick hungry. His tea and slice of pineapple had long ago been burned up.

"Bonjour," the man called out. Jean Patrick had just jumped over the side of the canoe and was about to dive under. He looked around, expecting to find a white man behind him, the person for whom this greeting was meant.

"Bonjour," the muzungu said again. He waved in Jean Patrick's direction. "Parlez-vous français?"

"Bien sûr." Jean Patrick slumped in the water to hide his naked chest and ragged shorts.

The man leaned over the railing. "Can I ask you something?" A blue cap embossed with a red *B* shaded his eyes. A wild thickness of red hair, gathered in a long tail, tumbled down his back. "I was told to stay out of the water, but here you are swimming. Is it safe?" His French was ill pronounced and clumsy. "I'd love to jump in; I didn't expect Rwanda to be this hot."

"It's safe for us, but I don't know for muzungu." Jean Patrick had never seen a white person swim.

"Excuse me?"

Jean Patrick thought he must have been rude or said something wrong. He looked at Uncle, and Uncle shrugged.

"I'm sorry," the man said. "I didn't understand you."

The sun glared, a spotlight on Jean Patrick's face. "I said I don't know for muzungu." He pronounced each word slowly.

"Ah!" The man waved wildly. "Muzungu! Bonjour! Hello!"

Uncle watched. "Be careful," he said. "This muzungu might be crazy."

The instant the man flashed his broad smile, Jean Patrick understood. "You think *muzungu* means hello?" He choked back a laugh.

"That's not right? Wherever I go, people run and wave and call, 'Muzungu!' I just assumed they were greeting me." He scratched his ear. "So what are they saying?"

"It means a white person. We don't see many, so it's an exciting event." The man chuckled in a friendly way, and Jean Patrick smiled back. "Usually, muzungu brings money."

"Faranga." The man held out his cupped palms. "It didn't take me long to learn that." He leaned farther over the railing, and Jean Patrick wondered if he was going to jump in, clothes and all. "I'm Jonathan McKenzie. May I ask your name?"

"Nkuba Jean Patrick. People call me Jean Patrick."

"Nice to meet you, Jean Patrick. In America, we like things short. We'd call you J. P." He held out his hand.

Jean Patrick waded over. An American! No wonder his manners were strange. He reached up and touched the extended fingers. "Enchanté."

"And this is your brother?"

"Do I look so young?" Uncle Emmanuel laughed, obviously pleased. "I'm his uncle, more like his papa."

"What are you fishing for?"

Uncle Emmanuel held up a large tilapia. "These we fish for in daytime. At night we fish for sambaza—sardines—when they come to the surface looking for flies. The big ones we eat; the small ones we use for bait. Sometimes, if we're lucky, we catch a capitaine fish like this." He spread his arms wide.

Usually, Uncle's animation was reserved for politics or the motorboat he still swore he would soon—very soon—be able to buy. Jean Patrick watched Jonathan, sure he would find Emmanuel's talk foolish, but the man paid close attention, nodding his head as if listening to an important lecture. A waiter approached and pointed to the abandoned food.

"Excuse me," Jean Patrick said. "I think the waiter wants to know if you've finished."

"Oh my God, I completely forgot. My breakfast must be ice cold." Jonathan whirled around. "Sorry. I'm coming. Could you please bring more coffee?" And then to Jean Patrick and Emmanuel: "Thank you for talking to me. I've enjoyed it." He jogged back to his plate.

Jean Patrick thought about the strange muzungu as they paddled to the fish market. He thought about him when they pulled the pirogue ashore by the docks to scrub the bilge. He decided to go for a long, easy run and loop by l'Hôtel du Lac Kivu. Maybe the muzungu would still be there. When Jean Patrick left for university and trained full-time with Coach, the pleasure of casual runs would exist in memory alone.

JONATHAN HAD MOVED to the hotel bar by the time Jean Patrick jogged onto the grass. He waved, and Jonathan beckoned him over. A Primus and a book shared space with the rocks.

"J. P! I went for a swim! Come sit down. Can I buy you a beer? Are you old enough?" He marked his place in the book and closed it.

Jean Patrick pointed at his shorts. "They'll run me off for begging." He peered at the book title, something in English about Mount Nyiragongo. "What are you reading?"

"It's about an expedition to explore the inside of the volcano. A crazy French geologist named Tazieff. Have you been?" Jean Patrick almost laughed aloud at the thought of visiting a volcano, but decided against it.

"Sit down. I won't let them chase you away." Jonathan patted a chair. "I'd love to go there, but it's threatening eruption. How inconvenient. But I do have these samples from the slopes." He chose a particularly shiny one covered with white speckles. "If I'm right, it's quite rare." Jean Patrick held the rock close to his face and squinted. "Here. Use this." Jonathan gave him the lens.

A tiny world opened up, speckles and dark turning into landscapes with rainbow colors and strange shapes. "You're a geologist?" He remembered the pictures in his schoolbook, the earth sliced like a layered cake.

Jonathan beamed. "Yes, I am. In the U.S., most people don't know what that is." He turned the rock. "This is nepheline—rare in itself—but I think there are two even rarer minerals here: leucite and melilite. You only find the combination on Nyiragongo."

Once more, Jean Patrick peered through the lens. "It looks like it comes from the sea."

The expression on Jonathan's face made Jean Patrick feel as if he were under a microscope, being examined. "Are you a student at the university?" Jonathan asked.

A waiter set down a saucer of peanuts and glared at Jean Patrick. "Are you making trouble for the muzungu?"

Jonathan flashed a friendly smile. "Is there a problem?" The waiter backed away. "Sorry, J. P. You were saying?"

"I've just finished secondary school. In two weeks, I start university in Butare. Are you here on vacation?"

"Yes and no. Actually, I'll be teaching geology at your university. I came a month early to travel." Jonathan scooped peanuts into his mouth. "These are hot," he said as his face flushed crimson. "By the way, I'll be teaching in French. Do you think I could practice on you?"

"I'd like that. Maybe you could teach me English."

The bar was getting crowded. Someone cranked the radio full blast. It was tuned to the new station, RTLM. In the strident tone typical of its anti-Tutsi broadcasts, the DJ shouted, *Hutu, listen up! This is Radio-Télévision Libre des Mille Collines, FM 106.* He spun a Congolese tune. Out of the corner of his eye, Jean Patrick caught the waiter with his hand on the volume, watching him.

Jonathan tapped Jean Patrick's arm. "Why don't you have dinner with me? We could have our first lesson tonight."

"I don't think it's possible. My family is expecting me home."

"What about tomorrow?"

"D'accord." They shook hands on the deal, and Jonathan returned to his rocks and his book. Jean Patrick sprinted toward the road. He wanted to get away before the waiter had a chance to catch him on the lawn.

JEAN PATRICK ARRIVED at the hotel in polished shoes and freshly pressed pants. Jonathan sat near the bar, studying a menu with complete concentration. He had on sandals and rumpled khaki shorts, an untucked shirt with large, bold flowers. Was this how they dressed in America?

"Come help me order," Jonathan said. "All I know is *brochettes et chips.*"

At the next table, a group of businessmen from Zaire shouted and joked in their choppy dialect. They molded balls of ugali with their fingers and scooped up fish and sauce. Men in loud dashikis strutted beside the pool table, fingers blue with chalk, Primus bottles in hand. Above them, fans whirred and hummed.

The restaurant was just a concrete porch with a metal roof and a waist-high brick wall. From beyond the lawn, the Rusizi River murmured. Cicadas sang a high-pitched chorus. The generator's hum competed with a football game on TV.

A waiter brought two beers, opened them, and poured. "No worries. I could order for us," Jean Patrick said. He chose brochettes and chips, grilled fish, bananas and peas with rice. As an afterthought, he called the waiter back and asked for ugali.

Silverware appeared, bottles of water. The waiter set the food on the table, and Jean Patrick cut two portions of ugali, spooning one onto Jonathan's plate.

"Now you will truly be Rwandan. This is ugali, made from cassava flour." Jean Patrick shaped a ball with his fingers. "You do like this." He surrounded a piece of fish and pulled it from the bone, then popped fish and ugali into his mouth. The waiters watched from behind the bar.

"Comme ça?" Jonathan copied him. With the first taste, his nose wrinkled. "Needs a little help. It reminds me of Play-Doh, the paste I played with when I was a kid. I ate enough of that to do for a lifetime." Before Jean Patrick could stop him, he picked up a bottle of pilipili and doused his food.

"Mana yanjye. Do you know what that is?" It was probably impolite to laugh, but Jean Patrick couldn't help it.

Jonathan grinned. "I love hot peppers." He smashed the pepper-stained ugali with a fork, put a piece of fish inside, and attempted to eat it with his fingers. Pilipili and sauce ran down his arm. Tears welled in his eyes. The waiters nudged each other and fired off a rapid burst of Kinyarwanda. "What are they saying?"

"They say you're one crazy muzungu."

Jonathan nodded. "They're right."

In the corner, the nightly news came on TV. More treaty violations by the RPF, more government victories, more vigilant measures required against the Inkotanyi. The scene switched to Habyarimana at a government rally.

Jonathan leaned in toward Jean Patrick. "Isn't that your president?"

Jean Patrick nodded as Habyarimana talked about the peace treaty he had signed at Arusha. "A meaningless scrap of paper," the president said.

"He certainly seems popular," Jonathan said. "Everyone I talk to loves him." Jean Patrick sucked a scrap of fish from a bone. Jonathan tipped back his glass and swallowed the last of his beer. "Didn't he just make a deal with the rebels?"

"Yes, he did." Jean Patrick stared at the drops of condensation on his glass.

"Hopefully your lives can return to normal soon."

One of the pool players made a fantastic shot to wild cheers. Jean Patrick glanced in their direction. *If we are not vigilant, the Inyenzi will enslave the Hutu once more,* the news anchor intoned. Normal? Jean Patrick no longer knew what that meant.

"So tell me, J. P., what are you going to study?"

"I want to study math and physics, but they've assigned me to engineering. I guess they think pure science is pretty useless."

Jonathan growled. "Useless? It's the cornerstone of the natural world. And who's *they*? Can't you study whatever you want?"

Jean Patrick glanced at his watch. If he didn't leave soon, he'd miss curfew. How could he even begin to explain to this crazy American what life in Rwanda was like?

A Simon Bikindi tune, "Bene Sebahinzi," played on RTLM. "Turn it up," a pool player called out, singing along. *Remember this evil that should be driven as far away as possible.*

"This music really makes you move," Jonathan said, snapping his fingers to Bikindi's extolment of the Hutu Ten Commandments.

"It's a great beat," Jean Patrick said. "I'm sorry, but I have to go now. Curfew."

"Did you know," Jonathan said as he walked Jean Patrick outside, "that Lake Kivu is the highest lake in Africa?" He tapped the concrete with his sandal. "And did you know that Africa is splitting in two beneath our feet?"

Jean Patrick wasn't sure he had heard correctly. "I'm not familiar with the theory," he said, leaving it at that.

Thirteen

On his last morning in Cyangugu, Jean Patrick awoke with a mountain oriole's persistent call in his head. The cry had been in his dream as a warning, shouted from a woman's mouth, and he had been trying urgently to interpret its meaning. Zachary slept beside him, back curved like a turtle's shell, vertebrae laddered up the center. Jean Patrick ran his hand lightly up the two ridges of muscle. Somehow, while he hadn't been looking, Zachary had taken the first steps toward manhood. In a month, he would turn thirteen.

"I'm up," Zachary said. "You can light the lantern if you want."

"I'm sorry I woke you." Jean Patrick struck a match. The flame caught Zachary stretching to his full, long height.

"It wasn't you. Those birds make too much noise."

Papa's journal lay beside the bed, open to the page Jean Patrick had been reading when he fell asleep. *In this complex world, it is up to us as teachers to shine a light on the darkness of misunderstanding.* He closed the journal and placed it on his suitcase. "I'm going for my last run," he said. To scare off bad luck, he added, "Until I come home again."

"What about curfew? It won't be light for a little while."

"I'll be careful. The soldiers are too lazy to climb up here."

"Those Hutu Power guys have been roaming around."

Jean Patrick rubbed Zachary's head. "You think they can catch me?" He pulled on his sweatpants, zipped his jacket, and stepped into the brisk air.

A skinny wedge of moon hovered above the trees. The first breath of dawn hung in the air, just enough light to see by. Jean Patrick stepped carefully, feeling the ground with his bare toes. At the crest of the first ridge, he stopped and looked across the landscape—his landscape—one last time. Lake Kivu opened below him like a yawn.

He had come to a clearing when he heard a rustle in the forest litter. Unlike the random scurry of animal feet, it sounded purposeful, human. He dove into the bush. From the same direction, twigs snapped.

"Yampayinka data."

Jean Patrick heard the whispered exclamation clearly. He pressed himself to the ground, dislodging a pebble that clattered down the hill. The movement around him stopped. Then, from a close-by clearing, a rifle's unmistakable *cachink*. His heart boomed. Level with his eye, the dark shapes of men emerged from the shadow into the clearing.

"There's no one here," a voice said. A machete slashed the brush. "Tsst! Hey, One Shot, monkeys scaring you again?" Soft laughter.

Another man joined them. "All clear," he said.

There was now enough light that Jean Patrick could follow their movements. The men squatted and lit cigarettes, talking easily among themselves. Jean Patrick thought he heard Ugandan accents. A soldier stood and drank from a canteen. He passed it to the man beside him.

"Eh, Captain!" The man spit loudly. "Did you find this in a latrine?"

"If you're going to insult my coffee, you don't have to drink it."

The captain let fly a barrage that was part Kinyarwanda, park Kiswahili, and part Luganda, one of the main languages of Uganda. Jean Patrick inhaled sharply — they must be RPF!

A soldier removed his boot and massaged a sockless foot. He appeared younger than the rest, a boy almost. "I won't complain," he said, holding his hand out for the canteen. "Me, I'm very thirsty."

It was still too dark to distinguish his features, but from somewhere, Jean Patrick knew his voice. There was no trace of accent — he was definitely Rwandan.

The captain gave the boy the canteen. He took a long swallow. "Mama weh! So strong."

"Like your women, eh, One Shot? Sweet and strong," the captain said.

One Shot groaned. He unknotted a green cloth from his neck and wrapped it around his foot. Wincing, he pushed the foot back into his boot. "Hey-yey-yey."

Jean Patrick knew this motion, this expressive sigh, too. It itched at his memory. Lying in the leaf litter, he imagined what it would be like to be

RPF, to drink and joke with them, go out on patrol. They rested until light took a firm hold on the forest, Jean Patrick watching from his nest of leaves. Then they shook themselves into motion, and the forest that had coughed them up swallowed them once more. Jean Patrick rose quietly and resumed his run, slowly at first, absorbing what he had witnessed, and then connecting to his speed, his power.

WHEN HE REACHED the fields, Jean Patrick stopped to take off his jacket. The sun had chased the cold from the air; heat lay heavy on the crops. Cassava leaves had begun to droop. He should have been home long ago.

Mukabera hailed him. "So you're off to school today?" She hilled earth around her squash plants with swift, certain strokes of her hoe.

"After the farewell meal. Are you coming to eat with us?"

"How could I miss it? I'll bring a package of food to keep up your strength for those Butare girls." Olivette, roasting potatoes over a crackling fire of twigs, looked up and giggled.

Simon paused from harvesting urubingo. "We should exterminate cockroaches, not help them breed." He brought down his machete in a smooth arc. A swath of grass shivered and fell.

Mukabera turned on him. "Eh-eh, is this how I brought up my son? Hutu, Tutsi—we all help each other in these hills."

A neighbor pointed her hoe toward Simon. "Don't listen to him. He's just speaking from the wrong side of his mouth. We're all your friends."

The women went back to talking and laughing, but the men cutting urubingo stood expressionless, watching each swing of Simon's machete. Mukabera took a potato from Olivette and peeled it with dirty fingers. She blew on it, then sank her teeth into the meat. Jean Patrick's Tutsi neighbors worked quietly, as if silence could turn them into trees.

HE LET HIS legs lead him as he careened down the last slope. From the red umushimi flowers came a brilliant blue flash. A purple-breasted sunbird took flight, wings ablaze, long purple tail streaming behind it. Jean Patrick paused to follow its trajectory through the branches.

"A sign of good luck; now your journey will be blessed." Jean Patrick whirled around. Roger grinned at him. He hugged Jean Patrick so hard it took his breath away.

"N'umwene wanjye! I can't believe it! Were you up there with those RPF guys? I was searching, but I never saw you." Jean Patrick held on tight. "More than one year now, I haven't seen you."

"I've seen you." Roger rubbed Jean Patrick's scalp. "More than once."

"You're crazy to be here. Your name was on a list of Inkotanyi in *Kangura*."

"I know. And Mama's name, and Uncle's and Auntie's." Roger led him toward the forest. "Everyone but you."

Jean Patrick wondered if Roger was going to hit him. "The burgomaster offered me a Hutu card. I *had* to take it. I ran a qualifying time for the Olympics, but the way things are, this card is my only chance to go. As a Tutsi, even though I have the fastest time in Rwanda, the national committee will pick a Hutu over me. They could simply make my A-standard times disappear from their books." He tripped over his tongue to get the words out. "I'm sorry."

Roger lifted him into the air and spun him around. "God help me! My brother going to the Olympics, and he says *sorry*!"

"You're not angry?"

"Aye! If I were any more proud, I'd burst." A flock of bats lifted from the trees, sailing on delicate wings, translucent in the sun. Roger shaded his eyes and smiled. Deep lines etched his face. "You do what you must to survive. Who could understand that more than me?"

Jean Patrick felt shamed. What he had imagined of RPF life while hiding in the bush was a child's dream, nothing to do with the flesh and blood of war. "I'm sorry," he said again.

Roger shook a cigarette from his pocket and lit it. The brother Jean Patrick remembered did not smoke. "For what?" Blue smoke slithered from his mouth.

No words existed to express Jean Patrick's regret. "Did you know I leave for university today?"

"I know many things. That is one of them." Jean Patrick put a hand on Roger's shoulder. He opened his mouth to speak, but Roger stopped him. "I also know you want to tell me now about Mathilde."

They embraced once more, and the touch was enough to call back Jean Patrick's tears. "How did you find out?"

"From Uncle."

"Eh? You've seen him?"

Roger pulled him toward a grove of eucalyptus. "Enough questions! Come. Someone wants to greet you."

One Shot stepped out from the trees. Of course his voice, his gesture, were familiar: they belonged to Isaka. Jean Patrick ran to him. "I can't believe it! How did you find my brother?"

"Inkotanyi find each other." Isaka squeezed Jean Patrick. He was still light and wiry, but the strength of his grip told Jean Patrick he could toss him to the ground like a sack of sorghum.

"At Gihundwe we heard you were killed."

"Killed!" Isaka spat. "My family are Abasesero. Where we come from, we fight for our land. Since 'fifty-nine, we can't lose. Everyone knows our reputation."

Jean Patrick understood then why he had liked Isaka the moment he heard him shout *I come from Bisesero* on the first day at Gihundwe. Although its heat drove them in different directions, the same fire burned in both of them. He thought of the meet in Butare where he beat the Kigali boys, and in a flash of insight, he realized that he needn't feel shame for his choices. Isaka and Roger chose to fight with bullets. He had chosen to fight with his legs. As Uncle told him, each time he won, he carried all Tutsi with him. And maybe it wasn't a matter of choice. Maybe, since birth, Ukubo kw'Imana, the Arm of God, had set them spinning one way or the other.

They remained in the clearing until sweat shone on their faces. They talked about the war, life among the rebels, Jean Patrick's year at school. On the road below, a colorful stream of walkers and cyclists climbed or descended, a river flowing in two directions. The sun ascended its well-worn arc, Roger and One Shot keeping one eye on its passage.

"We'll have to leave now," Roger said. He lit another cigarette. "Greet Mama and Auntie for me. Tell them I'm safe. Tell Uncle I think of him always."

"Good-bye, Mr. Olympics." One Shot shook Jean Patrick's hand. "Keep strong. I can't wait until we win this war so I can run for pleasure again. But me, I'll try for the marathon."

"Ko Mana! Such a long distance." Jean Patrick clasped Roger and One Shot to him. "I wish you both the peace of God."

"There are many, many things to wish for now," Roger said. He embraced Jean Patrick a final time, then exhaled a stream of smoke and started up the path.

"Wait!" Jean Patrick called. "What's your nickname?"

Roger crushed the ember from his cigarette and put the butt back in his pocket. "Mistah Cool." He wiped his brow and took One Shot's arm. "I wish that you run for us all, Little Brother. For us all."

Jean Patrick watched One Shot and Roger until they disappeared into the forest and Roger's shirt became the flash of a turaco's wings in the thick green growth. What good was a wish? In Rwanda a wish was an overturned bowl that nothing could right or fill as long as the war dragged on.

THERE WAS NO room in the house to walk without stepping on a hand or foot, barely room to sit on the floor with a bowl of igisafuria and eat without jostling an elbow. Mama and Aunt Esther had been in the cookhouse all morning preparing Jean Patrick's favorite dish, and the pots of peanutty stew disappeared as soon as they reached the table.

"Jean Patrick, I've saved the best for you. Look—two chicken legs," Mama said, putting a steaming bowl in front of him. He sat in the place of honor at the head of the table. Drops of oil gleamed on the stew's surface. Plump green bananas floated like islands in the reddish sea of sauce. Jean Patrick inhaled the earthy scent.

Every cousin and neighbor had come to see Jean Patrick off. Even some sisters from Ntura Church sat at the table laughing and joking, sucking the last drop of marrow from chicken bones. In his blue Sunday suit, Zachary looked like a prince in their midst. If fate were right or fair, he would have been starting secondary school next week. He wanted to study for the priesthood but had not been awarded a scholarship. Uncle had no money to send him. The twins, too, were finishing primary school, but they were not near the top of the class, and so there was neither money nor hope for them.

Jean Patrick took a fried sweet potato and dipped it in fresh milk. The cream floated to his lips, and his eyes closed with pleasure. "Mama," he announced, "every day at school I will think of this taste, and I will be happy."

"Jean Patrick—listen to me!" Mukabera called across the room, raising her bottle of urwagwa toward him. "When you get sick of that school of yours, you come back and marry my beautiful daughter, eh?"

Olivette tossed back her head in laughter, and it seemed to Jean Patrick as if she had just now stepped from the shadowy background and into day. He saw her white, straight teeth and lively eyes, her ocher skin, polished by the afternoon light that streamed through the windows. Like Jacqueline's, her hair fell straight and shining around her ears. When he next came home, he would have to take her for a walk.

"Oya, Mukabera—Jean Patrick will not have time for girls," Uwimana said.

Angelique rolled her eyes. "Umukunzi wanjye, there is always time for love."

Dipping into a fresh pot of igisafuria, Uwimana said, "Hear me—Jean Patrick is going to be a famous man in this country." With his fingers he picked out a bit of chicken and popped it into his mouth.

After oration from Mama, Uncle, and Uwimana, Uncle Emmanuel proposed a toast. Everyone whistled and raised a bottle. "Speech, Jean Patrick! Give us a speech!"

He took in the celebration. There was so much he wanted to say, but when he opened his mouth to begin his speech, only a long sigh came from his throat.

His suitcase overflowed, but still Jean Patrick kept finding one more thing he couldn't leave behind. Pili lay by his feet, following his movements with a distrustful eye. "Zachary, tell me which of Papa's books you want."

"Just the Bible and the hymnal. You can have your science—it thickens my head too much."

The suitcase wouldn't close. Zachary had to sit on it while Jean Patrick knotted twine crosswise and lengthwise to keep it from bursting open.

"This is a big fish you caught," Zachary said.

"From now on it's up to you." Jean Patrick cut the twine with his knife. "Next year you'll get a scholarship for secondary school, and it will be your turn to leave."

Zachary leaned against the bookshelf, his countenance rapturous. He could have been Saint Kizito, stepped down from his pedestal at Gihundwe and come to life. "I'm not worried," he said. "Imana has His plan for me."

On the shelf, carefully folded, was the suit that Uwimana and Angelique had given Jean Patrick for his journey. He shook out the pants and then the jacket. They were gray with faint silver pinstripes. "I'm an important man now, eh?" He pulled off his shorts and held the pants to his body. The pleasant scent of newness filled his nostrils as he pulled them on. He put on his blue shirt, freshly pressed, and then the suit jacket. The sleeves came exactly to the middle of his wrists, and he laughed, thinking of his mother secretly measuring him, passing the numbers on to Angelique for the tailor. He took a few prancing steps. "Smart, eh?"

Zachary gave a low whistle. "Big professor, weh!"

Jean Patrick hoisted the case onto his head. The weight was poorly distributed, and no matter how he tipped it, he couldn't find the balance point. It was Zachary who succeeded. "What have I always told you?" Jean Patrick joked. "You're good at science even if you don't want to be."

THE BRIGHTLY COLORED procession to the bus stop snaked down the path. Jean Patrick and Emmanuel formed the last segment of tail, Jean Patrick holding tight to Uncle's hand. A lifetime of hard work had callused those hands beyond healing; with his eyes closed, Jean Patrick doubted he could distinguish them from tree bark. Uncle wore his formal black suit and broad-brimmed black hat to mark the occasion. His carved herder's staff accompanied his step with a *toc*. Baby Pauline trotted to keep ahead of them.

They reached the stop just as the bus for Butare came into view. It strained up the hill, coughing out a thick plume of exhaust. At the tiny market that formed around the stop, market goers kicked up storms of red dust into air already thick with smoke from roasting corn and brochettes. Hawkers readied for the mad sprint to the windows, primping their baskets of sodas, breads, and candies, little sacks of fruit. As Jean

Patrick went to buy his ticket, Uncle pressed a wad of crumpled bills into his palm.

"Aye! This could buy half your motorboat."

"It's bad manners to refuse a gift. A motorboat can't run away."

"At least let me buy some intababara for the children." Jean Patrick picked out a handful of plump fruits from a stall and put the rest of the money in his pants pocket.

Emmanuel poked him. "Thief will take it there."

"Don't worry. As soon as I buy my ticket, I'll put the rest away."

Jean Patrick's entourage stood as if waiting to be photographed when he returned. Clemence and the twins ran in and out between them, chins, arms, and dresses stained purple from fruit. Clémentine and Clarisse still dressed in matching clothes and giggled when someone mistook one twin for the other. Jean Patrick pantomimed snapping photos. "These pictures I can sell to a fancy tourist magazine."

Mama pressed a heavy sack into Jean Patrick's hands. "So you don't go hungry." How many pairs of pants ironed for a loaf of bread? How many blouses for his favorite biscuits? "You better go now," she said. "While you can still get a seat."

Jean Patrick pressed his forehead to hers. "Kubana n'Imana," he said.

"May God keep us all safe," Uncle said, glowering at a group of Hutu Power boys. "There's something from me at the bottom of the sack. You can open it when you arrive."

Uwimana clasped Jean Patrick's hands. Unlike Emmanuel's coarse grip, the palms felt soft and giving. "I meant what I predicted; you'll be an important man in this country. My heart is full for you."

After hoisting his heavy suitcase up the step, Jean Patrick stopped to wave once more. It could go on forever, this thinning thread of good-byes. The driver sent out a blast from his horn.

The last empty seats were in the rear, next to the window. A large woman carrying a basket filled with produce shoved in beside Jean Patrick. He squeezed against the side of the bus, and his knee vibrated to the engine's hum. The bus door slammed shut, and Jean Patrick opened the window against the heat. The woman leaned across him and closed it again. "Leave it so," she said. "We'll all get sick from the dust."

With a loud clunk, the bus ground into forward gear. The driver turned up the radio, and the tinny speakers buzzed with song and static. *365 is my number.*

"Eh! That's my favorite Sunny Adé tune. More volume!" a boy in a red and gold boubou hollered.

"That's as high as it goes," the driver yelled.

The boy stood in his seat and harmonized with the lyrics.

"Lord bless us—we have the King right here on this bus," someone joked. A riotous hooting and whistling erupted from the passengers.

The bus lurched into motion. It snaked through the crowd and onto the main road, slowly gaining speed. Gears ground. The driver leaned on his horn. Animals and market goers scattered. Through the dust-caked window, Jean Patrick watched his family grow smaller and smaller as the distance between them increased. They still called and waved, but he could no longer make out the words. A crack in the glass split them precisely in half.

BOOK TWO

A BIRD BUILDS ITS NEST

Buhoro buhoro ni rwo urugendo.

Slowly, slowly, a bird builds its nest.

Fourteen

The bus arrived in Butare twenty minutes late, and Coach wasn't at the stop. In his last letter, he had mentioned he would be coming from out of town. People pushed and shoved past Jean Patrick. A woman stepped on his foot. He checked his watch, imagining a car wreck, Coach lying at the bottom of a cliff. Jean Patrick hoisted his suitcase onto his head and set off toward Coach's house. Dust coated his shoes and dirtied his pant legs. At the crossing with l'avenue de la Cathédrale, a group of nuns passed beneath the archway and strolled onto the main road. The breeze flapped their habits as they stepped carefully across the litter and rotted fruit in their path.

A boy pushing a bicycle taxi stepped in front of him. "Hey, mister, where you going?" He whipped a rag from his pocket and made a show of polishing the passenger seat.

"I'm going to the dirt road just before Ihuliro Hotel. How much to take me there?"

"That's where the rich people live. One hundred francs."

Jean Patrick sucked his teeth. "You be thief. Me, I'm not rich. For that I can walk."

"How much, then?"

"Fifty francs."

"How much you pay for this?" The boy leaned over his bicycle and rubbed the sleeve of Jean Patrick's suit between his dirty fingers. He dug his flip-flops into the pedals and peeled away. Over his shoulder he called, "Stingy! You got crocodile in your pocket, afraid he'll bite if you stick your hand inside?"

"OK: sixty."

The boy stopped pedaling and turned around. "Seventy. And pay now."

"All right. Seventy. Let's go."

Jean Patrick set down his suitcase and reached into his pocket. Uncle's money was gone. He felt someone brush his side, and he whirled around to see three boys in ragged shorts sprint toward the market. Two held his suitcase between them. The taxi boy pedaled furiously down the street, hurling insults over his shoulder. Jean Patrick charged after the boys.

The suitcase burst open, and clothes and books scattered across the dirt. The boys dropped it and disappeared into the swarm of foot traffic. Jean Patrick hurled a stone at their backs and slapped his head. What had Uncle told him about leaving money in his pocket? Dusting his things as best he could, he stuffed them back into his suitcase and dragged it to a spot beneath a tree. He retrieved the sack of food his mother had given him from his knapsack and took out a sandwich of fried sardine and tomato. It tasted of his mother's love and the fertile earth of Gashirabwoba. It tasted of home.

"SORRY," COACH SAID when he appeared in a swirl of dust. Dust covered the doors, windshield, and mirrors. "I had to take a goat trail, and it was rough going."

Jean Patrick grasped his outstretched hand. He could have kissed it. "I was beginning to think you were dead."

"You can't kill me off that easy." Coach inspected Jean Patrick. "Didn't your family feed you? You'll blow away in the first gust."

"I ate plenty, Coach, but also I grew too much." Jean Patrick maneuvered the broken suitcase into the trunk.

Coach frowned. "What happened?"

"My uncle gave me money, and I forgot to put it away. Some street kids tiefed it. My suitcase, too, but it came apart, so they dropped it."

"Let's get you out of here before you get in trouble again," Coach said. He opened the passenger door. The same red grit coated the dashboard.

"Were you on safari?" Jean Patrick joked.

Coach ignored the question. Jean Patrick rolled down the window and stared out at the town. He breathed in the clean, pungent scent of eucalyptus from cook fires. Buhoro, buhoro—slowly, slowly—he let go of anger and embarrassment.

Coach pointed at a small house on a corner, barely visible behind a thicket of evergreen. "There's Gicanda's house. Your queen."

"The mwami's wife?" Jean Patrick leaned out the window. On his tongue was the correction, She was queen for all Rwanda, not just Tutsi. But he swallowed it with a gulp of air, and instead said, "I hear she's so kind. Anyone can visit."

"I've arranged for you to room with Daniel at university," Coach said. "I have some pull where you're concerned."

Jean Patrick clapped. "Like old times, like Gihundwe."

"Yes. Like old times." Although Coach smiled, his mind seemed elsewhere. Maybe in the place he had just come from. Maybe with a girl, his secret umukunzi.

A new, higher gate guarded Coach's driveway, and a high wall surrounded the house. "Too many criminals," he said. He honked the horn loudly.

A grandmother in a muddied pagne shuffled to let them in. She grinned broadly, showing off her few remaining teeth. A strong scent of polish and soap permeated the front hall. As soon as Jean Patrick had removed his shoes, the grandmother clucked her tongue and took them. "To polish," she said.

"Jolie, bring us a beer and something to eat." Coach plopped down on the couch. "Jean Patrick—put your things in the spare room; it's all set up for you."

Jean Patrick rummaged through his suitcase and found a T-shirt and sweats. When he emerged from the room, Coach looked up from his running magazine and frowned. "You need to lift weights, eat more protein. You need plenty of meat if you want to tangle with world-class runners." He motioned to a chair beside the couch.

The smell of leather surrounded Jean Patrick as he sank into the seat. With all the new furnishings, he barely recognized the room. There were carvings of tribal art, large drums of varying types and sizes, and fancy lamps. A bookcase now took up most of one wall, with books in several languages, arranged by subject. Mostly history and government, but surprisingly he noticed titles of poetry, some traditional, in Kinyarwanda. Habyarimana still ruled the room from his place of honor above the mantel. Some things did not change.

Jolie set a dish of freshly boiled peanuts and two Primuses on the coffee table. She opened the beers, tipped Jean Patrick's glass, and poured. "For you. Muzehe pours his own."

"Jolie is the best cook in Butare," Coach said. "Once you taste her food, you will want it every day." Jolie cackled. Coach jiggled a handful of nuts and watched her shuffling gait in silence. When she had shut the door, he pushed the dish toward Jean Patrick. The nuts were still warm from the fire.

"Tell me, do you still have your Tutsi card?" From Coach's casual tone, he may as well have been inquiring about the weather.

Jean Patrick's hand stopped halfway to his mouth. "I do. Uwimana asked me to keep it."

"Good. I have a proposal for you." Coach brushed salt and bits of skins from his trousers. "Well, not a proposal exactly, because the decision's been made."

Suddenly, Jean Patrick couldn't swallow. He didn't know what to do with the nuts. Put them back in the dish? Pretend to eat them? He slid his clenched fist beneath his thigh.

"I think I can trust you," Coach continued, "if I speak frankly."

"Yego, Coach. You can trust me." Jean Patrick wondered if this trust was mutual.

"Our government is in trouble with the West. Important countries are threatening to cut off aid unless Rwanda shows progress with human rights." Coach spat out these last words as if ridding his mouth of some foul taste. He moved closer, and Jean Patrick resisted the urge to scoot to the far end of the chair. "Certain people have decided *you* will be our example. What could be more progressive than a Tutsi in the Olympics?"

Jean Patrick thought of the chess games between his father and Uwimana. When he was small, he used to watch, fascinated, as they picked up the mysterious pieces and moved them about the board. He felt like one of those pieces now, dangled from unknown hands. "I'm not clear. Are you saying you want me to be Tutsi again?"

A mosquito alighted on Coach's arm. He slapped it and flicked the body away. "You are the best runner this country has ever had. With the right training, you can medal. I don't say this just to flatter you. In the world of track, you are the jewel in Rwanda's crown. Why not give up the pretense and represent your people?"

If Roger or Uncle had said this, Jean Patrick would have been proud. But coming from Coach, it sounded like a dismissal, an insult. "My people are the people of Rwanda," he said. He slid his hand from beneath his thigh. One by one, he put the nuts in his mouth and chewed slowly. It was dizzying, this throwing down of one identity and picking up another. Outside the window, night bruised the sky. "If I am Tutsi again, can I still go to school?"

"Why not? You earned your scholarship."

"And travel to track meets?"

"You must. No one here can challenge you, and you need to get your name out there. Run qualifying times where they count."

"But it's so hard now for Tutsi to travel. What if I get stopped at the border?"

Coach roared. "You leave that to me. All you need to do is run." He poured the last of the beer into their glasses. "Good. It's settled, then. Let us drink to your future."

Of course, it had been settled from the first. On the one hand, Jean Patrick felt relief. He would not have to bite his tongue each time he presented his card, and as Uncle had said, he would truly lift up all Tutsi with each victory. But now, when he put his indangamuntu in a soldier's hand, he would once again know the feeling of surrendering his fate as well.

He glanced up at Habyarimana, then down at the volumes of *Kangura* stacked on a bookshelf. Although he did not see it now, there must be some advantage he could gain from this game. All he had to do was bide his time, hang back behind the leader, the way Coach told him to run the eight hundred. Like a chess player concealing his strategy, he smiled at Coach. "To my future," he said. They clinked glasses. "And my gold medal." They drank.

"Did you bring your Tutsi card?" Coach asked. Jean Patrick pointed toward the spare room. "Fetch it. And your Hutu card as well."

Jean Patrick took both booklets from his backpack. A piece of paper

Jonathan had given him with his address fluttered to the floor. With trembling fingers he picked it up and put it on the table beside his bed. Cyarwa Sumo. Later he would have to ask Coach where that was.

"You look like I'm going to shoot you," Coach said when Jean Patrick put the two booklets on the table. "Don't worry; everything will be all right. You have to trust me." That word again: *trust.* Coach upended his glass. A mustache of foam remained on his lip. "I have to take this." He wiped his mouth with the back of his hand and tapped the Hutu card.

"It's so dangerous for Tutsi now," Jean Patrick said. He looked at Coach and slid the card toward him. From the darkness, now complete, cicadas trilled a warning.

"Yego. You are right." Coach's hand hovered above the card as he held Jean Patrick's gaze. Then he slid the card back. "I threw this in the fire. You watched it burn. Do you understand?"

Jean Patrick touched the edge of his Hutu card. "Yes. I understand." He palmed the card. "Thank you."

"Hide it very carefully. Never use it again unless . . ." Coach left the sentence unfinished. He did not have to ask if Jean Patrick understood this last thing, and Jean Patrick did not have to answer that he did.

AFTER DINNER, JEAN Patrick sat on his bed with Uncle's gift on his lap, a framed photograph of Paul Ereng winning gold in the eight hundred at the 1988 Olympics. Ereng, a Kenyan middle-distance runner, had come out of nowhere, surprising the world with his win. How Uncle had managed to find the picture, Jean Patrick had no idea. The photographer had caught him just before he crossed the finish line a half step in front of another runner. On Ereng's face was an expression of ecstatic pain, an expression Jean Patrick believed he mirrored in the best of his races. *You have to suffer until suffering becomes an old friend,* Telesphore had said on the day he came to Jean Patrick's class, and Jean Patrick had tucked the words inside his heart.

Jean Patrick recognized Uncle's handiwork in the ironwood frame. In two diagonal corners he had carved a runner. They were stick figures, but Jean Patrick saw his own high, stretched-out kick. In a third corner was a running shoe, complete with a tiny Nike swoosh. A note tacked to the backing said, *Never forget we are your #1 fans. We love you.* Jean Patrick knew how difficult it must have been for Uncle to commit those three words to paper.

Jean Patrick turned the picture over, pried the nails loose that held the backing to the frame, and inserted the Hutu card behind it. In the morning, he would ask Coach for some glue so he could fasten it securely. If it ever came to that—if he needed the card in a hurry—the frame's destruction would be a necessary price to pay.

⁊

A flash of brightness startled Jean Patrick awake. Coach stood by the light switch dressed to run; a pair of Nikes dangled from his fingers. "I have a course mapped out, about ten kilometers, lots of long hills for intervals. The level of pain will please you."

"You're running with me?" Jean Patrick threw off the covers.

"I have trained for it." Coach set the shoes on the floor. "I figured you needed new ones. Lots of room for your toes." He tossed a bag onto the bed. "Courtesy of our government."

Jean Patrick removed a tracksuit, iridescent blue. His fingers slid across the satiny fabric as he lifted it from the bag. On the back of the jacket was a Rwandan flag. He let out a low whistle. It was the most beautiful jacket he had seen in his life.

SUNRISE CAUGHT THEM as they crested the first hill and approached the Junior Military Officers' School. The guard at the gates saluted, and Coach returned a clipped salute. "What are you gawking at?" he asked Jean Patrick.

"He saluted you, and you saluted him back like a soldier."

Coach waved off a fly. "I do some training, teach a few courses."

"You're in the army?"

"I was for many, many years. Not now."

Jean Patrick expected something further, but Coach just forced the pace harder.

They turned onto the main road and let gravity take them down the hill. Jean Patrick unzipped his jacket. The brisk morning tingled his skin. They ran past National University. In a few days, this would be his home.

At the bottom of the hill was a checkpoint. A group of guys with machetes on their belts loitered by the soldiers. When they noticed Jean Patrick, they stopped their bantering to stare.

"Relax," Coach said. "Just act calm." The soldier waved them through. Jean Patrick felt the stares at his back like a layer of cold sweat.

"Who are those guys?"

"Interahamwe. A government youth militia. I told you—don't worry." Coach turned down a narrow dirt lane and grinned wickedly. "Now comes the fun."

The road climbed sharply among large houses with tiled roofs. Tall trees shaded the route. Jean Patrick's lungs burned.

"Before you came, I drove around looking for the steepest hills," Coach said. He swept his hand across an expanse of rolling summits. "Today you have an easy day, a jog to see the scenery. Starting tomorrow, you'll do your intervals here. Hills in the morning, track in the afternoon. Resistance and endurance. Speed will come later, after you build your base."

"Where are we?"

"Cyarwa Sumo," Coach said.

"Eh! I have a friend who lives here."

Coach wiped the sweat from his forehead. "A friend?" From the expression on his face, Jean Patrick might just as well have said, I am Nkuba, King of Heaven.

"A geologist from America. He's teaching at National University, and he rented a house here." Jean Patrick paused to catch his breath. "I thought maybe I could take his class."

"Did you say geology?" Coach grimaced. "What good is that?"

IT WAS NOT yet light when Jean Patrick awoke. He dressed in the dark and tucked the paper with Jonathan's address into the pocket of his track pants. He nearly collided with Jolie on her way to the kitchen with a kettle.

"Sorry," she said. "I nearly burned you."

Jean Patrick took his shoes from the mat by the door. "Grandmother, I was at fault."

The old woman clucked. "Do you think you can go out so, no thought of curfew? If the crooks don't get you first, the soldiers will shoot you." She laughed at her joke.

"I'll be all right. I know how to hide. Can you let me out?"

Jolie removed the ring of keys from her pocket and unlocked the front door. "Imana bless us," she said. Jean Patrick stepped into the bracing air. She padded behind him in her flip-flops. "If muzehe wakes before sunrise and finds you gone, I'll say you stole the keys and let yourself out." She gave a throaty singsong and unlocked the gate.

"Yego, Grandmother. I did that."

JEAN PATRICK BEAT the dawn to the Cyarwa Sumo checkpoint, so he turned down a dirt lane to pass the time until daylight. Leaning against a signpost for the National University arboretum fields, he wondered what they were. He found a goat trail among them where he would not be seen. At the top he made out a small hut, and he chose this as his goal.

He took off his shoes and climbed, easy until he found his footing, then digging in until the effort burned his thighs. With each arm stroke, his jacket released a *ssshhh* like falling rain. The slope's steepness took his breath. He reached the hut simultaneously with the sun's arrival. Hands on knees, he caught his breath and watched the soldiers, tiny as ants at the bottom of the hill. The fields were filled with pungent, colorful crops he could not identify.

"Mwaramutse," a voice rang out. A wizened grandfather leaned against the door of the hut. Smoke from his pipe wound a blue ribbon about his head. He motioned to two chairs, one with a cup of tea, a knife, and a block of wood beside it. "Why are you running so? Please sit down." The old man sat and took up his knife. An animal head took shape in the wood.

"I'm training, Grandfather. I'm going to run in the Olympics for Rwanda."

"The Olympics? Imana bless you!" A scent of wood and smoke rose from his skin. Inside the hut, pots clanged, a baby cried, a woman sang a soothing tune.

"Is this your land?"

"I'm only the guard." The old man chuckled. "Aye-yay-yay! In all the years I've lived, I have never seen a human come up a hill like that." He drew a deep draft from his pipe. "Will you take tea?"

"Next time, Grandfather." Jean Patrick shook the guard's hand.

How pleasant it would be to linger and drink some tea, he thought as he ran back down. He jogged toward the checkpoint, taking deep breaths to calm the thudding of his heart.

"I REMEMBER YOU from yesterday," the soldier at the checkpoint said, jostling Jean Patrick's elbow. He popped a piece of gum into his mouth. "Your coach says you're our next Olympic hero." He inspected Jean Patrick's papers and thumped him on the back. "Run with a cheetah's legs," he said.

"I will do my best, muzehe."

JEAN PATRICK MUST have missed a turn. Now he started up an unfamiliar path, stopping beside a tree to get his bearings. The tree's strange geometry had caught his attention, three equal trunks split from a single base. At the top of the road a blue metal roof crowned a long ocher building. A series of smaller trails snaked through slopes dotted with well-groomed homes.

One hill is as good as another, he thought. He tied his jacket around his waist and began his intervals. Passersby turned their heads, children chased after him, goats scurried out of his way. Jean Patrick did high steps and butt kicks, forcing the cadence until he tasted tin on his tongue. Light streamed through the eucalyptus, melted into a luminous haze. By his third interval, he had to grit his teeth and half close his eyes to reach the end. In his wake, a chorus of dogs sounded an alarm. The goal was in sight when a gate opened directly in his path and startled him from his meditative state.

"Quickly! Come inside." A hand pulled him into the yard. The gate closed with a screech behind him. "Are you hurt?" The lilt of the woman's voice remained in the air like the first chord of a song. She locked the gate and slipped the key ring onto her wrist. The world jolted into focus, and an involuntary shudder passed through him. She looked as surprised as he, her eyes bright and round like a startled bushbuck.

"Did someone hurt you?" she asked again. "Come in the house. No one will search for you here." Her disheveled hair fell to her shoulders. Her clothing hung slightly askew, as if she had hastily thrown on her pagne and the shawl that draped nearly to her feet.

"I don't understand." Jean Patrick felt suddenly naked. "I thought *you* needed help." He fumbled with his jacket. "I thought maybe your husband—maybe something bad happened."

The woman hid her mouth with her hand. A sound between a sneeze and a laugh escaped. "Mana yanjye, you thought *that*? And here *I* thought someone was chasing *you*."

"No, madam."

"You looked like you were in terrible pain."

"No, madam. I was running."

"Because you wanted to? A jogger? Ko Mana!" She tucked a strand of hair behind her ear. Beneath her shawl she wore a pagne patterned with orange suns and pink-ringed planets. Gold zigzags of lightning streaked across the fabric.

"A *runner*," Jean Patrick corrected. "I'm *training*." Outside the gate, a crowd of children chattered. He could see the bottoms of their dirty legs, their broken flip-flops.

"You have a fan club," the woman said. "I heard the dogs, and when I saw you, I assumed some thugs were on your heels." She gathered her shawl around her. "It wouldn't have been the first time."

"And what if I had been a thief?" Jean Patrick said, stepping close. "What if you invited me into your home and I robbed you?"

She motioned toward the children who dashed back and forth against the gate. "You wouldn't have gotten far. My neighbors are very tough; they would have caught you and dragged you back."

Jean Patrick couldn't guess her age. At first he had thought her twenty-four or twenty-five, but in the sunlight, her features took on a schoolgirl look. Behind her, he glimpsed a garden and a yard thick with fruit trees.

A heady perfume of flowers came from her skin. He did not want to leave. He could have rested beside her and watched her pagne ripple about her feet until the waxed suns crossed the cloth sky.

Inside the house, dishes clattered and a radio clicked on. A woman's voice called out, "Bea, where are you?" A door banged. Two children, a girl and a boy, exploded through the opening, skin shiny with Vaseline. Bea opened her shawl and enfolded them like a bird taking her chicks beneath a wing. Jean Patrick's heart sank.

"I'm just coming," she called. She took the keys from her wrist and unlocked the gate. "Well, be safe, then," she said to Jean Patrick. She pushed the gate open, exposing a well-muscled calf. The little boy perched on her feet and rode her steps.

What could Jean Patrick do but thank her and walk into the morning through the space the children made for him? Bea. Beatrice. The blessed one.

He readjusted his jacket and jogged toward the next hill. It was useless. The girl called Bea had knocked the wind out of him. For the first time since a calf cramp had felled him on the day Rutembeza became his coach, Jean Patrick gave up. All the way back, her face remained in front of him. He could have placed a palm on her high cheekbones, felt her sun-warm skin, the color of strong tea, traced the almond slant of her eyes with a finger.

Coach's front door opened before Jean Patrick could knock. "We're safe," Jolie whispered. "Muzehe doesn't know." She pointed to his muddy Nikes. He removed them to give to her. "What happened? Tief chase you through the swamps?"

"No, Grandmother. I ran through the reeds myself."

She chortled. "Give me your dirty things, and I'll wash them."

It was only when he removed his track pants and found the directions in his pocket that he remembered Jonathan. He looked at the map. Bumps rose on his arms: a three-trunked tree, an ocher building with a blue metal roof. Most likely, Jonathan could throw a stone from his rooftop and have it land in Bea's yard.

• • •

WITH THE PHONE cord as his tether, Coach circled between bookcase and window and spoke loudly into the receiver. Jean Patrick lingered in the hallway, ears cocked to pick up the conversation, but as soon as Coach noticed him, he stopped and snapped his fingers. "Go and eat," he said, turning his back. Still trying to overhear, Jean Patrick went into the dining room and took a finger banana from a bowl on the table.

Coach strode in a little while later and pulled out a chair. "How was your workout?" he asked, drumming his fingers on the tablecloth.

"Good. I felt strong."

Jolie brought omelets sprinkled with onions and tiny red peppers. Coach put two pieces of bread on Jean Patrick's plate and pushed the tub of margarine toward him. "Eat. You need to build muscle." He watched Jean Patrick closely, fingers still tapping out a beat.

Jean Patrick's stomach shouted for food. He could have tipped the plate and shoveled the eggs into his mouth. Instead he cut slowly, dividing them into bites of equal size. Sooner or later, Coach would reveal what occupied his mind.

After Jean Patrick cleaned his plate and set down his knife and fork, Coach's fingers paused on the tabletop. He regarded Jean Patrick with a pleased, amused expression. "You are racing in Kigali next month," he said. "You haven't run an A-standard time in a while; do you think you can do it by then? It's important."

A switch flipped open in Jean Patrick's body, a current of excitement flowing through him. "I can run sub–one forty-five fifty in two weeks. I know it."

Coach slapped his palm on the table. "That's the spirit!" His mouth curved into a half smile. "Your Burundi friends will be there."

"Gilbert and Ndizeye? Those two that beat me?"

"The very same."

"I wasn't sure they could still race."

"Why? Because our Burundi brothers shook off the Tutsi yoke and elected a Hutu president?" The veins in Coach's temples pulsed. "Of course they can race. Burundi has a democracy now. Like Rwanda. The majority voted, and the majority chose Ndadaye. He is not like the Tutsi oppressors who have governed Burundi since independence. He will allow

Tutsi to be free." He took a breath as if he would continue his tirade, but instead he began drumming again.

Jean Patrick poured tea, stirred in sugar and milk. Bea's perfume reached his nostrils.

"This event," Coach said, "is a special occasion to celebrate the implementation of the peace process. Many Westerners will be there." His eyes penetrated Jean Patrick's. "World Championships are in Sweden next year. An A-standard time would qualify you. I want people to know who you are—important people in the international community. So you need to stay sharp. If you go and fall on your face, it will not be good for my reputation or your Olympic chances."

Blood rushed to Jean Patrick's head. "World Championships?" A long, low whistle escaped him. "No worry. I can do it."

Coach aimed his spoon at Jean Patrick's head. "You have to learn to run smart, so I want you racing with your competition as much as possible. Remember—you represent Rwanda by the grace of the National Olympic Committee and the Rwanda Athletics Federation. It is they who, according to their pleasure, verify your registration for the Olympics. Or not."

"Coach, that can't happen. I can run against anyone."

The spoon clinked against the edge of Coach's cup. "After the race, there's going to be a reception at the American Embassy. TV and radio reporters will be there. President Habyarimana will greet you."

Jean Patrick regarded Habyarimana's picture, just visible over Coach's shoulder. Bars of shadow from the half-open shutters turned him into a prisoner looking out from a cell.

"The president knows who I am?"

"Indeed he does."

"Can Daniel come to the reception?"

"Of course. His father will be there with the Presidential Guard." Coach traced circles with his spoon. "How about inviting your American friend, the geography professor?"

Geology, Jean Patrick corrected in his head. "That would be great!"

Coach swept crumbs from the tablecloth into his palm and disposed of them on his plate. "I'm going to arrange for you to take his class. It would be nice to have a Westerner who knows you and can tell your success story to his people."

"Did you say the race would be on TV?"

"I did. Your family can watch the entire day; in fact, the whole town can watch."

With a twinge of guilt, Jean Patrick realized he had not given a thought to his family. His mind was too much taken up by a woman with a pagne of planets and suns and the scent of sweet tea on her skin.

FIFTEEN

ON THE FIRST DAY OF CLASSES, Jean Patrick felt lucky and brave. On his way out the door, Jolie gave him a conspiratorial nod and pointed to his bare feet. "No fancy shoes?"

"No, Grandmother. Not today."

He warmed up with an easy jog. He waved at the guards at the Officers' School, and they waved back. He did strides, butt kicks, and pickups down the main road, then a steady pace to the arboretum. Finches trilled from the trees, showed off metallic flashes of feathers.

"Mwaramutse!" the soldiers at the Cyarwa checkpoint called. "How's the Olympics going?"

"Olympics are going well." On this morning, when he felt so bold, he could have looked them in the eye and said, My name is Nkuba Jean Patrick, and someday you will know it.

He passed the three-trunked tree. From the directions in his pocket, he found Jonathan's house, hidden behind a brick wall. He had been right: a straight shot down to Bea's garden. In the thick growth he spotted a place where he could see into her yard. A woman was hanging laundry, and Bea's pagne with its field of stars beckoned to him from the line. The boy and girl that Bea had taken into her shawl chased each other between the clothes. Fascinated, he watched until his muscles stiffened and the children darted back to the house.

When he stood to stretch, a group of scruffy children surrounded him. "Watch us!" they chirruped, pulling on his T-shirt and dashing up the slope with screwed-up faces, arms and legs flailing.

"Do I look so strange?"

"Like someone from the moon," they screamed, and they wheeled down the lane.

Jean Patrick had picked a rock from between his toes and was about to follow when he saw a man in Bea's yard. He walked stiffly along the path, stopping by a mango tree. Light limned his hair with silver. He reached to pick a fruit. Even from this distance, Jean Patrick saw that the act filled him with pleasure. Bea came out and stood beside him, and he put an arm around her waist. Together, they walked to the house. The man held the mango high, like a prize. He may as well have reached into Jean Patrick's chest and plucked his heart.

"THIS IS NKUBA Jean Patrick," Coach said to the guard at the university's main gate. "He's a student here. He runs for me — my star. Treat him well."

The guard held out a wrinkled hand to Jean Patrick. "Yes — I remember from last year. Such a pleasure to see you." He tipped his cap. "Welcome back, muzehe," he said.

Jean Patrick looked toward the eucalyptus grove that framed the track, his familiar world. As soon as his feet touched the packed red dirt, he could forget this woman called Bea.

Coach parked. "Your dorm is there." He pointed to the long rows of dormitories below. From the paths came the *scritch-scratch* song of women sweeping, punctuated by the commotion of the students' shouts and calls.

Jean Patrick touched the door handle. "Well, I guess I should go." He glanced at his suitcase in the backseat. Coach had repaired the lock and hinges. "Where's your office?" He let the car door swing open. "In case I need you."

Coach pointed toward a two-story building. "First floor, in the Government Department."

"Where is the Geology Department?"

Coach smirked. "I wouldn't know."

"I'll see you for practice this afternoon." Jean Patrick took his suitcase and stood beside the car. He watched a group of girls with arms linked sway down the path toward the cafeteria.

Coach started the engine. *"Imana gives you cows, but he doesn't tell you how to graze them,"* he quoted. He slammed the car into gear and drove off, leaving Jean Patrick in a blue haze of exhaust to puzzle out the meaning.

JEAN PATRICK HAD barely enough space to stretch his legs in the tiny room, but unlike in Gihundwe, he had only Daniel to share it with. On the bed next to the window, Daniel had left a note. *Welcome to the mwami's palace. I've left the view for you. My papa greets you and said he was sorry he couldn't wait. I got your last letter. FÉLICITATIONS!! We have much to discuss, my friend.* His suitcase lay open on the bed, clothes spilled across the blanket.

In the small mirror on the desk, Jean Patrick inspected his image. He liked the high crown of his forehead, the deep-set, serious eyes, but he found his nose a bit too long, his face perhaps too thin. He straightened his slacks, crisply pleated by Jolie, brushed off his jacket, and stepped out into his new life.

AFTER REGISTRATION, HE sat on a wall in the central courtyard. Students wandered the paths, crowded stairways, hung over balconies. Their singsong voices melted into a pleasant buzz in Jean Patrick's head. The heat lulled him into a trancelike state. Now and again he was jolted awake by a clap on the shoulder from someone who recognized him from track.

He looked up from a conversation with a fifteen-hundred-meter runner when the flash of a gold blouse and brilliant green skirt caught his eye. Gold bangles flashed from the girl's arm. Just before she disappeared into a stairwell, she turned and caught Jean Patrick's eye. Bea! She gave him an amused smile.

In the instant it took to say good-bye to the runner, Bea had vanished. Frantic, Jean Patrick dashed after her. She trotted up the stairs and then down a poorly lit hallway, bracelets ajangle. He stopped halfway up the stairs to regain his power of speech and compose the words he wished to say. An office door opened, and a man in a gray suit stepped into the hall. Bea walked into his embrace and kissed the air by his cheeks. The image of that same gray-suited arm plucking a mango flashed through Jean Patrick's mind.

JEAN PATRICK FOUND Daniel leaning against a giant plastic Primus bottle by the cafeteria, watching the girls. He wore blue jeans and a plaid shirt with the sleeves rolled halfway up his strapping arms. Jean Patrick had to look twice to make sure it really was him. He tried to lift him off the ground, but instead Daniel scooped him up and twirled him around.

"I guess Coach is right; I need to lift weights."

"Papa made me strong, eh?" Daniel grinned, and Jean Patrick saw the familiar dot of pink tongue. "I kept thinking he had secretly enlisted me in the army to cure my natural laziness."

Smoke from the cafeteria fanned out into the sky, carrying with it the smell of grilling meat. Jean Patrick poked Daniel. "Are you hungry?"

"If a cow walked by, I could catch it and eat it."

Jean Patrick hooked Daniel's arm, and they went inside. Hearing his friend's high-speed chatter, Jean Patrick gradually shook off his morning companion named Misery.

"Let me tell you—I'm glad to be here," Daniel said. They shoved through the crowd and found two seats at a long wooden table. They had to shout to make themselves heard. "Kigali and Butare are more like different countries than different cities. Kigali country I do not like anymore." He tore a piece of meat from his brochette. "In Kigali, you know every minute of the day there is war. Grenades, gunfire, explosions."

"What? The RPF are fighting in Kigali?"

"Not just RPF. Rival political parties. The MDR fights the CDR, CDR fights PSD, everyone fighting Habyarimana's MRND. Aye! So many letters—who can keep them straight? And then there's the crooks, blowing up shops just to steal from them. One day I almost tripped over a dead body. He was lying in the middle of the street, like he was asleep. They cut him in broad daylight." Daniel dunked a chip in pilipili. "Oof! These peppers are hot."

"What about the cease-fire? You said people danced in the streets. And what about the United Nations? They were supposed to send troops." Jean Patrick's sour mood returned. He had hoped Daniel would tell him the war had gone away.

"We have not seen UNAMIR." Daniel spoke in a low voice. "United Nations Assistance Mission for Rwanda—a fancy name for an invisible army. Habyarimana promises UN troops, and we see more government soldiers. He promises peace, and we get more killings, promises to honor the transitional government, and instead he tightens MRND's grip." Daniel made a kissing sound through his teeth. "Who knows if he will ever keep a promise?"

With a sweep of his hand, Jean Patrick dismissed Daniel's news. "These things take time. Eventually they will change. They must. Look at me, a Tutsi, competing in the Olympics. Habyarimana will come to greet me."

Daniel clapped his hands together. "Aye-yay. I forgot to say congratulations. My brain is too stupid from politics."

They talked about the race and the reception. Jean Patrick heard his voice, too loud, too insistent, in his ears, and he wondered if it was himself or Daniel he wanted to convince.

"Don't listen to me," Daniel said. "Papa's wrongheaded predictions have twisted my thinking. But now I'm here, in Butare, and all that disaster cooking on the coals is behind me in Kigali." He took in the commotion of a group of girls at the next table. "I had a few girlfriends while I was home. How about you?"

"I was too busy," Jean Patrick said. He took his books from his knapsack and lined them up on the table. Daniel plopped a pile of texts beside them. "A lot of biology and chemistry," Jean Patrick said. "Did they give you premed?"

"They did. I'll be a doctor after all, but I still have to take physics. That made my mama happy, since she teaches science. And you?"

"Mechanical engineering. I knew I wouldn't get physics or math, but I get to take a lot of the classes, so I'm happy." He handed Daniel his geology book. "And I'm taking this."

"*Physical Geology: An Introduction.*" Daniel wrinkled his nose. "What good is that?"

Jean Patrick recalled Jonathan's surprise when he mentioned that in Rwanda, students were not free to decide their course of study. He wondered what it would be like to pick from a list of courses as a diner picks from a menu. To say, I choose geology, or I choose physics. That was a world he could not even imagine.

Daniel gave him back the book, and Jean Patrick saw the splash of pink between his teeth. All vacation he had missed this face, this grin.

"I saw Coach," Daniel said. "He warned me we had a special practice, running up and down every stair on campus. Then he quoted some proverb about welcoming us to graze in his pastures, and laughed."

Suddenly, Jean Patrick understood what Coach had been trying to tell him as he sped off in his car. Imana had given him talent and a stubborn will. He needed to run as much as he needed to breathe, and he would endure any amount of pain to win. But now he saw that he depended on Coach to chisel his gifts into a shining, perfect gem. He realized, too, that this gem was more than his personal success. He remembered how Uncle and Roger had told him he was running for all Tutsi, and this seemed even truer after all this talk about the war.

Jean Patrick shook his head. All this time he had mistakenly believed he had only to trust in two legs that were quick enough to cleave the air. But that wasn't enough, would never be enough. He had to trust in Coach for guidance, in Habyarimana to allow him his Olympic dream, in the government to bring in the United Nations troops. And if it ever came to that, he would have to trust in those troops to protect his life.

Sixteen

COACH PULLED UP IN FRONT of Jonathan's house and grunted. "Look at that muzungu. He sticks out like a big white thumb."

Jonathan looked more tourist than professor, standing at his gate in the near darkness, cap on his head, knapsack on his back, camera case across his shoulder. Jean Patrick had learned that the *B* on the cap was for the Boston Red Sox, the baseball team from Jonathan's town.

"Mwaramutseho," Jonathan said, sliding into the front seat. "J. P., amakuru?"

"Ni meza," Jean Patrick said in response. "Jonathan, this is my coach, Rutembeza."

Jonathan extended his hand. "Mwaramutse," he said.

Coach's expression changed from scorn to smile, as if an unseen hand had erased one countenance and sketched another. "Good morning," he said in English. "Jean Patrick speaks highly of your class."

Jonathan placed his cap on Jean Patrick's head. He had cropped his wild hair into a neat, close cut. "Are you ready to win?"

"Me, I'm always ready."

"Today, he's going to beat the entire Burundi Olympic team," Daniel announced.

Jean Patrick felt the first nervous somersault of his stomach, and he turned his attention to the weather. It didn't look promising, rain clouds blotting out the smallest scrap of sun as the day took shape. As they left Butare Prefecture, rain plunked steadily on the roof.

"I'll never run a qualifying time like this; I'll be slipping in the mud."

Daniel rolled down the window and cupped his palm to catch the rain. "It could pass soon."

Jonathan pointed to a crack of blue gray and the faint edge of a rainbow. "Yes. I believe it will." He kept his camera in his lap, a finger on the shutter release.

Near the turnoff for Nyanza, the rain stopped. A flock of children burst from the grass, screaming, "Agachupa! Agachupa!"

Jonathan aimed his camera. "Beautiful! What are they saying?"

"They want this." Jean Patrick tapped him with an empty water bottle. "Containers are precious—especially from muzungu."

Jonathan threw the bottle out the window, and the children dove. A small girl surfaced from the fracas, bottle held high. She pumped her legs to outdistance her pursuers.

"Eh-eh—look at her go. Watch out, Marcianne Mukamurenzi," Jean Patrick said.

"Who's that?"

"I just read about her," Jean Patrick said. "She's run in the Olympics for Rwanda in the fifteen hundred *and* the marathon."

Coach dismissed her with a wave of his hand. "A girl."

Jean Patrick wouldn't let it go. "Eh—she beat that guy Telesphore Dusabe, who came to my school. Her time was a minute forty faster." He jiggled his leg. "She was a mail carrier, and she trained by running barefoot from village to village with the mail." Coach groaned, and Jean Patrick returned to watching the sky, hoping to coax a border of blue from the gray blanket.

THE KIGALI SKYLINE materialized beyond the swamps of the Nyabarongo River. Patches of blue sky appeared, and the land steamed dry. Jonathan leaned out the window with his camera.

"Maybe now the track won't be so slippery." Jean Patrick's jitters metamorphosed into a flock of butterflies in his stomach.

"Didn't I predict it?" Daniel high-fived him.

"Oh my God," Jonathan leaned out farther and frantically focused his lens.

Ahead, a crowd had formed around a group of machete-wielding men. The car crawled closer, and Jean Patrick saw that some of them had hand grenades clipped to their belts.

"Welcome to Kigali," Daniel whispered to Jean Patrick. "Now you see our Interahamwe."

"This doesn't look good," Jonathan said. He clicked the shutter, and Coach snapped his head around.

"You'll need to put your camera on the floor, where it can't be seen. Quickly." Ice could have formed on Coach's words. "Roll up your window and lock your door."

An old, bent herder stood at the center of the crowd, leaning heavily against his staff. Someone had pulled off one of the man's rubber boots and was brandishing it above his head. Although his clothes were patched and much roughed up, Jean Patrick could see that the man had dressed with care and attention. Earth stained his slacks, and his felt hat lay trampled in the mud. A torn sleeve dangled from his jacket. Schoolchildren picked among the vegetables from his overturned basket. But even through his fear, an air of dignity remained.

"Why is everyone harassing that poor farmer?" Jonathan pressed his forehead to the window.

"He's Tutsi," Jean Patrick said, shocked by his own boldness. Coach shot him a look.

The crowd swelled; drivers abandoned their cars to get a better view. Some taunted the herder or cheered on the Interahamwe. Some called out to leave him alone. A little boy hurled a tomato, and it burst against the old man's back. The boy's friends cheered.

Coach honked his horn and pointed at Jonathan. "You'd think they'd let a foreigner pass," he said in Kinyarwanda.

An Interahamwe picked up the cowherd's hat. He slapped it against the man's leg and threw it down again with exaggerated distaste. The mob whooped and whistled. The herder remained immobile, bared head bowed. Children ran off with armloads of produce.

"The guy probably tried to cheat them." Coach patted Jonathan as if pacifying a child. "It happens all the time. In Rwanda, people don't take thieving lightly."

Outrage swirled in Jean Patrick. The herder's shame burned his face. Although he knew better than to contradict an elder, he spoke up. "That's not—"

Daniel squeezed his hand. Leave it, he mouthed.

A second Interahamwe snatched the old man's glasses. He put them on and waved his arms like a political official working a rally. A gold chain glinted from his neck. The herder stood still, eyes blinking. Jean Patrick sensed the collective constriction in the mob like a boa squeezing its prey.

"Cut the Tutsi snake in two," someone yelled.

"Shouldn't we do something?" Jonathan's voice quavered. "Where are the police?" In the backseat, Jean Patrick fidgeted.

"The police are busy counting their *contributions*," Daniel whispered to Jean Patrick.

"Don't worry. Guys like this—they just want to scare him. They'll let him go in a minute," Coach said. Jean Patrick looked to Daniel for confirmation, but Daniel merely shrugged.

For an instant, the road opened up, and Coach accelerated, managing a few meters before the gap closed again. He blasted the horn, and the herder swiveled toward them, fear ablaze in his eyes.

Jean Patrick checked his watch. If they didn't get out of there soon, he would be late. He could have pummeled the seatback with his fists, but instead his voice came out a whimper. "We need to hurry," he said.

Coach rolled down his window. "Do you really want this muzungu to see what you're doing?" he shouted. At the mention of the word *muzungu,* Jonathan bolted upright.

"Fuck the muzungu," the Interahamwe with the gold chain yelled in English. "Fuck all Tutsi cockroaches." He pressed his face to the car window and leered at Jean Patrick, nose flattened against the glass. "Hutu Power! Umuzungu subira iwanyu!" He banged the glass with the handle of his machete. Spittle streaked a corner of his mouth. Then, reeling with laughter, he strolled back to his prey.

"What did that guy say to me?" Jonathan's shocked gaze locked with Coach's.

"He was welcoming you to our country," Coach said.

"No. He said, 'White man, go home,'" Jean Patrick said, unwilling to let this final humiliation stand.

Anger flared in Coach's eyes, but he said nothing.

The circle of the mob tightened. "Don't let the snake go; kill it!" The chant boiled in the already heated air.

"He's done nothing wrong—leave him," a woman yelled. "Go back to your business."

The Interahamwe scooped up the herder's hat and extended it toward him. When the old man reached for it, another Interahamwe pushed him full force into the mud. His staff flew from his hand. The man with the gold chain put a foot on the herder's back, leaned forward, and placed the blade of his machete on the old man's neck. A collective whoop rose from the mob.

"Please, no," Jonathan gasped.

Jean Patrick squeezed Daniel's hand. The alley behind the old baker's shop, the glint of Albert's knife, the boys closing, all flashed through his mind. He understood fate's balance could tip either way.

The car stopped directly in front of the herder. Jean Patrick could have counted the wrinkles in his weatherworn skin. He saw the rise and fall of the thug's chest, heard his breathy excitement.

"Enough," Coach shouted. "You've had your fun."

The Interahamwe with the gold chain spun and pointed his machete at Coach. "I'll remember you, icyitso," he said, but he stepped back. The cowherd struggled to his feet and collected his belongings. He limped off, one foot bare. Jean Patrick slumped lower, afraid the old man would see him sitting in the car, doing nothing to help.

The action over, traffic began to move. Uncapping a bottle of water with trembling fingers, Jean Patrick drank thirstily, greedily, as if the water would purify him, wash clean his slate. Shame burned inside him. But what could he have done, another tall, skinny Tutsi leaping into the fray while violence shimmered in the air like petrol fumes? Any small struck flame could have ignited it. Jean Patrick had a race to run.

AFTER THAT, THEY rode in silence. Only Coach spoke, pointing out a hotel here, a landmark there. Jean Patrick's nerves sizzled. He felt peeled bare, an insect specimen pinned on a card. Not until he saw the walls of Nyamirambo Stadium, the hawkers by the gates with their cigarettes and sweets, could he focus on the task at hand. In this meet there would be no prelims or semifinals. Only one race, one chance.

Jonathan's camera came out. He captured the ragged children, the women's bright parasols, the men balancing jerricans of urwagwa, sacks of sorghum, on their heads. He snapped photos of an athlete in silver shorts, her head full of plaits, her legs all muscle and shine. But when he aimed at the soldiers, Coach quickly covered the lens.

JEAN PATRICK WATCHED the runners while he loosened up on the grass. "I don't see those Hutu boys who gave me trouble in Butare," he said. Reflexively he ran his tongue across the edge of his chipped tooth and relived the slow-motion fall down the steps of National University.

"You might see two of them at Worlds," Coach said. "They've gone to Kenya to train." He pointed toward the field, where a stocky boy in red shorts did kick-outs and side-to-sides on the grass. "There's your rabbit, the new star on the École Technique team. He's a hundred-meter runner but doesn't know it. Goes off like a rocket, then detonates before the second lap."

"How do you know about all these runners?" Jean Patrick asked as the boy blazed past the Burundi runners.

"My job is to keep track of your competition; your job is to beat them." Coach licked his lips. "Aye! If I could get my hands on him, he'd be joining you at the Olympics." Jean Patrick gave him a look, and he chuckled. "In the hundred meters, of course. Look at him. He'll be exhausted by the time he has to race."

Jean Patrick noted the boy's pained expression. "I hope he has enough energy left for me to chase him."

"I want you right on his heels for the first lap. He'll pick up the pace with pressure, and that will destroy him. Turn it on as soon as you notice him fading."

"I feel great today. I don't think I need to follow anyone." The morning's tension had transformed into the desire for full-out speed.

Coach grabbed Jean Patrick's wrist. "When will you learn to listen? I'm counting on you to do as I say." He released his grip. "Now go warm up with your Burundi friends; you're no mystery to them anymore."

Ndizeye waved Jean Patrick over. "We hear you ran a qualifying time for the Olympics," Gilbert said. "Congratulations!"

Jean Patrick settled into an easy pace beside them. "Yego. If I can keep running them, I'll be seeing you in Atlanta." He watched them and committed their strides to memory. Maybe when he played back the tape in his head, he would find some weakness to exploit.

DANIEL WAS WAITING at the start line with a bottle of water. "Our president is waiting to greet you." He saluted Jean Patrick.

The front section of the stands had filled with dignitaries and the Presidential Guard. Habyarimana stood in their midst, a pair of binoculars trained on Jean Patrick. It seemed to him that the president had merely stepped from his photograph and come to life. The space he carved out for himself extended far beyond the boundaries of his body.

"Mana mfasha," Jean Patrick whispered. God help me.

Daniel led Jean Patrick toward the stands. "There are the TV cameras. You better look fast. They're here for you."

Jean Patrick caught the bright red *B* of Jonathan's baseball cap just to the president's left. His legs quivered, and it took every fiber of concentration to keep a jerky hip-hop from his stride. He took deep breaths to calm his pounding heart. Habyarimana extended his hand. Jean Patrick stepped close enough to count the beads of sweat on the president's forehead. Cameras clicked away.

Habyarimana beckoned. "I am flesh and blood," he said.

A firm hand pushed him forward, and over his shoulder he saw a dour-faced man, eyes hidden behind tinted glasses. "He won't bite," the man said.

Habyarimana yanked Jean Patrick to his side and spun him toward the cameras. He squinted into the sun to face the bank of lenses. "This boy is Rwanda's future," the president boomed, his smile candescent. "We are here to help him achieve his dream." He patted Jean Patrick firmly on the back as if he were in the midst of choking.

It took Jean Patrick a minute to realize the flash in the corner of his eye did not come from a camera. It came instead from the glint of bangles caught in a ray of sun. He blinked and focused. Bea was on the steps below, arm outstretched to hail someone in the crowd. She had on the same tea-leaf-green skirt he had followed up a stairwell, the same gold blouse. She supported her husband as he negotiated the steep stairs.

"THERE'S THE GIRL I want to marry," Jean Patrick said. He was warming up with Daniel along the edge of the field. Crews set up hurdles on the track for the first race. "Over there in the gold blouse."

Daniel jogged backward. "With the long hair, standing next to the old man?"

"Her husband." Jean Patrick watched the girl with the plaits and silver shorts who had taken up a roll of Jonathan's film. She was practicing her kick for hurdles.

"You're crazy. That grandfather? Are you sure?"

"I am sure."

"Well, maybe she has a younger sister."

"I don't want her sister. I only want her."

Daniel hummed softly. "Then you must break her husband's heart."

A pistol shot sent Jean Patrick diving to the ground. The echo reverberated from the walls, and the stadium erupted in cheers. Slowly, Jean Patrick opened his eyes. The hurdlers had cleared the first hurdle. The girl in silver shorts led the pack, plaits flung wild.

Daniel held his side. "Hey-hey! Haven't you heard a starter's gun before?"

Jean Patrick brushed grass from his track pants. "Mana yanjye, I thought that Interahamwe guy just shot me."

"Wa muturage, weh! You are still a country bumpkin. Do you think at World Championships or the Olympics they will bang two blocks of wood together?"

The girl cleared the eighth hurdle with no one else close. That was how he wanted his race to go. But then, in a moment too brief to capture, her foot caught the last hurdle, and she went down. Pain twisted her face. A runner passed her to capture the win. Jean Patrick felt a twinge of fear; how easily a path could veer from good fortune to bad.

THE EIGHT HUNDRED was the last event of the day. Photographers rushed onto the field to photograph Jean Patrick stretching.

"How do you feel?" Coach zeroed his watch. Jean Patrick's internal timer kicked in.

"Like nothing can stop me."

The boy in red shorts trotted onto the track, and Coach nudged Jean Patrick. "Tell me again—who's that guy?"

Jean Patrick observed the densely muscled thighs. "My rabbit." He searched for a flash of gold and green in the stands but found only the glare of the president's binoculars aimed at his chest. The announcer called the runners to the track, and his heart tripped into high gear.

He had lane five, flanked by Gilbert and Ndizeye. The rabbit had lane seven, near the outside. Jean Patrick swayed from foot to foot, shook out his legs and fingers. Gilbert and Ndizeye slapped their hamstrings, and Jean Patrick copied them. The rabbit jumped up and down in place and punched the air.

The runners crouched. The starter fired his pistol, and light blazed in Jean Patrick's head.

As Coach had predicted, the rabbit exploded off the line, arms pumping madly. Jean Patrick tucked in behind and sailed on the rabbit's air. He expected Gilbert and Ndizeye to flank him, but they hung back, a shadow's length behind. The rabbit set a furious pace. Jean Patrick ran at his heels and matched him acceleration for acceleration. He felt good; he felt unbeatable.

They passed the start line, and the bell clanged for the final lap. "The first four runners shatter the Rwandan record for four hundred meters!" the announcer shouted.

But as quickly as Imana had extended His hand to Jean Patrick, He snatched it back. The rabbit did not fade, and coming out of the turn, Jean Patrick wondered if he could push the pace much faster. He sensed Gilbert and Ndizeye at his heels. His lungs felt strained to bursting. The image of the hurdler flashed in front of his eyes, but it was his body, not the girl's, that he saw crash to the ground. Then, miraculously, on the back straight, Coach's prediction came true: the rabbit faded. Gilbert and Ndizeye surged. Now, when Jean Patrick ran on faith and hope alone, the race began.

Gilbert and Ndizeye fell back, leaving Jean Patrick to run unaided in front. From somewhere, he found the energy to maintain his lead. He imagined the president watching through his binoculars, envisioned the flash of Bea's bracelets as she shaded her eyes to see. Two shadows flanked him. He started his kick, but stones weighed down his legs. Metal bands squeezed his chest. Gilbert and Ndizeye glided beside him. He gritted his teeth and pushed. Fifty meters to go. While his stride was choppy, off balance, Gilbert and Ndizeye maintained their long, floaty kicks. Jean Patrick felt the first twinge of a cramp in his calf. He would not let it happen; he would not.

The Burundi boys dogged him as he had dogged the now forgotten rabbit. He dug deeper. Thirty meters. Black dots danced in his vision. The finish line blazed white, impossibly far away. In Coach's magazines, he had read about the wall. Now he crashed into it full force. They will not pass me, he repeated in his head. With ten meters to go, it became his chant.

He had a chance; all he had to do was hold on. But he couldn't, and first Gilbert, then Ndizeye, sailed past him. Riding the wave that had flung him off its crest, they stroked to the finish. Jean Patrick passed the line in a desperate lean. Even gravity defeated him, and he fell to the ground. It was only when Ndizeye shook his shoulder that he heard the announcer shout, "One forty-five forty-nine. Nkuba Jean Patrick breaks his own record!" Coach and Daniel bolted toward him, fists pumping the air.

"THEY BEAT ME AGAIN," Jean Patrick said. He lay on the grass while Coach rubbed out his legs. "They did exactly to me what I did to that guy from École Technique."

Coach kneaded Jean Patrick's calves, gently at first, then sinking in deeper. "What did you expect? They read you like a book."

An electric jolt ripped through him as Coach pressed a tender point. "I expected to win."

"You'll have another chance in Sweden, at World Championships," Coach said. "Now you have some idea what you need to learn."

"I won't make that mistake again."

"There are plenty of other mistakes to make. Your first lap was spectacular—I couldn't believe it. But if you had paced yourself, you would have given those boys a run for their money. Work on pace and closing speed, and we'll see whose flag flies on the podium next time you meet."

Jean Patrick wiggled his toes. His cramp relaxed. He watched Gilbert and Ndizeye, barefoot and stretching on the field. He grinned at Coach, and Coach grinned back.

JONATHAN BROKE THROUGH the mob of reporters and well-wishers and caught Jean Patrick in a hug. "Man, that was unbelievable!" He took Jean Patrick's picture with different lenses, in different poses.

"Even if I didn't win?"

"Who cares? You broke your own record, didn't you? And you made it look easy."

"Easy?" Jean Patrick snorted. "I thought it would kill me."

"I want to introduce you to someone while we have a free nanosecond," Jonathan said, pulling him toward the stands.

Bea stood with a woman reporter on the stairs. She looked up with the same expression of surprised amusement he had fallen in love with when she pulled him into her yard. She extended her braceleted arm. "I had no idea when we met that I was in the presence of such a celebrity." Jean Patrick enfolded her cool, dry hand in his sweaty, damp palms.

"You know J. P.?" Jonathan gave a pleased chuckle.

"One morning I had to rescue him from schoolchildren."

It was only when she squeezed his fingers that Jean Patrick realized he still held tightly to her hand. He didn't know what to do. If he pulled away, she would think him rude. If he did not, she might find him ruder. Words stuck to his tongue. "I'm glad to finally meet you and your husband," was all he could think of to say.

"My husband?" Bea laughed, throaty and full. "Ah yes. My husband who beats me."

"What's this?" the man said, regarding Jean Patrick curiously. Jean Patrick noticed that his nose was pushed slightly to the left side of his face.

Bea touched Jean Patrick's shoulder. "Let me introduce my father, Niyonzima."

Niyonzima gripped Jean Patrick's hand, and Jean Patrick was surprised by the strength. "Thank you for making me so young," Niyonzima said. He brushed Bea's back, and she leaned into his touch. How easily they could be taken for husband and wife. But they were not, and Jean Patrick dared to imagine the smoothness of her skin beneath his fingers.

"You make Rwanda proud," Niyonzima said. "You will send a message to the world."

Jean Patrick thought of his father, his face suddenly sharp and clear in his mind. He thought of his family cheering him on in Cyangugu. "I will do my best."

The Rwandan National Band marched onto the field and broke into "Rwanda Rwacu," the national anthem. Then the president and his guard joined them. In his sky-blue jacket, Habyarimana looked like a mythical king come down from the heavens.

"I think you're being summoned," Bea said. She pointed toward the field.

"Why don't you come to the reception?" Jean Patrick smiled and willed her to agree.

"We are not invited to the president's functions," she said, her expression still playful.

"But you must come for a meal in our home, you and Jonathan," Niyonzima said.

"That would make me very happy," Jean Patrick said.

Niyonzima leaned on his arm. "It was a pleasure to meet you. Here comes your coach to steal you away."

Coach marched up the steps. He did not offer his hand until Niyonzima offered his.

"We were just telling Jean Patrick how much we enjoyed watching him run," Niyonzima said. "It was truly an honor, and I congratulate both of you."

Coach clicked his heels in curt salute and guided Jean Patrick down the stairs. Jean Patrick turned to catch a final glimpse of Bea, but the crowd had swallowed her.

JEAN PATRICK FELT the thrum of the bass in his body even before the white-coated, white-gloved houseboy swung open the gate at the American ambassador's house. A crew of gardeners bent among rows of flowers. He gazed at the mansion at the end of the walk. Compared to this, the fancy houses of Cyangugu looked like huts.

"Americans need a lot of room," Coach said. He directed a smile at Jonathan.

"Now wait a minute. Not all of us live in luxury's lap." Jonathan took off his cap and stuffed it into his back pocket. "That's unfair." He ran his fingers through his hair.

"Me, I'm ready for a Coca-Cola," Daniel said. He took two cups from a tray and gave one to Jean Patrick. With the first icy sip, pain drilled a path from Jean Patrick's tooth to his eyes.

Guests milled about, tiny cups held high. A babel of languages swirled in the air. President Habyarimana moved through the crowd, sweat trickling down his cheeks. He shook hands, clapped backs, made jokes. Every so often, he threw an arm around someone's shoulder and posed for a photo. Catching Jean Patrick's eye, he thundered, "Here is our hero . . ." He paused, open mouthed, and Jean Patrick realized the president had forgotten his name. Pulling a photographer with him, he trapped Jean Patrick and Jonathan beneath his wings and beamed for the camera. "This young man embodies the new Rwanda," he declared. "A Rwanda where anyone can succeed." Jean Patrick waited at attention for the rest of the speech, but Habyarimana merely cleared his throat.

Jonathan excused himself to take pictures. The president strode off with his guard. Jean Patrick was left at the mercy of a woman who had fastened onto his wrist.

"So you're our hero," she said. She had electric-blond hair and wore a pink straw hat. He stepped back to dispel the rising sense of panic her nearness brought. "I didn't see you run — personally I detest sports of any kind — but I hear you are some kind of Rwandan wonder." She drew his hand to her lips, and he realized she was going to kiss it. "I admire you Africans," she said. Jean Patrick steeled himself against the warm, damp mouth and bowed as he had seen abazungu do in movies. As she disappeared into the crowd, he wiped his hand across his pants and went to search for Daniel.

He found him with his father, reclined against a tree. Its yellow trumpet blossoms carpeted the grass. "Finally, you can greet my papa. He's been waiting all day. Here is Pascal."

He was a head taller than Daniel, but with the same wide mouth, the same stocky build. Even in his informal posture, he maintained the bearing of a soldier. When he smiled, Jean Patrick saw the familiar gap between the two front teeth.

"I feel I've known you since your first day at Gihundwe, from all Daniel's stories." Pascal embraced Jean Patrick as a father embraces a son.

A waiter offered them a tray of yellow packages. A red *M* or *W* decorated the paper. "These were flown in from Belgium, so let's see what the fuss is about," Pascal said.

Jean Patrick sniffed carefully. "What is it?"

"It's called McDonald's, " Pascal said. "A kind of hamburger. I hear they're crazy about them in the U.S."

The woman in the pink hat held hers high. "Oh my God! When was the last time I had one of these?"

Pascal took a bite and shook his head. "I do not understand how Americans think."

Jean Patrick sampled the unidentifiable meat garnished with sweet red sauce. He didn't see what the fuss was about. "I better learn to enjoy these if I'm going to Atlanta." He washed the tasteless bread down with Coke.

The first peals of thunder echoed in the distance, competing with the American music that thumped from the speakers. Storm clouds hurried across the sky. The breeze picked up, and Jean Patrick zipped his jacket. A flurry of cups and McDonald's wrappers blew across the yard. Partygoers danced. Jonathan discoed beneath a tree with a woman in a gauzy headscarf whose hair was the color of scorched copper.

The Presidential Guard, somber and stiff, formed a loose circle around the president's entourage. Coach stood at the edge of the circle, head bent in conversation with an officer. Pascal spoke into Jean Patrick's ear. "Now you see the Akazu for yourself."

Habyarimana snapped his fingers, and a soldier came running. The president's wife spoke to the soldier, and he disappeared again.

"I don't get what you mean."

Daniel spoke in a low voice. "We call them the little house because it is they who surround Habyarimana—his inner circle—who squeeze the people dry, keep the cogs of government running smoothly and turning in their direction."

"By any means necessary," Pascal said. "They keep the money flowing, bribes and funds stolen from NGOs and who knows what other mischief."

"Which ones are they?"

With his eyes, Daniel indicated a group of men standing near the president's wife. One was the sour-faced man who had nudged Jean Patrick up the stadium steps.

"Not his wife, though, eh?"

Pascal made a sucking sound with his lips. "Madame Agathe is the most powerful of all." The soldier returned with a microphone, and Madame Agathe pointed. The soldier set up the microphone in front of the president. "Watch out. You are important now. If you misbehave, it is they who decide if you go to prison or if you die."

"Papa, don't frighten Jean Patrick with your catastrophes."

The music ended, and the loudspeakers squealed. Coach beckoned Jean Patrick toward him. The sudden tightness in his legs as he broke into a trot told him he had worked as hard as he could. The pleasure of well-earned fatigue filled his body.

With a hand on Jean Patrick's shoulder, Habyarimana began his speech. Jean Patrick quickly lost count of the times the president referred to him as an example of progress. Although he tried to dismiss Pascal's warnings, they kept whispering in his ears. Flashbulbs popped in the darkening afternoon. Thunder rumbled closer. A single raindrop splashed on Jean Patrick's scalp. The president concluded, and a few people clapped without enthusiasm.

A greenish light shimmered in the air, as if it had been wicked up from the lawn. Lightning forked over the hills, and guests jogged toward the gate. The ambassador's wife shook hands and said good-bye. The white-gloved waiters disappeared, replaced by a flock of women in headscarves and pagnes to collect the trash.

"J. P.! One more photo with your coach and the president," Jonathan shouted. His flushed skin glowed.

"Daniel, Pascal—come be in the picture," Jean Patrick said.

They gathered together, Jean Patrick between Coach and Habyarimana, Daniel and his father bookends on either side. Behind them, the tall poinsettia flamed. "Closer, so I can get all of you." They squeezed in until their bodies touched. Jean Patrick felt heat on either side.

Habyarimana's face glistened. Posing for Jonathan, Jean Patrick shook off Pascal's glum warnings, and his good humor returned. When he was a young boy running through the streets of Cyangugu, how could he have imagined he would be standing here, having his picture snapped with Rwanda's president? But as the shutter clicked, a member of the president's guard caught his eye. Pointedly holding Jean Patrick's gaze, the soldier smiled and drew his thumb across his throat.

"I'M STAYING IN Kigali tonight," Daniel said. He huddled with Jean Patrick in the driveway. They were the last to leave. "Papa will bring me back tomorrow, after church."

The ambassador's wife had returned to her palace. Pascal came toward them, straightening his jacket as he walked. He looked handsome and smart in his uniform, how Daniel would look in another ten years. "You're lucky to have him," Jean Patrick said.

Daniel looked at the ground. "Yes, I know."

Jean Patrick said, "You need to take care of each other."

"Until death do us part," Daniel said, smiling.

Rain swept toward them in a dark sheet. Any minute, the sky would rupture. By the open car door, Coach tapped his foot. Pascal drew Jean Patrick and Daniel into a farewell embrace. Aftershave lotion and tobacco whirled in Jean Patrick's nostrils, and he became a little boy, lifted into the air, held against Papa's intoxicating, sweet-smelling cheeks.

Pascal said, "You are blessed with a very special gift; use it wisely and well. Above all, be safe."

There were many ways to interpret this wish. "I will be safe, and in Sweden I will win," Jean Patrick said. He jogged to the car. In the ambassador's house, light came to the windows, one after another.

"Let's go," Coach said. "I want to get back to Butare tonight."

"Run as if your life depended on it," Pascal called. "As if all our lives depended on it."

Lightning struck close by. Thunder followed on its heels. Pascal and

Daniel raced to an army truck and climbed inside. The truck's driver followed Coach's car as it turned onto the street. The gate slammed shut behind them. Simultaneously, the storm cracked the sky open with a deafening roar.

Coach accelerated past a bus. Jean Patrick turned in his seat and watched the truck until rain engulfed everything but the headlights. Pascal's last entreaty had left an uneasy feeling in his chest. It brought back the image of the soldier, thumb to his throat. Jean Patrick shook it off. Hadn't Habyarimana arranged the party to celebrate his achievements? The soldier was a single stupid man, probably angry for having to waste an afternoon. And wasn't Daniel always saying that his papa smelled catastrophe cooking in every harmless puff of smoke?

SEVENTEEN

To cool down, Jean Patrick jogged through campus. It was a chance to strengthen his legs with a few extra intervals on the stairs. Since the race in Kigali, many people recognized him, and he spent this last portion of his run returning greetings. "Mr. Olympics!" they called out. He believed he had earned this name as much as Roger had earned Mistah Cool and Isaka earned One Shot. But he was also looking for Bea. He had not stopped looking for her since she opened her gate to call him inside.

He spotted her talking to Jonathan in a patch of sun, hugging an armload of books. Behind her, the flowers on the flame trees earned their name. Her right foot jutted out as if she were on the verge of motion, and she spoke to Jonathan in rapid English. A crushed orange-red blossom stuck to the sole of her sandal.

"J. P.! You remember Bea, don't you?" As if he could forget. "Did you know she's going to be the next president of Rwanda?"

"It would not surprise me." Jean Patrick smiled and extended his hand. Suddenly conscious of his chipped tooth, he covered his mouth.

Bea laughed. "You are very famous now; I see your picture all over the papers." She took his hand, and her books tumbled to the ground.

"So sorry. My fault." He bent to collect them, each title another piece of the puzzle that was Bea. Like Coach's books, most concerned government and history, but there was also a sketchbook, flung open to an intricate drawing of flowers. She bent to help. He could have reached over and touched her emerald-tinged eyelid.

"We're going for a coffee at the Ibis," Jonathan said. "Why don't you join us?"

"Yes, you must." Bea rose and straightened her pagne. Her cheek would fit perfectly, he imagined, in the hollow of his breastbone.

BEA WAS A second-year student, studying journalism and history. She had wished to be an artist like her mother, but art, like physics, was useless. Instead she would follow in her father's footsteps. "There's nothing wrong with that," she said. "Journalism is also in my blood."

She told Jean Patrick all this after Jonathan left, while she sipped a second cup of tea. She collected crumbs from the pastry they had shared and sucked them from her finger.

"You speak English like a native," he said. "How did you learn?"

"I spent nine years in London. We left Rwanda when I was four, to be with my father while he got his PhD. Later I went back for secondary school." Her hands on the table gave off a tingly heat. "I'm rusty—when you don't speak a language, you lose it so quickly—so I'm grateful to practice with Jonathan."

Now it made sense the way she walked through the world, the way she took life on her own terms and defied anyone to stop her. "Why did you come back?"

"At first I never wanted to. Great Britain felt like home." She added milk to her tea and stirred. "Everything so convenient. Hot water and electric light on demand, an inside stove you turn on with a button, clean buses and trains to take you everywhere. And no one on an English bus hits you on the head with a leaky sack of sorghum or pushes you off a seat with a filthy suitcase."

"I think I would get very fat." The waiter brought a fresh thermos of tea. Too much caffeine usually left Jean Patrick on edge, aware of his rapidly beating heart, but this morning he found the jolt pleasurably intense.

"When we first came home, I didn't know how to be African. My feet were soft, and I couldn't stand to go barefoot. But by the time I left for boarding school, I was Rwandan again. They nearly had to drag me to the plane."

Jean Patrick thought of the last day of Mathilde's life: the soldier pushing Aunt Esther, the rifle aimed at his heart. He thought of the soldier with the Presidential Guard who drew his thumb across his throat. "Some days I could get on a plane and never glance back." But there was also the lake, its bottomless blue eye. There was Uncle, standing in his pirogue as graceful as a stork to slap his pole and summon fish to the surface. "Other days I look around and feel only love for my country."

"*Imana yiriwa ahandi igataha i Rwanda,*" Bea quoted.

"True. God spends the day everywhere, but comes home to sleep in Rwanda." Sun streamed through the window, striping the tablecloth. Jean Patrick took off his jacket. "I don't think I could ever leave my family, and of course now I am representing Rwanda at Worlds."

"Did you grow up in Cyangugu?"

Jean Patrick momentarily lost himself in the light of Bea's eyes. He had to haul himself back. "Yes. My father was préfet des maîtres at Gihundwe."

"Is he still there?"

"No." He did a quick calculation and was shocked. "He's been dead nearly nine years."

"I'm sorry." Her gaze drifted to the door and back. "Cyangugu was one of my favorite places when I was small. We used to visit the lake during vacation, or go to Nyungwe Forest. I used to pick flowers and hide them under my dress. When my parents weren't looking, I threw them to the monkeys so they would have something to eat besides my arm. For some reason, they terrified me."

Jean Patrick couldn't imagine Bea terrified of anything.

"Did you live in one of those beautiful houses by Lake Kivu?" she asked.

How could he tell her that his mother cleaned floors and did laundry in those houses? "No," he said. "We live some distance away." He hoped she wouldn't guess that only country people lived there, scratching an existence from the earth and the lake. Many would never read a book. Some could barely scratch a few words in a letter.

A beggar came and squatted outside the café, his empty sleeve pinned at the elbow. Two police officers shooed him away, then came inside and sat at a nearby table. One nodded to Bea, and Jean Patrick thought he saw her spine straighten.

"Mwaramutse," the officer said. He offered her his hand. A row of braids and stripes adorned his uniform. "I see you 're acquainted with Butare's new celebrity." He smiled, revealing a mouth full of gold-rimmed teeth.

"I had the good fortune to watch him race in Kigali," Bea said.

"Perhaps I could see you next week." The man's eyes flicked over Jean Patrick's T-shirt. "If you aren't too busy."

Bea graced him with a smile that could have coaxed honey from a stone. "Next week I have exams. Perhaps after, when I've finished."

He lit a cigarette and extinguished the match in the pastry plate. A ribbon of smoke rose from the burned sugar. "It's nice to greet you here," he said, touching the brim of his cap to Bea. "Félicitations," he said to Jean Patrick, and then he turned on his heels.

Bea leaned across the table. "He uses the most awful aftershave," she whispered. Jean Patrick hid his smile. She gathered her books. "Let's go."

Bea marched so fast down the hill that Jean Patrick jogged to keep up. "How was your reception?" she asked. She hugged her books tightly, and her face was pinched.

"It was great. A big celebration: music, dancing, Coca-Cola. I even tasted MacDonard's."

"What?"

"MacDonard's. Some hamburger from U.S. It tastes like shoes."

"Ha! *McDonald's!*" For an instant, her bad mood lifted. "My God—where did they find those?"

"They flew them in from Belgium. Just for my reception." He waited for a response. When he got none, he said to fill the space, "President Habyarimana was so nice to me."

Bea's nostrils flared. "That's great." She would not look at him.

Jean Patrick stopped her. "What did I say wrong?"

She glanced around. "Do you mind if we keep walking?" Jean Patrick fell into step beside her as she picked up her pace again. "Habyarimana had my father arrested on November twelfth, 1990, a month after the RPF invasion," Bea said. "I was in boarding school. My auntie came to get me."

Jean Patrick felt as if he had set out for a stroll on a calm morning and headed into a storm. "Why did they arrest him?" He studied a little boy playing with a discarded tire.

"You can look at me," Bea said. "I'm not Queen Nyavirezi. I won't turn into a lioness and eat you. He was imprisoned for speaking—and writing—his mind." She touched Jean Patrick's elbow. "Don't look so shocked. Even we Hutu suffer Habyarimana's wrath. By my father's calculations, over ten thousand people—Hutu and Tutsi—were put in prison in late 1990, early 'ninety-one, and our president was not *nice* to any of them." Her voice shook. "My father spoke out because he loves Rwanda enough to die for her, and Habyarimana nearly made him prove it."

"Please." He started to wipe a tear from her cheek but thought better of it. "I'm sorry I caused you to think of these things."

"It's me who should be sorry." She touched a finger beneath her eye. The smudge her mascara left looked like ink. "What a gloomy subject to get started on. So. Tell me more about your fete."

There seemed nothing more to tell. What—or whom—did he love enough to die for? He needed to run, to win. He thought he would be willing to die for that. "Bea," he began, "I'm sorry for what happened to your papa. I don't know what else to say except I thank God he didn't die."

Bea said, "So do I. Every day."

When they reached campus, Bea stood on her toes, and for one giddy moment Jean Patrick thought she was going to kiss him. Instead she spoke into his ear. "Be careful, Mr. Olympics. I'll see you on Saturday night." Her sandals *tap-tapped* the brick pathway as she hurried away.

THAT NIGHT, JEAN Patrick awoke with the policeman's face so close, so real, he reached out to push it away. In the morning, he had two exams. In the afternoon, a hard workout. Shivering, he pulled the covers around him, closed his eyes, and tried to summon sleep. Dampness seeped from the sheets into his bones. A girl like Bea can marry anyone, he thought. A nice Hutu man, a doctor or a judge. What would she want with a Tutsi fisherman? The question troubled his mind.

But the next day, when his last exam was finished, he walked into town with his food money. In the first shop he entered, a store for tourists, he found her a gift. It was on a high shelf, between the clay pots and straw baskets: a pirogue carved from some soft, golden wood. When the shopkeeper lifted it down for him, Jean Patrick inhaled the musty tang of home. Inside the boat were two fishermen made from tightly woven imiseke, the reeds still smelling of the swampy earth they came from. They reminded him of the dog Mathilde had made him. They bent to their strokes with miniature oars, the delicate curves of their backs in perfect symmetry. Tiny fish made from shells flashed in the bilge. There *is* value to my life, he almost said aloud as he watched the merchant wrap his prize in pages torn from an old and yellowed issue of *Kangura*.

JEAN PATRICK AWOKE in a panic, daylight bright in his eyes. He bolted upright, then fell back against his pillow to keep his head from spinning. Instantly he regretted the late night, the third Primus he had shared with Daniel. Eyes half-shut, he sat up slowly, rubbed his temples, and searched for his running shoes.

The voice of RTLM pushed through the wall from the adjacent room. *Burundi first. That's where our eyes are looking now. The dog eaters have mutilated*—the rest of the sentence lost in static. Jean Patrick sucked his teeth. People loved this new radio station too much; he heard it day and night in students' rooms, as background at the cabarets and shops, traveling on guys' shoulders as they strutted about. Just after seven in the morning, and already the announcer was hard at it, heating up heads.

"Daniel, it's time to get up." Daniel pulled the covers over his head and turned to the wall. Jean Patrick yanked the covers down. "Don't make dead man's face at *me,* huh. I'm going. See you in class." He stood by their small desk and forced down a piece of bread, a few sips of water. Daniel's pillow slammed into the wall beside him as he opened the door.

It had not yet rained, but the morning threatened, the sky a dirty rag ready to be wrung out. A cold wind strummed the dark wires of the clouds. Jean Patrick pulled his collar close and started out at a slow jog. At his back, he heard the broadside of RTLM. *Even when the dog eaters are few, they discredit the whole family. Bahutu*—*be vigilant against them.* The voice kept pace behind him. Jean Patrick whirled around. He recognized the boy with the boom box, one or two others in the group. From time to time they greeted him on his morning runs. Sensing trouble, he nodded to them and picked up the pace.

"There goes a dog eater now," the boy with the boom box said.

Jean Patrick pushed harder, and the group fell back. His head throbbed; he wanted only to return to his room, crawl into bed, disappear beneath the blanket. A rock skittered by his feet, and then another.

On the main road, he forced himself to start his pickups and lunges. His lungs burned strangely, as if he had inhaled a toxic substance. Maybe today he would stop at the hut where the old guard lived and join him for a cup of hot, sweet tea. He neared the turnoff to the arboretum fields, and his breathing felt tighter. He couldn't puzzle it out, but then, turning onto the dirt road, he immediately understood. What he had taken for a cloud was a column of smoke, and it rose from the ridge where the guardhouse stood. A flower of orange flames bloomed at its center, where the old man's hut should have been.

Jean Patrick sprinted toward the ridge. His eyes watered, and his throat stung. A thick gray-blue haze rose from the earth. Usually by this hour, the women were hard at work, their ruckus carrying to his ears, but today he heard only the goats on the slopes, their high-pitched bleats and the tinkle of their bells piercing a preternatural quiet.

He reached the fields; sacks of different colors lay scattered among the rows, mist curling about them. When he drew close, an odor like none he had ever smelled brought him to his knees. It was the stench of death. The sacks, he saw now, were the bodies of the workers. They lay on the earth, heads oddly turned, limbs akimbo.

Kneeling in the dirt, he retched until his stomach was empty.

It took him a moment to connect the sound in his head with someone calling his name. He looked up. Bea stood beside a car on the side of the road, a scarf over her nose. "Come with me—hurry. Burundi's president has been assassinated, and everywhere, Hutu are blaming the Tutsi."

"Ndadaye? Killed?" Jean Patrick felt a chill as the morning clicked into place: the tirade on RTLM, the students hurling *dog eater* at his back, and now this scene of devastation. Slowly, Jean Patrick rose and stumbled toward Bea, forcing his legs to obey his crumbling will. When she opened the car door, he stooped inside and collapsed against the seat.

Bea reached behind him and pushed down the lock. "There's been a coup. It's not clear what happened, but the moment the news of Ndadaye's murder hit the streets, Burundi erupted like a volcano, and now violence has spilled like magma into Rwanda. No matter what you see, look straight ahead as if you didn't care." She accelerated onto the road. "In a few minutes we'll come to a mob. They're staggering drunk, blocking traffic, harassing everyone who passes." Her voice quavered. "You can see what they've been up to."

The men took shape from the mist. Dressed in rags, brandishing machetes, spears, and clubs, they fanned across the road.

"God will make us an exit," Bea said. "But you must stay relaxed. If they smell fear, they will devour us." Jean Patrick nodded. He tried to keep his hands from trembling in his lap.

The mob surrounded them, and Bea rolled down her window. The cloying sour-sweet of banana beer and blood, mixed with the stench of human filth, wafted into the car. "Good morning," she said.

A man pushed his head inside. Blood stained his club; his clothes were stiff with blood and dirt. "Are you Hutu?" he slurred. Jean Patrick held his breath against the fetor.

Bea bestowed on him a smile to melt sugar. "We're from the newspaper *Kangura*. Do you know it? We're covering reaction to Ndadaye's assassination. An important job." She spoke in the slow, cajoling tones reserved for young children. "Are you from Burundi?"

The man grunted. "What about him? He looks like a dog eater."

An exasperated breath escaped Bea's lips. "Do you think I'd let a Tutsi in the car with me? He's my assistant." She looked at Jean Patrick. "Show him." Jean Patrick gave her a puzzled look. "Your card. Your papers." She snapped her fingers, and he gave her his card. "There, you see?" Bea tapped the page in the man's face. "Hutu."

He examined Jean Patrick's picture and squinted at the writing, turning the booklet upside down, right side up, his brow furrowed with the effort. "Tell your paper we will make those dog eaters pay." He swept his arm across the scruffy group. "We are Burundians. We ran from our country because those Tutsi in charge slaughtered Hutu like dogs. We have been living first inside the stinking camps and now in Butare Town. We can't find jobs, can't find food, and just when we are thinking we can return to our land, because of those dog eaters, we're blocked again."

From a distance, Jean Patrick had seen the blue plastic roofs of the ramshackle huts in Gikongoro. The scent of their misery carried a distance in the wind. There were rumors, Uncle said, that Hutu militias were training them there.

With his bloodied club, the man pointed toward the arboretum fields. "At least those snakes can't poison us anymore." He waved his arms, and the mob parted to let the car through.

The mob turned their attention to the trunk, pounding it with clubs and fists. Bea's hands on the steering wheel were locked and rigid. Jean Patrick shoved his hands deep inside his pockets to hide their trembling. Neither spoke. Bea turned down a deserted goat trail, the car rattling and bumping across the ruts.

At a pullout hidden by a thicket of vines and brambles, she killed the engine. They both rolled down their windows. The air was clean, rain almost palpable in it. "If someone snapped our picture, we would see the same stupid expression on both our faces," Bea said. With a mixture of relief and terror, they both laughed.

"Where did you get the idea to say you were from *Kangura*? That was brilliant." Jean Patrick clutched the seat as if it held him to the earth.

"God gave it to me at the last second. Imana ishimwe, it worked, eh?"

"I can't believe you looked me in the eye and told me to hand that murderer my card." Tears flowed down his cheeks. "Mana yanjye, you were so calm—steady like a rock."

"*Know thine enemy.* I guessed he couldn't read. It's sad, really, but you have to take advantage where you can." Her hair hung over her face. Beneath the silky fabric of her blouse, her chest rose and fell.

A shiver passed through Jean Patrick. "If you hadn't found me, those guys could have killed me, too."

"When I heard RTLM last night, I knew things would be bad. I didn't sleep. As soon as it was light, I went to check on you. Daniel pointed me in the right direction."

"What's this about dog eaters?"

"The media has been shouting that Tutsi *dog eaters* tortured Ndadaye and mutilated his body. Who knows where the phrase came from, but they have pounced on it."

"But it was Tutsi who killed him?"

"Unfortunately, yes. In the spirit of reconciliation, Ndadaye had left the mostly Tutsi military in place after he came to power. They murdered him in an attempted coup. Whatever happens now, it will not be good for Burundi or Rwanda." Bea's fingers tapped out a rhythm against the steering wheel. "The funny thing is, if I lived in Burundi, it would be the Hutu I fought for."

"Why is that strange? After all, you are Hutu."

Anger flamed in Bea's eyes and then was gone. "It's not that at all. Hutu or Tutsi or green people from the moon, I fight injustice where I see it."

On the slope below, a woman prepared a field for planting. The hoe struck between her bare feet with a rhythmic *tac*. A red gash of soil opened in the stubbled remains of sorghum. Beside her, a little boy squatted and sucked on a piece of sugarcane.

"That hut," Jean Patrick began, "the one the mob burned." Bea turned toward him. "An old man lived there, the guard. I used to greet him when I ran. He would offer me tea, and each time, I said, 'Ejo hazaza,' tomorrow. Just now, before I saw, I said to myself, Today I will have tea with them." A sob wrenched free from his throat. "He had a daughter and a grandson."

"Promise me one thing," Bea said. Jean Patrick nodded. If she demanded a particular star, he would fly to the heavens to fetch it. "I'm going to bring you to our home now—Dadi has asked you to stay until we know it's safe. When you greet my mother, don't mention anything about this morning. She worries too much."

"Even if I wanted to tell someone, I have no words to speak it."

To the south and east, cloud banks rolled over Burundi's mountains. Rain fell in the high peaks. Streams would be bursting, tumbling down through the forests and denuded slopes to feed the Rusizi River as it journeyed southward from Lake Kivu. Jonathan had drawn pictures on the chalkboard in class. Before his eyes, Jean Patrick had watched the mountains form in thick yellow swoops from the violent upheaval of magma. He thought of Mama's sister Spéciose in Burundi, waking up to go to the fields, the children setting off for school. He thought of Gilbert and Ndizeye in Bujumbura, measuring their lives by the click of a stopwatch, the pure joy of motion radiant in their eyes. Yesterday he could have looked at the time and guessed what each of them would be doing, but from today, he could no longer predict the course of life beyond those mountains. He tasted bile in his mouth, sour and thick. He couldn't even answer the question *alive or dead* or say with certainty that the Rusizi River would not reverse course and spill back into Rwanda with its burden of ashes and blood. *Imana itanga ishaka.* God gives when he wants. And at any moment, he can take away again.

"Tomorrow, I will have to go to Cyangugu," Jean Patrick said. "I will have to see for myself that my family is safe."

On the path, schoolchildren laughed and sang. Goats bleated, the timbre of bells crisp and bright. Life went on. Bea gathered her hair into a clip. "Then I will drive you," she said.

"I DON'T KNOW why no one is coming." The car idled at the gate. Bea honked again.

Jean Patrick rested his head against the window's cool glass and recalled the day she had pulled him into her yard and permanently altered the spin of his world.

She bit her lip. "How am I going to get out of this car and act as if nothing has happened?"

Jean Patrick stepped out. He had to lean against the door for support. "The second step will be easier than the first," he said. "I will try it now, to let you know how it is." Strangely they both giggled. A woman came to open the gate. Jean Patrick followed the car into the yard and looked into the face of a smaller, thinner Bea.

"Welcome," she said. "I'm Ineza, Bea's mother." He stooped to receive her formal kiss: right cheek, left cheek, right again. "It's good to see you are safe. We were all anxious." She embraced Bea and led them to the door. "I've just now come from the market. I'm still putting things away."

"God help us, Mama, you went to market? Why didn't you send Claire?" Bea said. Jean Patrick noticed a tiny shudder before she recovered.

Ineza smiled at Jean Patrick. "My daughter, I have not yet reached an age where I can't walk to market."

"But *today,* Mama, you could have stayed home."

"As is our custom, we went together." A trace of worry underlay the casual banter. When Ineza balanced on one foot to remove a thin-strapped sandal, Jean Patrick thought of a bird preening delicate feathers. She disappeared into the kitchen.

Niyonzima stood by the curtains, looking out at the garden. Bea went to her father and kissed him. "I've brought Jean Patrick. He is unscathed."

Niyonzima squeezed Jean Patrick's hands. "Thank God. What did you discover?"

Bea spoke softly, her eye on the kitchen. "A gang of drunk Burundi refugees on a rampage. They burned down the guard's hut and murdered some workers at the arboretum fields. Closer to town, life seems as always." About their own confrontation, she said nothing.

"That is truly worrisome," Niyonzima said. "I've been making some calls. It appears most of the countryside remains calm."

"What about Cyangugu? Jean Patrick is anxious for his family."

"I have not heard. My few contacts there did not answer the phone."

Abruptly she put her hand on her father's shoulder. "Jean Patrick, come and see my mother's paintings," she said loudly. "Mama, leave the tea things for Claire and come be tour guide."

"With pleasure." Ineza took Jean Patrick's arm. "You're shaking. Are you cold?"

"A little bit. This jacket is thin."

"Then have tea first. That will warm you."

"Tea can wait. Let me see your paintings."

Ineza guided him toward the wall. "As you see, it is Rwanda's countryside that lives in my heart—the countryside of my childhood." Jean Patrick regarded the canvases: Intore dancers, farmers in terraced plots, tea pickers lost in a sea of foliage. Birds taking flight, green hills rising from mist. It took a moment to see that the golden light was a trick of the artist and not a swath of sun from the window. The last painting was of the children Bea had sheltered beneath her shawl. Ineza had caught them in the act of leaping for a ball, the illusion of motion so strong they looked about to leap from the canvas. Jean Patrick's heart twisted as he searched their faces for Bea's features. Maybe the boy's nose, the girl's broad shoulders; he couldn't be sure. "Your grandchildren are handsome," he said.

Bea shrieked. "Ko Mana—they are not my children!"

"My daughter has neither husband nor children," Ineza said. "Not even a suitor, as far as I know. Now come have tea, Jean Patrick, before you shiver out of your jacket."

A woman came from the cookhouse with bread and a bowl of fruit. Bea ran to her. "Here is Claire, the mother of those beautiful children." She touched her cheek to Claire's.

"I HAD TO put on something else," Bea whispered when she came outside. "I wanted to scrub my skin until the layers came off."

Jean Patrick was standing in the tentative sunlight, watching Claire shell peas. By pretending for Ineza that nothing had happened, he had almost come to believe it. But while he waited for Bea alone, his mind traveled back to the bodies, the drunk men. The blood smell was overmuch in his nostrils, and he wondered if it would ever wash away.

"I feel the same," he said.

"Dadi has asked if you will stay here, just to be safe. I can fetch what you need from Daniel, and we can leave for Cyangugu first thing in the morning." The children came running out in their blue school uniforms. Bea gathered them up and kissed their heads. "Sometimes," she said, "only innocence can bring you back to life."

JEAN PATRICK DID not know how he managed to survive the rest of the day. Ineza had presented him with an armload of books, and he occupied himself with trying to discover Bea through the pages. He approached it like a physics problem, gleaning the variables of her tastes and arranging them in orderly equations. He was staring at an English novel, trying to make sense of the words, when she returned with her father.

"I told him what happened," she said. "He went with a photographer, but someone had already removed the bodies. They found a few survivors and interviewed them. He sent the photos and the story to an American woman with Human Rights Watch. She knows Rwanda well and fights for us; the deaths will not go unnoticed."

"What about the old guard and his family? Did you hear any news?"

"Nothing, but it would have been difficult to catch them by surprise from such a lookout. Probably they saw and hid in the bush."

Jean Patrick wanted to believe it, just as he needed to believe his family had survived unharmed. The smallest line on a map separated them from Burundi. He looked out the window into the dusk. Claire and her

children picked tomatoes and squash from the garden. A chorus of birdsong came from the trees. All around them, the business of survival went
on unchanged.

"Since you are a guest, you will sleep in my room," Bea said. "Don't
look so frightened, eh! I will sleep in the study."

AFTER DINNER, JEAN Patrick slipped into bed beneath a pile of
blankets. He wrapped himself in the scent of Bea's body, her hair. He listened as she said good night to her parents in the hallway. One door closed
and then another. He shut his eyes and tossed from side to side until the
sheets tangled about his legs. It was no use. He flicked on the light and
walked about the room.

On wooden hooks behind the door hung a towel, the familiar gold
blouse, and a pair of red pantaloons rimmed with lace. He sat on the
small, wobbly stool beside her dressing table and examined her posses-
sions. A brush, a hair pick, a lipstick, a row of bottles. A few hairs remained in the brush, and he plucked them and rolled them between his
fingers. One by one he removed the stoppers of the perfume bottles and
inhaled until he grew dizzy.

Behind a stack of books, the corner of a picture frame was visible. He
knew he shouldn't, but unbidden, his fingers lifted the picture out. He saw
himself, caught as he leaned into the finish line at Nyamirambo Stadium,
his face twisted into an expression of exquisite pain. The angle his body
made was so far forward he seemed to defy the laws of gravity.

His heart wrenched, like an actual physical tearing, and with it, the
locked gate that guarded the morning's memory blew open. He set the photograph down on the table. Holding his head between his hands, he wept.
Tears fell on the picture, on the table, on Bea's brush, and on his bare,
goose-bumped legs.

RAIN TURNED THE road to Cyangugu slick, and small landslides
of rock and red mud fanned across it. Bea drove with her neck craned forward, face tense with concentration. "I feel like I'm driving underwater,"
she said.

"Since yesterday morning, I have been underwater." Jean Patrick studied his hands. "What I keep asking myself is why no one tried to stop them. Where were the soldiers, the police?" Bea stared out at the road in silence. "I mean, didn't Habyarimana give his troops orders to prevent violence? Can't he tell RTLM to stop their stupid talk?"

The windshield wipers whined. Bea wiped at the fogged glass with her palm. "The answer to the first question is, of course he didn't. And to the second: of course he could, if he chose to."

They entered Nyungwe Forest. Rain fell steadily; waterfalls tumbled from the rocks. A troop of baboons scampered across the road. They stopped in the undergrowth to regard the car, sitting up on their haunches, before continuing into the trees.

Jean Patrick laughed. "Shall I pick flowers to feed them?" In the hushed magic of the forest, his heart lightened.

"How wonderful. You remembered my story."

"I remember everything about you."

"You can stay dry. I've outgrown my childhood fear."

"Did you know all these rocks came from volcanoes? Jonathan says the Virungas are oldest — ten million years. Here, in the south, they are only two million years old."

"Eh! And how old does he say God is? God, who made all these pretty rocks?"

"That's what Coach said when I told him."

"That's one thing we agree on," Bea said. "Probably the only one."

Jean Patrick recalled Coach's chilly greeting to Bea's father in the stands at Nyamirambo. "How is it you know each other?"

"Butare is a small town, the university community, even smaller. Let's just say we do not look on Rwanda with the same eyes."

Jean Patrick stared out at the ancient, crumbling cliffs. Liana stubbornly took hold in every niche. He rolled the names of rocks silently over his tongue: granite, schist and metaschist, quartzite and metaquarzite. Obsidian, the vitreous secret of Bea's eyes, he saved for last.

CLIMBING OUT OF the forest, Jean Patrick caught the first glimpse of the tea plantations, like the flash of a sunbird's wing through the trees. They drew close, and the flash became rolling waves, a sea parted here and there by the red veins of irrigation ditches filled to bursting. Tea pickers bobbed like swimmers, their lower halves submerged, the huge leaf-filled baskets on their backs like floats to hold them up. Rain shimmered on the rows, a delicate lace.

This burst of green always told Jean Patrick he was home. Home tugged at his heart, and with it, a murmur of fear. Late last night, Niyonzima had reached a journalist who had passed through Cyangugu and found no sign of violence. Now, Jean Patrick willed it to be true. The tea plantations ended, replaced by the patchwork of terraced hills where women coaxed survival from the land. Bea stopped for a checkpoint. A soldier hitched his pants over his belly and strolled to the car.

"Good morning," he said, smiling. He took their cards. "Are you the husband?" He peered at Jean Patrick, and reflexively, Jean Patrick's heart fluttered.

Bea released a peal of laughter.

"No, muzehe. She's a friend from university. She's driving me to see my family."

The soldier continued to stare. Jean Patrick slid his hands beneath his thighs. Then the soldier exclaimed and struck his palm to his forehead. Jean Patrick's heart leapt into his throat.

"Wah! Now I remember." The soldier chuckled. "Last year—or maybe the year before—you were running very fast, and you fell down. At first I thought you were a thief, but when I came close, I saw you were just a skinny boy, crying. It was just outside Gihundwe School, on a Sunday. I gave you my handkerchief for the blood." He handed back their cards. "Aren't you a famous runner now?"

"Yego, officer." Jean Patrick remembered him from the day Mathilde died.

"Félicitations! I thought from your determined face you would succeed." He shook his head. "Wah! How time passes." He waved them through and called out, "Best of luck. May the Lord bless you both in everything."

Bea rolled up the window. "Is it true you're a thief?"

"Let me see." Jean Patrick scrutinized his card. "Ethnicity: Hutu, no; Twa, no; naturalisé, no." He traced each strike with his finger to symbolize the strikes on the card. "Tutsi, yes. But I don't see anything here about a thief." He tucked the booklet back into his jacket pocket. "I thought Habyarimana promised to abolish these."

Bea snapped her purse shut. "He did. Many, many times."

As they passed the welcome sign for Gashirabwoba, Jean Patrick scanned the horizon and took in the calm Saturday morning scene. He saw no sign that the flames of Burundi's fire had licked these hills. A sigh of relief escaped him.

But he needed to prepare Bea for what she would see. He needed to explain that he did not live in a house like hers, did not have water that came from a tap or light that came on at the flick of a switch. Now he had run out of time. To bargain for a few extra minutes, he let her drive on toward Cyangugu Town.

They crested a hill, and Lake Kivu appeared, winking like a mythical creature's eye. "Do you want to know what Jonathan taught us about Lake Kivu's beginnings?" Jean Patrick strung out his bartered seconds like beads on a length of twine.

Bea slowed, her half-closed eyes fixed on the water. "He can say whatever he wants. It was formed when Imana punished Nyiransibura. He made her squat in her fields. Try as she might, she could not stop her flow until urine covered the earth." A glow spread across her face. "That is what my mother told me when I was small, and therefore it is so."

"Can we stop here?" He pointed to a muddied patch of grass.

"Are you all right? Are you feeling sick?" She stopped the car.

"I'm fine. I have a present for you."

The rain had stopped completely. Sunlight threaded the clouds, and the hillsides in Zaire shone cobalt. Jean Patrick placed the pirogue on the seat between them.

Bea let out a tiny yelp. "Well, you finally found a good use for this newspaper." She cradled the carving in her hands, and Jean Patrick thought for a moment she would cry. "How beautiful," she said. "I can't believe you bought this for me."

A pleasant heat warmed Jean Patrick's legs. Fog drifted up from the valley, and he rolled down the window to breathe in the cool, rain-freshened air. The story of his life poured out in a long exhalation. He told Bea about his father's death, his life with Uncle's family, his love for running, and his struggle to make his way through school. He told her about Mathilde and the pain that filled him when he lost her. He did not tell her of his changing identities or the Hutu card sealed behind a picture of Paul Ereng.

A boy led a flock of goats on the trail above, a stack of firewood balanced on his head. Bea's shawl fell from her shoulders, and her skin shone against her collarbone. She stared in silence at the boy and then touched the pirogue. "This wood is so smooth," she said. Her eyes sparkled. He couldn't tell if it was from tears or the sun's reflection. "Did you think I didn't know about your family?"

"Since I never spoke of them, how could you?"

"Remember: my father is a journalist, and I am studying to be one. Your friend Jonathan is very proud of you, and it was not difficult to extract information."

"You investigated me?" He beamed.

"Americans are not private like Rwandans. A person's life is an open book to them." She turned the key in the ignition. "Are you angry?"

"How could I be?"

He took in the sweep of her forehead and the long, delicate curve of her neck, inherited from Ineza. He couldn't imagine anyone more perfect.

"I've been waiting all this time to meet your family," she said. She leaned her head out the window to check for traffic. "Shall we go?"

"We've passed it already; you'll have to turn around."

A giddy weightlessness lifted Jean Patrick. The liquid eye of the lake closed behind them. The pirogue rested on the seat, buoyed on the waves of *Kangura*. The shell-carved fish inside the bilge sparkled in the sun.

THE PATH WAS steeper than Jean Patrick remembered, channeled by erosion. Despite the grade and the mud, Bea kept pace beside him. She had taken off her sandals and lifted her pagne to her knees to keep it clean. As they walked, the earth sucked them in past their ankles with every step, then released them with a kissing sound. The compound took shape in the hills. When Jean Patrick saw smoke from the cook fire, a thin ribbon in the breeze, he released the last held breath of tension from his body. Passing the forked eucalyptus, he brushed his finger across the charred trunk.

He told her about Roger, how close they had been when the lightning struck. "When I touched him, electric current passed between us."

Bea brushed her fingers across the scar. "I can still feel it." She released her pagne, and it swayed about her muddied ankles.

"And your brother Roger. Where is he now?"

Momentarily, all thought flew from his head, and he had to think himself back to the present. "Kenya. He has a job in Kenya."

There was a new structure, half-completed and roofed with corrugated metal, attached like a bird's wing to the main house. With a smile, Jean Patrick imagined Uncle boasting to the neighbors, carrying the sheets as if they were made of gold. Glass panes glinted from all the windows. The fishing must be good once more. They stepped through the cypress gate into the yard. Clemence looked up from her game of hoop and stick and stopped midstride. She took Baby Pauline's arm and flew to greet them. "Jean Patrick is home! There's a lady with him!" she screeched.

Mama burst through the door. "Imana ishimwe—you're safe!" She embraced Jean Patrick and then turned to Bea. Bea stepped into her embrace as if she had been waiting her whole life to do it.

JEAN PATRICK WATCHED his family through the back windshield until they became specks at the base of the path. The cultivated hills disappeared from view and then Nyungwe Forest surrounded them in its aquamarine veil, dusk settling on the thickly forested slopes. Surrendering to the car's lullaby, he drifted, half-asleep and half-awake, not wanting to let go of the afternoon.

A violent jerk whipped his head against the window. Bea's hand closed around his mouth. "Not a word," she whispered.

She had stopped in a small thicket. Ahead, at a bend in the road, men emerged from the brush. They carried machetes and rifles and what must have been RPGs. They were dressed in dark clothes, caps pulled low over their faces, and they melted into the twilight like shades vanishing into mist. After they disappeared, Bea waited a few minutes before starting the car.

"Who were they?" Jean Patrick's heart raced. It was as if the forest had opened its mouth and revealed its dark, concealed secret.

Bea shrugged. "RPF? Interahamwe? Burundi rebels? Who can tell?" Somewhere near, thunder resonated. The storm would hit before they arrived in Butare.

Jean Patrick fished for something to say to break the silence. "Where are your brothers and sisters?" He was still trying to solve the equation of Bea.

Bea regarded him strangely. "I have none. I thought you knew. Thinking of it now, I wonder if this was one reason my parents sent me to boarding school in London, because kids used to torture me about it when I was small. One boy threw rocks and threatened me with a stick. He thought I was possessed by a devil because I was an only child."

"I'm sorry."

"Why? It made me strong." Her tongue against her teeth made a kissing sound. "Besides: all that love my parents have, and only me to take it." The evening breeze came in, and with it the smell of rain.

Her parents met, Bea told him, when Niyonzima covered Ineza's first exhibit at the National Museum. He had not been happy about the assignment. He had expected excitement and exposés, not dull social events. But the moment he saw Ineza, all his bad humor flew away. "I was a big surprise. I arrived when my father was forty, my mother thirty-six. By then, they had long given up hope. That's why they called me Bea—their blessing."

"They didn't want a brother or sister for you?"

"There were complications. Mama almost died, and the doctors told her if she had another child, it could kill her. It was a miracle, they said, we both survived."

"As favored as you have been, I guess you have a boyfriend." Jean Patrick ran his hand along the fabric of his jacket.

"As my mother told you, I have no child, no husband, no suitor."

"What about that policeman who came to talk to you in the café?"

She pursed her lips in disgust. "You are always jumping to strange conclusions. Don't give him another thought."

The engine thrummed, a slow, steady hymn. In the purplish light, Jean Patrick could just make out the stripes of pale and dark rocks, the abruptly discordant layers. In class, Jonathan had spoken of tectonic upheaval. Rwanda, he said, was a landscape twisted and folded, tied in knots by a history of pressure and heat. Its insides heaved and shifted, disgorging their molten contents.

"Stop the car," he said.

"Again? What's happened now?"

He threw back his head and gave a boisterous laugh. "I need a rock sample to take to Jonathan."

Bea pulled over. "If there are more soldiers, they could kill us."

"It will only take a minute. Come on; I want to show you." He jogged to the outcrop and held out his hand.

Bea hiked her pagne. "Claire will kill me, with all this mud." She picked her way to where he leaned against the wet cliff face. Wild begonias gave off a lemony scent.

"Give me your keys." She put them in his hand, and he dug into a vein of rock, extracting a small, multifaceted crystal. "I think it's quartz. If I scratched it on the window, I could tell—the glass would scratch, but not the rock."

Bea inspected the crystal. "I say it comes from the moon. I'm sure Jonathan will agree." She turned it around in her fingers, then placed it in Jean Patrick's palm. She let her hand linger.

A drop of rain hit Jean Patrick's jacket, and then another. He closed his fingers around hers. The edges of the crystal were sharp against his flesh. He leaned back against the cliff and pulled her with him. Dampness seeped through his jacket. He put the crystal in his pocket.

The forest was redolent with evening. Rain spattered the leaves. Bea's hair swept her shoulders, and he gathered a handful and held it to his lips. It felt slippery and soft, like fine cloth. He tasted her flower-scented soap, the coconut oil she rubbed into her scalp. Touching his forehead to hers, he smelled the sweet milk and pungent tea she had sipped at dinner. Gently, he traced the lines of her jaw and lifted her chin. Then, more gently still, he kissed her mouth.

EIGHTEEN

"YOU MISSED AGAIN," COACH SAID. He clicked his stopwatch. "One forty-nine fifty-nine. What's wrong with you? Are you sick?"

Jean Patrick shook his head, and pain knifed behind his eyes. "No, Coach. Just tired." He turned to hide his cough.

For nearly three weeks, he had failed to run an A-standard time. For the past week, fighting a cold, seconds attached themselves to his times and would not let go. He couldn't find his zone. His muscles felt sluggish; his rhythm, off. But it wasn't the cold. He knew the true cause: Bea was overmuch in his mind. At first, after their kiss, he'd drawn sustenance from the smell of her hair, the radiant heat in the hollow at the base of her neck, the way she tossed a shawl about her shoulders. He had blazed through workouts. Coach started talking about a medal at Worlds.

The change happened from one day to the next, as if his fibers suddenly forgot how to fire. As if Bea had overloaded his nerves and drained the current. Not knowing the reason, Coach told him not to worry. "These things happen even to the best runners," he said. But each time he stopped his watch, a knot worked up and down in his jaw. Jean Patrick thought of Samson and Delilah. He wondered if this was what love meant, a slow but steady sap of strength and spirit.

"One lap easy and we'll try again," Coach said. He zeroed his watch. "I don't want those boys in Sweden to eat you up next year."

Coach was trying a new plan, making Jean Patrick hold something back until he shouted, "Go!" at some point in the second four hundred. "That's exactly how those Burundi boys got you. For the eight hundred, you *have* to learn strategy."

Jean Patrick hated it; he couldn't run that way. Trickiness was not in his nature. And as if that wasn't enough, he was losing the battle with his cold. Cotton plugged his head. His chest burned. He ran again and failed again, and when he heard his time, he sneezed.

"Urachire," Coach said. Be rich. "Are you sure you're not sick?"

"Twese," Jean Patrick replied. All of us. The call and response that accompanied every sneeze in Rwanda. "No, Coach. I don't know what's wrong." Coach lifted Jean Patrick's chin. "Is there something you're not telling me?"

"No, Coach."

"Maybe you're overtrained. It's going to pour soon, anyway. How about a day off?"

"No, Coach. I need to run a qualifying time before I quit. All this doubt is too heavy." He fought off another sneeze. "Let me run my old way. If I can break through, I'll be all right. Just one eight hundred—I promise."

Coach placed a hand on Jean Patrick's belly. "I think you've forgotten. I don't know where your mind is lately, but this is where your power is. I want you to feel it here." He pressed hard. "Now hurry before you have to swim instead of run."

Jean Patrick did not hold back. At the signal, he ran as if his life depended on it. And it did. By the start of the second lap, he wanted to die. To keep from quitting, he recited physics laws in his head. He was onto harmonic oscillators when he reached the final straight. *Acceleration proportional to the negative of displacement from the midpoint of its motion.* He passed the line.

"One forty-six thirty-nine" Coach said. "You win."

Jean Patrick didn't have the energy to raise his arms into the air. A violent, heaving fit of coughing racked his body, and he doubled over.

"You are ill. I knew it." Coach helped him upright. At that instant, the sky tore open and rain came down in a sheet. "You're coming home with me. Jolie will make you soup, and you will drink it."

Jean Patrick peered up at the road. "Where's your car?"

"I ran." Coach brought an extra rain jacket from beneath the seats. "Put this on." He snapped the jacket open and shook it dry. "Let's go."

Already the ground was slick. They jogged down the road, mud sucking at their shoes. Jean Patrick observed his coach, his graceful cadence.

He could probably have been an Olympic runner in his own right. Jean Patrick didn't know whether to love or to hate him, if he was tyrant or father. Maybe he was both, all mixed up together in the same hardened soul.

"You taught me a lesson," Coach said.

Jean Patrick shook his head to clear it. "I don't understand." He wiped his streaming nose with the back of his hand.

"Your slump. Forcing you to change your style is like commanding a river to flow backward." He tugged Jean Patrick's jacket. "Slow down, eh? You plunge full force into the waters — no looking — with everything you do. It's why I like you, but in the eight hundred, I guarantee, you will drown *ev-ery time.*" He accompanied each syllable with a fist slapped against his palm. "I don't know how to make you do it, but somehow you must learn to hold back."

Jean Patrick wanted to laugh, but if he started, he would cough. He had a long road back to the times he was capable of, but at least he had broken the spell. He would not have to leave Bea; she had not cut off his invisible hair in the middle of the night.

JEAN PATRICK AND Coach shook off their wet clothes in the front hall. Water puddled on the floor, and Jolie scolded them loudly. "Jean Patrick," she said. "So many days, no news of you. Why are you a stranger?" Jean Patrick stooped to receive her cheek on his.

"He has been busy with a girl, and not a good one," Coach said.

Startled, Jean Patrick looked up. He had said not a word about Bea. "Don't worry, Jolie. She's not as beautiful as you," he said.

Jolie cackled. "The water is off again. I've brought some for a bath, and I'll heat some more. You are both drowned." She headed for the bathroom with her kettle. "I thought things would change with the peace treaty. I am waiting and waiting for the government to fix all the broken things."

"Don't worry," Coach called after her. "When Habyarimana comes back from peace talks in Arusha, milk and honey will flow from our pipes." He pushed Jean Patrick. "You first. We need to protect our Olympic future."

Jean Patrick squatted in the tub and breathed in steam from the basin.

Above him, wet laundry hung on a cord. There was no doubt about it now; the cold had won the war. He would ask Jolie for some herbs; old people knew such things. He could not afford to miss a workout. He needed to run another A-standard time to know that this was not a fluke. To be certain that Bea had not cast some spell.

Coach knocked at the door. "I have some clothes for you. I was saving them for Christmas, but take them now, since yours are wet. There's a leak in a pipe, and I'm going to try to fix it. Jolie will bring you soup."

"I could help you." Jean Patrick poured hot water over his head and wiggled his fingers in his ears to clear the soap. Coach was gone when he came out of the bathroom.

A sweat suit, neatly folded, lay on the bed in the spare room. Beside it was a pair of shimmery shorts and a long-sleeved jersey with a Nike swoosh. He put on the shorts and jersey and stood in front of the tiny mirror. The look pleased him.

Since the last time he had slept there, the room had changed. The bed had a thick blanket that hung down to the floor. He thought how pleasant it would be to wrap himself in its warmth and go to sleep. Jolie had hung his jacket on a chair. He shook it out, and something fell from the pocket and rolled under the bed. He bent to retrieve it and saw it was the crystal he had meant to give to Jonathan and forgotten. A wooden crate with Chinese writing had stopped its roll.

Curiosity won out over courtesy and common sense. He pulled on the crate, but it didn't budge. A dark substance had stained the wood, and when he drew his finger across it, a residue of oil remained on his skin.

"Inshyanutsi. Why are you nosing about?" Jolie's voice made him bump his head on the bed frame. She closed the door behind her and pushed a steamy towel at him. "I soaked it in herbs for your throat." Bending closer, she said, "I will teach you something I have learned. Stay out of places you have not been invited into. Otherwise, things will not go well for you."

Jean Patrick backed away from the bed.

"Come to the table," she said. "I brought you a special soup. Lucky for you, I am an old woman, and my memory is very short."

She touched his forehead, and he knew by the coolness of her fingers that he was burning up. He followed her out of the bedroom, and she closed and locked the door. Whatever the contents of the box, it would be better for him if his memory was short as well.

JONATHAN BOUNDED ACROSS the classroom, his voice booming with excitement. His constant motion made Jean Patrick woozy. Despite Jolie's herbs and two days of rest, his cold hung on. The subject of the lesson was geologic structures, and Jonathan described each one with wild swoops of chalk across the board. Students nudged each other and rolled their eyes. "Umuzungu yasaze," they hooted. The white man is crazy.

After class, Jonathan caught Jean Patrick. "Do you have a minute?"

"Sure." He followed Jonathan to his office.

The room looked as wild as Jonathan's class, every inch of space occupied by rocks and stacks of journals and books. "Tea?" Jonathan cleared a pile of papers. "Have a seat." He pushed a chair toward Jean Patrick. "You coughed and sneezed all through class. Are you sick?"

"A little. Just a cold."

Jonathan heated water in an electric kettle. "My new most prized possession." From the chaos on his desk, he retrieved an airmail letter. "And here's my Christmas present." He handed the envelope to Jean Patrick. Not sure what to do, Jean Patrick held it on his lap.

"Go ahead and open it. It's not top secret."

"This is from your umukunzi?"

"My what?"

"U-mu-*kun*-zi. Your girlfriend." Jean Patrick had studied Susanne's picture on Jonathan's desk. She posed on a mountaintop, feet wide, hands on hips. He thought she looked more like a boy than a young woman, but he liked her cheerful smile and the way the breeze had blown her hair into silky wisps around her head.

"Yup. She's coming January seventh."

"She really is your Christmas present."

"I couldn't ask for a better one." Jonathan sorted through a pile of letters, slitting the flaps with a wooden letter opener tipped with a carving of a giraffe. The kettle whistled, and he poured water into the teapot.

"Should you really let her come?"

Jonathan stared at Jean Patrick. "*Let* her come? J. P., in America, women make up their own minds." He removed a newspaper from a manila envelope and snapped it open. "Sorry. That was rude; I shouldn't have said it. Anyway, I've been missing her like crazy, and the CIA or the embassy or whoever her NGO consulted assured us the situation in Rwanda is stable."

Stable? Jean Patrick watched the changing clouds out the window. Wedges of slate-colored sky sliced their bellies. As stable as the weather in rainy season, he thought.

Of course U.S. agencies didn't understand. Even Jonathan, after what he had witnessed in Kigali, could not begin to understand. Rwanda's reality remained carefully hidden from foreigners so they could continue to float on the calm waters, conjured up for their benefit, above the turbulent sea Rwandans swam.

Jonathan poured tea. He no longer had to ask, spooning three sugars into Jean Patrick's cup. "Sorry, all I have is chemical milk."

Jean Patrick wrinkled his nose. "That's OK. I can drink it black."

"I am not quite man enough," Jonathan said, adding white powder from a plastic tub to his tea. He flattened the newspaper on top of the letters and paperwork. "I hate to divide my attention like this, but it's a newsletter from a French friend in Kigali. I just want to skim it before my next class."

"About Susanne, I only meant . . ." Jean Patrick searched his mind for words to complete the sentence.

"Dear God." Jonathan suddenly sat upright. His neck and face flushed, and he looked dumbly into Jean Patrick's eyes. For an instant, Jean Patrick thought he must have said or done something terribly wrong, but then he saw the tears. "Do you know anything about this?" Jonathan handed him the paper.

Stunned by the words, Jean Patrick dropped it into his lap.

"Did I get this right?" Jonathan asked. "Did someone bury a mine on a path where children walk to school? And the children *stepped* on it?"

Too numbed to speak, Jean Patrick nodded.

"How can one human being do this to another? To *children,* for God's sake: six- and seven-year old *children,*" Jonathan said. He cradled his head in his hands. "The cold, calculated brutality—to camouflage the damned thing with leaves."

Jean Patrick wished he could tell Jonathan that he was mistaken, that his translation was faulty, that twenty-one innocent children had not died. But he could not. Words unraveled; belief came unhinged. It had happened in Kigali, but it could have been anywhere. It could have been his sisters, his cousins. *"Iyo nyamunsi yaciye ishumi, nta mubyeyi uyihisha ikibando,"* he quoted.

"Which means?"

"Something like, 'When destiny cuts the link in the fence, no mother can hide her child.'"

Jonathan nodded slowly. Tears brimmed in his eyes, but he did not wipe them away. Instead his hands fluttered in a random fashion across the scatter on his desktop.

The clamor of students came to Jean Patrick slowly. He looked at his watch. "Sorry. I have a physics class."

"One second, before you go." Jonathan looked like a little boy pleading with his mother. "Do you think I should write Susanne and tell her not to come?"

"I'm sure it's OK. It's nothing against white people." As if his reassurance could hold the fence against death's machete. "I really have to go. If you want, we can talk about this later."

"Yes," Jonathan said. "I'd appreciate that very much." The words fell one at a time from his lips. "But who could have done this? Interahamwe? RPF?" He sighed. "I can't keep them straight, who stands for what."

Jean Patrick stood by the door. "These guys—they don't know themselves what they stand for, but I don't think it could be RPF. What you hear on the news about them—it's not like that. I'll come back after class, if you have time."

Jonathan stared out the window. "Hey—come for dinner," he said to the glass.

Jean Patrick's limbs ached. All he wanted was to retreat to his bed and fall into a dreamless sleep. "That would be great," he said, and he closed the door behind him.

The stairs swayed, and Jean Patrick grabbed the railing for support. What sense could he make of a child one minute chattering on a leaf-covered path, the next blown apart in the trees? What sense from a hand digging a hole, readying a mine, brushing the leaf litter back? Did the man wait to see his result? Did he smile or laugh? Did he feel anything at all? If Jean Patrick followed the hand to an arm, a shoulder, a face, whose face would he find, and what would he see inside those eyes? Would it, in the end, be better never to have seen at all? Yet here were Jonathan and Susanne believing in the world's order. Inviting love in. The last bell rang, and Jean Patrick took the stairs two at a time.

"I THOUGHT YOU drowned," Daniel whispered when Jean Patrick squeezed into the seat Daniel had saved for him. "I waited and waited, but you never came back from your workout."

The professor was already busy writing equations. RESONANCE, he wrote in bold letters across the board. He sketched a vibrating string fixed at one end with a weight and pulley and driven by a motor at the other end. He drew arrows of force.

Still sick? Daniel scrawled in his notepad.

Jean Patrick nodded. He opened his notebook to a fresh page and copied the professor's equations. Discordant frequencies jangled his nerves, and he needed to replace them with the steady, predictable vibrations of science.

The professor asked for examples of resonance. Jean Patrick raised his hand. "The waves on Lake Kivu, driven by wind."

"A tuning fork struck by a rod fastened to a turning wheel," a student in the front said.

And then, from the back row: "Rwanda driven crazy by Inkotanyi." Laughter rippled through the hall. Jean Patrick's cheeks burned hotter.

He tried to shout out a response, but only a cough came out. Daniel elbowed him and put a candy in his palm. *Good for the throat,* he scribbled in Jean Patrick's notebook. *From a muzungu girl in English class. She likes me.*

An explosion of mint filled Jean Patrick's sinuses and resonated in his throat. The professor wrote an equation on the board concerning the force, frequency, and density required to produce resonance. Jean Patrick's attention faded. The only equation in his head was a shock wave from a mine, resonant in the morning air, that traveled out across a school yard filled with children.

When Jean Patrick jogged onto the field for afternoon practice, Coach struck his hand to his forehead. "Are you completely without sense? Go back to your dorm. And I do not want to see you in the morning." Behind Coach's back, Daniel wagged a finger and smiled.

In his heart, Jean Patrick was relieved. As hard as he tried to deny it, he had no will to run. Every muscle in his body ached, and like a bad migraine, the headlines in Jonathan's paper kept flashing behind his eyes. Bea's art history class should just be ending, and if he hurried, he could catch her and walk her home. He needed to talk about the children. Only Bea could calm the angry spirits in his mind. Standing outside the building in the almost rain, he searched the swell of students for a flash of gold blouse, a blue shawl, but he saw no trace of her. He waited five minutes after the final bell rang and then set out for Cyarwa Sumo to find her.

Dusk brushed the arboretum fields. At the top of the ridge, someone had cleared the rubble of the guard's hut and piled freshly made bricks on the ground. Jean Patrick hoped it was the work of the old guard and his family. In this country, hope always chased close on the heels of despair. It was in the people's blood to try and try again.

For weeks after the killings, Jean Patrick had avoided the fields. Each time he set out for them, the smell of death overpowered him. It was an impossible situation; these were his favorite trails, the steepest for interval workouts, with plenty of action to distract him from pain. Bea had cured him. One morning, she met him after his workout, and without thinking about their destination, he set off with her. He was lost in conversation, and when he looked up, the fields surrounded him. The banter of the women in the plots filled his ears as before. He inhaled the morning, clear and fresh. Not one scrap of memory remained in his nostrils. Since that time, it had not returned. Now, at the church on the far side of the fields, evening mass had ended, and the worshippers poured out onto the road. A young woman picking her way down the trail caught his eye. With her broad shoulders, her considered and graceful step, it could only be Bea. He quickened his pace to meet her.

"It's good to see you," she said, kissing the air by his cheek. She could have been greeting a distant cousin, a friend of a friend at school.

Jean Patrick fell into step beside her, let her radiant heat temper his chills. She kept her eyes on the ground and marched forward. This gesture of displeasure he had also come to recognize. "I'm on my way to Jonathan's," he said. "He's invited me for dinner." He hoped she would ask if she could join him.

"Amos is a good cook."

"I've never been honored with a dinner invitation before." He searched her face for reaction, a spark of her usual fire; none was there. "I waited for you after class," he said. "I wanted—"

Bea cut him off. "You should not have bothered. I went straightaway to my father's office when the bell rang."

"Stop a minute." He stepped in front of her and held up his hands. "I don't understand you tonight. Did I do something to make you angry?"

A boy on a bicycle passed them. He stood as he reached the steepest part of the trail and pedaled with a rhythmic side-to-side sway. A woman sat sidesaddle behind him, steadying a basket on her head. A serene smile graced her features. "Good afternoon," they called together.

Bea watched them, a look of pain on her face. "It's nothing to do with you," she said.

"Then what? Tell me." He wished he could hook a finger beneath her chin, raise her face to his, and kiss her. Good customs would not allow it.

"Something horrible has happened in Kigali."

"I know. I read it in Jonathan's paper. It has been haunting me since. That's why I came to find you."

"One of Dadi's friends lost his daughter in the blast. That's why you found me at church." She took a step forward. "Let's walk; I feel this cold too much."

Maybe her mood had only to do with Kigali and not with him. He chided himself for putting his own selfish wishes above respectful grief for the children, but he allowed the thought to gather shape and substance in his mind. He walked stubbornly beside Bea, ready to pounce on any scrap of affection. He felt as if he were grabbing her little finger as she was swept downstream by a swift current. Although his mind told him to stop, his heart made him go forward. "You shouldn't let events we can't control stand in our way. It doesn't mean *we* have no chance for a future."

"Mon pauvre," Bea said, as if Jean Patrick were a little boy to slip inside the blue wing of a shawl. "If this crazy country made sense, we would stand a chance. But after what happened today, I can't believe in futures anymore. Not even with you. It is too painful."

They reached the Cyarwa checkpoint. Bea moved away from him. The soldiers patted him on the back and wished him good night. Even in darkness, he saw the way their eyes slid over Bea's body, the slight twist of their mouths into a sneer.

Jean Patrick had a list of arguments against Bea's worries, but none came out. He walked on in dumb silence, his head on fire with fever. It was clear she was determined to run away, and his mind wavered in doubt over every point he thought to bring up. Only when they came to Jonathan's gate did she catch his gaze and hold it.

"I'm sorry," she said. "You don't look well at all. I should have held my tongue."

"Is there something else? Did your father tell you to keep away from me?" The only explanation that came to him.

"You are *not* the center of the universe," she said. But then she touched her cheek to his, and her damp warmth remained on his skin. "How stupid. I didn't mean that." Her eyes glistened, and she wiped them with her sleeve. "Nkuba Jean Patrick." She released the syllables of his name like pebbles tossed into water. "How can you think of a future in a world where nothing is left of twenty-one children but bits and pieces in the leaves? Not even a body for a mother to bury."

"But Bea—"

"I'll be busy for a while, so I can't see you," she said. Jean Patrick opened his mouth to continue his protest, but she touched a finger to his lips. "Not a word. You can't change my mind."

She reached up on her toes and gently kissed his cheek. He thought to kiss her quickly on the mouth, but she stepped away. "You will catch my cold now," he said. Just to say something.

As he watched her hurry off toward her house, he had to believe he was still in her heart. He didn't know why she had done this. He almost wished her his cold, some small part of him to linger in her presence.

Jonathan's gate was unlocked, and Jean Patrick stepped into the yard. Coach had instructed him to be patient, to hang back and wait for the right moment to strike. The strategy hadn't worked on the track, but it might with Bea. If he bided his time, he thought he could reel her in again.

Before he could knock, Jonathan opened the door, his face nearly as red as the glass of wine he put into Jean Patrick's hand. "Come drink with me, J. P. I've finished half a bottle, but so far it hasn't helped. I can't even drown the day in alcohol."

Jean Patrick would have preferred a cup of Jolie's cyayi cyayi or even a beer, but he put the glass to his lips and sipped. He expected something sweet, like the fruit wines his father gave him when he was small, but this had a moldy, sour taste. He sipped again. "It's good," he said.

"You're not a skilled liar, but don't worry," Jonathan said. He led Jean Patrick to the table and filled both glasses to the brim. "Trust me—it will taste better with every mouthful."

With the next taste, a pleasant heat tingled his tongue. Amos came in with a tray, and when he saw Jean Patrick, he grinned from ear to ear.

"I believe you've met before?" Jonathan said.

"Yes, yes." Amos set the food on the table and grasped Jean Patrick's hands. "I watched your race on television—so wonderful!" He clucked his tongue. "It's an honor to greet you again. You make us proud." From his emphasis, Jean Patrick understood that *us* meant Tutsi. He remembered Uncle's words and smiled.

"Let's eat," Jonathan said. "I better get something in my stomach before I pass out under the table. Amos, will you join us?"

Amos smiled shyly. "I have just now eaten," he said, straightening the spoons in the bowls. He nodded to Jean Patrick. "Bon appétit. I cooked you a special meal."

Amos had cooked a feast of foods from his region, plenty of beans and green bananas, vegetables and spicy sauces. Jean Patrick wished his nose were less stuffy so he could inhale the aromas.

AFTER DINNER, JONATHAN emptied his wineglass and leaned his elbows on the table. "I told Susanne. She was pretty upset, but she's still coming. Of course there was no word in the American papers, and no one at the State Department had a clue—at least not that they shared." He tipped the last few drops of wine from the bottle into Jean Patrick's glass.

"No one back home cares about a few African children more or less in the world. It's business as usual to them."

They stayed at the table long after Amos cleared the dishes and brought tea and fruit. Jonathan patted his stomach. "I don't have any beer. Shall I send Amos for some?"

"If I drink any more, I will be the one to sleep beneath the table."

"I did not intend for you to go home tonight. Amos has already made up your bed."

The candles flickered in their clay holders. For a while, Jonathan and Jean Patrick watched in silence. Then Jonathan sighed and folded his hands on his chest. The ghosts of the children tiptoed in and sat in the empty chairs.

"I have learned that it is rude in Rwanda to ask prying questions, but we are both scientists," Jonathan began. "I am getting nowhere trying to figure this thing out on my own."

Jean Patrick's head swam; he couldn't hear his own thoughts, so muffled by congestion. He had planned to tell Jonathan a little of Rwanda's history as he understood it. But which story would he tell? He could say that the Tutsi were a Nilotic people: tall and thin, with narrow, graceful features. They came with their cattle and, shunning cultivation, tended cattle to survive. The Hutu were a Bantu tribe, farmers, a shorter, broader, and stronger people more suited to the constant toil that farm work required. Both groups settled in the territory that became Ruanda-Urundi and later Burundi and Rwanda. The Twa, a small and slight people, lived as hunters and gatherers in the forest and remained so until the forests diminished and the animals became scarce. This was one story, the most commonly accepted, and the one that was taught in school.

Much of it was true, but how much? It was true that the mwami, a Tutsi king, came to rule over all. But now Zachary came home from school with stories that the Tutsi were a haughty people, merciless oppressors of their Hutu brethren. One teacher told the class that the mwami forced his Hutu serfs to stand beside him and receive the points of his spears in their feet. This, Jean Patrick did not believe, and this he would not say to Jonathan.

Before the Belgians, Jean Patrick wanted to say, Hutu and Tutsi lived properly as neighbors. Perhaps, as Uwimana thought, Hutu and Tutsi were in fact one people. Had he lived, Jean Patrick's papa would most likely have taught him the same lesson. He would have said—as Uwimana did—that before the Belgians, distinctions were as fluid as the rivers, determined by marriage, convenience, and status. Names of rivers changed, but the water remained the same.

At least Jean Patrick thought this to be true. He had spent his early life not knowing the distinctions, and a country without distinctions was what his father had believed in and striven for. Jean Patrick believed, too, that examination of Rwandan blood under a microscope would yield mixed results, impossible to quantify or label. Bea's own mother was a perfect example. With her golden skin, her regal bearing, who would not look at her and say she was Tutsi?

And he wanted to explain to Jonathan what it meant to be Tutsi in a world where belief and order were blown apart daily, a world where he was constantly forced to navigate uncharted waters, the currents impossible to gauge. If the moment arose, he might also have attempted a careful defense of the RPF.

None of this came out. The history Jonathan's wine loosened on his tongue was the tale of Bea and of a need to be with her that burned almost— but not quite—as bright as his Olympic flame.

Nineteen

Jean Patrick knew it was foolishness, but he suspected his lingering cold and Bea's lingering absence grew from the same bitter seed. If he could chase sickness from his body, Bea would come back. Or if Bea came back first, she would sweep the aches and pains from his limbs, the congestion from his lungs.

The team had finished the warm-up—a series of lunges, strides, and butt kicks—and gathered to watch Coach struggle with something in the trunk of his car. He had his back to them, and no one could get a clear view through the dense eucalyptus that stood between them and the road above.

"It's a body," Daniel said. "A guy who cheated in Coach's government class."

A four-hundred-meter runner patted Jean Patrick on the back. "Oya! It's a wife for this guy. Coach found her in the bush, and if Jean Patrick survives the workout, he can have her."

The trunk lid banged shut. Coach rolled the object toward the edge of the road and shoved it down the slope. An immense truck tire careened down the embankment.

"Yampayinka!" Daniel said, and he let out a whistle. They all stood frozen, watching the tire's unpredictable passage as it crashed through the trees. At the last instant, they scattered. The effort sent Jean Patrick into a fit of coughing.

Coach howled. "You guys have to learn to relax. If you remain calm, your mind will tell your body what to do. It works on the track, and it works in your life."

The tire gyrated on the field. Its rotation slowed until it could no longer sustain the motion, and it toppled. Coach tapped it with his shoe. "Who's first?" He pulled a harness from his bag and let it swing from his fingers.

Despite the beating from his cold, Jean Patrick couldn't resist the challenge. "You want one of us to pull that thing?"

Coach held out the harness to Jean Patrick. "Did I hear you volunteer?"

"Wait. You mean, I race with that weight while the others run free?"

"Precisely. We'll start with two hundreds and work up to eights," Coach said.

Coach attached the lines. A crowd gathered in the stands. Just two days remained before Christmas vacation, and the students were boisterous, celebrations under way. Jean Patrick scanned the seats in vain for Bea. Since the evening two weeks ago when she had stood with him outside Jonathan's gate, she had truly vanished from his life.

"Coach is finally going to kill you," Daniel said, lining up beside him.

"We'll see. And if you run in your usual slack way, you'll be next."

"Six two hundreds," Coach shouted. "Tugende."

At first, inertia got the better of Jean Patrick. The tire's weight chopped his stride and sent him flailing. But by the third two hundred, persistence paid off, and he found a rhythm and stillness in his step that kept the tire straight and steady behind him. It was a matter of momentum; if he never quite stopped, if he conserved the tire's linear motion, he could keep the other runners in sight. He tasted the same sweet success that came from unraveling a stubborn equation after an evening of failure. From the stands came a rhythmic clapping. "Mr. Olympics!" the audience cheered.

Jean Patrick ate it up. When Coach said, "Enough!" after the last two hundred, he pleaded for a little more time, just one four hundred. To whistles of approval, he put his head down like a bull with a heavy cart and stomped his foot. He started off strong, but on the back straight, his strength gave out, and his legs began to quake. He barely made it back to the line. As Coach took the harness away, Jean Patrick doubted he could run a step farther. But freed from the burden, he flew, feet barely touching the ground. Life was like that, too, he thought, as he floated around the track. If only this weight of identity and politics could be lifted in the same way from his shoulders.

AT FOUR O'CLOCK, Coach called the runners off the track. "That's it for today. Short cooldown and then meet in the stands for a few words."

"Looks like I finally found a way to slow Jean Patrick down," Coach said when he had gathered the runners together.

"Now he knows how the rest of us feel," shouted Honorine, a distance runner, one of three other Tutsi on the team. A sprightly girl, skin shiny and brown like the shell of an umushwati nut, she gave many of the boys a challenge. A jovial drumbeat of heels reverberated to signal agreement.

Coach silenced the unruly group. "Tell us, Jean Patrick, did you learn anything?"

With his scratchy throat and thick head, Jean Patrick intended to say only a few words and then sit down. But in the middle of a sentence about the struggle between balance and weight, inspiration came to him, as if a hand had wiped clear a fogged windowpane.

"I learned that physics cannot be separated from running any more than running can be separated from physics. Everything in this world is about momentum and the conservation of energy, about motion deriving from a center of stillness." From somewhere in the stands, Jean Patrick heard runners groaning, a few suppressed bursts of laughter, but conviction kept him going. "What I saw is that if I want to win, I must focus every cell in my body on the shortest distance to the finish. We have all heard Coach's lectures once or twice"—again the laughter—"but when you are pulling such a weight behind you and you don't want to see the backs of eight runners getting small, small in front of you, then those words come into focus. Today, I *felt* them, absorbed them into muscle memory."

Coach took over the lecture from there, but Jean Patrick's attention faded, lulled by the wind's rhythm on the roof above the stands. He started awake as the team shuffled down the stairs. The anesthesia of excitement had worn off, and his head burned, his legs wobbled.

Daniel caught him on the bottom stair and looped an arm through his. "You OK?"

"Just tired. Lately I don't sleep well. Especially with you snoring away."

"What? That's your own snore reflecting back to you." Daniel screwed up his face. "My English professor killed a cow on my paper. I'm not going to tell Papa."

"If you paid less attention to girls and more to your books, you wouldn't have so many red marks."

"It's one time, eh? Don't act so superior." Daniel made a kissing sound with his lips. "When are you going back to Cyangugu?"

"I'm not sure. I have some things to take care of."

"Would *some things* involve Bea?"

The first drops of rain fell with a hiss in the surrounding trees. Jean Patrick followed the tremble of the leaves. He was too tired to explain. "I just hope I feel better before I go."

"Papa can give you a ride tomorrow."

"To Cyangugu? It's the opposite direction."

"No problem. Papa likes to drive in circles."

The thought made Jean Patrick laugh, and once he laughed, he started to cough and could not stop. Tears brimmed in his eyes.

Daniel pulled one of his minty candies from his jacket pocket and smiled wickedly. "As many as you need, they are yours." He tossed the mint to Jean Patrick.

"Ah!" Jean Patrick nudged him. "Success with your muzungu."

There were footsteps behind them, and Jean Patrick moved aside to let the person pass.

"Excuse me," the man said. "I was looking for a bathroom." He fell into step beside them and pulled up the brim of his cap. Jean Patrick found himself staring into Roger's eyes. "You looked like someone who would know."

Jean Patrick folded the candy wrapper into tiny squares. "Daniel," he said, applying the same concentration to his tone that he had applied to the truck tire, "I'll show this guy where to go and then meet you in the room."

"Why don't I come with you, huh?"

"Can you go and put water on for tea? I don't feel so well."

Daniel showed Jean Patrick the mint on his tongue and trotted off toward the dorm. When he turned the corner, Jean Patrick gripped his brother. "Mistah Cool! What's your news?"

"My news is good. And you, Mr. Olympics?"

"As well. Wah! If I had passed you on the street, I would not have known you." Roger's face was leaner, cut to the bone, the high cheeks and square jaw more pronounced. A scar divided his cheek like a boundary line sketched on a map.

"Good. That is what I wanted to hear from you." Roger's eyes scanned the trees and the field, flitted to the horizon, came back to Jean Patrick. He pulled down his cap and began walking. "Come. You're supposed to be showing me where I can relieve myself."

Jean Patrick poked the wiry growth on Roger's chin. "Is this supposed to be a beard?"

"It is." Roger poked back. "Tough guy, eh? I saw you pull that tire around the track. Me, I remember when you fell in the dirt trying to catch me."

"You saw that? Mana mfasha. You are always spying on me from the trees."

Roger lit a cigarette and threw the match onto the wet earth, where it sizzled. "More than you know, Little Brother."

They had reached the bathroom. Students pushed and shoved along the path. Roger stood close to Jean Patrick, and with a shock Jean Patrick realized he was nearly a head taller than his older brother.

"Your water will be boiled away," Roger said. "There is a small restaurant called Aux Délices. Do you know it?" Jean Patrick shook his head. "It's on a small dirt road just up from the Ibis. You have to watch for the path or you will miss it. It's quiet there—private. We can talk. Can you meet me in forty-five minutes?"

"If I have to crawl." Jean Patrick squeezed Roger's arms, his unyielding biceps. "They keep you fit, eh? I am waiting to hear your news."

"And you." Roger returned the squeeze, but the mischievous joy that had always spilled from his eyes was gone. He turned on his heels in the same military way Jean Patrick had come to know in Coach, and veered toward the woods. He disappeared on a small, hidden path as if he were a student and walked the trail every day.

Aux Délices was just a few tables in the back of a store. By the shabby front door a tethered goat, most likely doomed for dinner, walked the circumference of its rope and complained loudly. Jean Patrick found Roger drinking a Primus at a table in the corner. Again the sight of his brother startled him: the angled face, the restless eyes half-hidden by his cap.

Roger stepped free of the tiny table and embraced Jean Patrick. At least now they could hold each other, stand together cheek against cheek. Roger touched Jean Patrick's forehead. "You're burning up."

"Just a cold. It's become an old friend, overlong in my company."

The storekeeper came by, and Roger ordered two Primuses, rice and peas, brochettes with chips and bananas. He must have seen Jean Patrick's raised eyebrows because he held up his hand. "Keep away from your pocket. I'm buying. In celebration of the end of your first term, which I can guess was brilliant."

"Some things went better than others."

"Ah. Sounds like a girl is involved."

"Finished. Past tense: *was.*" He unwrapped the remaining candy from Daniel and put it in his mouth. The thought of Bea left a sour taste in his mouth. The storekeeper brought their beers and poured.

"Was it you or she who said good-bye? Cheers."

Jean Patrick and Roger clinked glasses. "Cheers. *She* left *me,* but she'll be back." It was wrong to ask Imana favors, but Jean Patrick let his prediction float skyward, toward Imana's listening ears.

"You sound confident."

"You know me."

Roger drank deeply. "Yes, murumuna wanjye, my brother, I believe I do."

After the beer had loosened his tongue, Jean Patrick spoke his full and aching heart. "I can't say why I think such a fancy Hutu girl could like me. Her father, Niyonzima, is a professor at National University and a well-known journalist, writing for many journals. He was schooled in Britain."

"Niyonzima Augustin?"

"You've heard of him?"

"In the RPF, we know who our friends are. Niyonzima Augustin is a very good one."

Jean Patrick knew Roger was circling around the reason he had risked so much to come. He also knew that when his brother was ready, he would speak his mind.

A group of soldiers came into the store and sat down at a nearby table. They were dressed in green uniforms, green military caps. Roger nodded to them, and they nodded back. "RPF," Roger said. And then, in a low voice: "They are stationed in Mulindi, as I am now."

"You are in Mulindi and I am just now hearing it?" Jean Patrick could have danced an Intore step to know his brother was back in Rwanda, just sixty kilometers north of Kigali.

Roger pushed the last brochette toward Jean Patrick and laughed. "Those guys are here for a volleyball game against the Rwandan Army. A friendly competition. It's all official—see how they wear their uniforms proudly in the open air? Arranged by the government." His lips curled into a smile. "One of the few positive developments to come from the Arusha peace talks. The various parties decided we should get together and work things out eye to eye. I guess they see volleyball as a first step."

Jean Patrick watched the soldiers as he had watched Isaka and the others in the forest in Cyangugu—with a twinge of envy. Roger ordered more beers, and when they arrived, he leaned forward and folded his hands on the table. "Does your coach ask after me?" he said.

"Every once in a while. He keeps track of me, knows each time I move my little toe. I just try and change the subject so he's not asking, asking."

"And he doesn't press you? Do you think he suspects?"

Jean Patrick shrugged. "What can he do?" He sneezed twice in rapid succession. Roger gave him the customary blessing—urachire, be rich—and Jean Patrick responded in turn—twese, all of us.

"Did you know Rutembeza was Rwandan Army?"

"He told me—one of the few facts Coach has ever revealed about himself."

"My commander served with him. He said he was extremely tough—cold blooded but fair. You better watch yourself with that guy."

"Your major was Rwandan Army?"

"He was. He saw the way the army was going and fled to Uganda to save his life." Roger tapped the table. "I mean what I say; never sleep with both your eyes at the same time when Rutembeza's around. Are you hearing me?"

"I hear you, my brother," Jean Patrick said. But what choice did he have? He couldn't just leave Coach and train with someone else. "In this country, many people have served in the army. It means nothing. Anyway, that is all the past. Ejo hashize: yesterday." Done with his lecture, Jean Patrick wiped his mouth, crumpled his napkin, and put it on his plate. "Is this what you came to tell me?" Heat rose in his face. His head was not right, and if he didn't take care about what he said and how he said it, talk could boil up quickly.

"Not only that." Roger shook a cigarette from his pack, lit it, and let the match burn nearly to his finger. "Our friend Isaka — One Shot — stepped on a mine." Jean Patrick's throat constricted. Before he could ask, Roger said, "By some miracle he's alive, but his leg is gone below the knee." At the next table, the RPF soldiers laughed at some joke, whooping and drumming their palms on the plastic cloth. Roger glanced in their direction. "But he said now you will have to compete for him as well, so you better start training for the marathon."

"Isaka!" Jean Patrick smiled sadly and shook his head. "Too much he liked to talk. Sometimes we would go for a run, and he would tell me about his neighbors and cousins in Bisesero who stood up to the Hutu with bows and arrows if they came with mischief on their minds. He could run forever. Even me, he tired me out." Jean Patrick swallowed the last of his beer. "You know, the marathon is a very long way to run, but you tell One Shot that for him, I will do it."

A BLUSTERY RAIN fell as Jean Patrick and Roger left Aux Délices. They had remained far after everyone else had left, and they made their way toward the university, leaning on each other for warmth and stability. Jean Patrick's clothes clung to his skin. He tried to control his drunken sway, but the walk did him in. In the shadow of a tree, he vomited until the contents of his stomach lay at his feet. He began to shiver and could not stop.

Roger led him to a doorway, helped him out of his soaked jacket, and rubbed warmth back into his skin. A truck approached, the headlights momentarily pinning them. The window opened, and a bottle sailed out. It exploded in a spray of glass against the building where they stood. The wheels spun in the mud as the truck accelerated, leaving in its wake a rusty rooster tail.

"Let's wait here and see if the storm lets up," Roger said. He stripped to his shirt. "You really are sick. Stand next to me for warmth." Jean Patrick pressed against his brother. "Nearer still." The friction of Roger's hands took the edge off his shaking. "Don't be afraid. Pretend I'm that girl, the one you are chasing," Roger said.

"Bea," Jean Patrick said between chatters.

"OK. So I am Bea." He made kissing sounds. "Umukunzi wanjye, come and kiss me." They both laughed.

Jean Patrick saw Roger in the high forests of the Virungas, drenched to the marrow and no fire to keep him warm. "Were you with Isaka when it happened?" Slowly his brother's heat penetrated and spread through Jean Patrick's body.

"Like slow motion, I saw the whole thing. His leg extended, his foot ready to step, his head turning to slap at a bug. We thought we had cleared the area, but apparently we had not. I've witnessed much death, but this was different." As he told the story, he rubbed Jean Patrick's arms and shoulders. "One Shot was my brother. As close as I could get to you."

A river coursed through the center of the road. If he could have, Jean Patrick would have wept. Not just for Isaka, but for the children in Kigali, the women murdered behind the arboretum. He would have wept for Anastase, the confident, smiling woman from Bugesera whose memory lived in a photograph and in a flame that must still burn in Roger's heart. "If it happened to me," he said, "I'd wish for death. I could not live if I couldn't run."

"Don't ever say that." Roger held him at arm's length. "You never know until fate hunts you down and finds you. One Shot is a soldier. Death and injury lay down with him at night, and when he wakes, they are there to kiss him good morning. He will find a way to overcome, as you would." He shook out Jean Patrick's jacket and helped him into it. "May God never put you to the test. This rain is here to stay, eh? Let's go."

With his stomach cleansed of alcohol, Jean Patrick felt better. Roger was right. Jean Patrick couldn't compare himself to a soldier, but for every blow he suffered, he found a way to adjust, to seek a new equilibrium. "Where are you staying tonight?" He looked at his watch; it was nearly curfew. The lights and noise of town grew faint behind them. Rain and darkness stretched before them.

Roger shook another cigarette from the almost empty pack. "Just like a little boy: always questions, questions. I will walk you to school, and then I will leave you." He chortled. "Eh—I saw your picture with Habyarimana. You looked terrified, but don't worry—only a brother could notice. I showed the whole unit. *Look,* I said, *what a star my brother is.*"

If Jean Patrick hadn't seen the proud smile on Roger's face, he would have thought he mocked him. "They gave me a big party in Kigali, with hamburgers from Belgium."

"Imana bless us." Roger flicked his cigarette into the road and took Jean Patrick's arm. "Luxury meat while your brother eats rats in the jungle."

"Rats? True?"

"Next you will ask if Inkotanyi women sleep with the devil. You shouldn't believe everything you hear—that's a habit you need to break for your own safety." Roger's mood turned serious. "Remember that with your coach, and when you shake Habyarimana's hand."

"What can I do?" Jean Patrick said. "I have to get to the Olympics. Coach has been good to me. He treats me like his son." Jean Patrick's voice echoed too loud inside his head. Did he want to convince himself or Roger? But he had seen a look, fleeting, at certain moments. It was not a father's love, but it was something close, something to do with pride. "Coach needs me. Habyarimana needs me. I'm their example for the Europeans. Coach told me that."

"Need is a funny thing. Sometimes you can need someone, but when he is all used up, you toss what is left into the bush, like garbage."

"What kind of story are you telling me?" Rage boiled up in Jean Patrick.

"The story I am telling you is what I see with my two eyes. Time and time again."

They reached the university. The storm had worn itself out, now merely an inconstant sprinkle. Jean Patrick's clothes clung wetly to his body.

Roger placed two fingers against Jean Patrick's throat. "You must learn to read Rwanda's pulse. These Arusha accords are only to please the West. The government preaches peace but prepares for war. Something unimaginable is coming. I'll try to get to you if I can, to our family, but if you feel a sudden quickening of the pulse and I am not here, you must run. Alone if you have to."

"I don't understand what you are saying." Jean Patrick felt weak and dizzy. His eyes only wanted to close.

"Now go. Dry off and get warm." He pressed his face to Jean Patrick's, then disappeared into the bush. "May God keep you in his hands." Roger's blessing floated out, disembodied, from the darkness.

Faint strands of music carried from the guardhouse. The guard peered out from his shelter, eyes blurry with sleep and age. "Not two minutes to spare," he said with a chuckle when Jean Patrick presented his card. "Run home with Imana's blessings," the old man chanted, and he waved him through.

Jean Patrick wanted to chase after his brother, to hold him until he explained. It was too much. The whole evening had been too much. The news about Isaka, the strange warnings. What about the children? he wanted to shout. Who will protect them? Who will tell them to run when the time comes? Who will protect Isaka, now that he is all used up?

DAWN, DIRTY AND gray, invaded the room. Rain hissed on the roof and battered the window. Jean Patrick awoke with his fever still keeping him company. Glass splinters cut his throat when he swallowed. The onslaught of noise from Daniel's direction was like blows to his head. A balled shirt sailed past him and hit the wall. "Are you planning to greet Pascal from there?"

"I think so. I don't know if I'll ever get well." Jean Patrick rubbed his temples. "Do you have any more of those candies?" A handful of mints landed on the blanket. Jean Patrick raised his eyebrows.

Daniel said, "I wanted her to taste urwagwa, so I bought a jug."

"And she drank like a Rwandan?"

"With a straw. True Rwandan. Aye! She kisses nice." Daniel snapped a pair of pants to straighten them. "She's French. Papa hates the French."

"Your papa doesn't have to kiss her."

Daniel stuffed a last shirt into his overfull suitcase.

"Your papa would beat you if he saw the way you packed," Jean Patrick said.

"Is he here?" Daniel grunted, but he took out the shirt, folded it, and placed it carefully on top of his other clothes. He forced the suitcase shut.

Jean Patrick would have killed for a drink of water. "When is he coming?"

"I don't know. Did you change your mind about the ride?"

It was tempting. Bundle himself in warm clothes, lock the door, leave all his crazy thinking behind. "No. I have too much to do."

"You never answered my question yesterday about Bea."

Last evening's confidence had deserted him. "Bea can get a good Hutu man, a rich one. She doesn't need me."

"And you—you're going to win the Olympics. That's nothing?"

"I have not won yet. The way I feel right now, I might never win a race again."

The pin-striped suit landed on his bed. "Go and talk to her. Papa will give you a ride."

Jean Patrick sat up and cradled his pulsing head in his hands. "Bea is finished. Kwa heri—good-bye."

"I am telling you—I know what I'm talking about. Put on your fancy suit and knock on her door like the king of Rwanda."

"Mwami also is good-bye. You Hutu finished the monarchy." Jean Patrick crawled back beneath the blanket and closed his eyes.

It was afternoon when he awoke again. Daniel paced the small space between the beds. "Have you been walking all morning?" Jean Patrick said. "You could have traveled to Kigali by now, saved Pascal a trip."

"I don't like when Papa is late."

"You sound just like him now, predicting the end of the world. How do you know what late is, since you don't know when he is supposed to come?" He closed his eyes again and drifted. A rap at the door jolted him awake.

Pascal began speaking the minute he came into the room. He had blood on his raincoat and on his pants. "Don't worry," he said. He took off his jacket and his muddy boots. "This blood isn't mine. There was an accident on the road from Kigali, and I stopped to help."

Instinctively, Jean Patrick shivered. "Did someone die?"

"No, thank God. There was . . ." Pascal scowled. His hands jerked as if he were trying to pull from the air the right way to continue.

"I'm just glad it wasn't you. I was beginning to worry." Daniel hung Pascal's jacket on the chair. "Did the police come?"

"The man wouldn't wait; you know how long it takes to fetch them. Something, maybe a boulder, hit his car. Tore off the roof and smashed the windshield. He's lucky to be alive. I offered to take him to hospital, but he refused." Pascal lit a cigarette and exhaled a deep draft of smoke. "He was losing blood, so I bandaged him with my undershirt; it was all I had. He barely waited for that. I don't know how he will manage to drive in this rain." He looked first at Daniel and then at Jean Patrick as if noticing them for the first time. He swept each of them into a quick embrace.

Something—he couldn't put a finger on what—made Jean Patrick mistrust Pascal's story. He was too agitated, too upset. A soldier, after all, would be used to the sight of blood.

Pascal regarded Jean Patrick. "You're burning up. Even through my shirt I can feel it."

"Jean Patrick is sick from love," Daniel announced. "I told him we would take him home, but he refused. I told him we would take him to his umukunzi, but he refused. What else can I do?" He made a face and put on his boots.

"We'll need to hurry to get back to Kigali before curfew, but can we take you somewhere? A doctor?" Pascal put his palm to Jean Patrick's forehead. "You're hot as a coal."

"Go. I'll be fine." He shooed them toward the door.

"The rest of the candies are on the desk. Don't forget my advice." Daniel hefted his suitcase and followed his father into the rain.

MOST OF THE students had left for vacation. No music drifted through the walls, no loud talk interrupted his thoughts, no RTLM stirred up his blood. Jean Patrick put on socks and pulled a sweater over his sweatshirt. Trying to concentrate was hopeless, but a ragged energy, fed by his fever, simmered. He picked up the pin-striped suit, put it down again, picked it up, and returned it to the shelf. He picked up his jacket from the floor where he must have dropped it when he came home. A scrap of green cloth protruded from the pocket. He pulled out a green bandanna and a note.

I thought you might want this. It belonged to our friend. Suddenly, Jean Patrick recalled Isaka's taking the bandanna to wrap his foot in the forest near Cyangugu. How had Roger managed to slip note and scarf into his pocket? He hid the note inside his physics text. Then he pocketed the bandanna, put on shoes and his jacket, and stepped outside.

Only a few lights shone in the buildings. The rain had tapered into mist. It seemed pointless to remain in the dorm, sick and alone. It had been nearly twenty-four hours since he had eaten or even had a sip of water, and the cafeteria was dark. Behind his glazed eyes, the windows in Bea's house beckoned like glowing candles.

Once more he unfolded the pin-striped suit. He brushed out the creases and dressed. Over the suit he put on his tracksuit to keep him dry. Maybe Daniel was right: if he came to Bea's gate like a great king, she would reconsider. Taking a flashlight from Daniel's drawer, Jean Patrick set out. Near Cyarwa, he heard a faint bleating. He looked down to see a billy goat in step beside him. Either this journey is written, or my fever is talking, he thought. Here is Rugira, my ram, come to accompany me. And so I must be Gihanga, half of heaven and half of the earth, setting off to navigate my earthly domain.

JEAN PATRICK RESTED his forehead against the cool metal of Bea's gate. He called again, rattled the bolt; no one came. Night drifted down. Rain had soaked his clothing. Thirty seconds, and he would leave. At twenty-eight seconds, the front door opened.

"Jean Patrick, is that you?"

Jean Patrick let the sound of Bea's voice fill him. "It is."

"My God. You are completely insane." She unlocked the gate and let him in.

"I am."

Niyonzima stepped out from the doorway with his sleeves rolled up to his elbows. "Bea? Who's there?"

"It's Jean Patrick. He walked here in the storm. He has drowned."

"Don't keep him standing there. Bring him inside."

"Be strong, Jean Patrick," Bea said before locking the gate behind him.

Jean Patrick puzzled over her meaning, but the next moment he saw, pulled into the far corner of the yard, a car with the roof torn off, the windshield and windows gone. He felt his heart in his throat. Was he still in his room, wading through a fevered nightmare? Was Pascal still recounting his story of the accident, only to have it come to life in Jean Patrick's mind? The earth lurched up to meet him. If Bea had not taken his arm, he might have fallen.

"I shouldn't have come," he said.

Niyonzima came out into the rain and took his other arm. "Nonsense. You are always welcome. Come inside—you are indeed drowned." His shirt was spotted with blood.

At the table sat a shirtless man. He nodded to Jean Patrick, and despite his obvious pain, he smiled. His left arm was bandaged, supported by a sling; his left eye, swollen shut and purple beneath a jagged, seeping gash. Small wounds peppered his flesh. Ineza bent over him, picking out shards of glass with tweezers. Jean Patrick thought to pinch himself to see if he was awake. Could it be that here, in front of him, was the man Pascal had stopped to help?

The man extended his right hand. "Félicien Gatabazi. Sorry if I don't stand to greet you properly, but you should know I'm a big fan of yours." He squinted like a mole suddenly come up into the light.

Gingerly, Jean Patrick took his hand. "I'm sorry. Your name is familiar to me, but I can't say how or why. Did we meet at the reception in Kigali?" The room began to spin. Sweat beaded on his skin, and Jean Patrick worried that this friend of Bea's would judge him for his slippery palm.

Bea pursed her lips. "Félicien Gatabazi is the minister of public works, and head of our Parti Social Démocrate, the party to lead Rwanda into the future."

A sound like a mosquito's whine grew until it filled Jean Patrick's head.

His field of vision shrank, and he realized he was about to faint. If he sat, he might be all right, but a bloody shirt lay across the nearest chair. Instead he took a step toward the wall so he could lean against it. The floor opened beneath him, and he fell through.

He opened his eyes, believing he was underwater and had to swim to the surface. As awareness returned, the water became a bed. He breathed in Bea's scent from the sheets. Ineza's face orbited above him and then became still.

"Good evening." She held a cup in her hands. The steam smelled of grass and citrus. "You frightened us. The second scare of the day."

"I'm sorry. I should have stayed at the dorm."

"And be sick alone?" She set the cup on the nightstand and propped pillows behind his head. "You must drink."

The tea tasted of hot pepper and lemon, sweet with honey. It soothed the burn in his throat. "When I came, I was not thinking well."

"You were thinking with your heart, but I will keep your secret," she said. "Are you better now? Will you stay in the world awhile?"

The lilt of Ineza's voice, her tender care, unlocked Jean Patrick. Warmth spread through his chest. "I think so. Have I been sleeping a long time?"

"Maybe an hour."

He shifted his weight, and the cloth of someone's bulky shorts bunched between his legs. In a panic, he sat up and clutched the blanket to his chest.

"Claire is wringing the weather from your nice suit and your track clothes," Ineza said. "When did you last eat?"

Bea's voice drifted down the hall, and he cocked his head to hear. "Not since yesterday, I think."

"No wonder you fainted. I'll ask Bea to bring something for you."

Jean Patrick settled back against the pillow and swallowed more of Ineza's herbs. His eyes took in the room. His picture was there on Bea's desk. Beside the photo was the pirogue he had given her, the fishermen still bent to their oars. "I would like that," he said.

Bea brought a tray with soup and a piece of bread and margarine. "You made quite an entrance," she said. She pulled her stool next to the bed.

Jean Patrick took a spoonful of soup. It was thick and pungent, creamy with vegetables and cassava leaves. He thought he might live. "Did you make this?"

"If I had, you would not be smiling so."

He dunked the bread into the soup and ate it. "It was Daniel's father who helped Gatabazi on the road," he said, gauging Bea's face for reaction. "He told us a strange story. I thought maybe he was protecting me, because of what happened to my father."

Bea confirmed nothing, denied nothing. She rose and shut the curtains. "Finish your soup and get some rest." Before closing the door and turning off the lights, she smiled at him. It was a faint smile, but Jean Patrick held on to it. He did as Bea asked, wiping the bowl clean with the last of the bread. From the pillow, he breathed in the air Bea had breathed and let sleep carry him.

THE DAY RETURNED to Jean Patrick in fits and starts. He winced at the thought of the picture he must have made at her gate. He did not know how long he had slept. Claire had pressed his clothes—even the track pants and jacket—and hung them up to finish drying. In a flash, he saw himself tucking Isaka's bandanna into his jacket pocket. He kicked off the covers and searched; it was gone.

Ineza came in with a shirt and sweater and a pair of sweatpants. "These will have to do until your clothes dry, unless you want to wear one of my pagnes." She set a pair of flip-flops on the rug. Everything would be far too small. "Are you well enough to eat with us?"

"I could go back to the dorm now," he said. "I don't want to stick my head into your private matters."

"Don't talk foolishness. You are welcome here, as our son."

A polite silence greeted Jean Patrick when he came to the table. Bea laughed first to break the mood. "It's an improvement over your appearance at the gate," she said. "At least you no longer resemble a chicken swimming to its death."

Jean Patrick's fever had broken. He was happy when Ineza piled his plate high.

Gatabazi's clothes must also have been Niyonzima's, but the two men were nearly the same size. One sleeve of his shirt hung empty, his left arm immobilized against his chest. Although Ineza cut his meat into small pieces, he struggled to get his food onto the fork. "I miss my arm and my glasses," he said.

"The arm I can do nothing about, but if your eyesight is as bad as mine, I will lend you a pair of glasses," Niyonzima said.

"My good friend," Gatabazi said, "you know it is far worse." A car drove slowly down the road, and they all sat up to listen. Gatabazi squinted his good eye in the window's direction, and Jean Patrick realized he must be quite blind.

Talk wandered here and there. At some point, Niyonzima would fold his hands and begin to speak. Then Jean Patrick could make some sense of the afternoon. Ever since he had learned of the mine that killed the schoolchildren, the events in his life seemed to tumble down a path of their own making.

Claire cleared the dishes and set down a bowl of fruit and a thermos of tea. When she had closed the door behind her, Niyonzima cleared his throat and folded his hands on the table. "My daughter has been against speaking to you frankly," he said.

"In these times, ignorance is a blessing." Bea's eyes flashed. Her glance flitted to her mother, then back to Niyonzima. "Knowledge can be a dangerous thing."

Niyonzima shook his head. "Ineza and I think differently."

Jean Patrick could not think clearly. Since his head still swam, he let the current of Niyonzima's words carry him. He hoped that when he reached the shore, Bea would be there, extending her hand to him.

"As you doubtless know, this country becomes more dangerous every day for those who are not graced with the government's good favor," Niyonzima said. "You are in the spotlight, and you must be mindful of the company you keep." He put a hand on Bea's shoulder. "You risk your future if you are seen with those of us who openly oppose the government. It was Bea's wish to sweep you from her door and make that decision for you, but she has agreed that we should speak plainly to you and let you decide for yourself. Whatever your answer, it must be given from your mind and not your heart."

After days of crashing around without direction, Jean Patrick had found the pointing needle of the compass. "I don't have to decide. I know already."

Niyonzima held up his hand. "Consider carefully. If you stay, understand that you have walked into a dangerous room, and that once you have come inside, you cannot change your mind and go out again."

"And don't forget there is someone else to consider," Bea said. "Your coach holds your future in his hands. He watches the company you keep." She pointed her knife at Jean Patrick and then peeled and sliced the mango on her plate.

With the mention of his coach, the last variable in the equation fell into place. It was Coach who had refused to greet Niyonzima properly, who told Jolie that Jean Patrick was *involved with a girl, and not a good one.* All this time, Bea had been trying to protect him. He took the slice of mango she offered and let it slither down his throat.

He would not be forced to choose between one future and the other. He had come out in the rain, burning with fever, to say his piece, and now he would say it. He had two fists; he could grasp one dream in each. "I can't let worry beat me," he said. "Any more than I can let an opponent beat me on the track. From the first day I saw Bea, I knew I would do what I had to in order to win her."

"That is not the right reason," Bea said.

"It is the only reason I have."

"My father went to prison a strong man." Bea's voice trembled. "When he came out, I thought the white-haired grandfather limping toward us was a stranger. He looked like the walking dead, and I told the guard, 'You have made a mistake. This man is not my father.' As you see, he has never fully recovered. This is what Habyarimana does to his enemies. Do not think you will be immune."

Ineza covered Bea's hand with hers. "You must look with your eyes open into this room before you decide to enter."

Gatabazi pulled his chair closer. He had been so quiet that Jean Patrick had forgotten his presence. "Bea told us it was your friend's father who helped me on the road. You must thank him for me. I believe I owe him my life."

"Pascal said a rock hit your car."

"I can tell you don't believe it."

"As a student of physics and engineering, I was confused by the mechanics, especially when I saw your car. If such a big boulder hit the roof, how could you live?"

"One hundred percent!" Gatabazi nodded his approval. "I will tell you the truth. A truck came up behind me, going very fast. When he pulled out to pass, he came very close, and the passenger threw something out the window. I knew immediately it was a grenade, but all I could do was steer into the bush and dive for cover. This time they failed, but they will try again. Eventually they will succeed. No matter—they can't stop me from speaking out."

Jean Patrick recalled Bea's comment on the morning she first told him about her father. Like Niyonzima, Gatabazi loved Rwanda enough to die for her. "Do you know who it was?"

"Perhaps the extremists, perhaps someone from Habyarimana's inner circle. I am a thorn in all their sides. We in the PSD, the Parti Social Démocrate, are trying to free Rwanda from Habyarimana's stranglehold on power. We want a coalition government, and we want to share power with the RPF. The extremists can't accept that."

"I've been waiting for the government to grow impatient with my articles and speeches again," Niyonzima said. "Even with our Tutsi préfet, I don't know if I can remain safe, but that is a risk we have all accepted." Sweat shone on Niyonzima's skin, and it gave the appearance of a glow coming from within, from his passion.

Now that Jean Patrick understood why Bea had left him, he would plant his feet firmly and hold on. Just two months before, Habyarimana had thrown a party in his honor, and Jean Patrick had shaken his hand. It was foolish to think anyone would want to hurt him, and he wished everyone would stop worrying over him. All he wanted was to run and to have Bea beside him. "I understand what you are telling me. But as I said, I did not come here in the bad weather to let doubt beat me down."

ONLY BEA AND Jean Patrick remained awake. Gatabazi, asleep in Niyonzima's study, snored softly. Rain struck the window and slid down in tiny streams. Jean Patrick studied their trace on the glass a moment before he spoke. "There was a scarf, a green one, in my pocket. Do you know what happened to it?"

Bea put a hand to her mouth. "Just a minute." She went to the kitchen and returned with the bandanna. "This?" She held it out, crumpled and wet, to Jean Patrick. "I found it in the bathroom, on the clothesline. I thought it was a rag for cleaning."

Jean Patrick cupped it in his palm. "It belonged to a friend." Another door better left locked and guarded, but he opened it and invited Bea inside. "He stepped on a mine." Bea gasped again. "He didn't die, but he lost his leg."

"You surprise me, Nkuba Jean Patrick. I see we both have secrets." She looked out the window at the rain. "Is he RPF?"

Jean Patrick took a deep breath. "Yes. We ran together at Gihundwe. He was a great distance runner. Our last year, he just disappeared, never came back from vacation. People said he had been killed, but then I got a message—he wants me to run for him in the Olympics." He chuckled. "The marathon." None of this was a lie. Jean Patrick was merely selecting his truths, a lesson he was quickly learning. Roger's story jumped onto his tongue, trying to find a way into the room, but Jean Patrick stilled it. That was a secret he needed to let sleep.

"My God, you'll die," Bea said. "I've seen you after eight hundred meters."

Jean Patrick thought of the photograph in her room, and his heart grew full. "True enough. But I need some way to honor him. His spirit is so strong."

"I have an idea." Bea disappeared and came back with a sketchbook. She turned the pages—flowers, her backyard, Claire's children, portraits of Niyonzima and Ineza—until she came to a sketch of three men, two black and one white, standing on the medal podium at the Olympics. The two black athletes raised black-gloved fists. They wore no shoes, just black socks beneath rolled-up pants. All three athletes had large white buttons pinned to their warm-ups. The title of the sketch was *Mexico City, 1968.*

"I drew this from a scrapbook my father kept. Long before he heard my first cry, he saved important newspaper articles for his children." A faint smile graced her lips. "And of course to study how they were written."

"You drew this?"

"I did."

Jean Patrick passed his hand lightly above the page as if to absorb its energy. "Like your mama's painting, it comes alive."

"They were protesting apartheid in South Africa and racism in America. I was so moved. They could have lost their medals, but they were willing to take the chance for their beliefs."

"Why are you showing me this?" Jean Patrick felt a twinge of annoyance. He did not want to be pushed into anyone's politics.

Bea touched her finger to the gold medalist. "His name is Tommie Smith. You can't see it, but he also wore a black scarf to stand for black pride."

"A scarf! Mana yanjye! I don't have to run the marathon after all. I just have to wear my friend's scarf in the eight hundred. But me, when I win a medal, I will not chance anyone taking it away."

"One more thing," Bea said.

She leaned closer to flip the pages. He felt her quiet, steady breath, her heat. Suddenly, Jean Patrick was looking into his own face, sketched from the photograph on her desk. He believed she had captured him perfectly, down to the mix of pain and transcendent joy radiant in his eyes.

1994

TWENTY

JEAN PATRICK HAD BEEN HOME for Christmas vacation when he heard the announcement on the radio that Gatabazi's PSD party would get what they had struggled so hard to achieve—a role in a transitional government. For the first time, they would share in power and have a true voice in shaping Rwanda's future. Jean Patrick and Uncle had celebrated with urwagwa, sipping the banana beer from a common straw, but as they sat and watched evening swallow the lake, Uncle wagged a finger. "This does not mean Tutsi should sleep with both eyes at the same time," he said, the same words Roger had used to warn Jean Patrick about Coach. When he heard them again, uneasiness crept from the mist to sit beside him in his rickety chair. Its presence stuck with him for the rest of vacation and even on the bus ride back to Butare.

Now, the day of the swearing-in, Jean Patrick tried to shake nervousness from his fingers as he prepared for his workout. This morning, Bea and Niyonzima had gone to Kigali to watch the ceremony, and to keep his mind going in one direction, Jean Patrick had come to the track to run. The workout was pinned to his shorts: a series of four hundred meters, fast, followed by a two-hundred-meter recovery, then four eight hundreds at race pace. He was on his last four hundred, not looking forward to the eights. A trace of sluggishness from his cold still lingered. Much of the time he was home, he had been too sick to run. This was his first attempt to return to his training, and yesterday's rough bus journey from Cyangugu had not helped.

He passed the start line and glanced at his watch: not good. The watch was new—a Timex, a Christmas gift from Coach. He had found it folded inside the package of workouts Coach had left for him, along with a note.

This will substitute for me. The Americans have created a miracle, keeping track of ten laps at once. Which you will write down in my absence.

Seeing his four hundred time, Jean Patrick wished he didn't have the reminder. He wished he had Coach to push him, the rest of the team to challenge him. On his own, his muscles tired and out of shape from too much rest, he couldn't reach his goals. There was at least one good thing: the truck tire existed only in memory. Coach would reinstate this torture when he returned, but for the present he had disappeared. Jean Patrick had gone to see him as soon as he returned, but Jolie said he was not expected back before the end of vacation. When he asked where Coach had gone, Jolie called him inshyanutsi—a nosy one.

Jean Patrick slowed for his recovery, shook out his fingers, tried to find in his legs the tempo he had lost. At his peak, he felt as if he sliced the air when he ran. Now he pushed against it, left jagged flaps of it in his wake. Crossing the start for his first eight hundred, he called back the memory of New Year's Day with his family to keep him company.

"I AM TELLING YOU," Uncle Emanuel said. "These days, prosperity opens her arms to me. I have seen a motorboat and soon it will be mine." The table was crowded with family and neighbors, piled high with food. Mukabera brought a large dish of igisafuria, made from a plump hen and her own peanuts ground into a spicy sauce. The front door remained open, and all day people from the surrounding hills came to say umwaka mwiza, happy New Year, and to share food and urwagwa. Even now, on the track, the vision made Jean Patrick smile.

He brought back the taste of the ibijumba n'ikivuguto his mother had made him. He saw himself take a sip of thick, sweetened milk, a bite of sweet potato, letting the two mix and melt in his mouth. Surrounded by family, the smells and tastes of his childhood cooking, he could almost believe he had returned to his previous life, one with two feet planted on the earth.

"Uncle," he joked, "all these years I broke my back paddling, and now that I'm gone, you get a motor?"

"I have seen this boat with my own two eyes," Fulgence said, emphasizing his words with a long draft of urwagwa and a tug at his Saint Christopher medal. "The man says it is not for sale, but me, I say if your uncle wants it, he will have it. His talk his too sweet—like honey."

Zachary sat beside Uncle with his luminous smile. He had received a scholarship for school in Kibuye. In the new term, he would begin his studies for the priesthood.

The vision gave Jean Patrick enough strength for one last brutal kick. He wheeled past the line, and the numbers on his watch gave him a glimmer of hope.

The second eight hundred proved harder than the first. He probably went out too fast. Maybe, finally, he was beginning to understand what Coach meant by *pace*. For distraction he recited the names of minerals found in Rwanda: *cassiterite, columbite, tantalite, wolframite,* quickening the tempo of the chant as he pounded the dirt. Another tenth of a second shaved from his time. For the third eight hundred, he switched to physics: *Energy is the property of matter and radiation manifested as a capacity to perform work. Energy. Energy. Energy.* He was two-tenths slower and had to jog a little extra to regain his breath.

For the final eight hundred, he conjured up Bea in her blue shawl (*azurite, beryl, chrysocolla*) her skin (*cinnabar*) gleaming in the room's dim light (*serpentine, olivine, mysterious minerals of the sea*). She hovered in front, his rabbit, exiting turns as he entered. The finish wavered in front of him. He crossed and stopped his watch and then doubled over, nothing left to give. Three-tenths of a second shaved. Now he knew he was clawing his way back. For luck, he touched the knot of Isaka's bandanna at his neck.

When he regained his breath and looked up into the stands, Bea was watching him, as if he had truly called her forth. He waved and trotted toward her. Taking the steps two at a time, he shouted, "I broke my own record in the eight hundred. Could you tell?" Bea covered her face with her hands, and his stomach twisted. "What's wrong?" He took his track pants from the bench and pulled them on. "I thought you'd be happy today. You got your wish."

"There is no new government. Habyarimana had himself sworn in, and then he left. It was a complete joke."

Jean Patrick sat beside her. "I thought everything was settled. What happened?" He recalled Uncle's warning. The heat of exhilaration drained from his body, the sharp chill of afternoon taking its place.

Bea pulled her jacket around her. "Will you eat with us? You don't have to change; no one will care." The sheen of her tears gave her eyes a hard, polished look, like metal.

"I'm soaking wet. Let me get dry and put on clothes. Pass by my room with me." He looked out across the field, the road above the track. He saw no one there to watch or judge, so he put his arm around her and led her down the steps. "Shh," he said. "Shh. It's OK."

Bea shook her head. "No. Nothing is OK."

What heat was left in the day had fled. Soon the light would follow it, vanishing behind the hills. "Tell me," he said.

"None of us believed Habyarimana meant to proceed, so we went with our eyes open. There was a big crowd outside the parliament building, shouting, joking, milling about together. It felt festive. Dadi and I began to get excited. We thought maybe we had been wrong, maybe our dream would come to pass after all." She paused to wipe her cheek. Her malachite bracelets jangled. "Habyarimana and his convoy came zooming up like Hollywood gangsters, horns blaring, weaving so fast and crazy we all had to jump out of their way. Even UNAMIR troops—they almost ran them over. The Presidential Guard leapt from the trucks, waving their guns and machetes, and swarmed into the crowd. They had on civilian clothes, but no one was fooled." Bea trembled. Jean Patrick thought it was from cold, but when she turned to him and held his gaze, he saw the anger. "They were the petrol poured on the smoldering fire," she said. "Of course the mob ignited."

Jean Patrick knew the face of this force. Frenzy shimmering like chemical vapors, the flash point dangerously low. He had looked it in the eye. "Was anyone hurt?"

"Not seriously, as far as I know. But the crowd attacked the moderate candidates—PSD and the other allied parties—as they tried to enter the building. They couldn't pass. We planned to follow Habyarimana inside, but when we realized what was happening, we stayed in the street to help protect the delegates, because the police did nothing. I heard Dadi yell, and when I looked around, he was on the ground, someone hitting him. Finally some UNAMIR soldiers stepped in and saved him."

"And until then, UNAMIR did nothing?"

"They protected those few they could, but they did not step in." Bea stopped to remove a stone from her sandal. "I do not think we can count on them, if it comes to that."

They had reached Jean Patrick's dorm and stood outside the door. Aside from two women strolling arm in arm on the path to the library, the campus was deserted, everyone still home for vacation. "Come in with me," Jean Patrick said. "You can close your eyes while I dress." He opened the door and turned on the light.

Bea paused as if weighing her options in her two hands. For a moment, Jean Patrick thought the balance would tip against him, but then she pulled her jacket tighter and stepped inside. Jean Patrick shut the door behind her.

"What happened then?" he said.

She turned and leaned against the door, forehead pressed to the shabby wood. "We learned Habyarimana had himself sworn in with a fancy ceremony." She hugged herself. "Along with a gang of Hutu Power thugs whose names mysteriously appeared on the list instead of the true delegates— the moderates."

Jean Patrick watched Bea's back, her bowed head. He didn't know what to say, so he said nothing. He took off his clothes and toweled dry. Bea's nearness made him shiver. When he had dressed, he stood beside her.

She faced him, her body pressed against the door, as if without its support she would sink to her knees. Her cheeks shone with tears. "For the first time since my father was in prison, I'm frightened. This country is going to explode. That is what I felt today." She began to weep, and Jean Patrick raised a hand to her hair. A strand, straight and silky, had come loose from the tie that held it, and he tucked it carefully behind her ear. "God help us," she said, and she closed her fingers around his.

"You're safe now," he said. The air trembled, his words moving outward as a ripple moves out from a pebble tossed into the depths of a lake. Outside the window, a night bird whistled. A purplish dusk curled around the last wisps of daylight. They would be walking in darkness. Jean Patrick reached across her and turned out the light. Before opening the door and letting in the evening, he sang to her, "Cyusa," the song his mother used to sing to him when he was small and frightened by shadows. It was a lullaby, a mother telling her child to fear nothing because his parents would always watch over him. It was the only thing he could think of to do for Bea.

✑

It was Friday night, the Murakazaneza crowded beyond belief. Jean Patrick and Bea pushed their way inside. "I think Susanne will be easy to spot," Jean Patrick shouted into Bea's ear, in order to be heard above the onslaught.

Bea leaned into him. "What makes you so sure?" She was already moving toward the cap of blond-white hair at the center table, the focus of all eyes in the restaurant. Not even the football game on TV could compete.

In person, Susanne did not resemble a boy. She was tiny and thin, hair cropped closer than in her photo, flyaway spikes caught in a current of air. "These are my very best friends, J. P. and Bea," Jonathan announced to anyone who cared to hear. Susanne raised her head, and Jean Patrick looked into two flakes of malachite.

Jonathan called the waiter to the table. "Brochettes et chips? Plantains?"

"Sounds wonderful," Bea said as she claimed the chair beside Susanne. "It's nice to finally greet you—we hear so much of you." She kissed Susanne's cheeks Rwandan-style.

Jonathan ordered in a mixture of French, Kinyarwanda, and English. The waiter, who knew him well by now, teased him with a rapid-fire Kinyarwanda response. "And beer. Inshi, inshi Primuses!" Jonathan spread his arms wide to pantomime *many*. The waiter chuckled and disappeared into the kitchen.

Jean Patrick understood Jonathan's fire now, the way love lit him up from the inside.

The waiter returned with food and beer. Susanne's eyes looked glazed. "Excuse me if I seem a bit out of it," she said. "I've been traveling for two days; it's been a really long and insane journey." She picked up a stick of gizzards from the plate of brochettes, and Jonathan gasped.

"Probably not the best first choice," he said as he took them from her fingers.

"Try this instead." Jean Patrick gave her a goat brochette.

With the tine of her fork she pulled the meat from the stick. "Mmm! What is it?"

Jonathan spoke over Jean Patrick's response. "Beef."

Bea looked at Susanne and smiled. "How do you find our country?"

Before Jonathan could stop her, Susanne spooned pilipili over her chips. "Wow," she said, her eyes watering. "Not quite ready for that." She gulped her beer and turned to Bea. "I love Rwanda. The beautiful landscape, the friendly people. I've never seen so many breathtaking smiles. Although tonight I may need a little coffee to stay awake." She slumped against Jonathan.

Raising her beer glass, Bea said, "A toast for our New Year's celebration. Uzakubere uw'amata n'ubuki." She translated for Susanne. "May you have a year of milk and honey."

Susanne gave Bea a sleepy smile. "How funny! We say that, too — halav oo d'vash — only I think it has to do with the land of Israel instead of the New Year."

"Ha-rav oo vache." Jean Patrick tried. He couldn't get his tongue around the sounds. "*Vache* like cow?"

"Oh no — sorry — it's Hebrew." Susanne giggled.

"To milk and honey — whatever the language," Jonathan said.

Everyone clinked and drank. Jean Patrick prayed their wish would come true in any language Imana heard.

All through dinner, Susanne and Jonathan swayed into each other like drunks. Jean Patrick envied them their bold and easy touch. If he lived in a place where such things were possible, he would sweep away hesitation, throw an arm across Bea's shoulder, and kiss her in front of the world.

Empty bottles disappeared; full ones took their place. Fresh brochettes arrived to replace the piles of empty sticks. Beneath the table, Jean Patrick sought Bea's sandal. She tapped his toe with her foot. An American movie, muted, flickered in the TV's blue light. Something about a war. A haze of cigarette smoke blurred the evening's edges.

Susanne talked about her NGO, their plans to plant new trees on denuded slopes. She had majored in forestry, minored in French, and when she confessed to having been Jonathan's student, she blushed. She ate a boiled plantain slice with her fingers. "C'est si bon," she said.

"Biraryoshye cyane," Jean Patrick taught her.

Susanne would spend two weeks in Gisenyi for training, then work in a small town near Ruhengeri, on the slopes of the Virungas.

"Aren't you afraid?" Bea asked. "That's right next to the DMZ."

"Should I be?" Susanne's brow furrowed. "The State Department told us it was safe."

"Of course," Bea said. Magma flared and then extinguished in her eyes.

"I can't wait to see the mountain gorillas. I was stunned when someone murdered Dian Fossey. And when I think of poachers killing those poor animals—" She broke off the sentence and sighed.

Bea scowled. Jean Patrick could see her boiling up. There are Rwandans in the Virungas, too, she was thinking. Innocent Rwandans are murdered every day.

WHEN SUSANNE PASSED out on Jonathan's shoulder, Jonathan signaled for the bill. Jean Patrick glanced at his watch. Less than half an hour until curfew. What was it like not to scurry into hiding when a certain hour arrived? He could scarcely remember. With Susanne's arrival, he saw his life with new eyes, all its faults and restrictions.

Jonathan had rented a car for the weekend, and he offered Jean Patrick and Bea a ride. Bea had calmed down, her resentment blunted into friendly goodwill. She watched, amused, as Jonathan fumbled with the key. The grating voice of an RTLM journalist came from a radio down the street. *We expect this government to be reasonable and not help the RPF create problems.*

Bea maneuvered into the tiny backseat, and her pagne flared open. A red pantaloon leg flashed in the light from the overhead bulb. Jean Patrick ducked in beside her, his bony knees nearly in his chest.

Jonathan drove carefully, Susanne asleep against his shoulder despite the skull-jarring bumps from the road. At the checkpoint, she half awoke and gave the soldier an angelic smile.

"Welcome to Rwanda," he said with a salute. He returned her smile. His finger brushed hers when he returned the passport.

"Thank you. I may never leave."

The soldier slid his flashlight beam over Bea and Jean Patrick and then

made a sweeping circle to wave them through. Jonathan thanked him and
drove on toward Cyarwa Sumo.

"It helps to have a mnyamerikakazi in the car," Bea said in Kinyarwanda. "The guy was so crazy for her blond hair, he forgot about us completely." Jean Patrick grinned. Bea had a human side after all; she was
jealous.

Jonathan, brave as soon as he passed through town, sped around corners like a true Rwandan driver. Jean Patrick and Bea slanted one way
and then another, like fishermen on a stormy lake. A crescent moon swam
through the clouds. Jean Patrick pressed his mouth to Bea's ear. "Do you
know what Americans do in backseats?" Bea shook her head. He took her
face in his hands and kissed her.

"Eh! Who taught you that?" she whispered back.

Tossed about in the darkness, the engine's drone a song in Jean Patrick's
head, they could have been adrift, the bottom so far beneath them they
might sink forever and never reach it.

"DADI AND I are going back to Kigali tomorrow," Bea said. She
spoke in a low voice, in Kinyarwanda. "Habyarimana is swearing in the
new government *again*. Or so he says. Why don't you come with us?" They
were stopped at the parking lot near Jean Patrick's dorm.

He paused with one foot on the ground, the other in the car, his eyes
on the slight rise and fall of her collarbone. "I would be glad to. Maybe
my presence will bring good luck."

"That's right," Bea said, a touch of bitterness in her voice. "I had forgotten you were one of the president's friends."

Jean Patrick leaned back into the car's warmth and touched his hand
to Bea's cheek. "Amahoro," he said to her. Peace. He switched to French.
"Jonathan and Susanne, thank you for a wonderful celebration. Susanne,
may your stay here be productive and peaceful."

Bea called through the open window. "We'll pick you up at eight."

Jean Patrick stood and watched the headlights slash the eucalyptus. He
watched and listened until the *clack-clack* of the bad suspension melted
into the night song.

Traffic jammed the road into Kigali, cars jostling for every centimeter of space. The excitement of a holiday sizzled in the air. In every direction, UNAMIR tanks and trucks lumbered, the blue helmeted troops looking out over the crowds.

"You see?" Jean Patrick said. "There are plenty of soldiers to protect us if anything goes wrong." Bea gave him a vexed stare but said nothing.

Niyonzima parked beside a small market at the edge of town and jumped from the car. "Let's walk from here. I want to see what's brewing." The sway and limp, reminders of his days in prison, did not slow him down.

"Mana yanjye, Dadi, are you trying for the Olympics, too?" Bea pulled her father's sleeve to slow him down.

From high on the hill came a commotion like a rowdy group of football fans. Jean Patrick was about to laugh when the din of whistles, chants, and shouts drew nearer, louder, and he heard the danger in it. The throng poured onto the road ahead of them, sweeping passersby into its turbulent flow. At its edge, the Interahamwe turned up the flame. They swung machetes and clubs, struck the ground with spears. Some dragged their machetes across the pavement to leave a trail of sparks in their wake.

"Now you see what I meant." Bea had to shout to be heard above the fray.

"Yes, I do." Fear set every cell in Jean Patrick's body on high alert.

"We have arrived at the Rwandan National Assembly. Did you know the RPF is headquartered there now?"

Jean Patrick followed her finger. He had expected something fancy for the parliament building, but the CND was just a group of run-down green buildings. Against all odds, he hoped Roger was somewhere on a balcony and could see him and—if necessary—protect him.

Bea pulled Jean Patrick and Niyonzima close. "This is even worse than last time."

Shouts coalesced into a deafening roar. Fury was a live wire at the crowd's center, explosion as close as a match against a fuse. A group of delegates tried to push through. The mob tore at their clothes, kicking and shoving them down. "They'll kill them," Jean Patrick yelled. "Why don't the soldiers *do* something?"

Outrage overwhelmed terror in Bea's eyes. "That, Jean Patrick, is a very good question."

The crowd engulfed them. Niyonzima gripped Bea and Jean Patrick. "Arm in arm," he shouted. "Do not let go."

More cars pulled up with opposition party placards. The moment the delegates emerged, they were swarmed, like storm winds whipping the sea into frenzy. Whistles screeched. Bottles crashed at their feet. One smashed into a UNAMIR tank, spraying a soldier with glass.

Jean Patrick searched the faces of the Rwandan Army soldiers in case Pascal was among them. He didn't realize the mistake of letting down his guard until he heard, "There's one—let's get him." He was ripped from Niyonzima's grasp, Niyonzima's and Bea's outstretched hands disappearing as he was pushed to the ground. Then only legs and feet, kicking and stepping. Arms reaching down and hitting. His favorite jacket, the one with the Rwandan flag, torn from his body. He rolled into a ball to protect himself. Pain, sudden and searing, tore through his shoulder. He heard Bea scream his name as if from a great distance.

Memory called up the vision of the truck tire as it careened down the hill. *If you remain calm, your mind will tell your body what to do,* Coach had said. Amid the press of legs and feet, the smallest clearing opened. Like a tiny miracle he saw them, Bea and Niyonzima, rushing toward him. He struggled to his feet and pushed through the fray to reach them.

Niyonzima grabbed him. "Are you OK?"

"Yes, I think so."

"Good. We've seen enough. I think we can safely say, no new government today—let's get out of here."

"Wait—they thieved my jacket!" Jean Patrick stepped back toward the mob.

"Are you completely insane? Leave it!" Bea shouted. They were walking quickly now, almost running down the hill, away from the CND. The mob had disappeared behind them; the air felt cleaner, fresher. Bea looked at Jean Patrick and out of nowhere began to laugh. "No one but you," she said, "would think of a jacket at such a time." And then, as if the timbre of her voice had opened a crack in the air, nervous laughter bubbled to the surface in all of them, and none of them could stop.

"Before we go," Niyonzima said, "I want to buy some batteries for the radio. They are cheaper here than in Butare." They were standing by the car, watching the colorful stream into and out of the market entrance. A hawker grilled meat over a charcoal fire, and the smell and sizzle awoke Jean Patrick's hunger. He had not eaten in the morning, and his few coins had vanished with his jacket.

"Aren't you ashamed to be seen with me?" Jean Patrick showed off his dirt-stained shirt. His shoulder throbbed, and he wondered if it had been bruised.

"Never," Bea said. "Your war wounds make us even prouder." She pushed through the gate and into the expanse of stalls and garish umbrellas. Niyonzima and Jean Patrick followed.

They stopped to look at a display of guns laid out like fruit or appliances at a hawker's table. "Can you believe this?" Niyonzima picked up an AK-47 and held it in the air.

The blast came out of nowhere and knocked them to the ground. A thick, choking dust rained down on them, and a sulfurous stench filled Jean Patrick's nose, burned his throat and lungs. He raised his head and realized he could hear nothing except a loud ringing in his ears. Bea and Niyonzima sprawled beside him. They were all covered with dust and debris.

Out of the cloud came two men, running full tilt. One clutched a TV; the other, a large radio still in its box. They looked like TV actors, pistols and grenades at their belts. Behind them ran another man, his arm and shirt bloodied. His mouth was open, and he was obviously screaming, but Jean Patrick still couldn't hear. All around them, market goers picked themselves up, brushed themselves off, and went back to the business of shopping as if nothing out of the ordinary had happened.

"I had heard about these things, but in my wildest dreams I couldn't have imagined such a scene," Niyonzima said.

They had left Kigali behind. The brown waters of the Nyabarongo ponded in thickets of papyrus close beside the road. Jean Patrick looked out over the landscape and drew comfort from the quiet. "They set off a grenade to steal things?"

Bea drove while Niyonzima wrote notes in his little book. A white powdery dust still clung to their skin and speckled their hair. "Why not?" Niyonzima said. "All those weapons there for the taking. Available and cheap." He leaned over and turned on the radio. "Let's see if there is any news about events at the CND."

They didn't have to wait long. *At the last minute, something came up,* the announcer said. *Habyarimana did not attend, and the delegates were not sworn in.*

"This will go on forever," Niyonzima said, "until finally Habyarimana and his henchmen ignite the fuse they have so carefully readied."

Bea snorted. Jean Patrick had neither the strength nor the conviction to contradict them.

Niyonzima went back to writing but soon looked up again and waved his pen in the air like a conductor leading an orchestra. "In telling this story, it is difficult to find the balance between comic absurdity and outrage." He struck through a phrase, wrote another. "And to report in a way that will not get me jailed." He struck a second phrase. "Or worse."

Jean Patrick let fatigue wash over him. He didn't want to think about the morning, about how such violence affected the country's future. Instead he brought back his early workout, the cool mist on his face, the first bluish light, the slap of his Nikes on the road. He had managed to shake off the headache from the previous night's beer and press through. His times were getting better, his kick sharper, his effort more focused.

On Monday, classes would resume. Coach would be back to push him. Even the truck tire: Jean Patrick welcomed it. Surely then the balance of life would tip back toward equilibrium. He closed his eyes and sank into a welcome sleep. When he opened them again, the sign that welcomed travelers to Butare greeted him. "We're home already," he said.

Niyonzima sighed and sank back against the seat. "At last. Our little island of peace and sanity." He pocketed pen and notebook.

At that moment, the sun broke free from the clouds and sprinkled Niyonzima's hair with a silver brilliance. Jean Patrick found in this sign a quivering hint of promise. He snatched the promise, gathered it up into his fist.

JONATHAN HAD INVITED Jean Patrick and Bea for dinner that night, but Bea did not want to go. She sat on the floor while Ineza combed and braided her hair. "If you stay at home and sink into misery, you are letting those criminals win," Ineza said. She dipped her fingers into the jar of pomade, releasing its coconut scent. Every so often, she had to tease out a tiny splinter or a scrap of debris that had survived the hair washing.

Bea whimpered, "Mama, are you trying to torture me into agreeing?"

"I am, daughter, I am."

"Ow!" Bea grabbed her mother's hand and held it. "You have succeeded; I will go."

Jean Patrick was relieved. He looked forward to discussing the day with Jonathan, to get an outsider's point of view. From Niyonzima's office came the steady *tap-tap* of typewriter keys as Niyonzima wrested from the chaos a story with meaning and purpose. Jean Patrick had been to the dorm to shower. He had collected his books so he could study. After what had happened, he didn't want to be alone. He tried to concentrate on his physics. *A natural process will always go in the direction that causes entropy to increase.* Jean Patrick put down the book and looked out at the garden. Would disorder accelerate until no law remained? His father had believed that all things had a mathematical expression. In the small, square plot, Claire and her daughter harvested beans, a brightly colored basket on the ground between them. The little girl laughed and held a bean in her hair like a bow. No, Jean Patrick thought, not entropy but momentum: *A body in motion remains in motion.* He glanced at Bea, head resting against her mother's knee, hair transformed into a crown of braids. We will keep moving forward as we have always done, as surely we will continue to do in the future.

AT JONATHAN'S HOUSE, Jonathan and Susanne were slow-dancing across the floor. A sweet, jazzy song melted around them.

"J. P.! Bea! Come dance!" Jonathan welcomed them inside.

"Yes," Susanne said. "Dance, dance!"

Jean Patrick took Bea's hands and pulled her close. "Like this?" He twirled her around. Quickly his shoulder reminded him he had been roughed up.

Amos came from the cookhouse with a platter of spaghetti, and Bea laughed. "Nkuba, you are saved by dinner."

Susanne cheered. "Pasta. Just like home."

Jean Patrick thought he wouldn't be hungry. The mob's ugly mood still jangled his nerves, and a sulfurous tang lingered in his mouth. But now that food was on the table, his appetite perked up, and he heaped spaghetti onto his plate. Jonathan poured wine. They toasted and drank, dug into their food.

"Beer-a-joshee-cyanee!" Susanne said. "Did I say that right?"

Bea leveled a vexed look at Jean Patrick. Susanne leaned her head on Jonathan's shoulder. Like two pieces of a puzzle, Jean Patrick thought.

"How was the ceremony?" Jonathan asked. "We missed the news." He grinned. Susanne turned red.

"Postponed again," Bea said. She held her glass to the light. Sparks danced in the wine, and when she drank, she swallowed them. "Susanne, tell us about your first day in Butare."

"Actually, we bought a car."

Jonathan said, "*Imodoka,* right?"

"That's right." Bea took a studied bite of pasta. Jean Patrick could feel the heat of her anger like a flame. His toe sought out her ankle beneath the table.

"I had been thinking about it for a while. I need to take Susanne to Gisenyi, and then to the Virungas."

"What color is the new imodoka?" Jean Patrick asked.

"Red." Susanne held up her wineglass, and Jonathan filled it. "The color of wine." She sipped. "And of the heart."

"To the heart," Jonathan said, and he raised his glass.

"To the heart," Susanne said. "That strong yet fragile organ." They toasted the heart.

It was after curfew when Jean Patrick and Bea left. Jonathan gave them a flashlight, and they kept to the trail. Bea snagged the fringe of her shawl on a thorny vine, and Jean Patrick bent to untangle her. He held her foot in his hand. "Why did you refuse to tell Jonathan what happened?" He hadn't meant to ask, but all evening the question had been sitting on his tongue, waiting to jump off.

"He doesn't need to know."

"Because he's muzungu?"

"That's not it. He can't be trusted. He doesn't understand."

"It's *you* who doesn't understand." Jean Patrick's voice rose, anger finally boiling up. "Your father wants to tell the world, but you won't enlighten one human being—a personal friend to both of us."

"It's not the same," Bea said. "My father knows Rwanda. He knows who to write to and what to say. What he tells the world helps us. With Jonathan, that is not the case. The word is a dangerous weapon. He could say one wrong thing to one wrong person, and my father could be jailed. Or killed. You saw what happened to Gatabazi. The university is filled with the government's listening ears."

"What nonsense are you telling me?" Jean Patrick quickened his pace. The flashlight's beam swept the darkness. "Maybe, as a Westerner, he *is* the one to tell our story."

Bea stopped him. "Are you blind? The West doesn't care. All those UNAMIR troops watching while Hutu riot? You saw how quickly savagery overtook them. How long until Western troops stand around while those same Hutu start their killing?"

Jean Patrick turned off the flashlight and set it in the bush. He traced the outline of her mouth, her full, pouty lips. "Don't be cross with me," he said. "I think you're not being fair to Jonathan, that's all."

Bea panted. "It's not you I'm cross with. I just can't stop thinking about today. I go over it and over it in my mind. I don't know how many more days like this I can stand." She rested her head on his chest. "I'm so frightened," she said. "For Dadi, for you, for all of us." She raised her chin, and the dark V at the base of her throat opened up to Jean Patrick. "Stay with us tonight, Nkuba."

He placed his lips against the V, the delicate angle of bone. "Your parents won't mind?"

"My parents love you like a son."

"And you?"

"Eh? No, I do not love you like a son." She spread her shawl wide to envelop him. His head spun. The earth spun beneath him.

"Will you stay in my bed, then?" He touched her, nose to nose.

She pushed him away, laughing. "Mana yanjye. And what do we tell Mama and Dadi?"

"That we're getting married," Jean Patrick said. "Tonight. Right now." Bea looked down at her feet. "I am speaking from my heart," he said. "I mean it." He might as well have asked Miseke, the Dawn Girl, to marry him.

"Jean Patrick, this is not a time for marriage."

"Then when?" He pulled her back to him. "When will it be time?"

She sighed, her arms tight about his hips. "Ejo," she said, the word for both yesterday and tomorrow.

"Please clarify," Jean Patrick said. "Do you mean *ejo* hashize, yesterday, or *ejo* hazaza, tomorrow?"

"Either one. We'll get married in Jonathan's new red car."

Jean Patrick kissed her until neither of them could breathe. On the road below, a jeep whined up the hill, headlights pointing askew. The soldiers' talk drifted through the brush.

Bea pulled away. "We better go."

Jean Patrick picked up the flashlight but left it off. Taking Bea's hand, he guided her down the path he now knew by the feel of every bump, every tree root beneath his foot. When they reached Bea's gate, they kissed again. Inside the safety of her shawl, he unbuttoned her blouse and found her breast, its taut nipple. She whispered, "Your hope is the most beautiful and the saddest in the world."

Jean Patrick knew he could never let her go again. "Let's find a spot in the bush."

"Eh? In the stinging nettles?" She fastened her blouse and called for her parents to open the gate. "*Ejo,* my Nkuba. *Ejo* hazaza: tomorrow."

TWENTY-ONE

IF YOU STRETCH A SPRING long enough, far enough, the metal will fail and the spring will snap. The same with a human body. The same with a human heart. The same, even, with a country. This is what came to Jean Patrick on his Monday morning workout in a moment of reprieve between hard intervals. Coach ran at a steady pace somewhere behind him. Dawn broke across the fields, the birds shrill and constant in the trees, the air sharp enough to cut the lungs.

Coach seemed to know exactly where Jean Patrick's breaking point was, and he kept Jean Patrick just at its edge. Instead of snapping, his body turned harder, stronger, faster. Coach had abandoned the truck tire for a new method from his magazines, a technique called fartlek. It was a system for distance runners modified for Jean Patrick's torture. "I will make you suffer for kilometers at a time," Coach said with his typical smirk. "That way, the eight hundred will seem like a walk."

Since the beginning of the new semester, they had been working out together in the mornings, then weights and breakfast at Coach's house. Coach said he wanted to keep a closer eye on Jean Patrick's training and nutrition, and anyway, it was time he got back in shape himself. Coach had grown lean like a leopard, the angle of his jaw sharper. Jean Patrick wondered if a woman had caused this change, and his mind pondered what she must be like.

"Go! Last and fastest!" Coach shouted at his back.

Jean Patrick accelerated. Three minutes of pain until Coach yelled "Stop." As he surged, he tried to focus on the political situation. The transitional government had yet to be sworn in. Always the tease of success and then another excuse: a procedural difficulty, a delegate whose name had been omitted. He could no longer tell Bea to have faith, to trust that Habyarimana would keep his word.

"I can't stand this anymore," Bea said on one of the rare days Jean Patrick managed to capture her for a walk. "This cycle of hope and disappointment breaks my heart every day."

Jean Patrick knew too much about the behavior of hearts. His own was breaking. Bea had jumped headfirst into politics. She started a club, organized student meetings, wrote articles and opinions for an underground newspaper. Jean Patrick saw little more of her than a skirt disappearing around a corner, a fringe of shawl beckoning from the stairwell. He tracked her news through Jonathan, greeted Niyonzima to catch a glimmer of her scent. He wondered if all this passion had at its heart the fear of losing her father for good. Jean Patrick glanced at his watch. Forty seconds to go. He let emotion fuel a final burst of speed.

"Stop!" Coach said, surprisingly close behind him.

Jean Patrick took a welcome gulp of cool air, turned back, and jogged toward his coach. His legs quivered, and sweat burned his eyes. "You're getting fast, Coach."

"Or you're slowing down," Coach said. He took off his sweatband and shook it out. "You'll turn heads at World Championships, put Rwanda on the map."

"Turn heads? I'm going to win."

Jean Patrick was half joking, but Coach didn't laugh. "It's possible. I've been thinking. We should travel this spring, race in countries like Kenya that are serious about running. People outside Rwanda need to know your name, and you need to get a taste of real competition. You have to get experience fighting through a pack with guys who've been around a track once or twice, guys you can't shake off so easily."

"Those boys from Kigali—didn't you say they went to Kenya?"

"Those boys," Coach said, "are specks beneath your heels."

THE PHONE RANG the instant Jean Patrick and Coach walked in the door, as if their entrance had set it off. Coach sprinted to answer. He listened in silence a moment, then covered the mouthpiece and turned to Jean Patrick. "Wait in the dining room. I'll just be a minute."

Taking off his shoes, Jean Patrick strained to catch some scrap of Coach's conversation. Jolie came in from the yard, chicken feathers stuck to her arms and clothing. "Where were you five minutes ago when I needed a fast runner to chase down a hen?"

"It looks like you did fine without me." He thought he heard Coach say *icyitso,* and he cocked his ear toward the living room.

Jolie slapped his arm. "Inshyanutsi! Mind your business, nosy one. What did I warn you?"

Coach strode into the hall. "Bring us tea and something to eat, Jolie." The toothpick between his pursed lips worked up and down. "No weights today. Something's come up."

Sitting at the table, Jean Patrick watched Coach out of the corner of his eye. Whatever news he had received was important enough to change a schedule that was as rigid as stone. He waited for a hint, a crumb of information, but Coach remained silent except for the rhythmic tap of his knife against the tablecloth.

Jolie brought bread and fruit, a thermos of tea. She set down plates and cups.

"Jean Patrick takes milk," Coach said.

"Milk is finished. Four days now I haven't seen that Tutsi woman I buy from at the market. She must have joined the Inkotanyi."

Coach pushed the bread basket toward Jean Patrick. "Eat. You worked hard."

"I'm not very hungry, Coach."

"You need to rebuild muscle; you're far too skinny." He sliced a tomato and slid it onto Jean Patrick's plate. "What's the matter? You're not sick again, are you?"

Jean Patrick picked at his food. He spooned extra sugar into his tea to make up for the lack of milk. It tasted strong and bitter. "No, Coach, I'm not sick."

Coach's eyes flitted to the window, stared out toward the road and came back to rest on Jean Patrick's face. Jean Patrick remembered how Roger had done the same thing, his mind never coming to a state of ease.

With half his food left on his plate, Coach pushed it away. "I'll drive you to school."

"Coach, I can walk. I have time before class."

A crumb remained on Coach's lip, and he swiped his napkin across his mouth. "Today, you're not walking."

A CHILLY WIND whipped at Jean Patrick's neck as he leaned against the car door, waiting for Coach to unlock it. He wiggled the zipper on his jacket to force it closed. Clouds gathered over the mountains and left Burundi in shadow. Coach remained in the doorway, a bundle of clothes in his arm, talking to Jolie. RTLM blared from an open window and competed with their conversation. Jean Patrick couldn't make out the words, but the announcer's animated tone made him nervous. He recalled the same rapid-fire, accusatory delivery from the day Ndadaye was killed. By the time Coach came to let him into the car, both RTLM and the cold had seeped into his bones.

Coach tossed a newspaper onto the seat. He handed the clothes to Jean Patrick. "I never could have imagined, that day at Gihundwe when you collapsed on the track, how far you would go. They gave you a different brand this time."

There was a new green tracksuit with PUMA across the front and RWANDA across the back of the jacket in the colors of the flag. "To replace the one you lost. I hope you're more careful with this one."

"How did you know?"

"You don't need to be an engineer to use deductive reasoning. You are wearing a rag with a broken zipper when I gave you a shiny new jacket. Until last month, you never took it off."

Jean Patrick took off his old jacket and tried on the new one. Folded inside the tracksuit were white running shorts with red-striped matching singlets that said PUMA on the sides. At the bundle's center was a pair of running shoes, also Puma. He held up a singlet. For years he had seen them in the magazines, dreamed how it would feel to wear one. There was a small Rwandan flag above the breast and the Puma logo — a leaping cougar — by his heart. RWANDA, in bold red letters, spanned his chest. His heart drummed a high-speed rhythm.

"For World Championships," Coach said. "They will be here before you know it."

"Suddenly it is very real." Jean Patrick touched the cougar. He touched each letter of RWANDA. But as he settled into his reverie, unease returned. Every time he received one of these packages, something more was required of him. He glanced at the headlines of *Kangura,* which had come open beside him. UNAMIR SHOULD CONSIDER ITS DANGER.

Coach stopped in the university parking lot, but instead of getting out, he let the engine idle. "I want you to stay on campus today. I have some business. Someone will substitute for afternoon practice. By now, you know what I expect."

"When will you be back?"

"Tomorrow. I mean what I say. On campus. Understand?" He put the car in gear.

"Yego, Coach. I wasn't planning to leave anyway." Again he thought that something bad had happened, something Coach was not revealing. Then Jean Patrick shook his head, unhinged his long body, and stepped from the car.

FROM A DISTANCE, Jean Patrick saw that the door to his room was open and that Bea sat on his bed, Daniel in a chair facing her. He sprinted the remaining steps.

"Félicien Gatabazi is dead. Assassinated last night in Kigali," Bea said as Jean Patrick entered the room. He sat down heavily beside her. She did not look up. "He called us as he was dying. We had a late dinner, and we were lingering at the table, discussing this and that, when the phone rang."

As if it were happening right now, right here, he saw Félicien Gatabazi at Bea's table, his squinted eyes, one swollen shut, face bruised, arm in a makeshift sling. He had looked at Jean Patrick and predicted his own death. And then he had smiled.

"There's going to be a huge demonstration," Bea said. "Many students are going to march. I came to ask if you will join us."

Daniel jumped up. "Let's go! Let another voice besides Interahamwe be heard in this town."

Jean Patrick retrieved Isaka's bandanna from his drawer and fastened it around his neck. Coach's stone expression came back to him. Never before had he so brazenly defied him. "I'm ready," he said. "Let's go."

ON THE ROAD to town, there was barely room to walk. A wall of demonstrators spanned the asphalt and spread out onto the grass. On the hillsides, small groups of spectators sporting caps of Habyarimana's MRND and other antimoderate parties shouted insults and threats and waved anti-PSD signs.

The protest was a river of color crested by raised fists. Jean Patrick was buoyed along by the powerful tide. "Félicien can be proud," he said. "So many Hutu and Tutsi marching together to remember him." A small political fire sparked in his belly.

Two women Jean Patrick recognized from school carried a hand-painted banner: WE ARE ALL ONE PEOPLE. Bea raised a fist into the air, her eyes candescent. A lightning bolt struck Jean Patrick's heart. For the first time since the riot in Kigali, hope returned, blunting memory the way a stream blunts a rock's sharp edges with its steady flow. Maybe in death, Félicien Gatabazi had achieved what he had struggled so hard for in life. Maybe now they could learn to walk in peace and unity, AMAHORO N'UBUMWE, as one banner demanded.

"Look," Daniel said. A group of boys in RPF T-shirts marched toward them from l'avenue de la Cathédrale. "In Kigali, they'd be torn apart for that."

"Probably in Cyangugu, too." Jean Patrick touched a finger to Isaka's scarf and scanned the marchers, the buildings, the trees, his eyes turning every shadow into Roger.

Bea brushed against him. "Who are you looking for?"

"No one. Just watching."

"Well, I hope you find this No One. You are searching hard."

JEAN PATRICK WALKED hand in hand with Daniel and Bea on the path. She had invited them for dinner so they could watch the coverage of the demonstrations on TV. They were keyed up from the march, charged with its giddy energy.

Ineza opened the gate. "The news is not good," she said. Like wet fingers touched to a candle's wick, her tone extinguished the flame of Jean Patrick's wishes. She kissed them in turn. "Come in."

The TV flickered, the nightly news barely discernible from the static.

The audio hissed and crackled. "Kigali has erupted," she said, "violence spilling onto every street."

"What happened?" Life appeared to drain from Bea's body, bone by bone. She sat on the couch and stared dully at the screen.

Ineza took her hand. "In retaliation for Gatabazi's murder, someone here in Butare lynched Martin Bucyana, leader of one of the extremist anti-PSD parties. Revenge for his death came swiftly. Interahamwe blocked the roads and set half of Kigali on fire. They've taken over."

Jean Patrick slumped down in a chair. The horizontal on the TV was out of control. What appeared to be scenes of burning tires and buildings in flames scrolled between black lines.

Ineza said, "I'm so angry. On RTLM they are screaming that Gatabazi was icyitso and deserved to die."

Bea snorted. "What did you expect? At any rate, if you're not angry now, you are either stupid or crazy." She got up and turned on the lights, and Jean Patrick realized they had been sitting in darkness.

Daniel squeezed beside Jean Patrick on the chair. "The peace process is dead," he said. "Murdered along with Gatabazi."

Bea shot back, "It was never alive." She looked up suddenly. "Where's Dadi? He isn't back yet?"

Worry on her face, Ineza glanced at the door. "He should be here soon."

Bea brought beer and Fanta from the cookhouse. "He shouldn't have gone; he was half-dead from exhaustion. After Félicien called, Dadi was on the phone half the night, and he left for Kigali with the dawn, to help with arrangements for the funeral." Defiance lit her face. "We will fill an entire football stadium. We will not let the extremists have the last word."

A program of Rwandan dance came on the television. With every sound of a car, Ineza went to the window. "Don't worry, Mama," Bea said. "He's lost track of time, as usual."

"WE'LL HAVE TO eat without him, or Jean Patrick and Daniel will never get back before curfew," Ineza said. It was nearly eight, and Niyonzima had not returned.

A car honked outside. Claire set down the food she had just brought and scurried to the gate to let the visitor in. Ineza and Bea exchanged glances. "I'll go to the door," Bea said.

"There's been an accident." The voice came, disembodied, from the hall. Jean Patrick had heard the voice before. Where? The man stepped from the shadow. It was the policeman who had spoken with Bea at the Ibis.

"I'm sorry to bring you this news." Butter could have dripped from his mouth. "Your husband was found near Murambi. He had gone off the road. He had been drinking." A flash of surprise metamorphosed into a smile when he noticed Jean Patrick. He gave a mock bow and said, "Good evening, Mr. . . . ." He raised his eyebrows.

"Nkuba. Jean Patrick Nkuba."

Shakily, Ineza rose from her seat. "Is my husband alive?"

"Madam, I wish I could tell you. I was only instructed to take you to the hospital."

Bea put an arm around her mother. "Be strong," she said, her face stony. Turning to the policeman, she added, "My father drinks only at home. He had no plans to go to Murambi."

The officer slid his glance over her. "Ah, but that is where we found him."

Ineza collected her shawl and purse and slipped on her sandals. "You must stay and eat," she said to Jean Patrick and Daniel. Her back straight and regal, she took the arm Bea offered and followed the policeman out the front door.

The car rattled down the road. After a time, the sound melted into the night's hum and click. "It wasn't an accident," Daniel said.

"I know." Jean Patrick had had enough of secrets. Gatabazi had been murdered. They didn't know if Niyonzima was dead or alive. Now, it was up to him and Daniel to carry the truth forward. No matter what Bea thought, Jean Patrick knew he could trust Jonathan. Down to the smallest cell in his heart, he knew it. "I think we should tell Jonathan," he said.

"Right now?"

"Right now." Jean Patrick put on his jacket and his shoes. He pounced on this small promise. Jonathan would find a voice to shout into America's listening ear.

The trademark spot of tongue showed between Daniel's teeth. "I'm with you."

Twenty-two

AT LEAST NIYONZIMA WAS ALIVE; they had that to be thankful for. Leg shattered, unable to move, he had lain against the car door where he was thrown and made his peace. But just as he had abandoned all hope, out of nowhere the police arrived to rescue him. At the hospital, he asked about his car, and they told him not to worry, they would see to having it towed. When no car appeared, Jonathan drove Bea and Jean Patrick to find it, but they could not. Several times they drove far past Gikongoro, searching the ravines and bushes. Jean Patrick asked the workers in the fields. No one had seen it. The earth, it seemed, had swallowed Niyonzima's vehicle. When they inquired at the station, the officer at the desk shrugged his shoulders and launched into a complaint about the lawlessness of the countryside.

Of course it had not been an accident. Opening his office door on the day of Gatabazi's death, Niyonzima found a letter slipped beneath it. The sender promised details on the secret arming of Interahamwe and asked Niyonzima to meet him at a restaurant near Murambi. He claimed to be a friend of a close colleague. "It was a novice's mistake not to verify the details," Niyonzima said. "But the colleague was away, and the bait, too delicious." A truck forced him off the road. It had happened so quickly; he had recognized neither vehicle nor occupants.

As the days passed, Jonathan called and wrote letters to the police chief suggesting an investigation. When his attempts went unanswered, he requested an interview with the burgomaster. He was received politely, given tea, promised results with a smile as sweet as the icing that glazed the cakes he was offered. "The man was drunk," the burgomaster said, wiping crumbs from his hands. "He could not tell us what happened or where he lost control of his car."

"You are asking a lion to investigate a calf killing," Niyonzima said when Jonathan told him of his failures.

"I always get the same smile," Jonathan said. "I call it the make-the-muzungu-go-away smile." Seeing Jonathan's exasperated expression, Jean Patrick felt his own hope fade.

Hope rose again when Jonathan wrote a formal complaint to the U.S. Embassy, but weeks later, he was still waiting for a response. Jonathan's voice simply rose into the mist with the rest of their voices. The ear of America remained deaf.

After a week in the hospital, Niyonzima came home. He was healing, putting on weight and muscle. On mornings when Jean Patrick could escape from Coach's watchful eye, he joined Niyonzima when he finished his workout. Together they walked up and down the lane, each time a bit farther, a bit faster. "Soon, even with your crutches you'll beat me," Jean Patrick joked.

"Ha! *That which does not kill us makes us stronger*," Niyonzima said. "Do you know the saying?" Ashamed, Jean Patrick shook his head. "It's Nietzsche, a German philosopher. I repeated it every day I was in prison."

"I have seen his book on Coach's shelf." The words were no sooner out of Jean Patrick's mouth than he wished he could snatch them back out of the air.

"Of course," Niyonzima said. Jean Patrick could taste the bitterness in his smile.

EASTER CAME EARLY that year: April 3, now only three days away. Jean Patrick stretched out on his bed. He was trying to study, but his mind traveled here and there. The milk and honey they had all wished for at the start of the year seemed as far away as the moon. Letters from Mama sighed with bad news. For the crime of being Tutsi, classmates had chased Clemence until her feet bled. Hutu Power toughs jumped Zachary on a morning walk near his school. *Luckily,* Mama wrote, *he has legs like yours to run.*

Jean Patrick returned to his geology book, a chapter on stress and strain in rocks. If stress was applied too quickly, he read, the strain could not be supported, and the rock snapped. This was how faults formed. But when the same stress was applied buhoro, buhoro, little by little, the rock adjusted. Folds formed instead of faults. "Like toothpaste squeezed from a tube," Jonathan told the class.

And if pressure kept increasing in Rwanda, what would happen then? Would they break or bend? Disgusted, Jean Patrick set the book aside. I will die in the wreckage of all this confusion, he thought.

Commotion erupted outside the door, and Daniel burst through, dancing and whooping. He took off his jacket and shook out the rain. "Classes are over! Papers finished!"

"Aye! Couldn't you do that outside?" Jean Patrick shoved Daniel out and wiped the floor with a dirty shirt.

"Let me in, huh?" Daniel kicked off his shoes and hurled himself on top of Jean Patrick, who was still on hands and knees, mopping. They rolled across the floor, wrestling.

"No more slaughtered cows on your essays?"

"Just a few drops of blood." Daniel jumped up and wiggled his hips like a rock 'n' roll singer.

The bass from a radio vibrated the walls. In the small square of space between the beds, Daniel twirled and swayed to the beat. Jean Patrick joined in.

"When are you leaving for Cyangugu?" Daniel asked.

"Saturday morning, after practice. Coach wants to destroy me one last time before I go. He's been too cross. Maybe he needs a wife to take his mind off his troubles."

Daniel howled. "Wah! Can you picture it?" He jabbed his elbow into Jean Patrick. "Anyway, I found out he had one."

"Eh-eh! Never."

"She ran away to Tanzania because she didn't want to be second wife, behind the army."

"I think he's still married to the army, the way he acts."

Daniel took two candies from his pocket. He gave one to Jean Patrick and popped the other in his mouth. These were red, a sweet burst of cinnamon and spice on the tongue.

"From your muzungu sweetheart?"

"I am in love!" Daniel grinned, openmouthed, showing off the candy on his tongue. "Let's get some food. I could devour a cow by myself."

AN ONSLAUGHT OF noise hit them when they walked through the cafeteria door, students shouting and pushing, every seat taken, students sharing the tiny chairs. After they got their dinner, Jean Patrick and Daniel waited by the front. Daniel attacked his chips with his fingers, dragging them through a pile of mayonnaise sauce on his plate.

"Tsst! Tsst! Share our seats." The call came from a table in the corner where two girls stood and waved. Jean Patrick recognized them from the protest, the ones who carried the banner that said WE ARE ALL ONE PEOPLE. Daniel and Jean Patrick squeezed into one chair, the girls into the other.

"Aren't you that famous runner? Mr. Olympics?" The girl pointed her fork at Jean Patrick.

"I am." Jean Patrick held out his hand.

"I'm called Valerie." She wore a PL beret over her close-cropped hair. "You're friends with Bea—why don't you come to our Parti Libéral meetings?"

"I didn't think Tutsi could come."

Valerie rolled her eyes. "Anyone can join. We can't believe in exclusion."

Daniel looked up from his food. "Tell me when your next meeting is, and I'll be there." He shook Valerie's hand. "My friend has no time for politics. He's too busy training."

"No time for politics when justice is disappearing?"

Like something too hot or too cold causing pain in Jean Patrick's chipped tooth, the question went straight to his nerve, the same raw nerve Bea always probed. He cut his food into small, neat squares. In two days' time, he would sit with his family, scooping up stew with ugali, all talk of politics forgotten for a while—except, of course, for Uncle. Daniel and Valerie debated Rwanda's problems, and the more they heated up each other's heads, the closer they sat. More than politics boiled Daniel's blood.

"I'm going to marry her," Daniel sang. They walked back to the dorm hand in hand. A light rain fell. The moon, almost full, gave off a ghostly glow from behind the clouds.

"You think you can marry an activist? She will break your heart."

"Bea's an activist."

"You see? That one breaks my heart every day."

"But you will marry her."

"She is not fast enough to run away forever." Jean Patrick matched his long stride to Daniel's shorter one. He traveled back in memory to the day he and Daniel met. That gap-toothed boy was far away from the young man who now walked beside him, sturdy and lean, talking of marriage. "You need to pack," Jean Patrick said. "Your papa will be here early, and he will not want to be kept waiting."

Daniel stopped in the path. "I wonder why Jonathan and Susanne don't get married."

"Americans are different from us," Jean Patrick said. "They don't get married, and they don't have kids. Not until they are old already."

"Did I tell you my sister Rosine is getting married?"

Jean Patrick counted on his fingers. "Only nine times."

Rain kept a steady beat on the roof as Daniel threw clothes into his suitcase, took them out and folded them, put them back in. Charged with excitement, he kept up a steady banter with the radio, with Jean Patrick, with himself. When Bob Marley came on, he broke into a dance and hollered. *Them belly full but we hungry.* "After vacaion, we'll go dancing," he said. "You and Bea and me and Valerie. Forget curfew. We'll dance till morning." *A hungry man is an angry man.*

"What about your muzungu sweetheart?"

With a brush of his hand, Daniel dismissed her. "Valerie is *true* love." Twirling between the beds, he slow-danced with the shirt he had been about to pack. "But I'm going to meet the muzungu in Kigali. She's spending Easter at l'Hôtel des Mille Collines. Her parents are coming from Paris."

"Oh là là," Jean Patrick teased. "The Mille Collines! Maybe you should reconsider." Dancing to the desk, he picked up Daniel's books. "Don't forget to take these. We still have exams when we get back."

Shrill laughter, female, came from the walkway. Daniel pulled aside the curtain to look. He stood by the window, head cocked, fingering the fabric of the curtain. Light from the dim ceiling bulb illuminated his face like a half moon. A small corner of his tongue peeked through in his usual gesture of concentration. If Jean Patrick had a camera, he would have taken a picture just so. Something to remind Daniel of this time when he was older, with kids of his own.

TWENTY-THREE

JEAN PATRICK ARRIVED EARLY FOR DINNER, dressed in his suit. Already he was outgrowing it, slivers of ankle and wrist poking out if he moved the wrong way. His legs jiggled with nervous agitation. He had something to ask Niyonzima and Ineza, and he wanted to ask it before Susanne and Jonathan arrived. This business of the heart's turmoil did not come easily to him. If Daniel hadn't gone home, he would have asked for his help. When it came to matters of the heart, Daniel knew how to make persuasion flow from his mouth.

In a moment of inspiration, Jean Patrick had thought of his father. If Papa had been alive, Jean Patrick would have gone to him for advice. The closest he could come was Papa's journal. He analyzed his father's turns of phrase and sentence structure and practiced them aloud. Even so, as he stood at the window with Ineza, he was still crossing out in his mind, replacing weak words with stronger ones. They were watching the spectacle beyond the window, where workers fortified the garden wall. Bea and Niyonzima walked the base, inspecting the work and making small talk with the workers. Niyonzima had traded his crutches for a sturdy staff, and he leaned against it, accepting Bea's support with his other arm.

The wall had been extended upward until it blocked all but the treetops in the forest beyond. Pieces of broken bottle cemented into the top turned the house and yard into an impenetrable fortress. At least this was the hope.

"After what's happened, we have no choice," Ineza said.

Trapped inside the broken glass, sunset became a row of colored flames: blues, greens, reds, and browns. "You will find a way to use your painting to turn this wall into a thing of beauty," Jean Patrick said.

Bringing with him the blustery wind, Niyonzima came inside. He shook Jean Patrick's hand warmly. "What do you think of our new structure? Have you noticed—all our neighbors copy us." It was true. Every day Jean Patrick counted more walls armed with sharp teeth, more coils of barbed wire rising from cement and brick. For a country moving toward peace, the impression was more one of preparing for war.

"We have urwagwa!" Bea announced, coming in from the kitchen with two large bottles of banana beer. "Jean Patrick—look at you." She touched her cool cheek to his warm one and ran her hand along his jacket sleeve. "Movie star, eh? At least this time, your suit is dry." She embraced her father as he stood by the window, leaning on his ornately carved cane. "And you with your staff—like the mwami."

"Ah! Finally you see it," Ineza said. She helped Niyonzima to a chair. "I knew from the first glance, when he walked into my exhibit and raised his pen as if extending a blessing."

Jean Patrick pondered Bea's cheer. She was like fire in the wind: he never knew in what direction she would burn. Ineza filled their glasses. The beer's yeasty tang wafted out into the room, and with the first sip, Jean Patrick felt it go to his head. Tonight, he needed the alcohol's strength to pry his speech from his tongue. But by the third sip, the potent brew had swept away half the words he had so carefully stored there.

His intention was to wait until a polite amount of time had passed and then, at the proper opening, to address Niyonzima and Ineza directly. Bea sat beside him on the couch, the nearness of her thigh boiling the pot the urwagwa had set on the flame. They discussed the rain, the government that was still to be sworn in, the huge crowd at Gatabazi's funeral. They praised Niyonzima's stirring eulogy, delivered on crutches. Then, just as Jean Patrick drew a breath and prepared to speak, Jonathan and Susanne called out, "Mwiriwe," from the gate, and opportunity vanished.

CLAIRE PILED DISHES of traditional food on the table: green bananas and beans, carrots cooked with cabbage and onions in a tomatoey sauce, goat meat swimming in thick broth. Bea brought in a dish of pasta and placed it in front of Susanne with a flourish. "Especially for you," she said.

Susanne let out a peal of laughter and clapped her hands. "Murakoze cyane!" she said, thanking Bea like a true Rwandan.

They all dug in and ate. They drank more urwagwa. Neither Jonathan nor Susanne had tried it before, and Ineza insisted on showing them the traditional way, sharing it with a straw. "Of course, in the country," Ineza said, "they use reed instead of plastic for the straw." With every bite of food, every sip of beer, Jean Patrick's speech retreated into a farther corner of his mind.

Susanne had brought a box of photographs, and after dinner, she laid them out across the table. Bea examined them beside her, and soon they sat as close as sisters. Susanne was pink faced and giddy from the beer.

Bea held a picture of ragged, waving children. "They're beautiful. Who are they?"

"Aren't they sweet? They go to primary school near my project slopes, when they're not too busy helping in the fields. I wish I could adopt every one of them."

Bea stiffened. "Probably they are happy where they are." Susanne had stumbled into another sin, but she didn't seem to notice. Bea's anger faded with the next photo, the children's smiles bright and filled with hope.

"I don't know how they manage," Susanne said. "We're just beyond the DMZ, and some days the shelling never stops. I thought there was supposed to be a cease-fire."

Bea said, "There is."

Susanne pointed to one of the boys. "His cousin was killed by a mortar. What is the point? By the end of the first week, I was ready to ask Jonathan to come and rescue me. But then, I guess I got used to it." She looked to Bea. "You do, don't you. Get used to it, I mean."

"Yes," Bea said, sweeping a grain of rice into her palm. "I suppose you do."

Susanne picked out a photo of a skinny black dog with matted fur. "Here's our new puppy. She was wandering around my hut in the mornings, so I started sharing my breakfast. Once she had me pegged as a primary food source, she wasn't going anywhere. We've named her Kweli, after one of Dian Fossey's beloved gorillas. The children about died when I told them we named a dog."

Ineza put her arms around Jonathan and Susanne. "Why don't you join us for Easter? It's such a beautiful time in Rwanda, long parades of people walking to church in their best clothes, everyone singing together. It's one of the few times we can forget our troubles."

Jean Patrick gulped the last of his urwagwa. Here was the opening he had been waiting for. He was half-underwater, but he forced himself up for air. "Tomorrow I leave for Cyangugu," he said to Niyonzima and Ineza, "and I want Bea to come with me." He glanced sidelong at her. "It is my greatest wish for her to celebrate Easter with my family."

"It's not possible," Bea said. "I'm needed here to help my father."

"Don't be silly," Niyonzima said. "Lately you forget *you* are *my* child, not the other way around. I'm perfectly capable of caring for myself, and if not, I have my wife."

Ineza gathered Bea into her shawl. "You must go. We can get through a day without you."

"How will I get home? I'm sure the bus doesn't run on Easter."

"Stay with us. You can sleep with my sister Jacqueline." Jean Patrick would leave her no way out. "There is a bus first thing Monday morning."

Bea's jaw relaxed, and Jean Patrick saw he had won. "You could have asked me first," she said. "Here in Butare, we live in modern times."

Jean Patrick smiled at her. "But I knew you would refuse me."

Bea raised her glass to her lips. The muscles in her neck formed taut ropes, and Jean Patrick imagined climbing them with his fingertips to feel her quickened pulse.

"We could drive you," Jonathan said. "We had planned to go to Nyungwe and stay in a cabin, hike around if the weather cooperated. But now we have this puppy, and Amos has gone home for Easter. This way, Susanne gets to see the forest, and we'll be back in time to feed Kweli."

"You can still have your vacation," Ineza said. "I'll take care of Kweli until Bea comes back, and then Bea will take over until you return. Just tell us what to do."

Bea opened her mouth to speak, but Ineza's expression shushed her.

"We could be back Tuesday," Jonathan said. "Would that be too long?"

"Perfect," Ineza said. "Then we'll have our own Easter on Wednesday, when everyone is here."

"It's a deal," Jean Patrick said in English.

At first he thought he had said it wrong, because Jonathan frowned, but when he followed Jonathan's gaze, he saw that his words had nothing to do with the expression of concern.

Susanne sat with a photo of schoolchildren in her lap. She stared intently at their faces. They were lined up on the steps of the school, laughing for the camera. Tears streaked her cheeks, and at first she didn't respond when Jonathan spoke. She was still with the children, taking their picture, loving them.

"Do you know what someone told me? At least I think I got this right." The back door opened, and Claire came in to clear the table. The candles flickered. Susanne sheltered a single flame with her cupped palm and waited for Claire to leave before continuing. "A government biologist, one who speaks English, said the teachers have made lists of all the Tutsi children. He said the burgomaster demanded it."

Bea and Niyonzima looked at Ineza. Ineza looked at the floor.

Susanne said, "And it's worse than that. The burgomaster wanted a list of every Tutsi household, every Tutsi business in the commune, with explicit directions to each one. The biologist is Tutsi himself, and I think he told me all this because he was afraid they were going to be killed. Because he thought there was something I could do, as an American, to stop it." She let her hands fall on top of the photo, palms up, as if waiting for good fortune to drop into them.

☙

Jean Patrick had been right in his prediction: on Saturday morning, Coach seemed determined to drive him into the ground one last time before Easter vacation. Fartlek training had been abandoned; the tire was back. Up and down the arboretum hills, its dead weight pulling Jean Patrick backward. Again and again in a cold mist until he doubled over, gasping for air.

"One more," Coach said. Jean Patrick did not think he could do it, but at the last moment, Coach took off the harness, and Jean Patrick floated, weightless, on his sprint to the top. He reached the crest where the new guardhouse stood and flung his hands into the air. "I'm a bird!"

The new guard was a surly man, solitary and silent. The old guard had never returned, although once or twice, Jean Patrick thought he had seen him around town. A few weeks after the burning, one of the women in the fields told Jean Patrick that the guard and his family had walked to Burundi. Jean Patrick prayed it was so.

Coach jogged up the slope, grinning from ear to ear. "When you get to Worlds, this is how the race will feel—like flying," he said. Jean Patrick wasn't sure. The sensation was already fading, and he wondered if even Coach believed himself.

"I'll run easy with you for cooldown, then drive you back to your dorm," Coach said. They looped together between plots verdant with new growth. It was Itumba, the main rainy season, bean plants hanging from their stakes, pendulous with pods ripe for picking. The fog thinned, and a pale sun broke through.

"I'm pleased," Coach said. "This is a good time to leave for a break." He stopped and faced Jean Patrick. "You said you'd be back on Tuesday?"

"Just for a couple of days. Then again to Cyangugu for the rest of vacation. Uncle is getting a new boat—a motorboat—and he needs my help."

Coach took a toothpick from his shirt and put it in his mouth. "That's not possible. From Tuesday, you stay in Butare."

It was a command, not a request. It made no sense; Jean Patrick was sure Coach had said that he would be away. He wanted to ask, but they were at the car already, and suddenly Coach was no longer in a mood to talk. They loaded the tire into the trunk. Coach looked off into the forest as if he had already left.

BACK IN HIS dorm, Jean Patrick packed his clothes and books and a few gifts for the family. He picked up the photo of Paul Ereng. The backing still held, his Hutu card safely hidden behind it. His conversation with Coach had rattled him; this would be a good time to have the card. He was about to put it in his bag when Jonathan knocked at the door and the thought flew from his mind.

The instant Jean Patrick got in the car, he felt Bea's wrath. She greeted him with a cool hand and a slight tip of the chin. He puzzled over the previous evening, combing in vain through the smallest details to discover his offence. Then, while discussing Rwandan culture, she said in a loud voice, "Some of us have come into agreement with Western ways, while others still believe a woman has no rights, not even the choice of where to spend a holy day." Susanne made an amused uh-oh with her mouth, and Jean Patrick grinned, the answer suddenly clear. He could be patient. As surely as her temper had flared, it would burn out again, like a brush fire in dry grass.

Curious troops of colobus monkeys came out of the forest, and Bea sidled closer on the seat. When Jonathan passed the spot where Jean Patrick had kissed her, she brushed his leg with forgiving fingers.

Jonathan pointed out faults and folds, the mineral veins in the cliffs. "It absolutely shouts out geologic upheaval!" he said.

The roar of waterfalls echoed around them. They climbed out of the forest's shadow into the tea plantations, where the pickers appeared like swimmers, half their bodies lost in a green lake of leaves. The emerald flash rising from the land brought Jean Patrick home.

"Amazing," Susanne said. She leaned out the window to take pictures, so far that Jean Patrick readied himself to grab her. A shaft of sunlight streamed through a cloud.

"It looks like the light around Jesus's head in paintings," Jean Patrick remarked.

Susanne took a picture. "Or God's spirit," she said.

Jonathan raised an eyebrow. "Actually, its just a phenomenon called crepuscular rays."

"Oh, come on!" Susanne said. "How can that *not* mean good luck?"

"I GUESS THIS is it." Jonathan parked by the bus stop in Gashirabwoba. Jean Patrick and Bea got out.

"Come greet my family and have something to eat," Jean Patrick said.

"We'd love to," Jonathan said, "but it's going to be a long hike to the cabin in this slime."

"In Rwanda, it's rude to refuse an invitation. We are always visiting, visiting. Our doors are never closed."

"Especially if you bring Primus or urwagwa," Bea added.

"In that case, we'd better come," Jonathan said, opening the door for Susanne. "Although we have no alcoholic gifts this time. Next time we'll make up for it—promise."

They climbed the path, mud sucking at their feet. Jean Patrick scanned the hillside. The moment his eyes distinguished the compound from the trees, smoke coming from the cookhouse, he would know his family was safe, and his heart could slow its racing tempo. He saw the smoke first, a thin blue ribbon, the eucalyptus scent sharp in his nostrils, and then the new addition, which was finished, a fresh coat of paint over everything. He took Susanne's hand to help her over a deep rut. "Can I ask you to take a picture of my family? I haven't had a new one for a long time."

Susanne squeezed his fingers. "I'd be honored."

Emmanuel noticed them first. Then a young man Jean Patrick barely recognized as Zachary walked through the door. Uncle shouted. Zachary whooped. They rushed toward Jean Patrick, and the three of them collided halfway.

Clemence and Baby Pauline tumbled down the hillside, tugging a goat behind them on a string. Baby Pauline was no longer a baby, reedy and graceful, but the name had stuck. Clemence leapt into Jean Patrick's arms. She had blossoms in her hair, and memory cut him. He saw Mathilde, copper skinned in the morning, reciting the taxonomic system as she struck at weeds with her hoe. Like Mathilde, Clemence had a dusting of henna in her feathery hair, and she had her same lively copper-flecked eyes.

The twins, Aunt Esther, and Mama came from the cookhouse and encircled Jean Patrick and Bea in a long embrace. From the affection obvious in their hugs, he knew they already saw Bea as his wife. He could tell by the smoke in their clothes and their hair that they had long been busy preparing food for Easter.

The girls swarmed Susanne, touching her hair, her skin.

"I'm Clémentine," said Clarisse, giggling.

"I'm Clarisse," said Clémentine, and left it up to Jean Patrick to tell Susanne the truth.

Clemence brought the radio outside, and they all sashayed across the yard. Uncle took the group on a tour of the land and then showed off his new addition to the house.

"Time for family portraits. Everybody squeeze in." Susanne waved them together.

"Wait! Jacqueline is coming now," Jean Patrick said. He watched her pick her way up the path in high-heeled sandals. She had grown strong and solid like Uncle's family; the tall, skinny frame he had inherited from Mama had passed her by. He took her by the wrists and spun her around. "Movie star!" he said, touching her satiny sleeve. "Why all these glamour clothes?"

"I have a sweetheart," she whispered.

"Me, too." Jean Patrick took her hand. "Come meet Bea and my two friends. Susanne is taking our picture." Before they reached the gathering, he stopped her. "There's something I need you to do." He whispered in her ear, and she giggled and nodded.

He made introductions and joined the group beside Bea. She laughed, chin tipped toward the sky. Susanne clicked. Zachary looked out, somber and formal for the camera. Jean Patrick poked him, and his serious face fell apart. Susanne caught his laughter. Mama and Aunt Esther tittered, shy as schoolgirls. Another frame. Then a picture of Jacqueline and Bea, posing together beside the jacaranda. Pili came up from her nest to see what she was missing.

"You have a dog," Susanne said. "He needs to be in the picture."

"*She*," Jean Patrick corrected. "Jonathan, you come, too."

"Perfect," Susanne said, and she took the picture. Then Jean Patrick traded places with her and got a shot with Susanne in the midst of the family. As he handed her the camera, he caught a bright flash like a glint of metal from the near ridge. It was so quick he doubted his own observation, but then it happened again. He scanned the ridge but saw no one, nothing. Stray lightning, he thought, although he could see no storm clouds.

"One more—a real family photo this time, a serious one." Susanne pulled Jean Patrick back into the huddle and directed them into position. "Ready? One, two three: fromage!"

"Fromage!" The shutter closed just as Jean Patrick caught the flash at the periphery of his vision, and this time he knew his eyesight was beyond doubt.

JEAN PATRICK ENTERED the cramped shop. Jacqueline had taken Bea for a long walk, as he had asked. The bell above the door jingled with a high, bright note. The shelves were crowded with appliances—electric irons, radios of various sizes and shapes, a few small TVs. There was even an electric sewing machine on a broken wooden table. A row of glass cases displayed watches and jewelry. The jeweler pushed up his magnifiers and looked up from his work.

"Last time I was here," Jean Patrick said, "I looked at a necklace, a gold cross. Do you still have it?"

The jeweler beamed. "I do! And I know who you are now. I thought you looked familiar, but I couldn't place you. The baker across the street told me. May God help you in your journey to the Olympics."

"Thank you, muzehe. I believe He helps me every day."

The jeweler took out a white box from behind the counter. "From the look on your face, I guessed you'd be back." He held out a small cross on a delicate chain, freshly polished.

"It's perfect. Thank you."

"I knew your father," the jeweler said. "He was my son's teacher." His gaze, pleased and distant, took in some faraway place. "Now my son is a father and a teacher himself." Taking the cloth from the counter, he shined the cross one last time and placed it carefully back in the box.

"I'm glad my father's spirit lives on." Jean Patrick took a sheaf of folded bills from his pocket and counted them. The day he brought Bea to meet his family, he'd begun saving—skipping meals, wearing socks until his toes poked through. He'd washed dishes at a restaurant when the boy who usually did them was sick. He was intent on finding a special gift for her, and when he saw the cross, he knew he had found it. Uncle Emmanuel gave him what he lacked. He asked for a loan, but Uncle wouldn't hear of it. The jeweler took a wooden box from beneath the counter and put the money inside.

"Aren't you afraid you'll be robbed?"

"Imana has taken care of me for seventy years. I believe He can manage for the meager amount of time remaining to me." He patted Jean Patrick's hands as if shaping a loaf of bread. "May your wife wear this in good health. God bless you both."

Walking out the door, Jean Patrick noticed a spiderweb of cracks that spread from a hole in the corner of the window. "What happened?"

The jeweler shook his head. "These young toughs. No job, no future. All they can think to do is cause mischief. They hit every Tutsi business in town. In broad daylight. They got your friend the baker, too. He had to throw out a day's worth of bread and cakes, ruined from glass."

On the way home, Jean Patrick walked through the market. He passed a line of women sewing on treadle machines. "Something for your miss for Easter?" Their feet pushed the pedals with a quick, steady rhythm.

"I have what I need," Jean Patrick called out. Hungry, he picked out plump passion fruits from a hawker, and she put them in a sack.

From somewhere behind him, a voice called out, "Hey, you—Inyenzi." Jean Patrick kept walking. "Nkuba Jean Patrick. I'm talking to you. What are you these days? Uri umuhutu cyangwa umututsi?"

The question struck Jean Patrick like a slap, and he whirled around. Albert's face, his zigzag scar, confronted him. He was sitting with a group of guys, drinking beer. "I haven't forgotten you," Albert said, sighting down his finger. "Soon we'll meet again, and if I were you, I'd choose Hutu." His smile curdled Jean Patrick's blood. "Something big is coming, and when it does, you won't want to be Tutsi."

Jean Patrick took a passion fruit from his sack, split it with his teeth, and sucked the sweet juice. He spit out the skin, turned, and walked away. Drunken laughter followed him. His body tingled, every cell alert. He sensed them at his back but refused to look. Pushing through the tumult of noisy shoppers, he walked briskly through the market. He kept up his pace until the market din faded, replaced by birdsong in the bush. He sensed someone watching him, like a chilly wind on his skin. It was a familiar feeling, the same one he had when he was jumped in the alley, a knife appearing in Albert's hand. Somewhere behind him, a twig snapped, and then another. Whirling around, he crouched and readied himself to spring.

"Yampayinka data—don't shoot." The shape materialized from the trees so quickly that Jean Patrick doubted his eyes for the second time that day. Then the man stepped from the shadow, hands up, laughing.

"Mistah Cool! You are always jumping at me from the bush. What if I *did* have a gun?"

Roger clasped him and held him firm. Jean Patrick squeezed back, inhaled his brother's scent of tobacco and sour sweat.

"In that case, Mr. Olympics, you'd be on the ground already, staring at heaven." He took Jean Patrick's arm. "Let's stay off the trail—follow me.

We need to talk." He took a small mirror from his pocket and flashed it at the sun. "I've been trying to get your attention all morning."

"Aye! That was you? I should have guessed." Jean Patrick gave Roger the sack of fruit. "Take some—they're sweet." They stood in the afternoon warmth and ate. Purple juice painted their fingers.

"Let's walk, eh? I don't have too much time." Roger wiped his hands on his pants and took off through the undergrowth, his pace steady and constant, his eyes scanning the bush. "Do you remember our conversation about Rwanda's pulse?"

"Of course." Jean Patrick couldn't forget even if he wanted to—which he did.

"So you remember I said I would try to warn you?"

"As well."

"That pulse is racing now, and there is no chance to slow it. The talk is that something very big is coming soon."

Jean Patrick felt as if he had been pushed down a hill, rolling faster and faster, out of control. "I just saw this guy in the market—Albert, the one who broke my foot at Gihundwe and later tried to cut me. He used those exact words, *something big is coming.*"

"The guy who sells junk with his father in the market? The one with that ugly scar?"

"The same."

"I remember him from primary school. He was rotten then. It's good you never told me before or I would have paid him back. But now you have to listen; there are more important things than that country boy to worry about."

"What makes you think today is any different from yesterday or the day before?" Jean Patrick touched Bea's gift in his pocket. Hope touched him back. "RTLM is just stoking the fire as usual."

"RPF is well placed to know what's going on. In every commune, on every level—teachers, sector leaders, burgomasters—lists of Tutsi and opposition Hutu have been collected. It's the same all over the country. This is not coincidence; it's a plan for total annihilation, and it *is* in place."

A cool breeze penetrated Jean Patrick's clothing. The pattern, the line connecting the graph points, was there in front of his eyes. It must have started in Kigali, as Pascal told Daniel when they were still at Gihundwe.

Then spread out, commune by commune, a cancerous growth. *The teachers have made lists of all the Tutsi children,* Susanne had said. The fit was too clear; he couldn't change variables, produce a different answer.

"What can we do?"

"Last month I was in Burundi, recruiting," Roger said. "I found Spéciose, Mama and Uncle's sister. She's waiting for the family." Roger stared out toward the lake. Clouds swooped down from the mountains in Zaire, turning the water to steel. "I know some guys, friends of mine, who can take you all across. A rowboat to Zaire, then overland to Burundi. I told them to be here Wednesday night."

"Can't it wait?" Jean Patrick was thinking of dinner with Bea. He couldn't miss it. He himself would never leave, but he wanted to be with his family, to see them off. If things happened as Roger said. If this craziness was anything more besides empty bluster. If, if, if.

"It's too urgent," Roger said. "I've spent three years in the middle of this war." He tapped his nose. "By now, I can smell the difference between smoke and fire. This fire is large."

"What about Thursday? Can't it wait till then?" Jean Patrick showed Roger the cross. "I plan to ask Bea to marry me," he said.

"Aye! The same? Last time I saw you, you said it was finished."

"And I also said she would be back."

"So she's the one I saw through my binoculars." Roger chuckled. "The one who's not muzungu. The beautiful one."

Jean Patrick grinned and nodded.

Roger flashed a smile and embraced Jean Patrick. "That's wonderful," he said. The smile lingered an instant before he turned serious again, jiggling his hand as if physically weighing the question. "I'll see what I can find out. If you don't hear from me, the answer is yes."

Jean Patrick thanked him. "But Uncle will never go." It was too fast, too soon. He couldn't think quickly enough to untangle the threads of his questions.

"That is the reason we are not going to tell him beforehand," Roger said.

"He'd be fighting with the RPF if he were younger."

"He is already. I couldn't tell you before, but for years he's been giving us money. He even smuggled weapons from Burundi once, in his pirogue."

Jean Patrick laughed. He could see it now so clearly, yet he had never suspected. "Why can't they cross in the new motorboat? He'll never leave it behind; he worked too hard to get it."

"No engine noise. But if these guys show up and we don't give Uncle the chance to go back and forth in his mind, maybe the two of us can persuade him. If not, he'll make sure everyone else goes. At the very least, we can get the rest of the family to safety."

"I don't think Auntie will ever leave without Uncle."

"True. Another reason I think we can persuade him."

"What about you?"

Roger shook a cigarette from his pack. "My fight is here. What I've trained for—my Olympics. And you? Do I have to put a gun to your head?"

"If you did, you would have to use it. I won't go. I have too much at stake."

"If they kill you, you can't run. If you are alive, in Burundi, you have a chance."

"They can't hurt me; I'm too well known. Habyarimana can never let it happen because he wants to look good for the West. As I told you, *he* needs *me.*"

They walked quickly. Smoke from Roger's cigarette fanned out behind him. "It is likely," Roger said, "your friend Habyarimana won't be around to help you."

"What are you saying?" Jean Patrick said.

"You should keep up with *Kangura* if you want to predict the future. They do quite well, much better, even, than the umupfumu with his sizzled spit and chicken entrails. They said Habyarimana would die in March."

"So you see? It's April already, and he is alive and well." Despite his effort to control it, Jean Patrick's voice came out shrill.

Roger stopped and took Jean Patrick's wrists. "I have to leave you here. If I can't change the date, is there any way you can come on Wednesday?"

"I will do my best, " Jean Patrick said, but in his heart he knew he would not.

Ahead of them, the familiar trail reached toward the compound, worn from years of traffic. Their lives, their world, were here. Every morning, fishermen went out to the lake, and women and children went to the fields. Hutu or Tutsi, they fetched water, gathered firewood, balanced loads on their heads. In the evening, they padded along paths up the ridge or down into the valley with bare and dusty feet. They cooked, ate, drank beer, and scolded children. In the darkness, men and women lay together and created new life. This was the dance of Rwanda. Jean Patrick could not let himself believe that this dance, as familiar as the beat of his heart, would suddenly end. And how could they leave it behind?

Roger stubbed out his cigarette and flicked it into the bush. He put his arms around Jean Patrick, and they held each other. How strange, Jean Patrick thought, to be looking down at his older brother's face. With his eyes, he traced the square, strong jaw, the scar that ran the length of his cheek, the thin and wiry beard. He committed them firmly to memory.

"In the meantime," Roger said, "take very good care of yourself."

"Always. And you the same."

Although Jean Patrick was well trained in tracking movement in the forest, it was not long before his brother's form melted into the tree shadows he had stepped from.

A ROARING SOUND invaded Jean Patrick's sleep. He bolted up, unsure where he was. Then he felt Zachary beside him, heard the warm, rhythmic breath he knew as intimately as his own. Slowly the walls gained form from darkness. The roar became rain on the metal roof, the familiar song. Worn out from all his tossing and turning, he nestled against Zachary and sank into a pleasant dream of the past, his family around him, even Papa.

When he next awoke, Zachary's hand touched his shoulder. "Are you up?"

"Yes, Little Brother."

"I'm going to pray now. Will you come?"

Jean Patrick took his hand. Quietly they felt their way down the hall and through the front room. The front door sighed open. They stepped out into the wet air, somewhere between mist and drizzle, the sky past night but not yet dawn. Hand in hand, they walked the path to the hut where they had slept all those years, and Jean Patrick with Roger before that.

Zachary lit a lantern. He had transformed the hut into a shrine. The bookshelf served as an altar, an image of the sacred Virgin flanked by two candles. A painting hung on the wall, and Jean Patrick brought the light closer to inspect it. Two lambs, one black and one white, drank from a stream. Orchids and lilies grew along the banks, and creatures—birds or angels—floated in an amethyst sky. In the blocky, primitive shapes, Jean Patrick saw a child's view of heaven.

"Did you paint this? It looks like paradise."

"It is." Zachary's countenance took on the innocence of a child. "For so long this vision came to my eyes. I think there was a similar painting at Gihundwe where we used to pray with Papa." Jean Patrick couldn't remember. Certainly, it hadn't been there when he went to school. "I miss this place when I'm at Kibuye." Zachary talked in low tones, as if speech would disturb some sleeping spirit. "It's the best place for me to worship, the place I feel closest to God."

Strange, Jean Patrick mused, how a person's traits passed from one generation to the next. Papa had a gift for science, but he could also turn his passion into lyric phrases on the page. As if these two halves had unraveled, the scientific side had passed to Jean Patrick and the artist to Zachary.

Papa's Bible lay open on the altar to the Acts of the Apostles, and Jean Patrick read. *And being assembled together with them, He commanded them not to depart from Jerusalem, but to wait for the promise of the Father.* No, Jean Patrick thought. Zachary will never leave this place, not even if Uncle commands him.

IN ALL DIRECTIONS, a stream of colors looped through the trails, people from the hills coming down to church. Most of their bright clothes were not new, but had been saved for Easter: hemmed, mended, scrubbed in Omo, and pressed with a hot charcoal iron. Sunlight dappled the road, but the ground had not yet dried, pulling at their feet as if it did not want to let them go. Jean Patrick watched Bea, strolling ahead with the women. The girls chittered beside them, dashed in and out. They wound flowers they had picked through the ribbons in their hair. Jacqueline whispered something into Bea's ear. When Bea threw her head back to laugh, the single feather in her hat shivered.

Jean Patrick walked between Zachary and Uncle Emmanuel, hand in hand. Feeling his uncle's callused palm in his, it occurred to him that Uncle had long ago lost all recollection that Jean Patrick, Roger, and Zachary were not his blood sons. And then Jean Patrick realized that he, too, had long ago stopped making any such distinction.

ON THE WAY back from church, Jean Patrick asked Bea if she would walk with him a little farther. "I want to show you something of Gashirabwoba, something of where I come from." Together they walked down the wide dirt roads where paths plunged into the valley or rose dizzily into the hills. He showed her where his cousins lived, where he had raced Roger and honed the power in his legs, the stubbornness of his mind. Stopping beside a runneled trail into the bush, he pointed. "And that is where I finally beat him," he said. "Far, far up there."

Bea laughed and brushed his hand. "Shall we put up a shrine?"

"After my gold medal, we will do so." Jean Patrick wished he could take her in his arms and tell her about Roger, but the heaviness in his heart was not a burden he would share.

As if she had read his mind, Bea asked, "This famous Roger—he couldn't come home for Easter? Kenya is not so far off."

"We should get back, eh?" he said.

He had stopped again, this time to point out the eucalyptus grove where meetings were held, when a group of boys in Hutu Power garb walked by, RTLM blaring from a hulking radio one of them carried. *On the third or the fourth or fifth there will be a little something here in Kigali. You will hear the sound of bullets or grenades exploding.* Was there no rest from the station's fool nonsense? Not even on the day of the resurrection?

EVERYONE FROM THE neighboring hills came to the house to eat. They crowded together at the table or sat with a plate on a chair. Children spread out across the floor. Mukabera came with Olivette and her new husband. Olivette's belly was already swollen; by the time Jean Patrick came home at the end of the term, there would be a naming ceremony to attend.

Angelique and Uwimana flanked Jean Patrick; Fulgence and his family sat like royalty beside Uncle at the head of the table. The center of the table was piled with a feast: grilled fish, crispy sambaza, stews with cabbage and tomato and bits of chicken and goat meat. There were bowls of ibitoki bigeretse kub'ibishyimbo, the green bananas and beans that Uncle always piled high on his plate.

Bea dove into the center of commotion as if she had always been there, cleft from the same country clay. Jean Patrick wished he could just watch her, just eat, joke with his family. But trouble bunched under his skin. He could not sweep it away, not even for this one afternoon.

AFTER DINNER, JEAN Patrick and Bea walked with Uwimana and Angelique to their car. The clouds had scattered, and the earth, hardened. With a tenderness that made him ache, Jean Patrick watched Uwimana's long-familiar rolling gait, his round body, the expression on his face as if he were always listening for something essential and was afraid he would miss it.

Angelique whispered in Jean Patrick's ear, "I hope next time we see you, you will be man and wife. You must not let this wonderful woman go."

For luck, Jean Patrick touched the gold cross. "It is most certainly my wish."

They said good-bye at the bus stop, where Uwimana had parked. Jean Patrick held Bea's hand and watched the car bump and rattle toward the main road. If Roger was right, who among them would be safe? Would Uwimana, who had more than once been called icyitso? Would Bea's own mother, who could easily be taken for Tutsi? He pulled Bea close. "Are you glad you came?"

"Yes." She leaned her head against his chest. "So much."

"You're not angry with me anymore?"

"Eh? For what?"

"For kidnapping you against your will." Bea shook her head. Jean Patrick took her hand and placed his gift inside it. "Open it." He wished for a sudden splash of sun to glint from the gold, as it had done in the shop, but that did not happen.

Bea held the necklace, the delicate chain turning. "You are always buying me gifts."

"Not always: only twice."

She held it out to him, and he fastened it around her throat.

"I saw the necklace when I was home at Christmas, and I knew instantly how well it would fit right here." He touched the shadow where her collarbones came together. Such a miracle, this thing we call life, he thought, feeling the rise and fall of her breath against his finger.

Quickly he kissed her. She kissed him back, and he savored the salt and spice of her mouth, the sweetness of tea on her tongue. He took her hand and led her back toward the house.

Their lives were only starting. How could they be wrenched apart? How could any of them be picked up suddenly, cast down somewhere else, over mere politics that should not concern them? For his part, no matter what happened, he would be safe. He had bartered a future with his legs and his sweat and his pain.

IN THE MORNING, Jean Patrick took Bea to the bus stop in a slanting rain. He held Mama's parasol above their heads. Bea held her sandals in her hand. Jean Patrick also walked barefoot, and with every step he sank to his ankles. The earth released his feet with a loud sucking sound.

"Are you tired?" Bea said. "You're not talking—it's not the Nkuba I know."

"You also are not talking."

"Did you run this morning?"

"Aye! In such a storm?" But he had, setting out in darkness, seeking the grass, the drier paths in the forest, pulling his feet high in the places where mud nibbled at his legs with swampy lips. Only when he ran, when every fiber in his body strained to propel him forward, could he sort out these problems that went round and round in his head. "Even for one day I will miss you," he said.

"Me, also—I will miss you."

Jean Patrick was about to kiss her, hidden by the umbrella, when a loud horn stopped him. A truck idled beside them, and Uwimana's head poked out from the window. "I was hoping to find you," he shouted. "In this rain I thought you could wait in the truck."

Jean Patrick and Bea climbed in, raindrops pooling on the seat. They squeezed together in the cab. Uwimana kept the engine idling, and steamy warmth surrounded them. Bea's internal heat spread across Jean Patrick's thigh. He had barely slept, and now he couldn't keep his eyes from closing. Indirimbo za buracyeye, Rwanda's soothing morning music, hummed softly on the radio. A river flowed on the road. Tails of water arced from tires of passing cars. The bus lumbered up the grade like a great beast, two round eyes of headlights glaring through the deluge.

Jean Patrick took Mama's parasol, and he and Bea ran across the road. "I'll meet you at the stop tomorrow when you come in," she said. Her fingers touched the cross at her neck, and Jean Patrick smiled.

Jean Patrick ran back to Uwimana's truck and climbed in. "I would offer you a ride home," Uwimana said, "but soon I would be stuck, and we would both be pushing." He turned up the radio. "I love this music more than any other. It always reminds me of my childhood." He hummed along.

"Me, too. We had a plug-in radio, and when I was small, I thought the singers were somehow inside it. I thought they had slipped in through the wire." Jean Patrick smiled at the memory. "I kept that radio forever, even though we had no electricity in Gashirabwoba."

Uwimana chuckled. "I remember."

"Aye!" Jean Patrick slapped his knee. "Now that I think of it, that radio still sits on a shelf in Zachary's room. Maybe someday electricity will come and they can use it again."

Neither of them moved. A fresh onslaught of rain hit the windshield. Uwimana turned the wipers on, turned them off again. "You can stay here," he said, "until this storm eases."

"Thank you. I'm happy for your company." Jean Patrick looked over at Uwimana, and Uwimana looked back, a faint, dreamy smile on his lips. An invisible thread bound them together inside the safe island of the cab. Jean Patrick did not want to be the one to break it.

&

The next morning, it was Jean Patrick's turn to say good-bye. He pushed open the bus window and waved to his family one last time. "I'll see you Thursday," he shouted. Roger had not returned, and so their plan held; he would not have to choose between Bea and his flesh and blood. It was nearly ten o'clock, and although he had eaten some bread and fruit, he had run hard intervals first thing, and already his stomach grumbled. A woman squeezed sideways into the seat beside him, her swollen belly nearly in the aisle. She placed a basket of fruit between them, and a ripe sweetness came through the skins of mangoes and guavas to stir up Jean Patrick's hunger even more.

By the time the bus stopped in Gikongoro, he couldn't stand it. Although it was against Rwandan custom to eat in such a public place, he whistled to a hawker and bought an ear of roasted corn. Turning toward the window, he took a bite and chewed slowly.

"Eh-eh," the pregnant woman chided. "Have you no respect for our ways? You—a grown man—how can you eat so, in front of all of us?"

Jean Patrick slumped in his seat. "I'm very hungry, Mama. I am feeling weak."

From across the aisle a grandmother called out. "He's a boy still. And so skinny! Ko Mana—leave him be."

"We are all hungry," a toothless old farmer said. "And yet only he is eating."

The pregnant woman rested her hand on her belly and smiled. "Maybe he is eating for his children." She turned to him, her face radiant. "Is that what you are doing?"

Jean Patrick had hidden the corn beside him on the seat. "I have no children yet, Mama, but I am hoping to."

A young woman with a head full of plaits turned toward him. "Do you have umukunzi?" In the crowded bus, everyone's eyes were on Jean Patrick.

"Yes, I have a sweetheart," he said. "A very beautiful one."

"Well, then it is settled," the grandmother said. She addressed her comments to the passengers. "He is eating for the children that are still inside him." She showed a row of small white teeth.

"Yes, it's settled," the pregnant woman said. "He has children inside him that need his food, and also, he is little more than a boy himself." She prodded Jean Patrick. "Eat well. We won't scold you anymore."

She returned her hand to her belly and cocked her head as if listening to her child, hearing its steady, beating heart. Jean Patrick took another bite of his corn. A kernel fell onto his jacket, and he brushed it away. Such a blessing to have life swimming and turning inside you, he thought, readying itself to push out into the world.

AT THE STATION, Jean Patrick didn't see Bea, and his stomach twisted. He pushed through the crowd, scanning the sea of bright headscarves crowned with basins filled to the brim. There was a small market at the bus stop on Tuesdays, and a row of blankets and stalls had sprouted up beneath the ocher brick walls. The sharp smells of raw meat and fermented fruit greeted his nostrils. One after another, scenarios of disaster went through his mind: Bea was angry again; she had found someone else, a good Hutu boy; she was involved in some politics and had forgotten he was coming. Then he spotted her. She was merely haggling with a woman over a bunch of green bananas. Catastrophe vanished from his mind.

Bea's back was to him. She wore a purple and red pagne with a design of birds in flight, a yellow shawl tied about her shoulders. Beside her were Ineza's two market baskets, already full. Bea and the woman's voices rose and fell in an ancient song that seemed to please them both. Bea won the bananas. The hawker, also victorious, pocketed her coins.

Jean Patrick could have stood and watched in secret for a long time, but as she stooped to pick up her baskets, her gaze fell on him. "Just in time. I couldn't imagine how I was going to carry all my things without putting these dirty bananas on my head." Jean Patrick laughed at the thought. He took the heavy stalk from her. "For tomorrow night," she said. "Mama and Claire have already started cooking. You would think an entire RPF garrison was coming for dinner." She jangled a set of keys. "I borrowed a car from Dadi's friend, but first we have to feed Kweli. She's very cute but also very spoiled, a muzungu dog."

Jean Patrick stretched out his legs. His hamstrings had started to cramp in the bus, his muscles sore from the morning workout. A pleasant burn told him he had worked as hard as he could. They walked toward a row of parked vehicles where bicycle-taxi boys called out and rang their bells. The air had been swept clean by rain. It tingled his cheeks, cold and vibrant. He felt truly alive, and for this moment at least, hope won out over the night's long moments of despair.

BEA UNLOCKED JONATHAN'S gate and then the front door. Kweli's plaintive yowl greeted them. They took off their shoes and entered the darkened house. It smelled of absence, unaired and dank. Jean Patrick slid along the floor in his socks. "Someday, I will have a house like this," he said. "It's as big as my dorm — the entire building, I mean."

Bea pulled back the curtains and threw open the windows. Sunlight poured in, falling in stripes across the floor. From behind a closed door, the puppy yelped again.

"She's demanding her dinner," Bea said. "She eats and eats and eats, that one." She headed toward the room.

"Do you know when they're coming back?" Jean Patrick's skin buzzed with Bea's nearness.

"They told Mama not to expect them until after dark."

"And Amos is still gone?"

Bea spun around. "Why do you ask, huh?"

"I am concerned for the dog is all. Me, I like dogs too well."

Kweli whined and scratched at the door. "Ko Mana, stop!" Bea opened the door, and Kweli bounded out. Laughing, Bea chased after her, and Jean Patrick followed. Before they could catch her, she squatted and peed. "You!" Bea said, but she was still laughing.

She picked her up, dripping, and carried her outside while Jean Patrick found a cloth to clean up the mess. When he was done, he went inside the room where Kweli had been confined. It was a bedroom, a small bed pushed against the wall, but Jonathan had turned it into an office, books and rocks spilling into every available space. Jean Patrick adjusted the shutters at the window to let in the sun and peeked between the slats. Bea was on her knees in the grass, calling the puppy. The dog ignored her and continued to run in circles around the yard. Bea cooed and wiggled her fingers as if showing a special treat. The puppy trotted to her then, her whole body an enormous wiggle, and Bea scooped her into her arms.

"Success," she said, putting Kweli down on her blanket. "She's finished her business for a while." She bolted for the door, and Bea closed it just in time. "I'll have to feed her now."

"Come here by the window," Jean Patrick said. "I want to look at you." He grabbed the edges of her shawl and pulled her over. The sun through the shutters drew lines of light and dark across her blouse. He pulled off the shawl. The puppy chewed on a leg of the bed, and Bea took a pen from the desk and threw it. "Aye-yay. Stop!"

With his arm around her waist, Jean Patrick reeled her in. "Her or me?"

Bea laughed. "Both."

Jean Patrick began beneath her chin, planting small kisses until he reached the base of her throat. He lifted the necklace and took the muscle beneath it in his teeth. His slow-burning hunger became a hard-edged flame.

"It's not a good time," Bea said. "I can't."

"What do you mean?" His voice was hoarse, as if need scalded his larynx.

"I could get pregnant," she said.

"Even better." He undid a button of her blouse and then another. "If your belly grows, you'll have to marry me."

"I mean it. We can't do this."

But when he kissed her, she kissed him back. He unfastened the rest of her blouse and slid it down her shoulders. She wriggled her arms, and it fell to the floor with a whispered *shush*. Zigzags of light streaked her breasts, her dark, encircled nipples. Kneeling in front of her, he unwound her pagne, pulled down her lacy leggings. She stepped free of them. He traced the angled patterns on her skin, first with a finger and then with his tongue.

BOOK THREE

DEATH BECOMES HUNGRY

Urupfu rurarya ntiruhaga.

Death eats and is never full.

TWENTY-FOUR

THE NEXT MORNING, Jean Patrick would leave for Cyangugu to spend the day with his family. In the darkest hour of night, Roger would come with his friends. They would walk silently to the lake beneath a sky heavy with clouds, no moon to guide them. They would embrace. Uncle would refuse to abandon his land, Auntie would refuse to abandon her husband. Jean Patrick and Roger would try to persuade them, and then, with everyone else in the boat, Uncle would ask Jean Patrick one last time to go. No, he would tell him. Although it struck a blow to his heart to defy the man who had been his father, to say good-bye to his family, he couldn't let go of his dream. He knew that in the end, Emmanuel would understand.

Whenever he shut his eyes, the scene came to him, so close he could put his arms around each member of his family, feel the pressure of their embrace, their warm breath on his skin. But it was the last moment that bothered him, the moment after he told Uncle he would not go. In his mind, he saw Uncle's foot inside the boat. Which way would he turn? Was there a chance he would step in with his other foot, take Auntie's hand, and guide her in as well? Or would they turn back, walk up the path, hand in hand?

Each time he tried to think of something else, there it was again, calling him. He could not tear himself away to return here, to Butare, to this moment of the life he called his own. He might as well have stuck to Roger's original plan so he could live the scene in reality instead of this torture of wait and imagine, imagine and wait.

From the dinner table, Jean Patrick watched the Cup of Nations game out of the corner of his eye. At least football could distract him from his mental twists and turns. Michel Bassolé, his favorite player, had just scored his second goal of the night for Côte d'Ivoire. The game was tied again.

Jean Patrick wanted the Francophones to win. So far, it had been a very exciting game.

This was supposed to be a celebration, an introduction for Jonathan and Susanne to Easter Rwandan-style, but Jean Patrick couldn't keep his mind in the present. Before dinner, when they sat together and watched the game, not even Bea's thigh against his leg could anchor him. When Ineza called them to eat, he had not wanted to move.

Jonathan and Niyonzima were discussing politics. Habyarimana had gone to Dar es Salaam to sign the final peace accord with the RPF. At this moment, he was flying home.

"This will be the turning point, don't you think?" Jonathan said. "The opposing sides sat down and came to an agreement. Habyarimana has stood up to the extremists and decided to compromise." No one answered, and Jonathan fidgeted with his fork. "I mean, this time, the door is open for peace, isn't it? Even the president of Burundi was at the table," he said.

Once more, Jean Patrick allowed himself to believe. If Jonathan's wish came true, Roger's plan would be called off, and Tutsi could begin to live in peace again with their Hutu neighbors. Maybe there would be an announcement on TV tonight, after the president landed.

Bea shook her head. "How many times have we thought this, only to have our hopes trampled beneath the feet of a rioting mob?"

Jean Patrick returned his attention to the television. Enough was enough. All he wanted right now was to replace confusion with the all-absorbing pursuit of a world-class game. Claire cleared the dishes and brought fruit, coffee, and tea. Jean Patrick was tired from his afternoon run—twelve kilometers at a steady pace, out and back to the National Museum, then eight times around the track. The two glasses of wine had gone to his head, and his eyes kept closing. The Cup of Nations went into extra time, and he was just about to suggest they watch the rest of the game when the screen went blank.

"What's this?" Niyonzima asked. The power had not gone off. He pushed himself up on his cane and went into the living room. He pounded the TV set, turned it off and on, off and on. The screen flashed—it clearly had current—but the picture did not return.

The set could not have gone dead at a more inconvenient moment. "Is it broken?" Jean Patrick asked.

Bea turned on the radio. Classical music played. "That's odd," she said. She switched from Radio Rwanda to RTLM. The usual diatribe burst through the speakers. Then the classical piece came on the television, too, but the screen stayed blank.

"No," Bea said. "It isn't broken. I believe something has happened in Kigali."

THE INYENZI-INKOTANYI HAVE killed our beloved president. Now they want to kill you. Hutu, we ask that you do patrols, as you are used to doing. Remember how to use your usual tools. Defend yourselves. Clear the brush, search the houses and the marshes, put up barriers so that nothing can escape.

These were the words that spewed from RTLM as dawn approached, a grisly shift of color out of the mist of night. The announcements had come the previous evening. First, that the president's plane had crashed on approach to the runway, and then that it had been shot down and there were no survivors. For the first time in Rwanda, the radio did not go off at ten o'clock, and everyone had remained in the living room all night, listening. It hadn't taken long to blame the RPF, UNIMAR, all Tutsi. By ten o'clock came the curfew declaration. Anyone found violating the order would be killed.

"How convenient that makes it," Niyonzima said grimly. "Just kick down the doors and start shooting." Jean Patrick knew he was thinking of his friends and colleagues.

Despite the edict to stay off the streets, Jonathan and Susanne had made their way home at midnight, terrified for Amos's safety. He was due back that evening from vacation, and they had been calling and calling the house, but there was no answer. They phoned when they got home to say he was safe, asleep in his hut, and they didn't have the heart to wake him. Since then, they'd been phoning every hour to ask if there was anything they could do. In the midst of the maelstrom, such tiny miracles: connections still worked, and the power was still on.

Now the TV was on, sound mute, and there, in front of Jean Patrick, was a scene he could not have conjured up in the wildest and most terrible regions of his imagination. On road after road, at roadblock after roadblock, some no more than tree limbs or cases of beer, Interahamwe and their cohorts killed methodically, mechanically. Machetes and spears, staffs and clubs, a rhythmic rise and fall as if pounding sacks of grain. Cars and trucks abandoned, smashed, burning. Bodies stacked by the side of the road, limbs splayed, dark stains spreading beneath them. Streets a scatter of clothing and belongings.

The incantations on RTLM buzzed in Jean Patrick's brain. *Here are the names of RPF traitors. You must act very fast! Force them out!*

"We should leave right now," Ineza said. For the first time, Jean Patrick saw terror in her eyes.

Niyonzima leaned both hands on his cane and rose stiffly from his chair to comfort her. It was an impossible wish, of course. They had no car, and Niyonzima could barely walk. "We're safe here," he said. "We have our Tutsi préfet to protect us. We know him well enough; he has shared our food, our hospitality. He will never stand for this madness." Ineza patted his hand, but Jean Patrick saw no conviction in her gesture.

Day broke colorless and wet, rain a dirty bandage fraying from the clouds. Niyonzima looked up with glazed eyes. "Is there someone I can phone in Cyangugu?"

Uwimana, of course. But Jean Patrick had never had reason to know his number. Coach would know, but he was gone. No one was at school, with Easter. Thoughts came one numbed word at a time. Today was Thursday. He was supposed to be in Cyangugu. Roger's friends were supposed to take his family to safety. Too late, too late. Without hope, Jean Patrick could only pray that Roger's plan would come to pass without him.

"No," Jean Patrick said. "There is no one."

Ineza pointed at the television and then she fainted. Bea screamed and collected her into her lap. On the screen, a group of shirtless men were poised above a pregnant woman, a machete blade at her naked belly.

Claire had just come in from the cookhouse. "We are all dead now," she said. She knelt beside Bea and put a hand to Ineza's forehead. "Niyonzima—muzehe—I am asking. Please turn this thing off so your wife can come back to the living with a few seconds of peace."

TIME DRIFTED SIDEWAYS. They orbited the television like moths drawn to an intoxicating, deadly flame. As many times as Jean Patrick turned away, his eyes came back to the wreckage. Ineza sat beside him, wrapped in a shawl. Her untouched cup of tea cooled on the table. Rain slammed the window. How long would this go on? Jean Patrick paced, sat, paced again. Every muscle in his body screamed until finally he leapt up.

"I have a Hutu card at school. I'm going to fetch it. I need to get to Cyangugu."

"Mon pauvre," Ineza said. "Once you leave the safety of Butare, how far do you think you will get before someone catches you? With your long fingers and skinny legs, who in a crazed mob will think you Hutu? Did you not hear? At roadblocks, they are inspecting fingers, forcing people to roll up their pants and show their calves."

"Mama is right," Bea said, slipping inside Ineza's shawl with her. "Your Hutu card will buy you nothing."

Jean Patrick felt a jolt of fear pass between them. The realization came to him like a snap of the fingers: with her high forehead, her thin artist's hands and golden skin, her Hutu card would be just as useless; her blood would mix with his in the street.

It rained all morning. Water pooled in the garden, the sky waxen, no way to tell the hour. From the top of the wall, glass teeth gnashed at the mist. Sometime in the early afternoon, a lively traditional tune interrupted the rant on RTLM. At the end of the song, the announcer came back. *The traitor prime minister, Agathe Uwilingiyimana, is not working anymore. She has been killed. We know our enemies, and we will seek them out.* The Rwandan Army had also captured ten Belgian soldiers who had been assigned to protect her, the announcer bragged. They were taken to the army camp, where they were beaten to death. *UNAMIR will soon flee in terror, its tail between its legs, and then the rest of the whites will follow. Soon no one will remain to judge us. We will carry out our work with their blessing.*

Soon after came more announcements of executions: candidates for the presidency of the transitional government, leaders of opposition parties, the president of the Constitutional Court, who would have sworn the new president in.

"God help us," Ineza said. "We have descended into hell." She wept openly. Jean Patrick was ashamed because he found no tears to shed.

BY LATE AFTERNOON, there were boastful reports of killings in Gisenyi. In Byangabo, Busogo, Gikongoro. In Kivumu, Murambi, Mudende, and Ruhuha.

"My God. Beyond Butare, no safe or sane place remains in this country," Bea said.

And then came reports of killings in Cyangugu. Jean Patrick listened to the names with his head in his hands until the need to move drove him from his chair. The absence of his family from the lists did little to console him. He escaped into the rain, ran laps around the garden until he was soaked to his core, but he could not run fast enough to leave his guilt behind. He came in, stood shivering and trembling by the fire.

Bea came to stand beside him, and he took her in his arms. "My brother Roger," he began. "He is not working in Kenya. He is RPF."

Bea nodded and took a breath, but Jean Patrick put a finger to her lips before she could speak.

"I know you well enough to have read the suspicion in your mind about my story," he said. And then he told her of his last meeting with his brother, about the plan to flee. "If only I had not been so selfish, had not begged for an extra day. If I had listened more closely, believed more urgently what he told me. I should have been there on Wednesday to persuade Uncle eye to eye. If I had been, I would know now that our family was safe. I would have seen it for myself." *If, if, if.* An endless, pointless march of *ifs*.

Bea held his hands to her cheek. "You cannot blame yourself. None of us could have predicted *this*," she said.

Niyonzima was busy phoning journalists and friends in Europe. Someone had to send soldiers; someone would rescue them from this madness. He tried to telephone Kigali but could not get through. Most likely, none of his friends were left to answer. Jonathan phoned to say he was in constant touch with the U.S. Embassy, and it was only a matter of time. The world would not stand by. He phoned again later to say he was still trying, promising that he would not leave, would not abandon them, no matter what.

"You must eat," Claire said. She brought dishes of food and set them on the table.

"Thank you," Bea said. She hugged Claire, rocked her. "You save us."

Ineza rose to draw the curtains as night drew its curtain over day. RTLM was a hiss in the background, a force too strong to resist. *RPF ibyitso were found hiding in the home of a Tutsi businessman. Now they are being grilled right there. Now they are burning.*

Jean Patrick pressed his hands to his ears. "I shouldn't stay here. I'm putting all of you in danger. I will go to the church or some other place of refuge. I know all the hidden routes."

"Don't be foolish," Niyonzima said. "Do you think with my politics I am any less a dead man than you?" He wobbled to his feet. "Eh — let me stop this talk. Claire has been kind enough to cook for us. Let us eat." His hand reached to silence the radio, but the announcer's message stopped him.

We will tell you the names of these traitors as we learn them. We will tell you how to find them. We will tell you the ones we have already found and killed.

The announcer reeled off names as if reporting the day's football scores. Niyonzima turned up the volume. He moaned for his friends. Ineza gasped for her cousin. Jean Patrick heard Pascal's name, and then he heard Daniel's.

ALONE AND SLEEPLESS in Bea's room, Jean Patrick tossed from side to side. When he closed his eyes, it was Daniel he saw, his face at the window, the dot of tongue like a tiny berry he was enjoying. Ear cocked to the sound of a woman's laughter in the night.

The house hummed with silence. Jean Patrick listened for a noise from the road, an insect's whir from the bush. Nothing moved. Not a dog barked, not a night bird shrieked. Even the land held its breath and waited. The world teetered on its axis, its center of gravity skewed. And then a thought took root: he could run. All these months of running, avoiding checkpoints, remaining hidden before first light, had taught Jean Patrick the trails to take. He could get to the marshes. He could fight his way through the mud and urubingo, the cutting fronds of umunyeganyege and the choking thickness of papyrus. He could make it to Burundi. He could take Bea's hand and leave all this behind.

❦

As one day lapsed into the next, Jean Patrick felt like a caged animal pacing the boundaries of his enclosure. Nervous energy sparked between the fibers of his calves. He did push-ups beside the desk in Bea's room until his arms collapsed, sit-ups until his stomach twisted. Time no longer kept its neat divisions of day and night. Before falling into bed, he would listen at the door of her parents' bedroom for Bea's quiet breath as she slept beside Ineza, the tick of her life his one constant clock.

Niyonzima stayed in his office and spoke on the phone in low, cajoling tones. He slept there now so he could maintain contact with the world at all hours. In Kigali, the list of his friends grew shorter. One by one, he heard their names announced on RTLM. In Europe, his contacts apologized and said there was nothing they could do. They would keep trying, but no one was listening. Rwanda had no oil or strategic interest, no diamonds or gold.

Niyonzima had been trying to get information from Cyangugu, but no one he knew could get out. Days of rain had left the roads in the countryside impassable. Helpless and powerless, all Jean Patrick could do was pray that Imana had looked down with pity and, with a breath of wind, had blown his family safely down the river to Burundi.

Butare persisted as an island of uneasy calm in a sea of complete madness. The Tutsi préfet appealed for Hutu and Tutsi to patrol together and keep the killers out. *Amahoro n'ubumwe* was the message: peace and unity. At least for now.

On the third day, Jean Patrick woke up and went to sit near the fire. No matter how he tried to change the conclusion, his mind came back to the thought that Coach, and only Coach, could help him now. Claire came in from the cookhouse and knocked on Niyonzima's door. "We're out of milk and margarine. Tomorrow, we'll be out of bread. I have slaughtered my girl's favorite rooster, and she is grieving."

The back door burst open, and the children ran in. The boy fired a machine gun made from a stick. "Tutsi snake, I'll kill you!" he shouted. The girl squealed with laughter.

"Mana yanjye." Claire clapped her son's head. "I never want to hear you say that again."

"They can't help it," Niyonzima said. He stepped from his office and held the sobbing child close. The stick gun clattered to the floor. "It's all they hear now, day and night." He let the boy go and straightened his shorts. "This can't go on much longer. They will have to let us go to market. Until then, we must live on our garden and whatever else remains." As he turned to go back inside his office, Jean Patrick caught him.

"Yes—please come in," Niyonzima said.

They went through the necessary dance of polite conversation. "I've been thinking," Jean Patrick said then. "The headmaster at Gihundwe was like a father to me since Papa's death. He may have news of my family. If I could get to my coach, I could get his phone number from him. Rutembeza was préfet de discipline when I was there."

A curtain closed over Niyonzima's face, but he put a hand on Jean Patrick's shoulder. They walked down the hall, Niyonzima supported by Jean Patrick. "It's quite possible your headmaster has returned to school," Niyonzima said. "I imagine Tutsi have been streaming there for protection, especially if he is known to be kind. Just let me have some tea and a little something to eat. Then I will find out the number. I will call him."

A tiny seed of hope took root—why hadn't he thought of it? Uncle knew all the ways through the bush. Even if they had not left Cyangugu, he could have taken everyone to safety at Gihundwe. They had lived through this before. They were strong. They knew what to do.

CLAIRE STRUGGLED WITH a stack of kindling, and Jean Patrick jumped up from the chair where he was reading, waiting for Niyonzima to place the call to Gihundwe. Niyonzima had asked him to come in, but he refused. He wanted to give Niyonzima the opportunity to compose himself in private if the news was bad.

"Here, let me help you," Jean Patrick said. He bent to take the load from Claire, but she was shaking, and the twigs tumbled to the floor.

"I'm so sorry," she said. Tears streaked her face.

"It's no problem. I can sweep it. I'm glad for something to do." Jean Patrick touched her shoulder gently. "Eh—such a small thing. Don't cry," he said.

"These people who are doing this, they are not my people," she said, weeping. "May God forgive them their wickedness."

Jean Patrick gathered sticks from the floor, on his knees like a suppliant. *Imana yirwa ahandi igataha i Rwanda,* he thought then. Wherever God spends the day, He comes home to sleep in Rwanda. But perhaps for God—like Coach—something had come up. Jean Patrick wondered if He was coming home at all or if He, along with the rest of the world, had forsaken Rwanda. Then, as if someone had slapped him, he bit down on his tongue. "Imana, forgive me my wicked unbeliever's mind," he whispered.

Niyonzima came out from his office. "I got through to Gihundwe. Uwimana is there. The woman who answered told me the classrooms are overflowing with refugees, many of them wounded. She had gone to fetch him when the connection went dead. I tried again but did not succeed." Jean Patrick's heart dropped down to his stomach, and Niyonzima must have seen. "Don't worry," he said. "That is the nature of communications now. I'll try again in a little while. Maybe then you will get a chance to talk to him," he said. "Keep up your hope. Inside the schools, the people are safe. If your family are there, they will be protected."

Jean Patrick thought of equations and mathematical proofs, chalk symbols filling a blackboard, a life that was no longer his own. Was that *if* or was that *if and only if*?

THE RAIN ENDED, but large drops still fell from the trees onto the walkway. Jean Patrick turned the radio noise into a hiss of rain, canceled it with a frequency of his own internal humming. He sat on the floor, legs crossed, the igisoro board on the low table in front of him. Niyonzima had taught him to play, but he wasn't very good. Niyonzima kept landing in his cups and stealing his seeds.

Ineza looked up from plaiting Bea's hair and scolded him. "So you thought igisoro was a game for old people, huh? It's not as easy as it looks." She went back to her plaits.

"Ouch, Mama. That hurts," Bea said. A floral fragrance came from her hair. Coconut pomade glistened on Ineza's fingers.

How strange, Jean Patrick thought. If someone from a foreign country were to drop down suddenly from the sky and land in this room, the scene would look like a peaceful day in the life of a Rwandan family. The person would never guess they clung to these simple acts as they would cling to bits of wreckage in the final flood.

FOR THE FIRST few hours of the first day, Jean Patrick had hoped the killing would not spread beyond Kigali. Then he had hoped and waited and prayed for the RPF to be victorious or for UNAMIR to take up arms and defeat the extremists. When the Belgians were killed, he believed surely the West would not stand by while their own were slaughtered. His vision of Americans landing at the airport was so vivid he felt joy and relief in his chest.

Today, the killers themselves came to speak on RTLM. A man from Nyakizu, just south of Butare, boasted that his group had caught eight Tutsi on the road to Burundi. They had tortured and killed them and left their bodies to rot, a message for any Tutsi who thought of escaping the country.

IN HIS DREAM, Jean Patrick was fishing with Uncle. The sun on Lake Kivu was like a surface of scattered diamonds. The voice that called him became Mathilde's voice. She had made another dog for him, this one no bigger than a thumbnail. As she stood on the shore and held it out to him, it came alive and grew and then jumped from her hands. She squealed with glee, and in his dream he thought of Miseke, the Dawn Girl, who turned her laughter into pearls. "Jean Patrick," she called to him.

The little dog barked. The bark became a knock. "Jean Patrick, wake up. Jonathan is here. We are free to leave the house, to go to market. The préfet has declared Butare safe." The voice belonged to Bea, but beyond the window, the high-pitched delight continued.

Jean Patrick rubbed his hands across his scalp. He sat up and straightened Niyonzima's ill-fitting sweatpants on his waist and went to the window. Beyond the shutters, Claire's children streaked through the wet grass.

"Jean Patrick—did you hear?"

"Yes. I'm coming."

"Freedom!" Bea said when he came out. "I can find out if Rwanda still exists or if we have been wrenched from the earth and thrown down in another galaxy."

Jean Patrick embraced Jonathan. "Many days I have not seen you," he said. Jonathan looked beaten down, dark circles like bruises beneath his eyes.

"It feels great to hold on to you," Jonathan said, squeezing Jean Patrick. "How are you holding up?"

"We manage." Jean Patrick squeezed back. What else could he say?

"I came to see if I could give you a ride to town. It might be"—he sighed—"safer."

Jean Patrick looked at the front door as if it were some foreign object he no longer knew the use of. His near-dead hope stirred. "How is Susanne?"

"Struggling a bit, but strong. She's home with Amos."

Ineza came in with tea and a packet of Belgian biscuits. "A hidden treasure from a corner of the cupboard." Bea clapped, and suddenly, Jean Patrick saw Mathilde's face in her simple joy.

Niyonzima came from his office and turned off the radio. "How about a little peace and quiet for our celebration."

They sat at the table. Tea steamed in their cups, lightened with powdered milk. Jean Patrick dunked his biscuit and savored its crumbly sweetness bite by bite. He thought of bears in cold climates emerging from winter's hibernation, blinking in the unexpected light.

First thing, he would go back to campus. Then he would see if his coach had returned. In his head, he made a list of everything he had missed: his new Puma running shoes, new running clothes, his tracksuit and books. Jeans and shirts, Isaka's scarf, Paul Ereng's photo with his Hutu card. He wondered if he was expected to return to the dorm, if the crisis in Butare had passed and he could resume his life. He wished to sweep this nightmare into the hole of forgetfulness, but he knew that was not possible. When he walked into his room, he would face Daniel's empty bed, and Daniel's spirit, his restless umuzimu, would wrap around him.

Across the table from him, Bea gathered crumbs with a fingertip and put them into her mouth. The gesture swelled Jean Patrick's heart, and he remembered the first time they had shared a pastry at the Ibis and he had watched this same ritual, warm sunlight washing the tablecloth. In the past week, her presence had become as much a part of him as an arm, a leg, his beating heart. It had happened gradually, naturally, and now he could not imagine losing it. Not even for an hour.

JONATHAN LET JEAN Patrick off by the university road. Rain had returned. Water dripped from branches, from the closed and curled blossoms of poinsettia and flame trees. The road that had always teemed with bright and colorful life was empty, and Jean Patrick felt as if he had stepped onto a strange, deserted shore.

"Are you sure you want to do this alone?" Jonathan said.

"I'll be all right."

"We can take you — I should go check on my office, and it's going to pour any second."

Jean Patrick looked up toward the gate. Well-armed soldiers stood by the guardhouse, and he didn't know if he should be frightened or re-assured. "I need to walk. It's the only way I can think. I know how to hide if I have to."

"Be careful," Bea said. Her plaits glistened. She brushed his fingers. "You're coming back, aren't you?"

"As long as I am welcome."

"You're family now. Of course you are."

JEAN PATRICK TRIED to keep his body from shaking as he put his identity card into the soldier's outstretched hand. The old, rheumy guard was gone; the gate was manned by the soldiers.

"You're not on the list," the soldier said. "You can't pass."

Fear squeezed Jean Patrick's throat. "The list?"

"You're not listed as a student present on campus." The soldier rattled a sheaf of papers.

A hand clapped Jean Patrick on the back. "Eh! Let him go. It's that famous runner." Jean Patrick looked into the face of the officer from the Cyarwa checkpoint, the one who was always friendly to him. "Hey, Rutembeza's boy. Amakuru?" He patted his round belly and snatched the card from the soldier. "This guy's OK. Remember him; he's going to the Olympics." He handed Jean Patrick his card. "Wah! What a crazy guy! A storm like this, and just a flimsy jacket to protect you? How is your coach? Lately we have no news."

"He's well, thank you. I will greet him for you." With his shaky hand, it took Jean Patrick three tries to get his card back in his pocket. He broke into a jog up the hill, but his legs moved in random directions, all signals from the brain on hold. He barely knew how to move one foot in front of the other.

THE CAMPUS WAS as deserted as the roads, only ghosts moving about. A familiar-looking woman walked quickly toward him from the direction of the cafeteria, and Jean Patrick soon realized that it was Valerie, the last woman Daniel fell in love with, the last on his long list of women he was going to marry. He waved her over. She peered at him blankly, rain dripping from the visor of a cap with the logo of a Hutu extremist party.

"How are you doing?" Jean Patrick said. He held out his hand, but she didn't accept it. He pointed to her cap. "I see you've switched sides. No more Parti Libéral?"

"Times change," she said. "We have banded together for the common Hutu good. What do you want?"

Jean Patrick stared back at her. "My friend Daniel. We had dinner with you and your girlfriends. You sat with him. Did you know he was killed?"

"He was icyitso. He deserved to die. As you do."

Jean Patrick observed her impassive expression, trying to bring forth something human in her. "He was eighteen years old, and he wanted to be a doctor, to help people. He did not have an evil thought in his head. What happened to all your talk about unity and justice?"

She shrugged. "We will not allow Tutsi to enslave us again. If we have to kill, we will kill. We adapt to the situation as we see fit." She turned away and continued down the path.

"Yego," Jean Patrick said to the space she left behind. "As we see fit."

JEAN PATRICK STOOD outside his room and stared in at what remained of his world. Shards of glass, splinters of wood, a few rags of clothing. The door listed drunkenly on a single hinge. Windblown rain slanted through the broken window. All the furniture, their clothes and books, gone. In the center of the floor, a small fire had been built, fueled by his and Daniel's belongings, those few deemed unworthy to be carried off.

Out in the yard, an occasional student passed. Strands of RTLM's noise floated, disconnected, in the air. *Inyenzi are disappearing. They disappear gradually as bombs continue to fall on them.* Simon Bikindi's hate-filled lyrics vibrated the walls of students' rooms. Jean Patrick stepped through the doorway, and glass crunched beneath his shoes. The stink of smoke and moldering ash infused the air. On the wall, someone had written TUBATSEMBATSEMBE!, Kill Them All. The red paint had dripped and pooled on the floor.

As he searched frantically through the wreckage, a piece of glass sliced his palm. In the charred remains of the fire he saw flakes of Paul Ereng's picture, a corner of ironwood frame, blackened scraps of his father's journal. He dug further and found the Hutu card, curled like a dead insect's shell. It was open to his photo, his own sad, burned eyes peering out at him. He brushed off the card and put it in his pocket along with the corner of frame, an entry of his father's journal that was readable, and a page of Daniel's physiology text, underlined, with notes in Daniel's careless writing. *Tibia = flute bone!*

On his way out the door, he glimpsed a pair of shorts tossed into a corner of the room. They were his Puma shorts, white with the red stripe, the last threads of his dream. They were filthy, trampled with muddy footprints, but whole—savable. He used them to wrap his hand.

JEAN PATRICK HEARD whistles, a high-pitched din. His skin went cold. A woman burst into the yard, running with long-legged strides, arms pumping. With a sinking feeling in his belly, he recognized Honorine, the distance runner. A group of guys chased her, slipping and sliding in the wet grass. A bottle hit her on the back of the head. She kept going. In the pack, Jean Patrick recognized teammates and friends he used to sit beside in class. He took off after them as Honorine disappeared around the corner of a building. They didn't follow, the heart gone from their chase. They staggered off toward the dorms.

When they had gone, Honorine emerged from her hiding place. "Jean Patrick, thank God you're safe." Her chest heaved with the effort of her sprint. She collapsed into his arms, trembling, no more weight to her than a leaf in the wind.

"Shh. It's all right. Are you staying here, on campus?"

She started to cry. "I have nowhere else to go. What about you? I looked and looked for you. I was so afraid you were . . ."

Rain had soaked their clothes, and they clung together like drowned creatures. "I'm staying with friends. I was there when . . ." When what? The world ended? He, also, could not finish his sentence.

Honorine nodded. "That's good. You should leave this place now and not come back. The Hutu Power students terrorize us night and day. We've banded together for safety, but I don't know how long it can last. I was stupid to think I could go out by myself." She wiped her face with the back of her hand. "As you see."

"Come—I'll walk with you."

She grabbed his arm. "Nkuba, we are gupfa uhagaze, the walking dead."

Jean Patrick wanted to comfort her, to tell her this was not so, but the lie would not pass his lips. He accompanied her past the rows of rooms, past doors, like his own, hanging off hinges or missing altogether.

She stopped beside a room. Inside, the shadows of students moved. "Will you come in? We can make you some tea."

Jean Patrick touched his cheek to hers. "I should get back," he said. "May God keep you safe." It seemed an empty phrase.

A CRUDE BARRIER of rocks and tree limbs blocked the trail that led from the woods to the road, manned by a citizen patrol. One was a fellow student who waited tables at the Ibis. "Hey, my friend," he called to Jean Patrick. They shook hands. "I'm glad to see you're well."

"Yes—thanks to God. And you, too—it's good to see you on patrol."

A ragged man demanded Jean Patrick's papers and examined them with a puzzled look. Jean Patrick remembered the day at the arboretum, the man with the bloodied club holding his card upside down. "Here," Jean Patrick said, pointing at the word *Tutsi*. "Hu-tu."

"OK," the man said. "You can pass."

"Lord bless us," the waiter said. He switched to French then so the man would not understand. "This fine fellow would much rather slit my Tutsi throat than stand here with me, but in these times we do what we can, huh?" He waved Jean Patrick through.

JEAN PATRICK COULD see through the slit in the gate that Coach was not in. One last time he called out to Jolie. "It's me, Jean Patrick. Can you let me in?" The windows glared at him, dark and empty. The wall surrounding the house had grown a crown of broken bottles.

Blood from his cut palm seeped through the makeshift bandage of his shorts. He turned to leave but then did not leave. If he waited long enough, Coach must come. Just as he made up his mind to go, he saw Jolie trundling up the road, arms wide to balance two baskets of food. He ran to help her.

"Your coach is not here," she said. She walked forward, eyes on the road.

"Let me carry these." He took the baskets from her.

"I can't let you in."

"Grandmother, when will he be back?"

"Inshyanutsi!" she said. "Someday your nosiness will kill you." But she smiled when she unlocked the gate. "You look like a drowned bush rat. Come and dry off for a minute."

Jean Patrick followed her into the yard. "Are you cross with me?" he asked.

"I am angry with all Tutsi for killing our president. You have destroyed everything good in our country."

"Grandmother, I am not a killer. I am the same person I was two weeks ago, last month, last year." Though this was a lie. He had been turned upside down, shaken, emptied out. They walked into the house, and he gave her the baskets, one handle stained with his blood.

"What happened?" Jolie removed the bandage and inspected his hand, holding it in her gnarled fingers.

"I slipped. On campus there is broken glass everywhere."

After lighting the fire, Jolie sat him at the table and brought a towel. Then she went to the cookhouse and came back with a steaming bowl filled with a potion of grasses. She cleaned off his hand and bound it with a cloth soaked in the pungent liquid. "I'll get your clothes for you." She took the ring of house keys from the hook and unlocked the door to the room where he used to sleep, emerging with shorts and a sweat suit, an older pair of running shoes, a T-shirt, a sweater that was now too small for him. She pulled the door to and locked it. "You can change your clothes in the bathroom." She cackled, conspiratorial. "Take one of your coach's old ponchos to keep you dry. He'll never notice its absence."

When he came from the bathroom, there was fruit on the table, a bowl of soup, a piece of bread and margarine, a cup of cyayi cyayi, the lemony brew Jolie always nursed him with when he was tired or sick. "Eat quickly. You'll have to leave soon," she said.

He ate hungrily. "Jolie, your food still melts my heart." Through the window he watched the weather. He listened for Coach's car. Not even the whistle of a bird broke the rain's monotonous song.

Full and warm, he let his eyes shut. Dozing off, he dreamed he heard the gate swing open, the clink of a key in the lock. When he started awake, he was smiling.

"You better go now," Jolie said. She held a cracked green poncho and a sack with Jean Patrick's wet clothes. She gave him a second sack. "Put the rest of your dry clothes in here."

"When can I come back? When will Coach be here?"

She hastened him toward the door. "I don't know. I haven't seen him since . . ." The sentence hung in the air, unfinished.

"I have to speak to him. He's my one hope to help my family," he said. "To help me."

"He will find you when he can. He cares for you."

"How will he find me?" He did not want to say where he was. "My room at the dorm was destroyed. I can't go back there anymore."

"You have to trust him," she said. She unlocked the front door. "He will come for you."

Jean Patrick touched his cheek to hers before stepping out into the wet. Trust Coach? If Coach told him that tomorrow the sun would rise in the east, it seemed to Jean Patrick there was a fifty-fifty chance it would rise in the west.

TWENTY-FIVE

BEA'S BELLY WAS SOFT AND WARM. Jean Patrick lay on the couch with his ear against it, listening to the secret sounds. The voice of RTLM that came from Niyonzima's office was like fingers scraped across a blackboard.

"Do you think there's a baby inside?"

Hutu, when you see people gathering in schools and churches, this is not good at all, because there are Inyenzi-Inkotanyi among them. You must take action against them.

"Eh! I don't know."

Bea's head bent over his, and he wound a plait of hair about his finger. "I say yes. I say it's a boy." He examined the cut on his palm; it was healing.

Bea kissed her teeth and pushed him away. "Why not a girl? What's wrong with a girl?"

Go after those Inkotanyi. Blood flows in their veins as it does in yours. All those who sympathize with both sides, they are ibyitso. They will pay for what they have done.

She pressed her hands to her ears. "How long do we have to endure this?" She rose from the couch and paced.

Jean Patrick had no answer. A span of time marked only by the count of the dead on RTLM.

Niyonzima had finally made contact with Uwimana, and Jean Patrick had spoken with him. He closed his eyes and imagined life and love coursing through the wires. Although Niyonzima called every day, connections were unpredictable, the distance from Butare to Cyangugu no longer measurable by any method Jean Patrick understood. His family had not come to Gihundwe, and Jean Patrick could only hope they were safe in Burundi. People inside the school were starving. Some had died. Angelique could not keep up with the sick, the wounded, more coming every hour.

A slate sky promised rain. Claire's children played in the yard, soft laughter rising and falling. Jean Patrick reached out to Bea with both his hands. "Come back. I want to touch you again."

"I cannot sit still."

Who could? But what was there to do besides sit still? Go for another run, read another book, play igisoro, write a letter. Soon enough, there would be no one left to write. Jean Patrick heard the name of the baker and the jeweler from Cyangugu announced on RTLM. Then a teacher from primary school. *All Tutsi will perish. They will disappear from the earth. We will kill them like rats.* He buried his face in his hands.

Ineza came into the room. She was knitting a shawl, a blue and green one, for a niece in London. She sat beside them. Slowly the scarf swallowed the colorful skeins, and Jean Patrick imagined it growing and growing, becoming a bright path of wool and color for them to walk on, all the way across the ocean.

LIGHT LEFT THE sky. A new voice on RTLM took the place of the old. This particular announcer was famous for her rapid-fire delivery. How else could she get it all in, leave time for the music, the reports, live, from the roadblocks? At least the deaths of his mother, his uncle and aunt, his brothers and sisters, had not come to Jean Patrick through the mouthpiece of Hutu Power. At least he had that.

Now the Interahamwe were setting fire to churches filled with Tutsi. Niyonzima shook his head. "The clever planning of these extremists chills me to the bone. They call everyone to the churches and . . ." He swallowed a word. "It's like sweeping dead banana leaves into a pile to burn them more easily." Jean Patrick knew the word he had not said. It was *schools*.

Muhutu, here are more ibyitso helping the Inkotanyi: Uwimana and his wife, Angelique. He's headmaster at Gihundwe. Those not yet finished off have crawled inside there. His school is swarming with snakes. Do your work. Clean the house.

Before the announcer reached the end of her list, Niyonzima had dialed the phone.

"I'm here," Jean Patrick said into the receiver.

"It's so good to hear your voice," Uwimana said. The greeting Jean

Patrick had heard all the years of his childhood. "I will tell you quickly. Interahamwe came yesterday. They said all Hutu were free to leave. They told me to send them out, and they would be safe. I gave everyone the choice. Many refused to go. They say, 'We have lived together, we will die together.' I cannot play God, deciding who lives and who dies. I asked Angelique to go, but she will not." In the background, whistles and chants joined in a frenzied beat. The line crackled. "Jean Patrick, are you there? They'll break through soon."

"I'm here."

"I have no news of your family. I'm sorry. I prayed they would come, but as it turns out, I could not have protected them. Angelique wants you to know she loves you. To both of us, you have been a son."

"And you have been father and mother to me."

Terrified screams, as close as Jean Patrick's ear. "They're inside now. Let me hear your voice one more time."

"May God protect you," Jean Patrick said. "Ndagukunda cyane. I love you very much."

"And you. May Imana walk with you — run with you — always. We'll meet again."

"We will."

A hissing filled the earpiece, as if the connection had been cut, but then Jean Patrick heard, "Are you still there? Can you hear me?"

"Yes, I'm here; I can hear you."

"Remember: they can kill our bodies, but they can never kill our spirits." Then dead air.

Jean Patrick pressed the phone to his chest. He could not put the receiver back in its cradle, could not hear the final click. He remembered his first day at Gihundwe, when he had looked out at Saint Kizito and joy had filled him. "Ndishimye," he had whispered. I am happy. He remembered that the sun's geometry had combined with his angle of vision to give the appearance of light flowing from the saint's arms, as if Imana's blessings emanated directly from the shining black skin.

JEAN PATRICK'S OWN cry awoke him, his calf in a knot. Pain knifed through his leg, but when he bolted upright, his hamstring seized.

He stuffed his fist into his mouth to keep from crying out. It was as if his muscles, so unused to days without running, had rebelled, found a life of their own. *Breathe into your belly. Send your breath through your body,* Coach used to say, in that other life. Gently, Jean Patrick kneaded the tangled fibers, as his coach used to do. No one stirred in the house. Rain, eternal, slogged across the roof.

He had to flee. The decision was fully formed before he knew it was there. When the line to Cyangugu was cut, so was Jean Patrick's chance of finding his family alive in Rwanda. Surely, if he tried, he would be caught and killed. To the south, the mountains of Burundi rose like a beacon. If Roger's plan had gone forward, he would find his family with Spéciose. If not, at least he would survive. The thought sent a chill through his body, but from this day forward, the only way left to help those he loved was to save himself.

He would leave in the morning. He would ask Bea to go, but if she would not, he would go alone. She was Hutu. She would be safe. But the killing was a cancerous growth that soon enough would spread to Butare. Soon the machete would fall on his head. Better to run like a dog than die like a dog. But what if Bea was pregnant? He could not leave her, unmarried, carrying his child. He would give it another day. Maybe two or three. Surely he had that much time. Surely, by then, the West would give the UN troops the help and the weapons they needed.

THEY SAT AT the dining room table — Jean Patrick, Bea, Niyonzima, and Ineza — tea steaming before them. Day had once more dragged itself from night's belly. *It is the Tutsi who are burning down their own houses! They want to lure the Hutu there. Then they will trap them and kill them.*

Ineza silenced the radio. "A moment's peace," she said.

"I have decided to try for Burundi," Jean Patrick said. He looked at Niyonzima. "Will you allow Bea to come with me?"

"We are modern here," Bea said. "You can ask me directly, and the answer is no. I will not crawl through the marsh like some kind of swamp animal, and I will not leave my family."

Jean Patrick had not slept since pain awoke him. Only his jagged energy, nothing useful to do with it, kept him moving. Before daybreak, he had gone for a run to untangle his head, keeping to the bush, barefoot like the muturage he was, the country boy. More than once, he had to stop and rub out his calf. The answer that came to him in the night did not change. With or without her, he had to flee. What good would he be to her or his unborn child if he was dead?

"Don't be a fool. You must go," Ineza said. Her knitting needles clicked. The green-blue wave of scarf unfurled toward the floor.

Niyonzima took off his glasses and rubbed his eyes, then put his glasses on again. "Maybe there is something I can do." He looked at Ineza. "If I can get travel passes for the three of you, will you go?"

The knitting needles stopped. "That is a silly question, my husband."

"And you, Bea?" Niyonzima's voice was cajoling. "It won't be for long. It can't be. This insanity must stop soon. Burundi is not so far away. Or Tanzania."

Bea went to the window and drew back the curtain, as if she would find her answer written in the patterns the rain made on the glass. She glanced up toward the soggy sky. Then she came back and hugged her mother and her father. "Dadi, you won't go?"

He held up his cane. "I am too old and tired to run. My voice is needed here, for whatever good it will do."

"Mama? You won't come with us?"

Ineza put down her knitting and took Bea's hands in hers. "It will just be for a little while. For us, please, go."

For a minute, Jean Patrick thought she would refuse again. The pain in her face made him regret that he had asked. But then she said, "All right. I will go."

Niyonzima clapped and got up from the table. "Please tell Claire to bring me coffee. I need to clear my head." He disappeared into his office.

Bea wandered into the living room and slumped onto a chair. A single cry heaved her shoulders. Ineza went to her. "Come," she said. "Let's go and see our beautiful garden."

"Mama, it's raining."

"We'll just stand beneath the roof and look out." She helped Bea to her feet. With their arms around each other, they walked to the door. Then

Ineza opened the door, and Jean Patrick smelled the wet grass, the bracing morning air.

INEZA HAD PUT on her painting clothes—a huge shirt, mottled with color, that she was lost inside. Bea came from her room in her pagne of planets and stars, malachite bracelets on her wrists. "Mama wants to paint us today." Her fingers trailed along the wall, and the bracelets jangled.

Niyonzima opened his door. "There is no more long-distance service, and no further travel permits will be issued. From now on, no Rwandan can leave the country." He limped to his chair. "But I think if I go in person to the police station and offer the chief a very fat bribe, he will take it. I've known him a long time." He leaned forward, hands folded on top of his cane. "Let me call Jonathan and see if he will drive me."

JEAN PATRICK LEANED on the gate and watched Jonathan's car slip and slide before gaining traction. The four silhouettes behind the steamy glass strained visibly as if they willed the struggling imodoka forward—Jonathan and Niyonzima in front, Ineza and Claire in back. After they disappeared, Jean Patrick stood in the rain and let the water streak down his skin, a baptismal shower.

This time, he told himself, Imana would hear them. Niyonzima knew the game of Rwandan politics; he had been around it long enough. He wouldn't ask Jonathan to come out in this storm if he had not been certain of success.

"You've lost your mind," Bea said when he came back inside.

"Say it again." Jean Patrick gathered her close, felt her heartbeat against his wet shirt.

"Eh? You really have." She struggled free. "I'm soaked now."

"I want to hear the sound of your voice, that's all." He kissed her head, her two eyes, her nose, and then her mouth. "Come lie down with me. Who knows when we can be alone again."

"Only a minute. I don't think I can stay still."

Jean Patrick led Bea to her room, the need to have her beside him, skin against skin, so strong he could barely breathe. He closed the door.

Rain drummed on the roof. The wind in the trees made a sound like the plucked string of inanga. He held the flat of his palm to her belly. "Is a baby inside?"

"Ko Mana—you ask every ten minutes." She sighed. "I don't know. Everything is off balance. Not even my own body makes sense anymore."

"No. Nothing makes sense. Except you." The room breathed softly around them. He guided her to the bed, undid the gold knots of her buttons, and kissed her breasts. "Will this hurt him?"

"I don't think so. If *she's* in there, *she* is strong."

She stepped from her pagne. Planets and suns spiraled from her body. Then she lay down and drew the pagne over them. Slowly, gently, they made love beneath this bright galaxy. Jean Patrick unwound inside her dark earth. The taut cord of death in his belly uncoiled. He buried himself inside her, seeking the slow, steady pulse of life, its perpetual seed.

THE CLICK OF a key in the front door startled them both from sleep. Bea dressed and quickly kissed Jean Patrick's cheek. "Let me go now and see if I can fasten myself together." Jean Patrick pulled on his sweatpants. He could have drowned in shame. She slipped out the door before he could kiss her back.

Niyonzima and Ineza were at the table when Jean Patrick came out. They looked up with a single motion, and he knew from their faces that once more, Imana's ear had remained deaf to them.

"Everything was going well," Niyonzima said. He regarded Jean Patrick with pained eyes. "I had a good conversation with the chief—a little joke, a little laugh. I showed him the envelope, nice and fat. He seemed about to take it, but then he told me to wait. When he returned, he said he could not accept the payment." Niyonzima cleared his throat and folded his hands, one on top of the other. "I am certain he checked a list, and our names were on it."

Twenty-six

THERE WAS A BREAK IN THE WEATHER. The sun climbed into a clear, crisp sky. Bea and her family still slept. Exhaustion had pulled them under. Niyonzima typed in his study. Jean Patrick heard the keys like some crazy syncopation to the voice of RTLM, both coming together through the thin walls. *There will be no more Inkotanyi; there will be none in this country anymore. When you see how many of them die, you would think they came back to life. They themselves believe they come back to life, but they deceive themselves. They are disappearing.*

Quietly, Jean Patrick tiptoed to the hall and put on his running shoes. He closed the gate behind him and stepped into the road. *"Kare kare mu museke,"* he sang softly, a line cast out to his former life, this simple greeting of the dawn. Blue mist hid the hills. Burundi's mountains floated in a sea of mist. Here and there along the paths, farmers climbed toward the fields. He felt like Rutegaminsi from his father's book of stories, tunneling through the earth with his mole guide to emerge into a terrible beauty on the far side of the world. He remembered reading the story to Mathilde, time and again, thankful that she never had to emerge into a land like this.

Checking one last time that his identity card was in his jacket pocket, he set off at a slow jog toward town. He settled into the motion his legs had ached for. Into his Nikes he willed the power of Nkuba, the Thunder God for whom he was named. He imagined tucking everyone he loved beneath his arms and carrying them across the Akanyaru swamps, away from Rwanda and into Burundi, away from this war in which they would almost certainly all die.

For now, Butare remained a place of safe haven. Little by little, women returned to their plots, men appeared on the trails with bicycles and carts.

Streams of Tutsi, filthy and bleeding, poured in from the rest of the country to seek refuge in churches and hospitals. They came from every direction like the walking dead. They were dazed, in shock. Some appeared to have gone mad. Behind them, children with sticks ran to the roadblocks and waited for the action to begin.

Jean Patrick spotted the convoy from a long distance off. Then he recognized the UN vehicles, flags flying, and his heart hammered. He nearly jumped into the air. They were saved. He ran toward them, praying fiercely. He wondered why no crowds lined up along the streets to cheer.

But the convoy barreled down the hill. He could make out the faces of the soldiers now, the scowling expressions. He stopped to watch, afraid to come closer. Mixed in with the UN vehicles was a parade of cars and trucks with the flags of their countries taped to the windows. Inside were the whites, looking out on the countryside with dull, shocked stares. He realized the rescue was only for them. They were fleeing, abandoning the fast-sinking ship. Jean Patrick's excitement fled with them. He saw, relieved, that Jonathan's imodoka was not among them. A ragged group of refugees jumped from the bush and sprinted after the vehicles, shouting and pleading to be taken in. As the procession stopped for a checkpoint, the refugees swarmed. A few managed to cling to the tailgates.

"Why won't you take us?" a mama wailed. "Can't you see they will kill us all?" She tried to push her baby into the arms of a woman inside a truck. "Mana mfasha—at least take my child."

A UNAMIR soldier shoved her with his rifle butt. A second soldier shot into the air.

In the last flatbed truck was a young girl, two tails of brown hair sticking out from her head. She was crying. Clutched to her chest was a carrying case with wire mesh, and a little dog peeked out from inside it. She caught Jean Patrick's gaze and held it. The convoy started up again. Imbazazi, the girl mouthed, forgive me, over and over until she faded into the haze of distance. Jean Patrick wondered if this was the only word of Kinyarwanda she knew.

THE MIST SHREDDED and then vanished, and Jean Patrick turned onto the trail to the arboretum fields. When he reached the first field, he

lifted onto the balls of his feet and sprinted to the top. He trotted back
down, then fast up, as hard as he could push. Again. And again. He recited the names of the minerals he had studied for geology class, the names
he would be writing today for his exams if Rwanda had not spun away
from the Earth's common axis.

Beryl. Cinnabar. Lepidolite. He continued until he had no breath left
in his lungs, no choice but to collapse into the grass. He bathed his face
in it and let the chocolaty perfume of freshly turned earth fill his nostrils.
Flopping onto his back, he watched the sky, the bright, shattered clouds.
The sun warmed his face. He dreamed of peace.

JEAN PATRICK WAS startled awake by a truck rattling along the
road, axles squeaking. He rolled onto his stomach, pressed into the ground.
The engine whinnied closer. The casual chatter of men drifted from the
open window. The truck, filled with soldiers, came to a stop directly above
him. In the bed, the Tutsi cargo. Jean Patrick wiggled deeper into the grass
and held his breath. Doors slammed. The tailgate clanked down.

"Move, Inyenzi, move! Tugende!"

From his hiding place, Jean Patrick heard the thud of feet hitting the
ground. A moan as someone fell. There were nine shots, one resonant in
the echo of the last. A bird started from the bush. It was a green-headed
sunbird, rare in this part of Rwanda. Captivated, Jean Patrick shifted to
follow its flight. The bird wheeled into sunlight, a metallic glint of wings
and tail feathers. *Pyrite. Chalcopyrite.* Fool's gold.

JONATHAN GREETED JEAN Patrick at the door when he returned,
shadows as dark as ink stains beneath his eyes. "Come and sit," he said.
"We have something to discuss."

Niyonzima looked up from his tea. "Jonathan has a plan to help us.
Our préfet was removed from office today. I'm sure he will be killed, if he's
not dead already." He poured tea from the thermos and motioned to Jean
Patrick to sit. "A man sympathetic to the government's program has taken
the préfet's place, and so the situation is suddenly urgent."

"That would explain the convoys I saw," Jean Patrick said.

"Susanne is sick. She can't stay any longer," Jonathan said. "The last convoy leaves tomorrow. The skeleton staffers, the holdouts who planned to stay but couldn't make it."

Jean Patrick thought of the line of somber faces, the little girl's plea for forgiveness. "I understand. We'll all miss you."

"Wait," Niyonzima said. "Hear him."

"We want to take you and Bea with us."

With their tails between their legs, the whites will leave, the RTLM announcer said on the day the prime minister was murdered. Everything had come to pass as RTLM had predicted.

"Thank you for your offer," Jean Patrick said, "but the soldiers will never let Rwandans into the convoy. I saw them today, pushing Tutsi away with their guns."

A faint smile lifted the corners of Jonathan's lips. "I'm building a compartment in the imodoka's trunk. It will be cramped, but if you and Bea don't fight, you can manage."

"No," Bea said. "I've changed my mind. I can't leave. If we die, we die together." She took Jean Patrick's hands. "But you go. Our last hope here is gone."

Ineza rocked Bea and stroked her hair. "My daughter, do you remember what you once said when I asked you who would carry on the fight if Dadi and I died?"

"Yes, Mama. I remember, but that was a very long time ago."

"I will ask you the same question again. If we all die, who will tell the world what happened here? Who will bring justice for all these unjust deaths?" She held Bea's hands to her cheek as if cooling a fever. "You are our voice — our future. Your father and I want nothing more than for you to carry our lives forward. You must go with Jean Patrick."

With her mouth slightly open, Bea turned to her parents and then to Jean Patrick. The silence was so thick he could have shaped it between his hands.

"All right," she said then. "I will do as you ask, Mama. I will go."

☙

Ineza insisted on a last dinner together, the traditional meal that always began a journey. She had been in the cookhouse for much of the day, preparing igisafuria, the chicken stew that was Jean Patrick's favorite meal.

The aroma had been teasing his nostrils each time the back door was opened, the momentary pleasure calming his troubled thoughts.

The power had been off since morning; they ate by lantern light. A few stars shone, the moon's larger half dangling between them. Jean Patrick and Bea would have to keep to the high bushes on the way to Jonathan's in order to avoid being seen. Bea held on to her mother's hand while she ate, neither of them capable of letting go. A tape of Rwandan music played, the sound tinny on Niyonzima's portable machine. When the scream came from the cookhouse, it took Jean Patrick a moment to realize it was not part of a song. The scream became a wail, a keen.

Claire burst into the room. "Queen Gicanda's been murdered. Soldiers broke into her house and took her to the National Museum." Her face crumpled. "In a truck, like a dog. They just announced it on RTLM."

Niyonzima pushed away his plate. "You must leave quickly," he said. "All of you. If they can kill such a woman, none of us are safe. They'll be coming house to house soon, as they've done everywhere."

Jean Patrick let his fork fall from his fingers, the last of his will drained. God had truly abandoned them now. The mwami's wife murdered, an old woman who had been only a symbol of kindness—it was unthinkable, even in this world that had been turned on its head. The burst of gunfire from the road brought him to his feet, and he tipped over his bowl. A stain spread on the cloth. Sauce and meat slid to the floor.

"We're too late," Ineza cried.

They heard shots, screams. Then gunfire, continuous, shredded the evening. A grenade blast rattled the windows.

"Go! Ineza—please, go with them." Niyonzima took a pocketknife from the bureau drawer. "Take this." He gave the knife to Jean Patrick and blew out the lantern. "Claire, fetch them the machete and then lock yourself and the children in your hut."

"I'm staying." Ineza's voice floated in the darkness. "Jean Patrick, take Bea. No arguments." Outside, above the clamor of drums and whistles, they heard the chant, *"Tubatsembatsembe!"* Exterminate them all.

"Mama! Dadi!" In the faint light, Jean Patrick watched Bea move toward them. He was afraid she would fall to her knees. The whistles shrieked, coming closer.

"There's no more time," Ineza said. She kissed Bea and turned away. "God protect you both."

Jean Patrick pulled Bea toward the garden. Objects lurched from the darkness. He stumbled into Ineza's easel, and it crashed to the ground. "We'll have to go over the wall, into the woods. They'd kill us the minute we came out the gate."

The noise became a single stream: screams, gunshots, chants, and whistles mingled together. Trucks moved up the hill—gears grinding, soldiers barking out orders. In the dining room, Ineza and Niyonzima spoke softly. Jean Patrick's fingers closed around the doorknob, and he led Bea out into the yard. Orange flames lit the hillsides. In every direction, houses burned. He felt the cold grass on the soles of his feet, and he realized they were both in flip-flops. He removed his shirt and cut off the sleeves. He cut the body in half and gave the two halves to Bea. "Wrap your hands," he said. "Quickly."

The trucks stopped one house away, maybe two. Close enough so that Jean Patrick could make out the words to the killers' song. *Umwanzi wacu n'umwe turamuzi n'umututsi.* Our enemy is one, we know him, it is the Tutsi. The near, sweet scent of orange blossoms pierced his lungs.

Bea dropped the shirt, and a cry of anguish came from her throat. "I can't leave them—I can't." Next door: screams and gunfire, then the whistles and drums. She ran back toward the house.

"Bea!" Jean Patrick bolted after her but slipped in the wet grass, twisting his ankle. She disappeared through the door.

The truck engines started and stopped. They were in front of the gate. This gate. He picked up the shirt Bea had dropped and put the two halves in the pocket of his sweatpants. The gate shrieked, ripped from its hinges.

He ran to the base of the garden wall, wrapping his hands as he went. Ashen light illuminated the broken glass. He took a breath, a running start, and leapt. The cloth on the left hand held. Glass sank into his right as deep as bone, the flesh there new and barely healed. From inside the house, he heard gunfire and then a woman's scream, abruptly silenced. Ineza? Bea? He could not tell. He bit his lip and vaulted over but did not quite clear the top. Glass opened his ankle as he jerked free and tumbled.

His body twisted, and he landed awkwardly, all his weight on his weak-ened leg.

"There's a cockroach hiding here. Catch him," someone shouted.

Jean Patrick got his bearings and tried to sprint for the forest's cover, but his right foot wobbled and dragged as if not quite attached to his leg. He tumbled down the steep slope, feet tangling in the vines. Behind him, the earth erupted. He felt the pressure wave against his eardrums and then its oscillating aftermath.

He went down onto hands and knees and crawled, his ankle wet with blood. When he reached the forest, he pulled himself upright and looked back toward Cyarwa. Flames rose from the houses, a brightness like plan-ets and stars, a heaven upside down. He forced himself to turn away. Smoke was heavy on his skin and in his eyes, acrid and oily in his lungs. Stopping beside a fallen and rotted tree trunk, he began to dig, pounding and clawing with a rage that welled up from his core. Soil, leaves, and blood mingled. Like a rat, he burrowed inside the hole and waited for the silence of the grave.

THE MOON WAS still out when Jean Patrick emerged, its fierce ge-ography blotted by the passage of fast-moving clouds. Watery light turned leaf and branch shadow into spilled blood. Clotted blood stuck his legs to his pants, coated his arms. He pulled up his sweatpants and saw fibers of torn calf, a cord of tendon, shiny and white. With what remained of his shirt, he bandaged his wounds.

Walking was difficult. His swollen ankle offered no support, and he couldn't push off with his right foot. He tripped on a log and fell. No. Not a log—a body, eyes level with his own, wide with final terror. The boy's hand was raised to his head, fingers splayed across his crushed skull. He was naked except for a sock. Jean Patrick scrambled to his feet. The ground was littered with bodies, as if they had all fallen suddenly into a nightmarish sleep. Dizzy and weak, he stumbled deeper into the thick-ness of eucalyptus and pine. By a combination of walking and crawling, he headed in a direction he believed would lead him south to the border, to Burundi.

Stars blink, not planets, Jean Patrick said, over and over, thinking of
anything to avoid thinking of Bea. The moon's light diffused through
the clouds. He had neither stars nor planets to guide him. His uncle had
taught him the constellations, pointing out the heavenly bodies as they
wheeled across the night sky while he and Uncle fished. He tried to bring
them to mind, dredge them up from his childhood. Only the hunter surfaced, tipped onto his side in equatorial laziness. *In other places, he runs
across the night chasing the bear. Here it's too hot, so he just sleeps.* That's what
Uncle told him. But in this terrible darkness, even the lazy hunter had fled.

Time doubled back on itself. Direction lost meaning. Jean Patrick listened for a night bird, a bushpig, a monkey's warning cry, a rat scurrying
through leaf litter. Nothing moved. Nothing breathed. He shivered, suddenly cold. The smell of pine cut his nostrils. He crushed a carpet of pine
needles, vines, and wild begonias beneath his feet. Pain cracked his skull.

HE FOUND THE trace of a footpath, but then the moon set, and
he had to crawl to follow the faint trail. A frantic trill burst from the trees
around him. At first he thought it was wood pigeons, confused and singing at the wrong time. Then shouts and chants rose above the whistles'
din; *"Tubatsembatsembe!"* they whooped, a wild song of celebration.

Hand over hand he hoisted himself into a densely branched tree. The
rough bark pierced his wounded palm. Above him was an abandoned
monkey's nest, and he curled inside its stink. Held in the cradle of inter-
woven branches, he watched in silence. The Tutsi ran before their pursuers, mute and ragged, the young and the old dragged by the hand or
abandoned to fate. Women carried babies in their arms, some clearly dead.
Torchlight turned night into an unnatural day.

The killers wore banana leaves around their necks, and capes of banana
leaves draped their shoulders. Gray paint, ash, and mud masked their
faces. Even so, he recognized a guard from the university, a farmer he used
to greet in the fields, the shopkeeper who had sold him the pirogue. They
carried nail-studded clubs, machetes, and spears; the Interahamwe had
guns and grenades, cans of petrol strapped to their backs.

Jean Patrick tried to shut his eyes, but every thud of a weapon drove
them open. He had no free hand to cover his ears. Some Tutsi cried out,

some begged for life, some died in silence, not even a hand raised against the blows. He held his breath against the reek of blood and petrol, the fetid monkey refuse, until he thought he would faint. With the first air he drew, he vomited onto his chest. The tree shook, and twigs and leaves rained down. Through the crisscrossed branches, two killers stared directly at him.

"Eh! That's just a monkey. Leave it."

"Let's get it down. Let's grill it."

"Here we are, bellies full from Tutsi cows, and you want to grill a monkey? Muturage! Let's go."

"Me, I'm going to catch him." The man took a grenade from his belt and yanked the pin. He drew back his arm. In the torchlight, his ash-caked face gleamed ghostlike, transformed by blood hunger into a profane shape. Jean Patrick coiled himself into a spring, drew himself into his center. *If you remain calm, your mind will tell your body what to do.*

"Igicucu! Are you crazy? Don't move!" The second killer grabbed his friend's hand in both of his. "It's us you'll kill like that—forget the fucking monkey." He yanked the grenade away and threw it after a young boy and a woman dodging among the trees, sprinting for their lives. The blast sent them flying into the night's embrace.

Trees bent and shook. A rain of leaves, wood, earth, and flesh fell. The world expanded and contracted, resonant, swinging on its hinges. Jean Patrick's head became a struck bell.

Stillness returned, and the attackers hurried off after the few Tutsi who had managed to flee. The shrieks of whistles faded. Bodies lay scattered on the ground, caught in the last stunned moment of flight. Life flowed away beneath them, sweet and dark, seeking the earth. Jean Patrick waited to descend until his arms were too tired to hold him. He did not know which way to go; his choice was random. Behind him, a survivor begged for a sip of water, but he did not turn back.

TWENTY-SEVEN

A BIBLICAL RAIN FELL as Jean Patrick slogged through the marsh. When the killers came, he sank into the muck and papyrus. He felt rather than saw the others hiding beside him. They were all ghosts—the hunters and the hunted—invisible to the living.

Blood soaked his bandages. He had tied his foot to his leg to keep them going in the same direction, but the bandage was too tight, and his ankle pulsed and swelled. Vultures circled, and clouds of flies fed. A vapor of death, oily and cloying, rose from the umunyeganyege palms and clung to his hair and skin.

Jean Patrick waded and crawled, hid and waited and crawled again, until fatigue and dizziness forced him to rest. At night, when the killers went home, he slunk into the forest to dry. Sometimes a few refugees gathered together to share what food they had. Jean Patrick lost track of when one day ended and another began. Only the chants of the killers, coming and going, told him. He licked droplets from leaves, drank swamp water polluted with rotting corpses. He found wild fruit, dug up roots and grubs, and put them in his mouth though he was not hungry. Only death was hungry now. *Urupfu rurarya ntiruhaga.* Death eats and is never full.

THE KILLERS FOUND a group of Tutsi and dragged them from the reeds, a mama and children, one a young baby. Jean Patrick was close enough to reach out and touch them. They slumped in silence and waited for the blows. Not even the baby wailed. Death had long since eaten their voices.

AT SOME POINT, while he slept, the rain had ended, the stars emerged from hiding. Jean Patrick knew from the trembling hint of light around him that dawn approached, but no bird sang it into the sky. He checked his ankle. The previous night, a grandmother had rested beside him. Before lying on the ground to sleep, she had collected some leaves from the bush and, with a rock, pounded them into a poultice for his wound. He thought it had helped. The pain, at least, was less, and the murky discharge had stopped. In the distance, a dog barked, and then another. After tightening the cloth, Jean Patrick limped back toward the swamp. Around him, others emerged from the trees, a procession of shades.

A young boy came up beside him and whispered good morning. "Mwaramutse ho."

"Mwaramutse," Jean Patrick said. The boy slipped his hand into Jean Patrick's. "Are you alone?"

The boy nodded, and then he was gone. Soon the sun came out. It shone, indifferent, on the killers and on those who waited to be killed.

HE COULD NOT have taken Bea through this; even she could not have withstood it. He thought of her eyes, their obsidian shine. What was the green basaltic mineral? Yes! Olivine, mineral of the sea. Jean Patrick had never seen the sea, but he envisioned it now, green waves lapping a warm shore. Something in his heart told him Bea lived. This kept him going. For himself, he could have slipped into the filth and slept forever.

THERE WAS A photograph. He must have been about three. Mama and Papa tall as trees. Jacqueline a baby in Mama's arms, pink ribbon tied around her head. A bundle of pink and white, skin the color of ironwood, little red shoes. A church function? He thought so. The girls in lacy white dresses, white veils flowing from pearled crowns. All these cousins he couldn't name, who were probably now dead, crowded together. He and Roger in little suits, holding hands, such serious, grown-up faces. Mama wore a pearl necklace, a long satiny shawl. Papa had on a tie with silver moons, flashes of gold. Jean Patrick couldn't remember what had happened to the picture. If he had it now, he would swallow it. A glowing ember inside him, a sign of life.

Night fell. The vultures slept. Jean Patrick crawled from the water like a prehistoric creature that had sprouted prehensile digits. He staggered to the bushes, found a hole, and hid within it. When dawn broke, he did not return to the swamp. The forest was dangerous in daylight, but he could not stand the mud's stench any longer: the sharp-edged palm fronds, the bodies he fell over, soft, swollen, and decomposing. He wanted to be dry for just one more hour, and so he let himself sink back into the sleep of the dead.

ๆ

"Lieutenant, look at the snake we found crawling in the brush." Hands in Jean Patrick's armpits jerked him from sleep, pulled him from his hole. He struggled, slipped free. The hands caught him again, stood him up. It was day, a gentle drizzle. "It's a tall one. And strong." The hands held him firm, squeezed him.

An officer strolled over, shirt untucked from his pants, round belly protruding. Jean Patrick couldn't believe his good fortune; it was the soldier from the Cyarwa checkpoint. "It's me, Lieutenant," he said. "Mr. Olympics." He extended his hand, but the lieutenant did not take it. "Remember? Rutembeza is my coach."

The lieutenant took Jean Patrick's chin and twisted his head from side to side. "Aye! Look what we've caught!" His eyes were empty, as if everything human had spilled from them. "We can't kill this cockroach here. I'll take him to the major." He laughed and poked at Jean Patrick. "Your Olympic coach, eh? Your Rutembeza."

Jean Patrick shook his head to clear it. He was missing a connection, a conclusion he needed to come to.

With the butt of his rifle, the lieutenant prodded Jean Patrick toward a truck. "If you run, I can catch you now. If not, I can shoot you." He laughed, then shoved Jean Patrick into the bed and slammed the tailgate shut. Jean Patrick struggled to a sitting position and tightened the wrap against his foot. If he could slip from the truck unnoticed at a stop, maybe he could run.

"Hey, Mr. Olympics, you almost made it, huh?" The lieutenant pointed to the mountains, close, blue, and shimmering. "Only a few more kilometers to the border. Oh. I almost forgot." He leapt into the bed of the truck.

A swift, graceful movement for such a fat man. He tied Jean Patrick's
hands behind his back.

They banged along the muddy road, bodies sprawled across it: women
naked from the waist down, a man with a single shoe, the other placed
neatly beside him, two small children curled in an embrace. Littered belongings scattered in the wind, hung from tree limbs. Identity cards fluttered like dying butterflies. Interahamwe sat on couches and fancy chairs
in the open air. Women walked with televisions in their arms, carried
stereos, clothing, and cooking pots. Men balanced sheets of corrugated
metal on their heads. A child ran with a toy giraffe clutched to his chest.
Wild dogs tore at the dead. Jean Patrick's head kept hitting the rear window. No Olympics now, he thought. Then, inexplicably, he laughed. And
then he slept again.

HE WAS JARRED awake with the cessation of motion. When he
opened his eyes, Coach stared down at him. His ankle pulsed beneath the
bandage. He shook his head to clear the fog.

"I'll take care of him." Coach opened the tailgate and helped Jean
Patrick down. He took him to a jeep and pushed him inside.

"Eh, Major. Why don't you leave it in this truck? It stinks."

"That's all right. By now, I am used to the reek." Coach climbed into
the driver's side. He turned the key in the ignition, put the jeep in gear,
and headed up the road. "Jean Patrick, amakuru?"

Jean Patrick couldn't help it. He smiled at the question. "I am well,
Coach. And you?"

"Me, I'm not so well." Coach's face was drawn and hard. His uniform
smelled of blood, and blood stained his jacket, his pants. "You should have
listened. This one time, you should have done as I told you." What was it
Coach had told him? Jean Patrick couldn't remember now. "I went to find
you in your room, to take you somewhere, but you had disappeared. Jolie
told me you came to the house. I knew where you'd gone, but I couldn't
fetch you there." He regarded Jean Patrick. "Why did you disobey me?"

Jean Patrick thought it was sadness hiding in the creases around Coach's
eyes. Sadness and weariness. He said, "Coach, did you know Daniel is
dead?"

"I heard it on the radio."

"That house . . . where I was." He refused to say Bea's name to Coach. "Do you know what happened?"

"Yes."

"Were you there when . . ." He couldn't finish the sentence. Could not make it real.

"No. But I told them if they found you to bring you to me. Even then, I could have helped you."

"But it wasn't you."

"No."

"They would not have brought me anywhere. They would have killed me." Jean Patrick grasped his thigh and moved his leg; it had fallen asleep. "Do you think someone could have escaped?"

"No. It's not possible."

All things were possible. Jean Patrick would not believe otherwise.

"I will have to kill you now," Coach said.

"I know," Jean Patrick said.

COACH TOOK HIM to the arboretum fields. With the rains, the crops had burst into life. Coach opened the door, and the sweet, clean fragrance hit Jean Patrick, so vibrant it was painful.

"What happened to your foot?" Coach kneeled and tightened the bandage.

"I cut it when I went over a wall. On the bottles." He twisted to show Coach his palm, and the rope burned his wrists. "My hand, too."

"The stigmata."

"Yes."

"Can you run?"

"I think so. I'm not feeling very strong, but if I have to run, I will do it." A half smile. "You know me."

"Yes, Jean Patrick. I do." Coach's hand lingered on Jean Patrick's foot. "I'll give you one chance. If you make it, you'll be on your own again."

"You won't untie me?"

"No. That, I could not explain if they catch you." A truck whinnied up the road, sliding in the mud. "Get out. You need to be quick." The truck came closer. At least, if he did not make it, he would be running when he left this world. Coach pulled him out of the jeep and stood him up. "Go! Go! Go!" He pushed him.

Jean Patrick struggled to remain upright. The truck was close enough for him to hear the soldiers' voices. He didn't need to look to know the cargo. With strength he pulled from the air, he sprang forward, an awkward, bumbling gait. If he could stand the pain and zigzag, he might make it.

"Next time we meet will be Atlanta," Coach called after him. "For the Olympics."

The crack of the shot came at once from far away and inside his head. Falling took forever, a feeling of release. He had time to wonder at the course of the pain, traveling simultaneously upward from his ankle and down from his skull, to anticipate its coming together like two rivers colliding. For a second, he swam. And then he drowned.

BOOK FOUR

THE FAR SIDE OF THE EARTH
Umuntu asiga ikimwirukaho ariko ntawusiga ikimwirukamo.
You can outdistance that which is running after you,
but not what is running inside you.

Twenty-eight

Gihanga, Burundi

THE MAN WAS VISIBLE from far off in the bright morning as he climbed the trail. He walked quickly, head down, face shaded by a dark cap. He hefted a large pack, and his arms kept time with his legs in a way that branded him as a soldier. There was something teasingly familiar about his way of moving, but at this distance, it was hard to tell. Jean Patrick felt his heart quicken, but after so much disappointment, he was wary of its sting. Behind the soldier, a trail of red dust billowed and swirled.

Jean Patrick had been working in the garden when the man caught his attention. From the hours spent weeding, his ankle pulsed. He limped to the edge of the plot and watched carefully for some small, definitive gesture, something that would tell him that this once, he had been right to believe, that Imana had indeed turned his ear in Jean Patrick's direction.

After a few more steps, the soldier looked up toward the house. He stopped, took a few steps forward, stopped and looked again. Jean Patrick waved to encourage him. Probably he was just Auntie Spéciose's friend, uncertain about the stranger in her garden. The war that in Rwanda had ignited like a nuclear explosion and been extinguished by the victory of the RPF had continued as a never-ending smolder in Burundi.

The soldier's pace quickened. He threw his arms in the air and called out, but the wind swept his words away. He took a few more steps and then broke into a run. Jean Patrick heard his own name shouted from the soldier's lips. He took in the square jaw, the familiar sprinting stride he had spent so much energy chasing. He saw that after so much time spent shutting hope out, he could open his heart and let it hit him full force. He threw down his hoe, picked up his cane, and stepped out into the road.

Jean Patrick and Roger stood in the sunlight and held on to each other, swaying in silence, only the familiar notes of their breathing between them. The words to bring them back across the chasm of so much death had not yet been invented.

"You're alive! I knew it," Jean Patrick finally whispered. He stepped back and studied Roger's face. War had carved a geologic epoch into his skin.

"Me, I also knew *you* were alive, and I knew that if I did not find you in Rwanda, I would find you here. Still, I can't believe I am touching you again, flesh and blood." Roger laid his hands on Jean Patrick's shoulders. "Everyone else is gone."

Jean Patrick fought off collapse. In his heart, he had known it. If any of them had been alive, they would have found a way to contact Auntie Spéciose. But until Roger's words extinguished it, he had nurtured a tiny flicker of belief. "Come to the house. Auntie has gone to the market, and Uncle Damien is at work." He wiped dirt and sweat from his face and smiled weakly. "He's a teacher, like Papa."

"Yes, I remember. He told me when I came — *before*." The words that divided Rwandan time in two: *before* and *after*. *After*, only a month's worth of days.

Jean Patrick said, "When I first saw Auntie from a distance, my heart flew. She resembles Mama so much I thought it was her. It was only when I was nearly face-to-face that I saw I had been mistaken." One hand on Roger's shoulder, one hand on his cane, Jean Patrick started toward the house.

"Aye! What happened to you?" Squatting in the dirt, Roger examined the purplish, swollen skin, the jagged scar between ankle and calf. "Did you know the person who cut you? I promise he will face justice, if he is still alive."

Justice? What was that? "You have found him, my brother. I did it to myself, jumping over a wall." He took off the felt hat Uncle Damien had given him and ran his fingers across the pink, hairless line above his ear. "This gunshot wound I did not inflict on myself."

"Eh?" Roger stood. "A bullet? Mana yanjye!"

"Yego. It's a long story, but we have plenty of time. Come and take something to drink, some nourishment. Wherever you came from, it is a hard journey here."

THEY SAT AT the tiny table carved by Damien's hand and drank orange Fanta. Jean Patrick sliced mangoes and papayas, peeled a cucumber and a tomato and sprinkled them with thick granules of salt. "I am ready to hear, if you are ready to tell."

Roger wiped his fingers on his pants. "I am ready."

"You went there?"

"Yes."

"And you are certain?"

"Yes. I talked to Mukabera. She's the only Hutu neighbor who didn't run to Zaire with the Interahamwe. My company would have killed her, too, if I hadn't stopped them. After all we witnessed, there were many angry boys." Roger looked around. "Is there beer?"

"Spéciose will bring it from the market."

"I can't be sure about Mama, Jacqueline, and the girls," Roger said. "Uncle told Mukabera he was taking them to the church at Ntura. After the killers did their work there, the Interahamwe bolted the doors and set fire to the building. There were few survivors. I posted the names on all the bulletin boards at the camps, and I studied every picture pinned up on them. I have had no word of them. I do not think they walk among the living."

"And the rest of the family — they were at home?"

Roger placed his hand over Jean Patrick's. It was rough and callused, as Uncle's had been. "They were. Mukabera said Uncle died fighting. She found him with an ax still in his hand. She left him with it; it was the one token of respect she could pay. The killers must have left it there for the same reason, but surely it was not long before someone else carried it off." A fly landed on the table, and Roger flicked it away. "They even killed your little dog. Mukabera said Pili's body was resting on Zachary's chest."

"Mana yanjye, they just left the bodies on the ground?"

Jean Patrick could have filled the world's oceans with his grief, but he found not one tear in his heart. Everything inside him had dried and shriveled. "Did you bury them?"

"By the time we got there, what was left had been scattered by animals. I won't pain you with details. We dug a single grave for the hillside, but we were not so thorough. I can only hope that someday, you and I will find the right bones so we can lay our family to rest properly and according to custom. That much we must do for them." Sunlight, dim and dusty, canted through the narrow window and fell across Roger's face, threading his eyes with topaz. They were Mathilde's eyes. Jean Patrick had never noticed before. "Will you come back to Rwanda with me?" Roger asked.

"I can't. I'm waiting for a visa for the States, which my American professor—Jonathan—is helping me to get. I've applied for refugee status, and if I return for any reason, they will deny me." Jean Patrick waved his hands. "But that's all part of my long story, which can wait. Spéciose will be back soon, and she will want your news. My tale, she has already heard." The bones only, Jean Patrick thought, not the raw flesh.

Roger shook a cigarette from his pack and pushed up from the table. "You can smoke in here," Jean Patrick said. "Uncle does all the time." He fetched a cracked clay ashtray. His eyes followed the struck match, the ember's glow, the two tendrils of smoke rising from Roger's nostrils. Only then did he ask, "Have you been to Butare?"

"I have. I thought by some miracle I might still find you there." Roger studied the cigarette's glow. "I'm sorry to tell you this," he said. "I saw Niyonzima's house, and it is burned to the ground. Is that where you were?"

Although he knew this to be true, hearing it from his brother was like a grave opening up, possibility falling into it. "Yes. The soldiers and Interahamwe came. I jumped over the wall, and that's how I destroyed my ankle. Bea was with me, but at the last moment, she turned back." It was the first time Jean Patrick had torn these words from memory, given them substance and shape. "What I am asking is if there is a chance. Remote. That someone escaped." In the theory of quantum physics, Jean Patrick had read, a person could be leaning against a wall and fall through to the other side if the molecules simultaneously realigned in just the right way.

Roger exhaled a thick blue ring of smoke. "I suppose." But his expression told Jean Patrick he did not believe it. There was an equal chance, the expression said, that they would wake in the morning in their house at Gihundwe, Mama and Papa at their bedside, the past ten years of their lives nothing more than a terrible nightmare.

"I heard their names announced on RTLM—the three of them—but then, I heard yours, too," Roger said.

"Eh? They announced my name on the radio?" Possibility stirred, put a bony finger on the edge of the grave.

"They boasted of it. We were fighting near Kigali. I had just returned to the truck and put the radio on. They said they caught you at a roadblock. I punched the dashboard so hard my hand was swollen for a week." He held up his fist to show the scarred knuckles. "But after the shock wore off, a little voice kept telling me it wasn't so. My brother, he is too crafty, I told myself. Since that time, I knew I would find you again."

Jean Patrick said, "The thought of greeting you again has kept me going." That and the smallest spark of belief that Bea lived.

The sun had started its descent, its angle now missing the tall window. The topaz was gone from Roger's eyes. "A funny thing," Roger said. "When they mentioned Niyonzima's wife, they said she was Tutsi. Do you know anything about this?"

Jean Patrick shook his head. "She could easily have been mistaken for one—most likely this happened—but she was Hutu."

IN THE EVENING, Roger sat outside with Jean Patrick. The full moon painted a path into the bush. Spéciose brought out a small table and two bottles of ikigage. The sorghum beer was strong, and Jean Patrick's head spun, although he was only halfway through his bottle. Smoke from a mosquito coil spiraled upward. An occasional volley of gunfire came from the forest. War, it seemed, would never be far away.

"Do you remember the roof Uncle made for us when we first moved in?" Roger asked.

"How could I forget? When I think how proud he was of his corrugated metal, and how we joked about it in private, I could crawl into the earth with shame."

"Those killers stole it. Every scrap of metal gone. When we were advancing, we saw so many Hutu fleeing with heavy, heavy piles of roofing on their heads. They could barely move forward under the weight."

Jean Patrick laughed at the image. A dance of looters and killers wobbling and weaving to the borders. He asked Roger if he had been to Gihundwe. He had. Nothing left of the school, the survivors counted on a single hand.

Spéciose came out with two more bottles. She touched Roger's cheek. "You have your mother's beautiful face." She wiped her eyes. "You'll have to come in soon; it's almost curfew."

Roger stared into the bush. "Is the fighting near?"

"It comes and goes," Jean Patrick said. "Not like Bujumbura, where you fear for your life going to market. But everywhere is dangerous after dark." He smiled weakly. "At least I'm on the right side now."

"Right side? Is there ever one?" Roger lit a cigarette. The match flared across his face. "I brought you something." Roger fished a bundle wrapped in newspaper from his pack. Inside the layers was Zachary's Bible, pages curled with dried blood. "Mukabera saved it. She found it clutched in his arms." He snorted. "Probably the killers knew there was too much deadly sin on their hands to tempt God's wrath by stealing it."

Jean Patrick held the Bible to his face and took the scent of his brother's blood deep into his lungs. He inhaled the decay, the ferruginous odor of death. Suddenly he was underwater, grief flowing over him like the sea.

"She found this, too." Roger uncurled his fist. "Do you recognize it?"

Jean Patrick examined the Saint Christopher's medal. "It's not Uncle's, but it's familiar."

"Think about fishing."

He saw it then, lantern light across a bare chest in the pirogue, the medal flashing and twirling in its gleam. "Fulgence. It used to mesmerize me when he pulled in the nets."

"He was one of the killers. Mukabera saw him."

"What are you going to do with it?" Jean Patrick gave the medal back to Roger.

"I'll keep it." He shoved it into his pocket. "So I can show it to him before I kill him."

Weariness filled Jean Patrick's bones. In this moment, he was too tired for vengeance. But in another moment, everything could change.

"I'm going to Boston as soon as my visa comes through," Jean Patrick said. He took a long swallow of beer. "Why don't you come with me?"

"My muzungu brother, huh!" Roger clapped Jean Patrick's knee. "Well, why not? There's nothing for me here. I don't think they'll appoint me president in the near future."

"You could join the American army."

"Fighting is finished."

"What about One Shot? Do you know what happened to him?"

Roger smiled. "He hooked up with some NGO about child soldiers. He's a big man now, goes around speaking everywhere. They paid for a brand-new leg—he may run his marathon yet. Mana yanjye, he was brave. Someone you could always count on." He leaned forward and touched Jean Patrick's scalp, the still-tender wound. "What about this?"

From the forest came a monkey's warning cry. Jean Patrick took another swallow of beer and waited for the pain in his ankle to blur. "Coach." He forced his ankle in a slow circle. "He took me to the arboretum to kill me but then gave me one chance to run. Truly, by that time, I should have been dead, but my body insisted on life. I heard the shot and felt a searing pain in my head. I'm finished, was my last thought. But then I woke up in his arms." Jean Patrick tunneled through the dark earth of memory. He wondered if he would ever emerge on the other side of the world. "Until now, I don't know if he is a good shot or if he missed by accident." He gave a little laugh. "Maybe someday I will get the chance to ask him."

Again, Roger went to his pack. He pulled out a piece of paper and dropped it onto the table. "Bad news and more bad news," he said.

Jean Patrick picked up the crumpled, filthy paper and read. *Iyo inzoka yizilitse ku gisabo ugomba kikimena ukabona uko uyica.* In killing a snake curled around a gourd, you break the gourd if you must, to kill him. It was an old Rwandan proverb, and there was no mistaking Coach's writing. "What's this?"

"We found that in his pocket when we went to his house. He was in the backyard. Like a true soldier, he shot himself in the head."

Jean Patrick felt an empty pit in his stomach. "What do you think he meant by that?"

"Probably, it is the same old thing—we Tutsi are the snake, and Rwanda the gourd."

Jean Patrick nodded. "I can think of no other meaning." He thought he should feel—what? Rage? Grief? No one else besides Bea had had such an influence on his life, but he could not begin to untangle the web of their long history together. At some point, there would be rage, and there would be grief; he knew that. But at this moment, there was only a dull ache in that place Coach had taught him was the source of all his power.

Jean Patrick turned to Roger. "What can you tell me now that you would not tell me before? If I had not been beyond feeling or thinking when I was taken to him, the shock of the man in his army uniform with his gun, stinking of blood, would have killed me."

"While he was training you, he also trained militias in the forest. Armed them. That's what I was trying to warn you about when I came to Butare. The killing did not take him by surprise; he was involved in the planning."

Coach always disappearing. The locked spare room and the heavy wooden crate beneath the bed. All the whispers Jean Patrick had blocked from his ears, swept from his eyes.

"And Jolie, his servant—did you find her?"

Roger shrugged. "Gone to Zaire, most likely."

"But I can't forget that in the end, he saved me," Jean Patrick said. "I was in and out of consciousness, in his arms, then in the jeep again. I thought he was taking me somewhere else to kill me, but I could not stay awake. I was no longer capable of caring. Next, I woke up in a bed at my friend Jonathan's house. He and his umukunzi, Susanne, were supposed to have left for Burundi, and they were going to hide Bea and me in the trunk, but the same night, the killing started. After that, they refused to flee. That is the reason Coach found them. Come to think of it, he must have known they were there." Jean Patrick gave a little laugh. "Coach had a way of knowing everything.

"Their cook, Amos, was Tutsi, too, and they were protecting him." Jean Patrick wiped the beer's sweet foam from his lips. He would have a headache in the morning. "Coach promised a military escort, so Jonathan's plan was executed after all. Only it was Amos instead of Bea who curled beside me in the trunk."

Jean Patrick rose unsteadily from his chair. "We better go in before the rebels come running through. Enough is enough." In the doorway, he held Roger back. "One request."

"Anything."

"Will you go back to Butare? Look around? Maybe you could find some news for me."

"It is as done."

Spéciose and Damien slept. Roger and Jean Patrick walked quietly through the dark house. They lay down together and pulled the blankets close around them. Jean Patrick tucked himself against Roger's back for warmth, as he had done every night when they were children, when the world was solid beneath their feet.

1995

TWENTY-NINE

AS HE STRAPPED HIMSELF into the tiny seat and looked through the wavering heat at the tarmac, Jean Patrick discovered he was scared. His body vibrated with the crescendo of engine noise, and he felt as squeezed as in any Onatracom bus. As instructed, he tucked the knapsack Jonathan had sent from America under the seat in front of him and pulled the uncomfortable seatback into an upright position. Rwandans always did as they were told, he reflected. His knees pressed into the seat in front.

The woman in the seat beside him tightened the shawl that held the wailing baby to her breast. She was floaty and tall, a breakable beauty, and when she smiled at Jean Patrick, life stirred in his heart.

"Girl or boy?"

"Boy," she said, untucking the baby's head from his cocoon to show him. The child's toothless, wide-eyed fear made Jean Patrick laugh.

"I know how he feels," he said.

"Is this your first time flying?" She rubbed the baby's nose with hers and cooed to him. Gold bracelets sparked on her arm.

"Yes, my first time on a plane. I come from Rwanda. Cyangugu." The plane moved slowly down the runway, the engine's pitch rising.

"I'm sorry." The woman settled back against her pillow and sighed. "Imana ikurinde." Then she sat up again and held out her hand. "I'm Eugénie. From Bujumbura."

It was strange to mention the country of his birth and receive always an apology and a blessing. "I'm going to Boston to live," Jean Patrick said, returning her firm handshake.

"We're going to Boston, too. But from there we go on to Montreal. At least you have some time to get used to the weather before winter.

The temperature change is quite a shock." She smiled again, and warmth spread through Jean Patrick.

The plane accelerated, the runway a black blur. There was a last jostling bump, and they were airborne. The city of Bujumbura wheeled away beneath them. Lake Tanganyika glistened, a black diamond. What was it Jonathan said? The second-deepest lake in the world? The lowest point in Africa? He remembered that, like Lake Kivu, Tanganyika was part of the East African Rift Valley, the continent of Africa tearing apart in fits and starts along a jagged seam beneath the hot and thinning crust.

Jean Patrick retrieved his knapsack and took out his Bible. It was a new one, a parting gift from Auntie Spéciose. Zachary's Bible was in his suitcase, bundled in newspapers and plastic bags. He hadn't been able to leave it behind.

Life always moved in a circle, he thought, flipping through the pages for a suitable section to read. He'd spent years trying to lift Papa's life from the words he had written, but the journal was destroyed before he succeeded. Now he had the Bible that had been passed from Papa to Zachary, and in his braver moments, he tried to face Zachary's final one, to discover the passage he took comfort from as he awaited death.

He let the book fall open, and it parted on Isaiah. *For the stars of heaven and their constellations will not give their light; The sun will be darkened in its going forth, and the moon will not cause its light to shine. Everyone who is found will be thrust through.* He could not read on. Instead he imagined his brother taking comfort from the Hymn of Praise: *For YAH, the Lord, is my strength and my song: He has also become my salvation. Therefore with joy you will draw water from the wells of salvation.*

He remembered Zachary as he had seen him at Easter, face rapturous, ribbons of stained-glass light streaming onto his white shirt. He remembered the walk to church—the sun shimmer on Jacqueline's hair, the dance of flowers on Mama and Auntie's pagnes—the recollection still sharp enough to cut him.

Reading brought on queasiness, and Jean Patrick set the Bible on his lap. Tentatively he closed his eyes. Sometimes, without warning, images loomed up before him. Already he recalled those days like fractals of broken glass plucked from his flesh shard by shard. This time, only light from the airplane window played behind his eyelids. He floated in the engines' thrum. He wondered if they had passed over Rwanda, the infected wound in the elephant ear of Africa.

It was Iki now, the long dry season spanning July and August. If he could have excised that wound, inserted the normal passage of time, Mama and Aunt Esther would have been in the fields, harvesting sorghum and maize. Clemence, Clémentine, and Clarisse would have been spread-legged on the ground, the ruby beads of sorghum berries spilling from a blanket between them. Uncle would have been a stork, balanced with his long pole in his pirogue, slapping the lake's surface. And Daniel? Jean Patrick thought of his friend's smile, pink berry of tongue between gapped front teeth. He would be preparing for his third year at university, falling daily in and out of love. Jean Patrick tucked his head under his arm and fell into a troubled sleep.

WHEN JEAN PATRICK AWOKE, darkness bathed the cabin. Eugénie read, illuminated by a halo of overhead light. Her baby played in the lap of the grandmother across the aisle.

"I put your Bible in the seat pocket," Eugénie said. "I rescued it from the floor." From between the pages of her book she removed a photograph. "This fell out," she said, handing it to him.

It was a picture of him with Bea that Susanne had taken the day before Easter. She had mailed it to him in Burundi, wrapped in purple paper—purple, the color of the genocide now—and folded into a long letter. *At first I didn't want to send this, but the more I looked at it, the more I knew I had to.*

In the photo, he and Bea leaned against each other and looked out at the camera with the sternest of expressions. It must have been a trick of the fickle light; he saw Bea lift her head and smile. He took the Bible from the pouch and opened it. The page fate chose was in Romans. *Do not be overcome by evil, but overcome evil with good.* He shuffled again: *For he is God's minister, an avenger to execute wrath on him who practices evil.* As he flipped through the books, it seemed that wherever he landed, he could choose either vengeance or forgiveness. He could not say which he chose for himself. He settled finally on Ephesians: *Walk in Unity, Walk in Love, Walk in Light and Wisdom.* The day had not yet come when he could live by this message.

If his future had followed its intended path, he would be on his way to Sweden for World Championships. A few months ago, he had reconciled with fate enough to contact Gilbert and Ndizeye after he saw their names in a newspaper. Ndizeye had switched to the 10K and was training for the Olympics. Gilbert was running close to world-record times in the eight hundred. In Burundi, they were idols. Jean Patrick went to Bujumbura to see them but stayed away from the track. Setting foot on that oval would have reopened a deeper wound than he could bear, as if he had jumped over the bottle-crowned wall once more and sliced open his belly. Even so, he was not yet ready to let go of the belief that he would heal and run again. This, and the voice that would not stop whispering to him that Bea lived, were what kept his heart contracting and relaxing: one beat and then another.

He tucked Bea's picture back inside the Bible. He had done everything he could to discover a trace of her. He asked Roger to track down anyone who knew her, asked him to find Claire, although he could not tell his brother where she lived or any way to find out. He wrote letters to professors in Butare, but the university no longer functioned.

Then, a week before Jean Patrick was to leave, Roger came to spend this last time with him. They sat at the table with bottles of urwagwa.

"I found an uncle of Niyonzima's in Kigali," Roger said, "and I went to see him." Slowly and deliberately, he tapped the ash from his cigarette into the ashtray. In the stuffy room, the smoke hovered, motionless. "I'm afraid in this, RTLM was right: there were no survivors from Niyonzima's house."

Jean Patrick shook his head. "Was he there? Did he see the bodies? Identify them?"

Roger begged him to leave it. "Don't keep digging up that chapter of your life. There is nothing else we can do. Now you must bury it, for your own good."

I will bury it, but I will always water this one seed, Jean Patrick thought. Before closing the Bible, he traced the outline of Bea's body. He brought forth the touch of her skin, the warmth of her breath on his neck. *Walk in Light and Wisdom,* he whispered. *Walk in Love.*

BOOK FIVE

THE THINGS OF TOMORROW
Iby'ejo bibara ab'ejo.
The things of tomorrow will be recounted
by the people of tomorrow.

1998

THIRTY

BEHIND THE INTORE DANCERS, musicians leapt into the air, pounded drums with hands and sticks. Stage lights caught sweat on their foreheads and shot pink and blue spears across their leopard-spotted ikindi. Dancers tossed their imigara, the headdresses flaring like arched tails.

Jonathan and Susanne knew how to throw a party. It was nearly eleven o'clock, and they were all going strong, waiting to ring in the New Year. Every Rwandan within a hundred-mile radius of Boston had squeezed into the hall, as well as the entire geology department at MIT, students and staff. The department head was there, and even she was dancing. There was much to celebrate. In two weeks' time, Jonathan and Susanne were getting married.

Jean Patrick leaned against a wall and watched the party. *A body in motion tends to remain in motion,* he mused. The clam-shaped bells around the dancers' ankles oscillated in harmonic motion with their stamping feet. Across the room, the door to the hall opened, and one of Jonathan's students came in, skin rubbed pink from cold. He dropped dollar bills into the five-gallon bottle marked FOR FORA. Once more, Jean Patrick checked his phone for messages.

The cell phone was a new thing, and Jean Patrick hated it; he did not like its weight or the way it banged around in his jacket pocket. But Roger had just left for Rwanda, and they wanted to keep in touch. He was in Kigali with his wife and daughter for Christmas. "I want my Mathilde to see the country where her parents were born," he said. In the intervening years, they had found a scattering of cousins who had survived, an aunt of Papa's, a few nephews and nieces who had returned to Rwanda from Uganda and Burundi to live. Roger and his family would meet those who could travel to Kigali. The rest of the country still reeled from the war. He couldn't expose his child to that; they would not go to Cyangugu.

Jean Patrick was not ready to return. He couldn't get beyond imagining the instant of landing: the fuel smell, fumes, and noise rising from the tarmac. He couldn't get past the fear that with his first footstep, he would fall into the rivers of the dead.

Jean Patrick had invited a girl to the party, and she had promised to be there by ten. Her name was Leslie, a grad student in physics of Ugandan descent, lively and lithe. They had gone to the movies, had dinner together, talked until four in the morning. At her door, he had kissed her, the kiss long and hard and hungry. Feeling the warmth of her body, inhaling her heady perfume, he believed he could open a corner of his heart to her. He checked his watch and sighed; she must be keeping African time.

The musicians announced a break. Bob Marley's "No Woman No Cry" wailed from the speakers. Jonathan and Susanne danced, Jonathan mimicking the Intore dancers, tossing his headdress of red hair, unhindered by ponytail or braid. He took a glass of champagne and drank. Susanne rolled her hips, exposed the taut bulge of her belly. The baby would be born in March.

The song ended, and Susanne brought Jean Patrick a Mutzig beer. "We must have raised a few hundred dollars tonight for the Friends of Rwanda Association," she said. "That's tuition for two and a half students."

Jean Patrick handed Susanne a five-dollar bill. "Now it's two and nine-sixteenths."

The door to the hall opened once more, and two Rwandan professors entered. Jean Patrick sucked his teeth. "I guess Leslie's stood me up," he said.

Paul Simon's "Graceland" came over the speakers, and Jonathan shouted to the DJ for full volume. The sad joy of the lyrics threaded Jean Patrick's heart.

"J. P.! Come dance!" Jonathan held out his hands to Jean Patrick.

"Yes," Susanne said. "Come dance."

Jonathan pulled Susanne to the center of the floor, and she pulled Jean Patrick with her. Besides Roger, they were the closest family he had. The three of them swayed to the music. That afternoon, he had spent too long on the treadmill, and his ankle let him know. A familiar but unnamable longing tugged at him. After all these years, he thought, we are still a nation in exile, a diaspora.

THE MUSICIANS HAD GRABBED their instruments but had not yet begun to play when Jean Patrick's cell phone rang. It took him a moment to distinguish his brother's voice from the static.

"Umwaka mwiza, Little Brother."

"Umwaka mwiza, Roger. Happy New Year. Is everything OK?" Jean Patrick realized he was shouting into the phone, the tingle of panic at his throat. He still felt always on the edge of disaster, as if at any moment the earth could open beneath his feet.

"Are you sitting down? I think you should be sitting down." Roger sounded strange—drunk or disoriented.

"Mana yanjye, what's happened? Is Marie hurt? Mathilde?"

"No! Everything's fine. I have someone here who wants to talk to you. Hold on."

Jean Patrick waited. There was static, followed by murmurs in the background.

"Uraho? Jean Patrick?" A female voice, woman or child, he couldn't be sure.

Jonathan trumpeted over the loudspeaker. "One minute to midnight by my official clock. Set your watches. Countdown in fifty seconds."

"Muraho? Who is this? Just a minute. I can't hear." Jean Patrick covered one ear and pressed the phone against the other.

"Are you there? Are you hearing me now?" A woman, but not Spéciose.

"Ten. Nine. Eight." The whole hall roared.

"I'm here. You'll have to speak up."

"Is that really your voice coming through this phone, Jean Patrick Nkuba?"

Jean Patrick found his way to the wall and sank against it. The light in the hall took on an unnatural color. His lips couldn't form the name; he was afraid that if they did, it would not be true. He closed his eyes and held the phone to his heart.

"Three. Two. One."

He brought the phone to his lips. "Bea?" He tried to absorb it. Tried to breathe. "Bea," he said again, louder, holding the sound on his tongue, a musical note. "Yes. It's me. I always believed one day I would hear you again."

Cheers bounced in standing waves across the hall. "Happy New Year!"

"Is it just New Year's there? Is that what I hear?"

Jean Patrick nodded before he realized she couldn't see. "Uzakubere uw'amata n'ubuki." The last time he had wished her a year of milk and honey was in Café Murakazaneza, in 1994.

"J. P.—what's wrong?" Susanne was at his side.

"It's Bea," he said. He handed her the phone while all at once the dam burst on a lake that had been filling for four and a half years.

JEAN PATRICK SAT in darkness. His bed remained undisturbed, sheets folded crisply over the blanket. Stripes from a streetlamp fell across his desk. The faint gray glow of dawn outlined the buildings against the skyline. In fifteen minutes, his alarm would ring. He opened the window and let the cool air hit his face. The hiss of falling snow filled his ears.

It was incredibly crazy. Roger sitting in the hotel bar in Kigali watching TV, Bea's face suddenly there, on the screen. She was being interviewed for her work with women survivors with HIV-AIDS. Roger said he knew instantly—absolutely—that it was the same woman whose face had greeted him from the photo on Jean Patrick's desk. When her name flashed on the screen, he hollered so loud the whole place looked around, although madness was something they were used to. He bought everyone a drink. Jean Patrick wanted to believe it was more than coincidence. He tried to convince himself it was fate.

"But how did she seem?" Jean Patrick had asked Roger when he called back to give him the details. Jean Patrick sat at his desk, staring into Bea's eyes. He had had enough time to let the shock settle, to wade out into the murky waters of speculation.

"She looked great. I can see why you fell in love with her."

"But I mean, she seemed *well*? Not skinny or something? She was never skinny before." He couldn't say the word *AIDS*. He could barely think it.

"She didn't look ill, if that's what you're asking."

Jean Patrick nodded. "You're sure?" Roger must understand what he meant.

"Yego, Little Brother. Yes, yes, yes."

Beside Jean Patrick's desk, the wastebasket overflowed with the detritus of discarded letters. All his attempts to smooth sweetness over the words he needed to say came out as schoolboy nonsense. Over and over, he tried to steer his mind away from the abyss beyond the instant of hurtling over the wall. Over and over his mind traveled back to that one second in time he could never undo. He didn't know what price she had paid to survive, but he knew it had been high. He picked up the pen again and wrote the only two words for which meaning remained: *Forgive me.*

Thirty-one

JEAN PATRICK STOOD IN THE FRONT HALLWAY of his apartment building, Bea's letter in his hand. Unlike the first two letters, short and chatty,
this one had substance and weight. Even the stamp appeared carefully chosen: a landscape of Lake Kivu. A cold draft came in through the door, but
despite the dampness of his clothes from a run in the snow, he did not move.

Jean Patrick had told Bea nothing of his time in the swamps, nothing
of his rescue by his coach. He merely said that in the end, he owed his life
to Jonathan and Susanne, and he mentioned in passing the journey in the
trunk, curled up with Amos like twins in the womb.

In turn, Bea's life as he knew it jumped from the shadows of the wall to
three years in London, where she received a degree in social work. She had
been back in Rwanda for less than a year. She did not mention to whom
she owed her life. Each letter sank beneath the burden of all that remained
unsaid, but where could either of them begin? How could they dig with
the blade of questions at a scab that had not even begun to heal? Neither
of them had sent a photo.

After her second letter, he hadn't been able to stand it anymore. *I want
to come and see you,* he had written. *I have no other way forward from here.*

Jean Patrick shivered. When he opened the letter and began to read, he
would find the word *yego,* yes, or *oya,* no. He did not think he could stand
a no, did not think he could bear to lose her one more time. Tucking the
letter into his inside jacket pocket, he took the three flights of stairs two
steps at a time.

Once inside his apartment, he made himself wait. From the cupboard
he took a box of Burundian tea—a gift from Spéciose—and brewed a
strong cup. He added milk, three teaspoons of raw sugar. Stirred. Only
then did he take a knife and slit the flap and sit down to read.

Dear Jean Patrick,

I cannot tell you how many times I have started my letters, found my words to have failed completely, and started again. I know it is the same for you. We are walking among land mines, eh? I wonder if we will ever be able to go back to speaking as we used to, living from one day to the next without memory seizing us by the throat.

Jean Patrick's blood went cold. He read on, scanning her descriptions of life in Kigali, the rubble of buildings cleared so that new, modern ones could replace them. She had enclosed a newsprint photo of the building where she worked, and this, not her thoughts, had made the letter bulky. A group of women stood beneath a purple banner that said, FIGHTING THE STIGMA OF AIDS. Holding the print close, he examined the gaunt faces; Bea's was not among them, he was sure.

I cannot begin to express how brave these women are or the sorrow I feel when I lose one of them. I have thought this over and over until I have worn holes in my mind. I do not think we should meet. At least not now. I cannot bear to take into my arms one more life I could lose.

Folding the letter in half, Jean Patrick set it down on the table where the spilled drops of tea would not wet it. He took his cup to the sink and emptied it, came back to his chair and rested his head on his hands. From somewhere came the sound of a young child laughing. Day faded into evening, but he did not turn on the light.

IT WAS THREE days later when the next letter came. The envelope was thin and square with the embossed image of a stork, made from reeds, in the corner. Jean Patrick almost missed it, tucked between the bills and the endless flyers of junk mail. This time, he did not wait. He tore the envelope open so he could read as he climbed. Bea's perfume embraced him, the familiar scent of flowers and perfumed tea bridging the gap between them as if they had been away from each other for a day, an hour, a minute.

It was a tourist card that, like the envelope, was made from woven reeds embossed on paper. Susanne had a box of similar ones that she sent to her closest friends. This one had a stork and a fisherman casting a line from his pirogue, and he nearly wept to see it. A letter was folded inside.

Dear Jean Patrick,

When I found this card in a shop, the past came back so clearly that my strength left me. Suddenly I was in my father's car on a ridge above Lake Kivu, sun beating through the windshield. It was the day you told me about your life. Do you remember?

As if he had forgotten one scrap.

You gave me a little pirogue with two fishermen inside made from imiseke. You placed it on the seat between us as if it were a crown of jewels. Only now have I realized that yes, it was.

Holding the card in my hands, it came to me that my true reason for refusing you had nothing to do with what I wrote. Please forgive me. I should never have sent that letter. I am writing you at my desk, and above me is a stained-glass bird. For some reason, it has begun to sway, and it is spilling rainbows onto the page. I wish I could send them to you. But what I want to tell you is yego, yes, please come. I will put this card in its envelope and lick it shut quickly, before I change my mind once more.

Softly, Jean Patrick kissed the ink. He was sitting on a step, although he did not remember the act of sitting. The dim light of the hallway quivered in the folds of his parka. The sound of footsteps came to him slowly, a steady musical *clup,* pause, *clup.*

"Dear, are you all right?"

His upstairs neighbor, Mrs. Greenbaum, peered into his face. Seated, he barely had to look up into the hazel of her eyes. She balanced two heavy shopping bags. Jean Patrick guessed her to be eighty years old, and yet she walked to the store and up three flights of stairs daily.

"Yes, Mrs. G., thank you. I am fine."

She set down a bag and patted his arm before continuing up the steps. The song of her boots faded and then became silence.

Jean Patrick stared down at his open suitcase. It had been snowing since early evening, and as midnight came and went, the snow still fell. His clothes were neatly folded, his presents for Auntie Spéciose, Uncle Damien, and the little cousins protected by sweatshirts and pants.

From Susanne and Jonathan, he had an album of photos to give to Bea. The pictures were all from Jean Patrick's new life. Jean Patrick leaping from a sand dune on Cape Cod, waving in front of the Green Building at MIT, his first snow, his first Red Sox game, Red Sox cap cocked over one eye and beer and hot dog in hand. Susanne and her pregnant belly.

"What do you think?" Susanne had asked him.

"I think it's OK. I think she will want to have them." But then he had wondered if the want was more his—pushing himself back into her life.

Rwanda, all the pictures from Easter, had been neatly excised. It had been only in the past year that he had found the strength to look at those himself.

He put his economic geology book into his backpack. Midterms were the week after he returned. With his thick sweaters and all his running gear, he worried about the weight. He took the album out. Flipping through the pages, he stopped at a picture of himself and Jonathan finishing a 5K, their joined hands held high. It had taken courage to sign up for his first race in his new life, courage to run without expectations. Standing at the start line, all those people crowded together, he had nearly panicked and walked away. Then, out of nowhere, Coach's voice had come to him: *Your mind will tell your body what to do.* A mixture of profound grief and a sense of nostalgia that felt almost like joy filled him. He was able to relax, to tell himself again that he was doing this for fun. But as soon as the horn sounded, his muscles fired with the mad surge that instinct brought to his legs, and Jonathan had had to call him back.

"Whoa, J. P.!" Jonathan shouted. "Run as one, right?" They had made a pact.

Far removed from the few at the front who cared about placing, it seemed so strange: no tight pack jockeying for position, no serious race faces. A jubilant tumult of noise instead of silence broken only by the *slap-slap* of eight pairs of shoes. So Jean Patrick had settled into an easy pace beside Jonathan and let the festive air of his fellow runners infect

him. And after the initial blow of finishing midpack in his age group, he
let that go as well.

It was a lot easier than it had been to watch that first Olympics, his physical and emotional wounds so close to the skin's surface. He had wedged
himself between Jonathan and Susanne, squeezing the edge of the couch so
tightly that he could barely uncurl his fingers when the eight-hundred final
was finished. Although Gilbert hadn't qualified, a Kenyan came in third,
and Jean Patrick was genuinely happy to see an African medal.

The next picture was of Kweli, taken shortly after Jonathan and Susanne
arrived home. She was in midstride, running through tall grass. Suddenly,
Jean Patrick was supplicant by the side of the bed, cold sweat trickling
from his armpits.

He was back in Jonathan's office, face pressed to the window, watching
Bea on the grass with the puppy, then seeing her shirtless in the window's
light, shadows tattooed across her breasts. With a vividness so sharp it cut,
he tasted her salt on his tongue, felt the warmth of being inside her.

And then gone. He repacked the album, drew himself up, and wiped his
face with the edge of his sweatshirt, dried his clammy fingers. Beside the
suitcase was a small white box. Inside the box was a gold cross, and its resem-
blance to the first was uncanny—the delicate plaited chain was nearly iden-
tical. The thought of putting this gift into her hand terrified him. Maybe
she believed God had abandoned her. Maybe she had abandoned Him.

ON THE PLANE, Jean Patrick opened his eyes and let them adjust
to the darkened cabin. He could not say if he had slept. Beyond the window, running lights pierced the dark. The engines droned, a comforting
hum in his head. He turned on the overhead light and checked his watch;
in five hours' time he would see her.

Once more, he took the letters and the card out of his knapsack. He
had read them so many times he was afraid they would disintegrate in his
fingers. With each reading, he pulled the lines apart and put them back
together again. Still, he couldn't find the hidden ones that whispered,
I have my health and there is no one else. Of course the first was most
important, but he couldn't stop himself from asking for both. He felt like
someone bargaining at the market. But if—God forbid—he could have

only the second, he would seize the chance. He would cup each moment he had with her in his palms, a precious gift.

It seemed unlikely that no one else had claimed her. In his moments of doubt, he cursed himself for his spontaneous travel plans. More than once he had held the phone in his hand to cancel his reservations. But even if Bea turned out to be an impossible dream, it was time to stand on the earth where his family had lived and hear for himself the stories of the bones. He had just needed this one push to see him through his fear.

He had written Bea that he would be going to Cyangugu, but he had not asked her to accompany him. He did not want to leave her in the uncomfortable position of refusing. When he had requested the name of a Kigali hotel so he could make a reservation, she told him she would take care of it. She had not offered to open her home to him. He put the letters back in his bag and pressed the pair of socks to ensure that the cross still nestled inside them. In the end, he had to keep moving forward, one foot in front of the other.

He maneuvered into the aisle to stretch his legs. Slowly he made circles with his foot: clockwise first, then counterclockwise. Sitting for long periods of time made him feel like an old man, his ankle perpetually stiff and prone to swelling. After what the doctors had told him, he was thankful he could run at all. If he had found a doctor immediately, the damage might have been repaired, they said. A chance he could have healed completely and even competed again. *If my grandmother had wheels, she'd be a trolley car,* Susanne liked to say. Jean Patrick rubbed out his Achilles tendon and headed for the back of the plane. He wondered if Bea would notice right away the slight favoring of his right leg.

In the galley, a stewardess loaded a cart with drinks, and Jean Patrick asked her for a water. He took the bottle and held it to his cheek a moment, letting the cold sink in. The electric jolt when he drank made him wince. Two weeks ago, he had bitten into a bagel and broken off a fresh fragment from his chipped tooth. He had meant to get the tooth fixed, had been meaning to get it capped for years, but the high-pitched whine of the dentist's drill left him breathless and faint, the sound too close to the whistles. There was always a reason to put it off. At least this way, Bea would recognize him when he smiled.

It was morning when Jean Patrick awoke, the lustrous African light penetrating his eyelids. Clean clothes tucked under his arm, he headed for the bathroom to wash up and brush his teeth. The seatbelt sign was on when he emerged, and he squeezed back into his seat. He took deep breaths and tried to relax into the first dizzying moments of descent.

Beneath the wing, a verdant landscape tilted. Soon his country would take shape from the blurred geology. Terraced hillsides would rise to his sight. At this time of year, the green was intense enough to damage him. He wondered what remained of Cyangugu. He wondered if children still waded into the waters to wash, if women brought basins of clothes to launder, if fishermen still sang the old songs when they returned from fishing. Jean Patrick brought his seat to the full upright position and prepared himself for landing. Lake Kivu gleamed beneath him—windswept, bejeweled. His longing for his family left a cavernous space inside him. He had heard that during the genocide, the bodies in the lake were so thick you could have walked across them to Zaire.

Jean Patrick cleared customs and stared through the glass at the crowded lobby below. After the third sweep, he panicked: Bea was not there. I never should have come, he thought. He shouldered his knapsack, waited for his suitcase, and then walked to the tourist information booth. His ankle hurt, and his head felt packed with cotton. He made a mental plan for an immediate journey home.

"Nkuba Jean Patrick, you said?"

Jean Patrick nodded, too shaky to speak another word. "Let me see if there is a message for you."

The woman behind the window shuffled sleepily through a sheaf of papers. "You are to wait by the door. Your friend has been delayed because of an accident." Quickly she gave him a sympathetic smile. "Don't worry," she added. "She was not involved."

He pushed through the bustle of travelers and luggage and stood in the long line to change money. His foot jiggled as he waited impatiently for his turn. I've become American, he thought, always in a hurry.

He had pocketed the colorful bills and was threading his way through the crowd when he heard the voice. "Mana yanjye! Nkuba, you haven't changed one bit. Even the sneakers are the same."

The bright timbre of words crashed through the years of lost time. He gripped the handle of his bag to steady himself. Then he turned around to greet Bea.

She was a flash of morning color: a cream-yellow pagne with red roses, a billowy orange blouse, gold sandals, thin strapped and glittery. The neck of her blouse was high, so he could not see if she wore a necklace. Her hair was straight, an ear-length bob, and her trademark gold hoop earrings swung with her step. She was thinner—yes—but she did not look unhealthy. In truth, she looked radiant, if possible more beautiful than he remembered. If possible, as if every instant of time since he had last seen her had merely glanced off the coppery shield of her skin.

"ARE YOU EXHAUSTED?" Bea opened the trunk of her tiny car—a Toyota, Jean Patrick noticed—and he put his bag inside.

Since his landing, the weather had turned; an anemic sun poked through a sky messy with charcoal clouds. The airport was high on a hill. Kigali unraveled, a multicolored skein, below them.

"How could I be?" he said. "I am looking at you."

"Soon you can have a sleep, but I wanted to welcome you properly first, and I am not much of a cook. That gift I did not inherit from my mother." Bea unlocked the car door, and he climbed inside, into the lap of her perfume. "Would you mind if I take you for lunch?" she said. "The place is not much to look at, but each time I go, I am reminded of the Murakazaneza."

At the mention of the restaurant where they had eaten together, Jean Patrick felt a yearning stir. Gingerly he put a toe into the river of the past. "I would like that," he said. "Nothing in Boston comes close." As if searching for a wallet or a piece of gum, he put his hand into his knapsack and found the pair of socks. With the tip of his finger, he felt the square corner of the box that contained the cross.

THE RESTAURANT WAS noisy, packed with a lunchtime crowd. Their table was small, covered with a shabby white cloth, and the plates

NAOMI BENARON

of brochettes and chips, isombe, green bananas, and beans took up most of the space. Jean Patrick inhaled the rich aromas and sank back against the chair. He did not know what to do with his long legs, his hands, his power of speech.

Bea spooned isombe onto their plates, and Jean Patrick closed his eyes with the first taste. His childhood floated before him in all its olfactory richness. He had bought the packets of dried cassava leaves in the States and tried to fix it for himself, but it wasn't the same. Even at the homes of his Rwandan friends who were excellent cooks, some important taste was always missing. "Biraryoshye cyane," he said. It's so good. He watched her expression carefully, but his exploration into shared memory went unanswered. He could not crack the mask of her face.

Over lunch, Jean Patrick told Bea a little of his life in Boston, his studies, his desire to go on for a PhD. She spoke of her work with the women, her plans to further her education as well. All around them was the sound of silverware clacking, plates and pots banging, a constant surge and ebb of conversation. Jean Patrick felt as if they were two ships navigating the waters of Antarctica, icebergs looming beneath them.

When she had finished, Bea folded her paper napkin and set it beside her empty plate. "I'm so glad for this chance to eat with you again," she said, "since our last meal together was interrupted."

Jean Patrick had been drinking water when she spoke up; he could barely swallow it. Where could he begin? "Yes," he said. "I believe it was." He set down the glass, and the ice clinked loudly against the side.

"I booked you a room in a hotel near my apartment. It's a nice place and not very dear."

Jean Patrick nodded. His skin went cold and then hot.

"I am happy to take you there if you want, but you are welcome in my home." Bea took a deep breath before continuing. "I have an extra bedroom, but my cousin and her daughter have been living with me while my cousin attends university. They've gone to stay with friends, but the bed is small." She smiled. "I think your feet will be in the air at the far end of it."

"Knowing you were in the next room, I would make my bed on cold ground, *rock was my pillow, too,*" Jean Patrick said, quoting the Bob Marley song to keep the mood light.

They got up from the table, and their arms brushed. Bea did not take hers away. Outside, in a corner behind a shop, he pulled her close and held her, and she, too, held him. The sound of a radio from a passing car, loud and intrusive, made him jump. But it was not RTLM, and no one leapt from the shadows to kill him.

℥

Jean Patrick stood at the window of Bea's apartment and looked out onto the Kigali night. Lights blinked like dirty stars against the black horizon. Hôtel des Mille Collines rose like a beacon of promise out of the ghost of war, windows bright. Car horns honked, tires clunked over potholed streets. Much of the rubble had been cleared; everywhere there was scaffolding and construction as a new city, fresh and scrubbed clean, without history, was birthed from the annihilation of the old.

In the room where Bea had led him to rest, he had felt like a giant bumbling around among the pieces of miniature furniture: a little desk neat with pens, crayons, and paper; a matching chair; a small dresser on which a collection of perfumes, pomades, and creams were aligned, the only evidence of a grown woman in the room. The child's drawings were tacked on the walls, and Jean Patrick wondered at her age; they were bold with color and possessed a sophisticated sense of design. Remembering Ineza's paintings, he smiled; the cousin must be on her side of the family. Like a true artist, the little girl had signed her work: Gabby.

He had slept a bit, fitfully, in the cramped bed, and he wondered how a mother and child could sleep there together night after night. When he woke, he had taken the box with the cross from his socks and put it in the pocket of his hooded sweatshirt. He fingered it now as he stood and from a distance watched the people of Rwanda go about the business of living.

Bea came and stood beside him, not quite touching, although her heat touched his. "Are you hungry?" she asked.

"Aye! Lunch has not yet moved from my stomach. Are you?"

Bea shook her head. "Shall I make you tea? Juice?"

"I don't need anything," Jean Patrick said. "I brought you a present."

He placed the box in her hand. She was still wearing her high-necked blouse, and when Jean Patrick moved to touch the collar and expose her skin, she recoiled. "What's wrong?" He felt her tremble, a slight movement of the air between them. "What is it?"

Bea took his hands and moved them down to his side. Then slowly she undid the top buttons of her blouse. Stepping from the shadow into the light, she pulled the collar down and tipped her chin slightly upward. Jean Patrick saw it then, the dark keloid like a smile across her throat. It left him without breath.

"Come. I will tell my story first," she said. "And then you will know if you still want to tell me yours." She led him to the couch, and he sank into the shabby fabric. He held on to her hands so he would not give in to the urge to press his own hands to his ears.

"The soldiers and Interahamwe had just burst through the front door when I ran inside," she said. "Mama and Dadi were already dead, lying on the floor in their last embrace. Selfishly I regret that I did not get to say good-bye, but I'm glad because in their moment of death, they thought that I had escaped with you, that I had a chance for life. What I will tell you next I remember little of, although lately it comes back of its own accord like bits and pieces of shrapnel rising to the skin's surface. Most of this story comes from Claire, who rescued me and nursed me back to life when I was past dead."

Bea paused to drink some water. Out of the corner of his eye, Jean Patrick caught the glass bird she had written of in her letter. It twirled a slow dance on its tether. The silence in the room hummed in his ear.

"I was wild. I ran back outside, into the yard. I suppose I had decided to run after you; I don't know. The Interahamwe caught me and tore off my clothes."

Jean Patrick's hand had come up without his mind's knowing it. He would have spoken then, begged her to stop, but she put a finger to his lips.

"A police officer came after them and fired a shot in the air. It was someone I knew. He said he wanted me for himself, so he sent the rest of the men to search for you while he had his way." She smiled then, merely a slight upturn at the corners of her mouth. "Claire said I fought like a lioness. She said I grabbed his machete and nearly succeeded in killing him. That was when he cut me."

"My Bea." Jean Patrick took her hands and kissed them. "I can imagine how you fought." He stroked her hair, and she collapsed against his shoulder. "This policeman," Jean Patrick said, "did I know him?"

Bea sat up. "What does it matter? He is probably dead now. I am past hating him; I feel nothing."

She didn't have to answer. Jean Patrick could see the man's gold-capped teeth, watch him put out his cigarette in the crumbs of their pastry at the Ibis, hear him tell Bea that Niyonzima had been in an accident. Had he materialized at this moment in the room, Jean Patrick could have killed him with his own two hands.

"Before the Interahamwe left, they poured petrol inside the house and started a fire. By some miracle, I lived. Claire was hiding in the shadows. They had told her to go, but she didn't. She bundled her children in blankets under her bed so they would not hear, and then she waited. The instant the men went on to do their business elsewhere, she dragged me to the cookhouse and put poultices on my wounds to stop the bleeding. Then she put me in a wagon like a sack of sorghum, covered me with clothes and sacking, and she and her two children pushed me to her sister's house. I remained there until the war's end, hidden in the grain room. Had her sister's husband found out, he would have killed the three of us. Every morning, I heard him leave to do his work, his killing."

"Mana yanjye, that tiny woman dragged you in the night? Through those wild mobs fueled on urwagwa?"

"She risked her life for me, and I owe her mine. She coaxed me back more than once from the arms of death. It was she who gave me the courage to continue, to step out into the air and seek the living."

"What happened to her?"

"She came to the UK with me, she and the children. My aunt — my mother's sister — found the money for all of us somehow. She is studying to be a nurse."

"And you, Bea." Jean Patrick floundered about to come up with the words, only a few to string together, but he could not.

"That is the second miracle," she said, jumping in to save him, "if AIDS is what you mean. I have been tested and retested. I escaped unscathed." There was that smile again, barely more than an illusion of the light. "As unscathed as one can be."

Bea lay back against his shoulder, and he felt the warmth and wet of tears. "There is one thing more I want to ask you, a silly thing," he said.

"I will tell you whatever you ask," she said. "I am sorry to have to speak this truth to you. You're not angry with me?"

"Shh," he said. "Shh. It is you who should be angry with me." She lifted her head to respond; he kissed her lips to quiet her. After such a drought, once more he drank in her salt. "My brother said when RTLM added your names to their lists, they announced your mother as Tutsi."

"I also heard this—from Claire," Bea said, sighing. "How much time and effort it must have taken to discover such a stupid, meaningless bit of information."

"It's true?"

"It was a secret only our family knew; her father was given a Hutu card as a favor before she was born. But, yes, she was Tutsi."

JEAN PATRICK SAT with Bea for some time without moving, feeling the rise and fall of her breath against his chest. He was wrung out. What was anything he had suffered compared to this? He turned over words in his mind, dug them up from the earth, but none stayed. The lights coughed and sputtered and then failed. Through the window, Jean Patrick saw Kigali drown in darkness.

"Some things never change," he said. "I see even General Kagame cannot bring forth light in this country."

"He is not God," Bea said.

"There is one more question," Jean Patrick said. The darkness gave him courage.

"And I have one more answer."

"Do you think what happened was because of me—because I was in your home?"

Bea answered without hesitation. "If you had never walked into our lives, it would have been the same." She stood and lit a candle. "So will you tell me your story now, or have I frightened you away?"

"How long have you been trying to scare me off? Have I gone?" They both laughed softly, and this seemed to bring them back among the living. "I will tell you ejo, if you want to hear."

"Will that be *ejo* hashize, yesterday, or *ejo* hazaza, tomorrow? Do you remember when you asked me that?"

"I believe it was the first time I asked you to marry me," Jean Patrick said. "And I believe I am still waiting for my answer."

Bea brought the candle close. "We have a long drive tomorrow, and I'm afraid you will not sleep in that tiny bed. Will you stay in my room?" She held out her hand to him, and he took it.

☙

Jean Patrick emerged from a deep sleep and for a moment did not know where he was. A white fog of mosquito netting surrounded him. He rolled over, and warmth greeted him: Bea's warmth. The world came back thickly and slowly. Gently he touched an arm, a leg. Rising onto his elbow, he kissed the scars on her breast, her belly. He lifted the gold cross and kissed the dark rope of scar at her throat. Bea awoke, and they held each other. It was all they had done, and it was all he needed.

"I want to make one stop on the way to Cyangugu," Bea said. She cupped his chin in her hands. "When I dug through the remains at our home, I found some bones and a few trinkets: a melted spoon, a bracelet of Mama's, a fountain pen of Dadi's. Bits and pieces of paintings and books. Last April, during the time of mourning, I brought everything to Murambi to be buried in the mass grave there. I find it difficult to pass without stopping."

Jean Patrick's hands grew clammy. He blew out a long breath through his lips. He had thought that a good night's sleep would help to clear his mind, but it hadn't. On his arrival, he had been thrown into a fast-moving current, and he couldn't remember how to swim. "That will be fine," he said. "I imagine there are others I knew who are buried there. I can pay my respects."

BEA PARKED AT the base of the Murambi Genocide Memorial. It had been raining, but now a ghostly sun was visible behind the thinning clouds. Jean Patrick looked out across the terraced hills, the flat-topped acacia. The land came back to him in a mixture of sharp recollection and blurred dream. Gravel pathways led up the hill to a collection of buildings that before the genocide had been a school. Bea told him that more than forty thousand people had gathered here for protection. Most did not survive. The French, she said, had been charged with their protection but did nothing to save them. She touched his arm. "You don't mind? You're OK?"

"I'm fine," Jean Patrick said.

He followed Bea up the path. "We'll stay outside. They have put the bodies in the rooms as a reminder of what happened, room after room of mummified corpses; it is too much," she said. Wind rippled through the thick grass fertilized by the dead. A sharp odor filled Jean Patrick's nostrils, and he sniffed the air.

"Do you recognize it?"

He did, then. "Yes." It was the smell of death.

They stopped beside a row of stones. "When I first came here, the scent terrified me," she said. "Now I can't live without it. I come here and take it into my lungs, and then I know for a while that, yes, I am still among the living. It's like breathing the blood of my country, this country I still love."

Jean Patrick did not understand, but he stood beside her, and after a little while, the odor melted into him, became a part of him, too. They stared out at the grass, a snapping field of green. Jean Patrick took Bea's hand. "Umukunzi wanjye," he said. My sweetheart.

"How beautiful to hear those words once more. It's what my parents called each other, even after so many years of marriage."

"I don't know how many times I have asked you to marry me."

Bea's gaze followed the whipping grass. "Seventeen, I think."

"Before, I thought I would ask you forever, until you said yes. Now, I will only ask you this one time more. Will you marry me? I knew then, and I know now—whatever you say—there will never be anyone else for me."

Bea held his hands against the deep hollow where her collarbones met, where the gold cross flashed against her scar. "Jean Patrick, I have a child."

"How wonderful! Boy or girl?"

"A little girl. Gabrielle Miseke. Gabby. She was born on January fifteenth, 1995. I cannot tell you if she is yours."

For a moment, a thought he couldn't quite form itched at his mind as he tried to take her words inside him. "Miseke, the Dawn Girl who laughs pearls," he said, buying time until his shock cleared. "Mathilde loved that story. We read it over and over." The thought clicked into place. "Gabby! The name on the paintings in the bedroom where I was," he said. "The room is hers, then."

"I had to wait until I knew that I could tell you, that it was something that could be between us. Can you forgive me?"

"How can you think there is anything to forgive?"

"It was a long time before my child received her Rwandan name. When she was born, there was only darkness in my life. More than once, as I stood at the sink to bathe her, I thought, How easy it would be to hold her under until she ceases to breathe. But in my heart I always believed she was yours, and I could not snuff out the last light of your life. Nor could I give her up." Bea took a Kleenex from her purse and dabbed at her cheeks. "As soon as I allowed Gabby's smile to reach me, it became obvious what she must be called. She swept night from my life as dawn sweeps night from the world."

Bea looked out toward the hills, the distant forested slopes. If her gaze kept going, it would find the swamps where he had hidden. A little girl rolled a metal hoop down a path, and sublime peace transformed Bea's face. Jean Patrick knew it was Gabby Miseke she watched.

He gathered her to him. If he could have opened his skin, tucked her inside his beating heart, he would have done so. He rested his chin on her hair. "You have not answered me. You have not said yes or no."

Bea's cheeks were wet and glistening, her eyes, a mineral, polished black. "You understand—I can't leave my work. There are not so many social workers in Rwanda, and my AIDS group has become my family— my sisters. I will never abandon them."

"Of course."

"And I don't expect you to come back here. We have no Harvards or MITs in Rwanda—not yet—so I don't know how it can work."

"None of that matters. There is always a way if you search for it. We have both learned this lesson, I think."

A shadow of pain passed across Bea's face. "There is one more thing.

Since finding you again, I knew I could have Gabby's DNA tested. I could find out. This question has been like a hook, twisting in my heart, but the answer is always the same: I cannot do it. I cannot let destruction sweep through my life again."

"There is no question," Jean Patrick said. "Gabrielle Miseke is my daughter."

THIRTY-TWO

JEAN PATRICK WAS ALONE when he awoke in another strange bed, and for a moment he panicked. In his dream, he had been sitting at the table with his family. Something about the room, the house, was not quite right. Proportions were askew, the distances between him and the rest of his family too great to bridge. When he tried to touch them, he found only air, and it unsettled him nearly to the point of terror. It was a dream he visited often.

It was not yet light; a candle flickered on the table beside him. Had he been so careless, letting it burn all night? The bed creaked, and Bea sat beside him. Ah, he thought, place and time slowly drifting back to him. *I am at the Peace Guest House in Cyangugu.* The accommodations had just been completed; the smell of new paint came from the bright walls.

"I better go back to my room," Bea said, "before someone discovers me and drowns me in the lake for my sins."

"Eh? I believe those old customs are gone from this country — even here in Cyangugu."

He blew out the candle, pulled her down, and took her into his arms. Thus tethered, he allowed himself to sleep again, a dreamless sleep like floating in deep water, until the plaintive *cree* of a brown kite over Lake Kivu woke him. Daylight, dank and dull, spilled through the space between the orange curtains. He walked to the door, opened it, and stepped outside, the concrete porch a sudden chill on his bare feet. Rain fell, a thin gauze of it, on the lawn and the plantings of trees, but here beneath the porch roof he remained protected.

"You are lucky," the concierge had told them. "Last week it was a deluge, but now everything is drying out."

Jean Patrick sat in the cane chair and looked out over the pleasant yard bordered by the chaos of grass and reeds. Potted plants framed the doorways of the rooms, and semicircles of blooming plants peppered the grass beyond them. A profusion of orange flowers like overturned cups dripped from tall bushes. Bea had found the guesthouse and made the reservation, and he was thankful. The Anglicans who had built it had wrested a small piece of the former paradise from the devastation that was still all around them.

A steep slope plunged down to the lake, where the silhouettes of the fishermen drew shape out of the fog, the sight familiar and foreign at the same time. He could not quite take in that he was here, seeing all this once more. Suddenly, loss tugged at his heart; he could have fallen to his knees with the weight of all that was gone. He went back into the room and shut the door behind him.

Bea was at the sink in the bathroom between their two rooms, brushing her teeth with bottled water. "There is no water," she said, her words muffled by toothpaste. She flicked the light switch. "No power."

Jean Patrick came up behind her and kidnapped her in his arms. He brushed his teeth beside her, and she kissed him with her minty mouth.

"I'll go now," he said. He put on a shirt and running tights, then changed the tights for shorts and track pants over them. "I don't know if Cyangugu is ready for such modern things."

"Will you be all right?"

"Yes. I'm ready."

"You'll run there in this rain with your foot?"

"It's barely wet. A little forward motion will give me time to prepare myself."

"Ko Mana! You never give up."

For courage, he held her one last time. He sucked in breath. It felt like a miracle. It felt like he would awaken and she would be gone.

JEAN PATRICK LOPED easily down the hill to l'Hôtel du Lac Kivu. With a shock, he saw that it was run-down and dirty, nothing like the palace he remembered. There were still bullet holes in the walls of the building. He walked across the lawn to where the tables used to be, where he had first seen Jonathan with his treasure trove of rocks. Lake Kivu yawned before him. The Rusizi River, where he once hauled fish lines and dove for his rusty prizes, murmured at his back. Foot traffic crowded the rickety bridge between Cyangugu and the DRC, the country he knew as Zaire. The Interahamwe still crept across the border, back into Rwanda, to stir up trouble. Just last year, Bea told him, five human rights workers had been murdered here.

A pirogue with an older man and two young boys came close to shore. Jean Patrick waved, and they waved back. The words of their songs drifted across the water. Jean Patrick could have sung along; they were still the same verses. He could have been watching himself, Zachary, and Uncle Emmanuel. He had to turn away.

At the docks by the old harbor, a freshly painted hull rested on a wooden framework—a flower of rebirth blooming amid the rusted hulks. There were new brick buildings, too, with bright blue metal roofs. At the fork in the road, he turned right, toward home. His heart pounded, and he didn't know if it was the altitude, the climb, the fear, or some combination of these factors. All along the hillsides, the old homes were gone. There was nothing left but crumbling walls, glassless windows, gardens overrun by vines. The road was steeper than he remembered, or perhaps it was just the difference in his fitness. Ghosts ran beside him. He picked up his pace, but the abazimu matched him stride for stride.

Farther on, swaths of forest had been cleared, and new buildings emerged from piles of bricks, concrete, mud, and metal. They were crowded and square, arranged in neat rows. Imidugudu, Bea had called them, adding to the many meanings of the word that of subsidized housing. He stopped to rub the dull ache from his ankle before continuing up the grade.

Far in the distance, Jean Patrick could pick out the ridges of Gashirabwoba. He must have logged a few thousand kilometers, running up and down them. He recalled the words Uncle had told Mama on that first night inside his house. *You've come back to Gashirabwoba now. Here, we live up to our village name: Fear Nothing.* During the genocide this had been so. Roger told him that some Tutsi gathered in the grove of eucalyptus where meetings were held and fought off the Interahamwe, only stones for weapons, for nearly a day. They held their ground fiercely until the Interahamwe retreated and returned with grenades.

AT THE MAIN dirt road where he used to catch the bus, Jean Patrick stopped. He could not distinguish one path from another. He turned a slow circle, disoriented and confused. Houses—his landmarks—were missing, and unfamiliar ones had sprouted up. Then he spotted the forked eucalyptus, blue and shimmering, rising above the forest canopy. The trail, overgrown now, where he had raced Roger and finally won appeared like a faint pencil mark in the undergrowth. The earth was slippery as he began to climb, but not liquid enough to suck in his shoes; he remembered days when mud swallowed all. He stopped to kneel and touch the earth. When he stood, his fingers were stained with rust, and a rubiginous circle remained on his knee. He was home.

The landscape of his childhood took shape before him, but as in his dream, it was off kilter and disjointed, overrun by high, wild grasses. The fence formed by cypress trees had disappeared without a trace. As he passed the spot where he guessed it had been, his skin grew cold. He was terrified he would step on a loved one's bones with the sole of his shoe.

One foot in front of the other, he climbed. A gnarled and scarred mango with tiny, unripe fruit survived, but the jacaranda that had once provided shade for their house now listed at a dangerous angle, naked and leafless. His family home was a blackened skeleton, vines crawling through the bones. Not one building stood. It had stopped drizzling, but a heavy mist remained, transforming the silence into something unearthly.

In the midst of the destruction, someone had scratched out a new plot in the old garden. Maize and sorghum, a few tomato vines and peas and spindly cabbages, pushed through the rubble and stones. Jean Patrick shivered. Did an umuzimu—a ghost—live here amid the ruin? A sense of violation and then of anger stirred in his chest.

An old woman approached, leaning heavily on a stick, and behind her, two small children pulled a goat by a string. She paused to greet Jean Patrick. "Mwaramutse," she said. The children pressed close and stared at him with sad, rheumy eyes.

"Mwaramutseho, Grandmother."

She peered intently at him. She was familiar to Jean Patrick, but he couldn't place her. Suddenly she cried out and pressed her fingers to her heart. "Ko Mana! It's not possible! We heard you were killed." She held her thin arms out to him and smiled a toothless smile. "Do you not know me?"

He shook his head, again unsettled by the suspicion that she was an umuzimu emerging from the earth to meet him.

"I'm Mukabera." She paused. "Your neighbor." Covering her face with her hands, she wept.

"Mukabera!" He stooped to hold her, palms resting on the sharp wings of her shoulder blades. Her musky, unwashed odor surrounded him. "Roger told me how you helped us. I have held you in my heart all these years." Her throaty laugh, the racy banter, the gifts of blue eggs and fat ducks, her joyful spirit and her courage, were still there, he had to believe, behind the frangible skin. "I feel blessed to thank you face-to-face. I still have Zachary's Bible, the one you saved."

"You must come and have tea," Mukabera said. She exhaled a sad breath. "It's not like old times—we have nothing. But something to drink I can offer you."

"Of course I will come."

She chuckled, fanning a small spark of her old fire. "From afar I thought you were a fancy tourist who had lost his way. A black muzungu."

THE HUT WAS smaller than Jean Patrick had remembered. "Welcome," Mukabera said. The children tethered the goat to a tree and tumbled in front of him through the doorway. Jean Patrick ducked through the narrow opening into the dank smoke, walls smudged with its residue. The children touched his track pants and giggled.

Jean Patrick took off his shoes, and they grabbed at the laces. "They're for running. Hold them," he said. "They feel like air in your hands." He tied the laces together and looped them over their upturned palms. They shrieked with joy.

A woman and two small children squatted on the floor, shelling beans, a pale tapestry of blues, pinks, and purples spread before them. The woman stood, wiped her hand on her ragged pagne, and held it out to him. Although a rough, young beauty shone through, she moved with the fatigue and stiffness of a grandmother.

"Olivette, it's Jean Patrick. He's come home."

"How can it be?" Olivette cried out. Then she placed an arm across her body as if hiding nakedness. "Yes—I see now—it really is." She bit her lip in shyness, a gesture Jean Patrick recalled with one more pang of loss. "Thanks to God," she said.

Mukabera came in with a thermos and three chipped cups ringed in pink roses. She poured tea and gave a cup to Jean Patrick. With a shock he saw this was his mother's tea set, the one she had cradled on the journey from Gihundwe to Gashirabwoba. The cup that now warmed his hands might be the same one he had held on the morning of any special occasion. He took a sip. The tea was little more than water, and the milk had soured.

"We're so sorry for what happened," Mukabera said. Olivette nodded. The spoiled milk churned in Jean Patrick's stomach. "Your uncle was a good man, strong and brave. Your mother and your aunt were my good friends—ego ko Mana, how we slaved together in the fields. Slaved and laughed."

This word *was,* his family relegated to the past tense. Mukabera gestured toward her daughter. "Olivette's husband died in the camps in Congo. And Simon, gone from cancer. We had to sell the cows and the goats, most of the chickens, to pay for the operations, but they didn't work."

Was this God's wrath? His retribution? Jean Patrick couldn't make himself care. The smallest child wobbled over and fell into his lap. She seized his jacket with both hands and rubbed the silky fabric against her cheek, kicking her feet with delight. Her unbridled joy brought him back into life. He tickled her under the chin, and her laugh was a tiny bell.

"That's Simon's daughter," Olivette said. "After Simon died, her mama went to Congo and left her behind, with us."

"Probably my son did bad things, but he was in Kigali," Mukabera said. "He wasn't one of them."

The soot-black walls, the cookhouse smoke that came inside, the damp earth: all closed in on him. Somehow he managed to finish his tea. Then he pulled a handful of franc notes from the money belt inside his track pants. He was too spent to think about conversion rates. It could have been five or fifty dollars. Mukabera gasped and pressed her hands together in a supplicant's gesture of thanks. "May God bless you, always."

"And you," he replied.

They escorted him as far as his family land, Mukabera and Olivette leading the way as mist turned once more to drizzle, a sad susurration. The procession of children clung to his hands. They stopped beneath the ghost of the cypress fence, in the overgrown grass, and Mukabera planted her stick in the mud. "My husband was lucky he died young. He never lived to see this." She spread her arms wide and gathered into them the pearled light, the silence and waste of the countryside.

Jean Patrick knew she spoke not only of the poverty of her family and of Rwanda, but of the terrible choice her husband would have had to make in 1994. How much easier it would have been if invading armies from a hostile land had done this instead of neighbor against neighbor. He clasped her hands and wished her well one last time.

"Nkwifurije amahoro," she called. She turned back toward her home.

"Yego. Amahoro." Peace. He was still watching them, cleaning his hands on his jacket, when he stepped backward across a vine and fell. His palm hit something sharp. He uncovered it and saw it was a triangular piece of bone. A cow's sacrum, he thought at first. He hefted it in his hand; the angles were wrong for a cow. On his knees in the wet earth he dug, scooping red clay with his fingers. He uncovered a femur, a fragment of pelvis, a piece of a skull. He gathered together the calcified pearls of teeth.

Gently he turned the remains over, searching for some identifying mark, some unique blemish to reveal to him whom he held. There was a small scrap of cloth still attached to the femur, a tuft of hair on the skull, but nothing told him, Yes, this is my uncle, my aunt, my brother. The bones held faintly the same musky odor he had recognized in Murambi. For some minutes he squatted there and took the scent into himself as if taking his family into his blood. Now he fully understood what Bea had meant when she said it was like breathing her country into her lungs.

Jean Patrick wanted to say a prayer. For a moment, none came to his mind, but then he remembered Papa's favorite verse from Ecclesiastes 9:10, the one he hadn't been able to bring himself to finish beside his father's coffin.

"Whatever your hand finds to do, do it with your might; for there is no work or device or knowledge or wisdom in the grave where you are going."

He recited the verse as he dug out a hollow as best he could and carefully placed the bones inside it. The teeth, he guarded in his palm. He let their last words pass through his flesh and into his heart.

It is love, the teeth told him, that resurrects life from death. Leave us here. Turn your head to the living.

Jean Patrick placed the teeth beside the bones, pressing them into the earth like seeds. He covered them over, hilling the grave, and made a cairn of stones so he could find it again. There must be some official process, but he couldn't think about that now. Mukabera would guard the site until he and Roger returned to lay his family properly to rest.

But now it was time he headed back. Bea was waiting.

ACKNOWLEDGMENTS

I am honored beyond belief to have been selected by Barbara Kingsolver for the Bellwether Prize, and I am grateful to her for her devotion to fiction in support of social change. Akil Pinckney, National Writers United Service Organization administrator, was always kind and patient, and his assistance proved invaluable. My editor, Kathy Pories, has been teacher, listener, guide, and so much more. My copy editor, Rachel Careau, brought my words to a careful polish. I am thankful to everyone at Algonquin for their kindness, their time, and their hard work, especially Ina Stern, Sarah Rose Nordgren, and Megan Fishmann. Special thanks to managing editor Brunson Hoole for his patience with my never-ending changes. My agent, Daniel Lazar, has given me great advice and lots of book wisdom.

When I first started to write this book, I found Dr. Alexandre Kimenyi's Web site. I wrote to him, and he immediately wrote back, and that was the start of a long and dear friendship with him and with his wife, Mathilde Mukantabana. This book would never have come to be if it weren't for their time, advice, mentorship, and love. Both Kimenyi and Mathilde have worked tirelessly to educate the world about genocide and to make this world a place in which genocide will never happen again. Kimenyi died suddenly on June 11, 2010. His passing leaves a void in many lives, but his work lives on in all of us. VCCA gave me a beautiful place to complete my final draft and the time in which to do it. Mark Bizimana shared his life with me, answered all my questions, and taught me that hope is always possible. Patrick Nduwimana, eight-hundred-meter runner for the Burundi Olympic team, taught me to love the eight-hundred-meter race, which I never thought possible. Jean Nganji provided advice, translation help, personal stories, and laughter when I most needed it. Euthalie Nyirabega was my Rwandan rock. She gave me sustenance and wisdom and introduced me to urwagwa. Tate—Julienne Nkundabiga—and Sophie Kantengwa made me feel welcome in their home. Beatrice Ufutingabire lent her name to my character and made sure that the women I wrote about were strong. Derick Burleson wrote the book of poetry that started me on this path and was kind enough to let me share the incident of McDonald's in Kigali. Rosamond Carr nurtured my body and my spirit. Her death in 2006 left a hole in the world. The children of her Imbabazi orphanage gave me inspiration and love. I spent many hours traversing Rwanda with Danny Bizimana, and I am grateful for his driving, his stories, and his company. His wife, Kayitesi Médiatrice, gave freely of her hospitality and taught me to eat ugali with my fingers. Jean Marie Kiguge took me to Nyamata, even though it was difficult. Noheli Twagiramungu read my work and helped me with my Kinyarwanda. Thank you to Uwamahoro Jean Claude, who guided me through the difficult trails in Nyungwe Forest. While researching this book, I relied heavily on the exhaustive work of Alison Des Forges. I am grateful for her book and for her personal communications. She, too, left this world before her time. For Rwandan customs and oral history, I relied on the Web site *Gakondo: The Royal Myths,* by Rose-Marie Mukarutabana, as well as scholarly texts by Dr. Alexandre Kimenyi. Quotations from *Kangura* and RTLM came from *Leave None to Tell the Story* and the *Genocide Archive Rwanda.* Commander Tom Coulter taught me about grenades, RPGs, and combat tactics. Thank you to Mary Brown, Barrie Ryan, and Gayle Brandeis, who read my drafts with care and attention, and to Emmanuel Sigauke, who believed in me enough to publish a chapter of this novel. Thanks to Maureen and Noheli Odenwald for opening doors, and to my adopted family, Halima Kasimu and Jaffar Mugaza, for opening their arms and their hearts to me. Thanks to my mentors at Antioch: Frank Gaspar, Dana Johnson, and Susan Taylor Chehak. To Meg Files, my first fiction teacher, and to Lorian Hemingway, who first put a red #1 on my writing, I owe an immeasurable debt of gratitude. And to my husband, Dan Coulter, who has walked with me no matter how hard and steep the journey.

The following books were invaluable to me in my research:

Leave None to Tell the Story, Alison Des Forges, a publication of
   Human Rights Watch
Ejo, Derick Burleson
Shake Hands with the Devil, Roméo Dallaire
Life Laid Bare and *Machete Season*, Jean Hatzfeld
Season of Blood, Fergal Keane
Resisting Genocide, Bisesero, April–June 1994, a publication of
   African Rights
*We Wish to Inform You That Tomorrow We Will Be Killed with Our
   Families: Stories from Rwanda*, Philip Gourevitch
The Shadow of Imana, Véronique Tadjo
Left to Tell, Immaculée Ilibagiza
Nyiragongo: The Forbidden Volcano, Haroun Tazieff
*Justice on the Grass: Three Rwandan Journalists, Their Trial
   for War Crimes, and a Nation's Quest for Redemption*, Dina
   Temple-Rasten
Murambi, the Book of Bones: A Novel, Boubacar Boris Diop
Killing Neighbors: Webs of Violence in Rwanda, Lee Ann Fujii

Running the Rift

A Conversation with Naomi Benaron

෩

Fiction and Social Responsibility:
Where Do They Intersect?

෩

Questions for Discussion

A Conversation with Naomi Benaron

How did Jean-Patrick's story come to be?
It started with a visit to Rwanda in 2002. I fell in love with the country and the people. At that point I knew I would have to tell a story to the world that grew from the people I met there and the histories they shared. Then, when I became friends with an eight-hundred-meter runner who ran for Burundi in the Olympics, Jean Patrick's specific tale began to unfold in my mind.

This novel feels so meticulously written. How long have you been working on it?
Running the Rift began as a short story in 2004. I committed to a novel in January 2005, so six years, although not continuously.

As I read it, it felt as if you were fluent in the language.
Hah! I am a beginner. I find Kinyarwanda to be a very difficult language to learn, but I try. I practice every chance I get.

How did you come to fall in love with this country, which seems like a second home to you?
The moment I first looked out the airplane window and saw an unending landscape of rolling green hills, I fell deeply in love. Watching the streams of people in their brightly colored clothing, greeting them on the streets and seeing their beautiful smiles, I felt something change in my heart. And it's funny that you said "second home," because I do have a feeling, in the first few minutes of being back on those streets, of coming home.

In addition to your intuitive way of writing about Rwanda, I was struck by how well you write about running: the sense of concentration, the training regimens, the pleasure of pain — things that only a serious runner knows. Which leads me to wonder, how serious of a runner are you?

I used to be a very serious runner and triathlete. I competed in road races and triathlons for many years, my favorite being the long distance ones: marathons, half-ironman, ironman. Not to brag, but I did well and was for many years in the top 10 percent of my age group nationally. My knees won't let me race anymore, but I still love running. I will never quit. It's funny, though: I used to train on the track, and I particularly hated running eight-hundreds. Although I love the theory and strategy, and I love to watch the race, I would rather run a marathon than race eight hundred meters on the track.

What was the most difficult part of writing this book?

I think the most difficult part of the book for me was the beginning, because it was hard to speak in the voice of a young boy without sounding childish. I wanted to capture Jean Patrick's innocence and the unreliability of a young narrator without making him seem simplistic or — frankly — boring. It was a hard balance to find.

You won the Bellwether Prize for Fiction, awarded to a novel that addresses issues of social justice. But rarely do novelists set out to write a novel that will address such serious political issues. What would you like readers to take away from this book?

What I do hope for is that I can in some small way bring the people and the country of Rwanda to life for readers. Maybe after finishing my novel, they will look at the world with a different eye, and they will recognize the insidious manipulations of governments on many levels and in many countries to create divisions and a sense of "othering" among peoples. Perhaps, then, they will do one small thing to fight it.

Your mother managed to escape from Europe during World War II. How did her history influence you in writing the book?

I would have to say that my mother's life and her stories have been the main influence in my writing. From a young age, I was brought up to fight injustice wherever I found it — my mother, throughout her life, was a very political person — and that has stuck with me. I know that the parallels between the Rwandan Genocide and the Holocaust are what drew me to Rwanda. I believe I told this story first because I was not ready to face the pain that the Holocaust caused my mother. She lost most of her family, her best friend, and her fiancé, and those losses hung over her life. Looking back on it, I see that she never managed to free herself from the burden of survivorship.

Who from Rwanda was your most important reader, and why?
I cannot, in all fairness, pick one person. There were three people who were central to shaping both the story's heart and its narrative: Mark Bizimana, my unofficially adopted son; Mathilde Mukantabana, my mentor and dear friend; and Jean Nganji, one of the first people from Rwanda I met, who has been my "go-to guy" throughout this long process. Mark comes from the town I picked as the birthplace of Jean Patrick (I had not yet met Mark when I chose Cyangugu), and their early lives were in many ways similar. He opened many windows into the mind of a young boy coming of age during the time preceding the genocide and answered many practical questions concerning the details of daily life. Mathilde helped me to understand the female protagonist, Bea, and she also taught me many lessons about culture, custom, and folklore. Kinyarwanda is an oral tradition that grew out of poetry, and Mathilde provided me with a sense of that. Jean Nganji taught me Kinyarwanda and answered the questions I was too embarrassed to ask Mark. He has always been an honest and wise critic of my work and has never shied away from sharing his own experience with me.

Despite the genocide, your novel is also rich with a sense of forgiveness among the survivors. Is this a sentiment you heard from those you met?
Let me address this in two parts. It's interesting that you say *Running the Rift* is "rich with a sense of forgiveness," because I'm not sure I feel that

way. What I wanted to convey was that the *possibility* of forgiveness exists but that the road will be hard and long. As for a sense of forgiveness among survivors, the answer to that is multifaceted and fraught with complexity. On June 18, 2012, the Gacaca, or community courts, where the "lesser" genocidaires have been tried since 2005, were shut down. Results from these courts have been mixed at best. From what I have read and heard, forgiveness seems to hinge on the perpetrators asking for it. These people are now being released into the community, so survivors who saw their families slaughtered now see those who committed the crimes living beside them once more. It is a tremendous source of stress. I have had friends who have been asked for forgiveness and have granted it, but I also have friends whose lives have been threatened for giving testimony at Gacaca. I think many survivors would say that forgiveness on some level is necessary if they are to go on with their lives, but I also think the wounds are so profound that the healing process can never be complete.

There is one character who is a genocidaire whom the reader gets to know fairly well. And one could argue that he is, in some small way, redeemed by his treatment of one person.

Strangely enough, Coach is the character who came most easily to me. He walked into my novel almost fully formed the minute he first jogged across the soccer field at Gihundwe. He was by no means an evil person but rather one who was raised taking orders and following the party doctrine. In short, he was a military man. It was not in his mindset to question orders or doctrine until a certain human being—Jean Patrick—came into his life. Coach was capable of redemption because he was capable of genuine human affection and because that affection, spontaneous and unanticipated, was enough to crack his comfortable worldview and to allow him to act outside of it.

No doubt you've been asked this many times, but did it give you pause to assume the perspective of another culture, a culture entirely different from your own?

Absolutely. It gave me pause every day while I was working on the novel, and it continues to give me pause today. The situation is particularly complicated because it is not just one person assuming the perspective of another. It is, in fact, a political question, because it involves the appropriation of a colonized culture by someone who stands for the colonizer. As much as I would like to refute this label, I could not be honest with myself if I did not come to terms with it. This meant that I had to approach Rwandan culture with humility, respect, and honesty; I had to be vigilant to avoid stereotypes and false representation. To accomplish that end, I had to live with Rwandans, learn something of their language, eat their food. In so doing, I came to love the culture on a profound level. On a personal level, Jean Patrick had to be someone I understood. Since I am a scientist and a triathlete, and since the love of running and the love of science transcend culture, it was a foregone conclusion that Jean Patrick would love these things as much as I do.

Fiction and Social Responsibility: Where Do They Intersect?

By Naomi Benaron

I recently attended the Third International Conference on Genocide, where I presented a paper on the rights and responsibilities of cultural appropriation. I wrote the paper because, having penned a novel from the point of view of a young Tutsi boy coming of age in the time surrounding the Rwandan genocide, it is a topic with which I frequently wrestle. During the Q&A, a Rwandan man raised his hand. "Don't you feel silly," he asked, "writing fiction about the Rwandan Genocide?"

After my initial shock and a few clarifying words, I realized that the question was not, as I had first thought, flippant but rather a query into the nature of fiction itself and into its ability to engage an event so vast and unspeakable as genocide. I realized, too, that for me, it was actually a conflation of the two central questions that define my writing. Why do I write about social justice? And, given that I am driven to address these issues, why indeed do I use fiction to address them?

Perhaps the answer to both these questions is that in my case, neither of them is a choice. I have written fiction since I was a young child; fiction is in large part the way I organize the confusion of this world in order to make sense of it. I was also raised in an environment that cultivated concern for issues of social responsibility. For me to conflate the two was therefore instinctive and reflexive. I cut my novelistic eyeteeth on the literature of social responsibility—it was much of what my parents gave me to read—so when I began to write as an adult, I naturally gravitated toward similar subjects. Until the gentleman from Rwanda called this conflation into question, I had never given it much thought.

One cannot talk about about the literature of social justice without speaking of social responsibility. The term *social responsibility* means that the awareness of social injustice, from the local to the global, necessitates specific actions to combat those injustices. In other words, social responsibility and social activism are inextricably intertwined; once aware of the injustice, one is morally obliged to act. Taking the logic one step further, fiction, in my case, becomes a form of social activism; it is one of the primary weapons I have chosen as a means to fight injustice.

The relationship between fiction writers and social responsibility is a long one. It began with Don Quixote when he became a knight-errant and set off on his quest to "right all manner of wrongs." It continued with Dickens and Jane Austen, with Elie Wiesel, Chinua Achebe, Ken Saro-Wiwa, Isabel Allende, J. M. Coetzee, and Nadine Gordimer. It continues today with Chimamanda Ngozi Adichie, Shahriar Mandanipour, Shahrnush Parsipur, and Orhan Pamuk. Social responsibility fuels passion, and passion fuels great writing. What would this world have lost if the great writers of social justice had not chosen to change the world through the written word and specifically through the art of fiction? Many of those writers live or lived in a place where speaking out in public is forbidden. By couching their message in allegory, they could slip their protests into the world.

Writers, to be sure, are not safe from imprisonment, torture, and death. Oppressive governments are well aware of the power of the book. Ken Saro-Wiwa, the Nigerian activist and writer, was hanged for his social activism against the government's environmental policies. A book burning campaign was one of the first coordinated actions when the Third Reich came to power in 1933.

I am a social activist. I am also a fiction writer. Both are part of my identity as a human being, as a teacher, and as a writer. To take either one away would be like cutting off a limb, and to have one without the other would not be possible. I chose Antioch University for my MFA in large part because it is a school devoted to "a social justice perspective."

Social justice infuses nearly all my fiction, whether directly or indirectly, and I cannot imagine what shape my stories would take if they did not in some manner address it. Issues concerning social justice are most often what first move me to put pen to paper, even if the threads of the injustice are woven into a seemingly unrelated arc. Conversely, my fiction also drives my awareness of social justice. It was the extensive research I undertook to understand the Rwandan genocide that led me to a commitment to the work of ending genocide on a global scale. It was one of the most important decisions I have made in my life, both as a writer and as a human being.

The awareness of social justice causes and the propensity to dwell inside a world of my own fictive creation have been with me since I can remember. I have been a storyteller since I knew how to speak. I was an extremely active child, and inventing stories was how my parents kept me calm and entertained. In the car, my mother and I concocted lives past, present, and future for the occupants of every house we passed. At home, my father wrote illustrated stories for all my stuffed animals, and I had quite a few.

One of the first role models my mother gave me was Joan of Arc, and what I loved about her was that she was willing to give up her life to defend her beliefs. Despite my young age, it was a message that went straight to my heart and burrowed in, and it has stuck with me all these years. My mother's choice of heroines was not accidental, even if unconscious. A refugee from the Bukovina region of Eastern Europe, she was born in a horse-drawn wagon while her parents fled World War I. Her great-grandmother, who refused to flee, was murdered with her own Shabbas candlestick. My mother and her parents settled in Zurich, and she came of age during Hitler's rise to power. As was the case with many Jews at that time, she was active in communist youth groups and in anti-Nazi activities. When the German ambassador visited Zurich, my mother climbed on his car and ripped off the Nazi flag. Her actions did not go unnoticed — my mother had flaming red hair — and her family was threatened with deportation. My grandfather, understanding what returning to the Bukovina meant, booked immediate passage on a ship bound for Australia. They never made it beyond Canada, but that is another long tale, the result of which was my birth.

I tell my mother's story for two reasons. The first is because I firmly believe that my own relationship with social activism was passed down to me through her DNA. She fought her way into medical school in Canada when there was a strict quota both for women and for Jews. When she married my father in 1944, she fought to retain her identity by hyphenating her last name. When my parents came to the United States, she fought her way into a professorship in psychiatry at Harvard Medical School and fought for the creation of a special department in women's studies at Peter Bent Brigham Hospital. Later, after I was born, she fought for civil rights and to end the war in Vietnam. I only hope that I have become half the fighter she was.

But I also tell my mother's story because nested in that same sequence of DNA is the need to tell stories. As I have said, the two are paired inside the double helix and cannot be unpaired. The story of Joan of Arc and the issues of justice for which she fought could not be divided in my mind, and so, when I came to understand that I had to tell the story of the Rwandan genocide, fiction was the only way I knew to tell it.

This brings us to the second part of the question, the part the gentleman from Rwanda directly addressed. Is fiction indeed an appropriate modality when dealing with atrocity and injustice on the scale of genocide, or does it somehow demean the topic? In the case of the Holocaust, this question has long been settled. During the symposia to honor the centennial celebration of the Nobel Prize, the literary symposium concentrated on the genre of "Witness Literature." As Michael Bachmann states in his paper, "Life, Writing, and the Problems of Genre in Elie Wiesel and Imre Kertész," the literature of witness is "the formative genre of the 20th century." Today's literary canon is replete with examples that extend witness literature to apartheid in South Africa, slavery and racism in the U.S., and dystopian societies that symbolize governmental injustices, to name a few.

What is it specifically about fiction that justifies its use as a weapon against social injustice on a massive scale? I believe it has to do with the empathy that the world of a novel creates. In her recent *New York Times* op-ed, "And the Winner Isn't . . . ," which addresses the failure of the fiction judges to pick a winner for the 2012 Pulitzer Prize, Ann Patchett states, "Reading fiction is important. It is a vital means of imagining a life other than our own, which in turn makes us more empathetic beings. Following complex story lines stretches our brains beyond the 140 characters of sound-bite thinking, and staying within the world of a novel gives us the ability to be quiet and alone, two skills that are disappearing faster than the polar icecaps."

I believe there is a second reason that is related to the specific craft of fiction. Although one is certainly constrained by the holistic sense of facts when writing a novel meant to represent historical events—surely one does not have the freedom to reinvent that history—as a fictional accounting, the writer does have the liberty to shape those truths into a broader "story-truth," as Tim O'Brien puts it. In painting story-truth, the writer can add a little lightness here, cast a shadow there, in order to heighten emotion and empathy, to guide the reader toward one certain picture of the world and away from another.

That I would tell the story of the Rwandan genocide through fiction was never a question for me. I returned to writing fiction, after a long hiatus, at the same time that I became involved with the local African refugee community. I returned to writing because after my father's death, I knew it would make me feel alive again. I decided to work with the local refugee community because the Lost Boys of Sudan were much in the news, and there was a large community of refugees from Darfur in Tucson, where I live. I knew I had to do something more than wear a green wristband and send thirty dollars to the Save Darfur Coalition, as worthy as those actions might be. Through a series of serendipitous events, I ended up working with the Somali Bantu community in Tucson as a volunteer with Jewish Family and Children's Services. Their personal stories broke my heart and took my breath, but what stayed with me was the spirit and determination of the people. Soon, fictional stories started to grow in my mind, seeded by the experiences of these quietly courageous human beings.

I decided to focus on the Rwandan genocide when I visited Rawanda in 2002. While walking on the beach at Lake Kivu, I discovered human bones in the sand. I got down on my hands and knees and gathered some of the bones together and held them in my palms. It was a seminal moment. I realized that what I cradled were not just bones but stories. I realized, too, that if someone did not tell the stories of the bones, those stories would be lost forever. That was the moment I decided to write a novel about Rwanda.

As much as I fought that decision (who was *I* to tell the stories?), it would not leave my mind or my heart. Before going to Rwanda, I knew a little bit about the genocide, but not much beyond the fact that it had happened, and that a lot of people were killed. The story resonated with me because I grew up with the ghosts of the Holocaust wandering around my house. Hardly anyone in my mother's extended family survived; her side of the family is a black hole around which a few old photographs orbit. The words *never again* formed the core of my mother's being; they lit the flame of her social activism, and she passed the flame on to me.

When I came back from Rwanda and began to talk about my experiences, I realized how little people in the West knew about what had happened there. I had made friends during that first trip, and their stories had become important to me. I wanted those stories to become important to others as well. I began the long process of researching the genocide. I read every book on Rwanda I could get my hands on. I went back to Rwanda for three more extended visits, staying with Rwandans who had become my friends, interviewing survivors, standing in the sites where genocide had occurred, and listening to testimonies given during the memorial services that mark the annual April commemoration of the onset of the event. I wanted Westerners to understand that the genocide was more than a few seconds of news footage to turn away from during dinner; it was an unspeakable event that changed the lives of everyone in the country forever. Its ripples spread out across the continent, and its effects are still felt today, far beyond the borders of Rwanda.

I also wanted Westerners to understand that the genocide was not just a fight that spontaneously erupted between two tribes. It was meticulously planned and carefully orchestrated, and in the case of Rwanda, the Hutu and Tutsi are not really two separate tribes; they are one people whose imposed permanent division was largely the result of colonial intervention. I wanted Westerners to understand that genocide could happen anywhere. It could happen here, in the United States. It could happen to us.

The only way I knew to tell this story was through fiction. I needed to create characters that lived and breathed as they moved through a world in which the noose of genocide slowly tightened around their necks. I needed human beings whom the reader would come not only to believe in but also to love. I needed the reader to come to understand the insidious beast of genocide by letting those human beings I created, partly from my own imagination and partly from the melting pot of my friends and their stories, into their hearts.

As a teenager, I chose to change the world by marching and sleeping on the steps of the Pentagon, but those days for me—at least for the moment—are over. Now I fight with the word. Just as I believed then that I could reach a wide audience by adding my voice and my footsteps to the crowd, I believe now that the power of the written word will effect change. I believe that someone can read a novel and be moved to say, "There must be something I can do," and beyond that, to do it.

The literature of social justice changes the world one reader at a time. Sometimes, the enormity of injustice can seem overwhelming. Rather than demean its scope, I believe fiction has the power to shape events so that the reader can grasp them rather than turn away. It has the power to shine a focused beam by actually deflecting it. I understood this when as a child I re-created the story of Joan of Arc in my head. My mother understood it when she first told it to me. At the time, I had no idea that the story that lay beneath the surface of this telling was of the near-annihilation of a people. Our people. But so it is with fiction. We fall in love with a world and the characters that populate it, and so, despite the unspoken horror, we keep reading.

QUESTIONS FOR DISCUSSION

1. Discuss the various ways in which you see the question of identity addressed in *Running the Rift*.

2. What reasons do you see for the Tutsi living in Uganda to invade Ruhengeri in 1991? How does it fit into the broader conflict between Hutu and Tutsi? Why do you think Roger joined the RPF?

3. What can you say about the class system in Rwanda after reading *Running the Rift*?

4. How did the Belgians exploit the class system, and how did this exploitation eventually contribute to the genocide?

5. Running can be seen as a metaphorical theme throughout *Running the Rift*. Why does Jean Patrick run from any awareness of politics? What challenges does the political reality in Rwanda pose in terms of his own belief system?

6. Physics and geology are two more themes that run through the novel. How do those subjects work as metaphors? Identify specific examples.

7. The title *Running the Rift* can have several meanings. Identify those meanings and discuss how they relate to the narrative.

8. Discuss the character of Coach. What do you see as his motivations concerning Jean Patrick? Do you see those motivations change over time?

9. Discuss how Coach's belief system may have changed once the genocide started. Why do you think he took his own life? Do you think he let Jean Patrick live, or did he miss?

10. Identify issues of "culture clash" with Jonathan and Susanne. Why does Bea sometimes bristle around them, and why does she mistrust Jonathan to speak out on behalf of the Rwandan people?

11. How do you see the role of the media in the genocide? Does the role change or intensify over the course of the years between 1991 and 1994?

12. Can you draw any parallels between the media campaign in Rwanda and that in Germany before and during the Holocaust? How about other genocides, such as those in Bosnia or Darfur? Any parallels between Rwanda and what you see happening in the United States?

13. Given all the disturbing warning signs regarding the approaching genocide, why do you think more Tutsi did not decide to leave before it started? Why do you think Roger didn't insist the family escape earlier?

14. How do you see Pascal's role in the genocide? Was he guilty of abetting it?

15. Who, if anyone, do you think acted heroically during the genocide?

16. There are many nonfiction books addressing the subjects of the Holocaust and genocide more generally. What role do you think fiction plays in telling this kind of story, and how is its role different than that of nonfiction? Why is literature of witness important?

Naomi Benaron holds an MFA from Antioch University and an MS from Scripps Institution of Oceanography. She is also an Ironman triathlete. She teaches for UCLA Extension Writers' Program, mentors for the Afghan Women's Writing Project, and has worked extensively with genocide survivor groups in Rwanda. For more information, visit www.naomibenaron.com. Naomi Benaron is available for select speaking engagements. Contact speakersbureau@workman.com.

Other Algonquin Readers Round Table Novels

Mudbound, a novel by Hillary Jordan

Mudbound is the saga of the McAllan family, who struggle to survive on a remote ramshackle farm, and the Jacksons, their black sharecroppers. When two men return from World War II to work the land, the unlikely friendship between these brothers-in-arms—one white, one black—arouses the passions of their neighbors. In this award-winning portrait of two families caught up in the blind hatred of a small Southern town, prejudice takes many forms, both subtle and ruthless.

Winner of the Bellwether Prize for Fiction

"This is storytelling at the height of its powers . . . Hillary Jordan writes with the force of a Delta storm." —Barbara Kingsolver

---

AN ALGONQUIN READERS ROUND TABLE EDITION WITH READING GROUP GUIDE AND OTHER SPECIAL FEATURES • FICTION • ISBN 978-1-56512-677-0

A Friend of the Family, a novel by Lauren Grodstein

Pete Dizinoff has a thriving medical practice in suburban New Jersey, a devoted wife, a network of close friends, an impressive house, and a son, Alec, now nineteen, on whom he's pinned all his hopes. But Pete never counted on Laura, his best friend's daughter, setting her sights on his only son. Lauren Grodstein's riveting novel charts a father's fall from grace as he struggles to save his family, his reputation, and himself.

"Suspense worthy of Hitchcock . . . [Grodstein] is a terrific storyteller."
—*The New York Times Book Review*

"A gripping portrayal of a suburban family in free-fall." —*Minneapolis Star Tribune*

AN ALGONQUIN READERS ROUND TABLE EDITION WITH READING GROUP GUIDE AND OTHER SPECIAL FEATURES • FICTION • ISBN 978-1-61620-017-6

The Girl Who Fell from the Sky, a novel by Heidi W. Durrow

In the aftermath of a family tragedy, a biracial girl must cope with society's ideas of race and class in this acclaimed novel, winner of the Bellwether Prize for fiction addressing issues of social justice.

"Affecting, exquisite . . . Durrow's powerful novel is poised to find a place among classic stories of the American experience." —*The Miami Herald*

"Durrow manages that remarkable achievement of telling a subtle, complex story that speaks in equal volumes to children and adults. Like *Catcher in the Rye* or *To Kill a Mockingbird,* Durrow's debut features voices that will ring in the ears long after the book is closed . . . It's a captivating and original tale that shouldn't be missed." —*The Denver Post*

Winner of the Bellwether Prize for Fiction

AN ALGONQUIN READERS ROUND TABLE EDITION WITH READING GROUP GUIDE AND OTHER SPECIAL FEATURES • FICTION • ISBN 978-1-61620-015-2

Pictures of You, a novel by Caroline Leavitt

Two women running away from their marriages collide on a foggy highway. The survivor of the fatal accident is left to pick up the pieces not only of her own life but of the lives of the devastated husband and fragile son that the other woman left behind. As these three lives intersect, the book asks, How well do we really know those we love and how do we open our hearts to forgive the unforgivable?

"An expert storyteller . . . Leavitt teases suspense out of the greatest mystery of all—the workings of the human heart." —*Booklist*

"Magically written, heartbreakingly honest . . . Caroline Leavitt is one of those fabulous, incisive writers you read and then ask yourself, Where has she been all my life?" —Jodi Picoult

AN ALGONQUIN READERS ROUND TABLE EDITION WITH READING GROUP GUIDE AND OTHER SPECIAL FEATURES • FICTION • ISBN 978-1-56512-631-2

In the Time of the Butterflies, a novel by Julia Alvarez

In this extraordinary novel, the voices of Las Mariposas (The Butterflies), Minerva, Patria, María Teresa, and Dedé, speak across the decades to tell their stories about life in the Dominican Republic under General Rafael Leonidas Trujillo's dictatorship. Through the art and magic of Julia Alvarez's imagination, the martyred butterflies live again in this novel of valor, love, and the human cost of political oppression.

A National Endowment for the Arts Big Read selection

"A gorgeous and sensitive novel . . . A compelling story of courage, patriotism, and familial devotion." —*People*

"A magnificent treasure for all cultures and all time." —*St. Petersburg Times*

AN ALGONQUIN READERS ROUND TABLE EDITION WITH READING GROUP GUIDE AND OTHER SPECIAL FEATURES • FICTION • ISBN 978-1-56512-976-4

How the García Girls Lost Their Accents, a novel by Julia Alvarez

In Julia Alvarez's brilliant and buoyant first novel, the García sisters, newly arrived from the Dominican Republic, tell their most intimate stories about how they came to be at home—and not at home—in America.

"A clear-eyed look at the insecurity and yearning for a sense of belonging that are part of the immigrant experience . . . Movingly told."
—*The Washington Post Book World*

"Subtle . . . Powerful . . . Reveals the intricacies of family, the impact of culture and place, and the profound power of language." —*The San Diego Tribune*

AN ALGONQUIN READERS ROUND TABLE EDITION WITH READING GROUP GUIDE AND OTHER SPECIAL FEATURES • FICTION • ISBN 978-1-56512-975-7

fee 12-14

Join us at **AlgonquinBooksBlog.com** for the latest news on all of our stellar titles, including weekly giveaways, behind-the-scenes snapshots, book and author updates, original videos, media praise, detailed tour information, and other exclusive material.

You'll also find information about the **Algonquin Book Club**, a selection of the perfect books—from award winners to international bestsellers—to stimulate engaging and lively discussion. Helpful book group materials are available, including

Book excerpts
Downloadable discussion guides
Author interviews
Original author essays
Live author chats and live-streaming interviews
Book club tips and ideas
Wine and recipe pairings

twitter🐦 Follow us on twitter.com/AlgonquinBooks
facebook Become a fan on facebook.com/AlgonquinBooks